THIS WAS A MAN

JEFFREY ARCHER, whose novels and short stories include the Clifton Chronicles, *Kane and Abel* and *Cat O' Nine Tales*, is one of the world's favourite storytellers and has topped the bestseller lists around the world in a career spanning four decades. His work has been sold in ninety-seven countries and in more than thirty-seven languages. He is the only author ever to have been a number one bestseller in fiction, short stories and non-fiction (The Prison Diaries).

Jeffrey is also an art collector and amateur auctioneer, who has raised more than £50 million for different charities over the years. A member of the House of Lords for over a quarter of a century, the author is married to Dame Mary Archer, and they have two sons, two granddaughters and two grandsons.

ALSO BY JEFFREY ARCHER

THE WILLIAM WARWICK NOVELS
Nothing Ventured   Hidden in Plain Sight
Turn a Blind Eye

THE CLIFTON CHRONICLES
Only Time Will Tell   The Sins of the Father
Best Kept Secret   Be Careful What You Wish For
Mightier than the Sword   Cometh the Hour   This Was a Man

NOVELS
Not a Penny More, Not a Penny Less
Shall We Tell the President?   Kane and Abel
The Prodigal Daughter   First Among Equals
A Matter of Honour   As the Crow Flies
Honour Among Thieves
The Fourth Estate   The Eleventh Commandment
Sons of Fortune   False Impression
The Gospel According to Judas
(with the assistance of Professor Francis J. Moloney)
A Prisoner of Birth   Paths of Glory   Heads You Win

SHORT STORIES
A Quiver Full of Arrows   A Twist in the Tale
Twelve Red Herrings   The Collected Short Stories
To Cut a Long Story Short   Cat O' Nine Tales
And Thereby Hangs a Tale   Tell Tale
The Short, the Long and the Tall

PLAYS
Beyond Reasonable Doubt   Exclusive   The Accused
Confession   Who Killed the Mayor?

PRISON DIARIES
Volume One – Belmarsh: Hell
Volume Two – Wayland: Purgatory
Volume Three – North Sea Camp: Heaven

SCREENPLAYS
Mallory: Walking Off the Map   False Impression

JEFFREY ARCHER

THE CLIFTON CHRONICLES
VOLUME SEVEN

THIS WAS A MAN

PAN BOOKS

First published 2016 by Macmillan

This edition published 2024 by Pan Books
An imprint of Pan Macmillan
The Smithson, 6 Briset Street, London EC1M 5NR
EU representative: Macmillan Publishers Ireland Ltd, 1st Floor,
The Liffey Trust Centre, 117–126 Sheriff Street Upper,
Dublin 1, D01 YC43
Associated companies throughout the world
www.panmacmillan.com

ISBN 978-1-0350-2283-0

1 3 5 7 9 8 6 4 2

A CIP catalogue record for this book is available from the British Library.

Printed and bound by CPI Group (UK) Ltd, Croydon, CR0 4YY

Visit **www.panmacmillan.com** to read more about all our books
and to buy them. You will also find features, author interviews and
news of any author events, and you can sign up for e-newsletters
so that you're always first to hear about our new releases.

TO VIVIEN

My many thanks to the following people for their invaluable advice and research:

Simon Bainbridge, Sir Win Bischoff,
Sir Victor Blank, Dr Harry Brunjes,
Professor Susan Collins, Eileen Cooper RA,
The Rt Hon The Lord Fowler PC,
The Reverend Canon Michael Hampel,
Professor Roger Kirby, Alison Prince,
Catherine Richards, Mari Roberts, Susan Watt,
Peter Watts, and David Weeden

THE BARRINGTONS

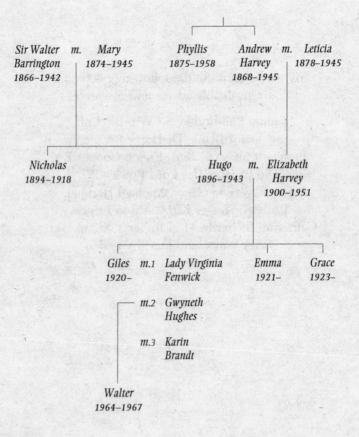

Sir Walter   m.   Mary
Barrington   1874–1945
1866–1942

Phyllis   Andrew   m.   Leticia
1875–1958   Harvey   1878–1945
      1868–1945

Nicholas
1894–1918

Hugo   m.   Elizabeth
1896–1943   Harvey
      1900–1951

Giles   m.1   Lady Virginia
1920–   Fenwick

Emma   Grace
1921–   1923–

m.2   Gwyneth
     Hughes

m.3   Karin
     Brandt

Walter
1964–1967

THE CLIFTONS

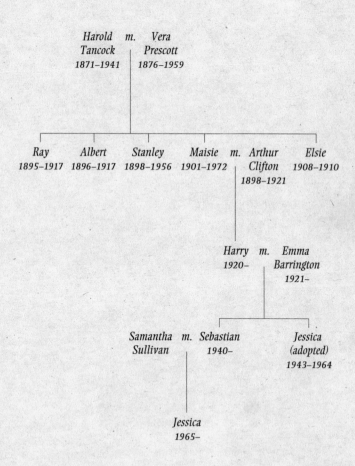

Harold Tancock *m.* Vera Prescott
1871–1941 · 1876–1959

Ray 1895–1917 · Albert 1896–1917 · Stanley 1898–1956 · Maisie *m.* Arthur Clifton 1901–1972 · 1898–1921 · Elsie 1908–1910

Harry *m.* Emma Barrington
1920– · 1921–

Samantha Sullivan *m.* Sebastian 1940– · Jessica (adopted) 1943–1964

Jessica 1965–

PROLOGUE

1978

EMMA ALWAYS TOOK a second look at any vessel that flew the Canadian flag from its stern. She would then check the name on the hull before her heartbeat would return to normal.

When she looked this time, her heartbeat almost doubled and her legs nearly buckled under her. She double-checked; not a name she was ever likely to forget. She stood and watched the two little tugs steaming up the estuary, black smoke billowing from their funnels as they piloted the rusting old cargo ship towards its final destination.

She changed direction, but as she made her way to the breakers' yard, she couldn't help wondering about the possible consequences of trying to find out the truth after all these years. Surely it would be more sensible just to go back to her office rather than rake over the past . . . the distant past.

But she didn't turn back, and when she reached the yard Emma headed straight for the chief ganger's office, as if she were simply carrying out her usual morning rounds. She stepped into the railway carriage and was relieved to find that Frank wasn't there, just a secretary typing away. She stood the moment she saw the chairman.

'I'm afraid Mr Gibson isn't here, Mrs Clifton. Shall I go and look for him?'

'No, that won't be necessary,' said Emma. She glanced at the large booking chart on the wall, only to have her worst fears confirmed. The SS *Maple Leaf* had been scheduled for breaking up and work was to begin on Tuesday week. At least that gave her a little time to decide whether to alert Harry or, like Nelson, turn a blind eye. But if Harry found out the *Maple Leaf* had returned to its graveyard and asked her if she'd known about it, she wouldn't be able to lie to him.

'I'm sure Mr Gibson will be back in a few minutes, Mrs Clifton.'

'Don't worry, it's not important. But would you ask him to drop in and see me when he's next passing my office?'

'Can I tell him what it's about?'

'He'll know.'

◀◦▶

Karin looked out of the window at the countryside rushing by as the train continued on its journey to Truro. But her thoughts were elsewhere as she tried to come to terms with the baroness's death.

She hadn't been in touch with Cynthia Forbes-Watson for several months, and MI6 had made no attempt to replace her as Karin's handler. Had they lost interest in her? Cynthia had given her nothing of any significance to pass on to Pengelly for some time, and their tea-room meetings had become less and less frequent.

Pengelly had hinted that it wouldn't be long before he expected to return to Moscow. It couldn't be soon enough for her. She was sick of deceiving Giles, the only man she'd ever loved, and was tired of travelling down to Cornwall on the pretence of visiting her father. Pengelly wasn't her father but her stepfather. She loathed him. She'd prayed her mother wouldn't marry him. But once her mother became Mrs Pengelly, Karin quickly realized she could use the petty party official to escape a regime she despised even more than she despised him, if that was possible. And then she'd met Giles Barrington, who'd made it all possible by falling in love with her.

Karin hated not being able to tell Giles the real reason she had tea at the House of Lords with the baroness so often. Now that Cynthia was dead, she would no longer have to live a lie. But when Giles discovered the truth, would he believe she'd escaped the tyranny of East Berlin only because she wanted to be with him? Had she lied once too often?

As the train pulled into Truro, she prayed it was for the last time.

◄o►

'How many years have you worked for the company, Frank?' asked Emma, looking up from her desk.

'Nigh on forty, ma'am. Served your father, and your grandfather before him.'

'So you'll have heard the story of the *Maple Leaf*?'

'Before my time, ma'am, but everyone in the yard is familiar with the tale, though few ever speak of it.'

'I have a favour to ask, Frank. Could you put together a small gang of men who can be trusted?'

'I've two brothers and a cousin who've never worked for anyone else but Barrington's.'

'They'll need to come in on a Sunday, when the yard is closed. I'll pay them double time, in cash, and there will be an incentive bonus of the same amount in twelve months' time, but only if I've heard nothing of the work they carried out that day.'

'Very generous, ma'am,' said Frank, touching the peak of his cap.

'When will they be able to start?'

'Next Sunday morning. The yard'll be closed until Tuesday, Monday being a bank holiday.'

'You do realize you haven't asked me what it is I want you to do?'

'No need to, ma'am. And if we find what you're lookin' for in the double bottom, what then?'

'I ask no more than that the remains of Arthur Clifton should be given a Christian burial.'

'And if we find nothing?'

'Then it will be a secret the five of us take to our graves.'

⌐o⌐

Karin's stepfather opened the front door of the cottage and welcomed her with an unusually warm smile.

'I have some good news to share with you,' he said as she stepped into the house, 'but it will have to wait until later.'

Could it just be possible, thought Karin, that this nightmare was finally coming to an end? Then she saw a copy of *The Times* lying on the kitchen table, open at the

4

obituaries page. She stared at the familiar photograph of Baroness Forbes-Watson and wondered if it was just a coincidence, or if he had left it open simply to provoke her.

Over coffee, they talked of nothing consequential, but Karin could hardly miss the three suitcases standing by the door, which appeared to herald imminent departure. Even so, she became more anxious by the minute, as Pengelly remained far too relaxed and friendly for her liking. What was the old army expression, 'demob happy'?

'Time for us to talk about more serious matters,' he said, placing a finger to his lips. He went out to the hallway and removed his heavy overcoat from a peg by the door. Karin thought about making a run for it, but if she did, and all he was going to tell her was that he was returning to Moscow, her cover would be blown. He helped her on with her coat and accompanied her outside.

Karin was taken by surprise when he gripped her arm firmly and almost marched her down the deserted street. Usually she linked her arm in his so that any passing stranger would assume they were father and daughter out for a walk, but not today. She decided that if they came across anyone, even the old colonel, she would stop and talk to him, because she knew Pengelly wouldn't dare take a risk if there was a witness present. Like all spies, he assumed everyone else was a spy.

Pengelly continued his jovial banter. This was so out of character Karin became even more apprehensive, her eyes darting warily in every direction, but no one appeared to be taking a constitutional on that bleak, grey day.

Once they reached the edge of the woods, Pengelly looked back, as he always did, to see if anyone was following them. If there was, they would retrace their steps and head back to the cottage. But not this afternoon.

Although it was barely four o'clock, the light was already beginning to fade and it was becoming darker by the minute. He gripped her elbow more firmly as they stepped off the road and on to a path that led into the woods. His voice changed to match the cold night air.

'I know you'll be pleased to hear, Karin' – he never called her Karin – 'that I've been promoted and will soon be returning to Moscow.'

'Congratulations, comrade. Well deserved.'

He didn't loosen his grip. 'So this will be our last meeting,' he continued. Could she possibly hope that . . . 'But Marshal Koshevoi has entrusted me with one final assignment.' Pengelly didn't elaborate, almost as if he wanted her to take her time thinking about it. As they walked deeper into the woods, it was becoming so dark that Karin could hardly see a yard in front of her. Pengelly, however, seemed to know exactly where he was going, as if every pace had been rehearsed.

'The head of counter-surveillance,' he said calmly, 'has finally uncovered the traitor in our ranks, the person who has for years been betraying the motherland. I have been chosen to carry out the appropriate retribution.'

His firm grip finally relaxed and he released her. Her first instinct was to run, but he had chosen the spot well. A clump of trees behind her, to her right the disused tin mine, to her left a narrow path she could barely make out in the darkness, and towering above her, Pengelly, who couldn't have looked calmer or more alert.

He slowly removed a pistol from the pocket of his overcoat, and held it menacingly by his side. Was he hoping she would make a run for it, so it would take more than a single bullet to kill her? But she remained rooted to the spot.

'You're a traitor,' said Pengelly, 'who has done more damage to our cause than any agent in the past. So you must die a traitor's death.' He glanced in the direction of the mine shaft. 'I'll be back in Moscow long before they discover your body, if they ever do.'

He raised the gun slowly until it was level with Karin's eyes. Her last thought before he pulled the trigger was of Giles.

The sound of a single shot echoed through the woods, and a flock of starlings flew high into the air as her body slumped to the ground.

HARRY AND EMMA
CLIFTON

1978–1979

1

NUMBER SIX squeezed the trigger. The bullet left the rifle at 212 miles per hour, hitting its target a couple of inches below the left collarbone, killing him instantly.

The second bullet embedded itself in a tree, yards from where both bodies had fallen. Moments later five SAS paratroopers stormed through the undergrowth past the disused tin mine and surrounded both bodies. Like highly trained mechanics at a Formula One pit stop, each of them carried out his duties without discussion or question.

Number One, a lieutenant in charge of the unit, picked up Pengelly's gun and placed it in a plastic bag, while Number Five, a doctor, knelt by the woman's side and felt for a pulse: weak, but still alive. She must have fainted on hearing the sound of the first shot, which is why men facing a firing squad are often strapped to a post.

Numbers Two and Three, both corporals, lifted the unknown woman gently on to a stretcher and carried her towards a clearing in the woods some hundred yards away, where a helicopter with its blades already whirring awaited them. Once the stretcher was strapped inside, Number Five, the medic, climbed aboard to join his patient. The moment he'd clipped on his safety harness, the helicopter lifted off. He checked her pulse again; a little steadier.

On the ground, Number Four, a sergeant and the regiment's heavyweight boxing champion, picked up the second body and threw it over his shoulder as if it were a sack of potatoes. The sergeant jogged off at his own pace, in the opposite direction to his colleagues. But then, he knew exactly where he was going.

A moment later a second helicopter appeared, and circled overhead, casting a wide beam of light on to the area of operation. Numbers Two and Three quickly returned from their stretcher-bearing duties and joined Number Six, the marksman, who'd climbed down from a tree, his rifle slung over his shoulder, as they began searching for the two bullets.

The first bullet was embedded in the ground just yards from where Pengelly had fallen. Number Six, who had followed its trajectory, located it within moments. Although every member of the unit was experienced in spotting ricochet marks or gunpowder residue, the second still took a little longer to discover. One of the corporals, on only his second mission, raised a hand the moment he spotted it. He dug it out of the tree with his knife and handed it to Number One, who dropped it into another plastic bag; a souvenir that would be mounted in a Mess that never had a guest night. Job done.

The four men ran back past the old tin mine towards the clearing and emerged just as the second helicopter was landing. The lieutenant waited until his men had clambered on board before he joined the pilot in the front and fastened his seat belt. As the helicopter lifted off, he pressed a stopwatch.

'Nine minutes, forty-three seconds. Just about accept-able,' he shouted above the roar of the rotating blades – he'd assured his commanding officer that the exercise would not only be successful, but would be completed in under ten minutes. He looked down on the terrain below and, other than a few footprints that would be washed away by the next rain shower, there was no sign of what had just taken place. If any of the locals had spotted the two helicopters heading off in different directions, they would not have given it a second thought. After all, RAF Bodmin was only twenty miles away, and daily ops were part of everyday life for the local residents.

One local, however, knew exactly what was going on. Colonel Henson MC (Rtd), had phoned RAF Bodmin within moments of seeing Pengelly leave the cottage firmly clutching his daughter's arm. He'd rung the number he'd been instructed to call if he thought she was in any danger. Although he had no idea who was on the other end of the line, he delivered the single word 'Tumbleweed' before the line went dead. Forty-eight seconds later, a brace of helicopters was in the air.

The commanding officer walked across to the window and watched as two Puma aircraft flew over his office and headed south. He paced around the room, checking his watch every few seconds. A man of action, he wasn't born to be a spectator, although he reluctantly accepted that at the age of thirty-nine, he was too old for covert operations. *They also serve who only stand and wait.*

When ten minutes had finally passed, he returned

to the window, but it was another three minutes before he spotted a single helicopter descending through the clouds. He waited a few more seconds before he felt it was safe to uncross his fingers, because if the second one was following in its wake, it would mean the operation had failed. His instructions from London could not have been clearer. If the woman was dead, her body was to be flown to Truro and placed in a private hospital wing, where a third team already had their instructions. If she had survived she was to be flown to London, where a fourth team would take over. The CO didn't know what their orders were and had no idea who the woman was; that information was way above his pay grade.

When the helicopter landed, the CO still didn't move. A door opened and the lieutenant jumped out, bending double as the blades were still rotating. He ran a few yards before he stood up straight and, seeing the colonel standing at the window, gave him a thumbs up. The CO breathed a sigh of relief, returned to his desk and phoned the number on his notepad. It would be the second and last time he spoke to the cabinet secretary.

'Colonel Dawes, sir.'

'Good evening, colonel,' said Sir Alan.

'Operation Tumbleweed completed and successful, sir. Puma One back at base. Puma Two on its way home.'

◄o►

'Thank you,' said Sir Alan, and put the phone down. There wasn't a moment to waste. His next appointment would be turning up at any minute. As if he was a prophet, the door opened and his secretary announced, 'Lord Barrington.'

'Giles,' Sir Alan said, getting up from behind his desk

and shaking hands with his guest. 'Can I offer you some tea or coffee?'

'No, thank you,' said Giles, who was only interested in one thing: finding out why the cabinet secretary had wanted to see him so urgently.

'Sorry to drag you out of the chamber,' said Sir Alan, 'but I need to discuss a private matter with you, on Privy Council terms.'

Giles hadn't heard those words since he'd been a cabinet minister, but he didn't need reminding that whatever he and Sir Alan were about to talk about could never be repeated, unless the other person present was also a privy councillor.

Giles nodded, and Sir Alan said, 'Let me begin by saying your wife Karin is not Pengelly's daughter.'

-◄O►-

One broken window and a moment later the six of them were inside. They didn't know exactly what they were looking for, but when they saw it, they wouldn't be in any doubt. The major in charge of the second unit, known as the litter collectors, didn't carry a stopwatch, because he wasn't in a hurry. His men had been trained to take their time and make sure they didn't miss anything. They were never given a second chance.

Unlike his colleagues in unit one, they were dressed in tracksuits and carried large black plastic bin liners. There was one exception, Number Four – but then he wasn't a permanent member of their unit. The curtains were all drawn before the lights were turned on and the search could begin. The men meticulously dismantled each room, swiftly, methodically, leaving nothing to chance. Two hours later they had filled eight plastic bags. They ignored the body that Number Four had placed on the carpet in the front room, although one of them did search his pockets.

The last things they went through were the three suitcases that had been left standing by the door in the hallway – a veritable treasure-trove. Their contents only filled one bag, but contained more information than the other seven put together: diaries, names, telephone numbers, addresses and confidential files that Pengelly had no doubt intended to take back to Moscow.

The unit then spent another hour double-checking, but came across little else of interest, but then they were pros, trained to get it right first time. Once the unit commander was convinced they could do no more, the six men made their way out of the back door and took separate well-rehearsed routes back to the depot, leaving only Number Four behind. He was not a litter collector, but a destroyer.

When the sergeant heard the back door close, he lit a cigarette and took a few drags before dropping the glowing stub on to the carpet next to the body. He then sprinkled the fuel from his lighter on to the dying embers and moments later a blue flame leapt up and set the carpet alight. He knew it would spread quickly throughout the small timbered cottage, but he needed to be certain so he didn't leave until the smoke caused him to cough, when he walked quickly out of the room and headed for the back door. After he'd left the cottage he turned around and, satisfied the fire was out of control, began to jog back to base. He wouldn't be calling the fire brigade.

All twelve men arrived back at barracks at different times, and only became a single unit again when they met in the Mess for a drink later that evening. The colonel joined them for dinner.

◄o►

The cabinet secretary stood by the window of his office on the first floor and waited until he saw Giles Barrington leave No. 10 and set off purposefully along Downing Street towards Whitehall. He then returned to his desk, sat down and thought carefully about his next call, and how much he would reveal.

Harry Clifton was in the kitchen when the phone rang. He picked it up, and when he heard the words, 'This is Number Ten, would you hold the line please,' he assumed it would be the Prime Minister for Emma. He couldn't remember if she was at the hospital or chairing a meeting at Barrington House.

'Good morning, Mr Clifton, it's Alan Redmayne. Is this a good time?'

Harry nearly laughed out loud. He was tempted to say, no, Sir Alan, it isn't, I'm in the kitchen making myself a cup of tea, and can't decide between one sugar lump or two, so perhaps you could call back later? But instead, he switched off the kettle. 'Of course, Sir Alan, how can I help?'

'I wanted you to be the first to know that John Pengelly is no longer a problem, and although you've been kept in the dark, you should be aware that your fears about Karin Brandt were unfounded, although understandable. Pengelly was not her father, and for the past five years she has been one of our most trusted operatives. Now that Pengelly is no longer an issue, she will be on gardening leave, and we have no plans for her to return to work.'

Harry assumed 'no longer an issue' was a euphemism

for 'Pengelly has been eliminated', and even though there were several questions he would have liked to ask the cabinet secretary, he kept his counsel. He knew that a man who kept secrets even from the Prime Minister would be unlikely to answer them.

'Thank you, Sir Alan. Is there anything else I ought to know?'

'Yes, your brother-in-law has also just found out the truth about his wife, but Lord Barrington doesn't know it was you who led us to Pengelly in the first place. Frankly, I'd prefer he never did.'

'But what do I say if he ever raises the subject?'

'No need to say anything. After all, he has no reason to suspect that you stumbled across the name Pengelly while you were in Moscow for a book conference, and I certainly haven't enlightened him.'

'Thank you, Sir Alan. It was good of you to brief me.'

'Not at all. And by the way, Mr Clifton, many con-gratulations. Well deserved.'

--<o>--

After Giles had left No. 10, he made his way quickly back to his home in Smith Square. He was relieved it was Markham's day off, and once he'd opened the front door, he immediately went upstairs to the bedroom. He switched on the bedside light, drew the curtains and pulled back the top sheet. Although it was only just after six o'clock, the street lamps in Smith Square were already ablaze.

He was halfway down the stairs when the front doorbell rang. He ran to open it and found a young man standing on the doorstep. Behind him was an unmarked black van, its back doors open. The man thrust out his hand. 'I'm Dr Weeden. I think you're expecting us?'

'I am,' said Giles, as two men emerged from the back of the van and gently offloaded a stretcher.

'Follow me,' said Giles, leading them upstairs to the bedroom. The two orderlies lifted the unconscious woman off the stretcher and placed her on the bed. Giles pulled the blanket over his wife, as the stretcher bearers left without a word.

The doctor checked her pulse. 'I've given her a sedative, so she'll be asleep for a couple of hours. When she wakes she may well imagine for a moment that it was all a nightmare, but once she finds she's in familiar surroundings she'll quickly recover and recall exactly what happened. She's bound to wonder how much you know, so you have a little time to think about that.'

'I already have,' said Giles, before accompanying Dr Weeden downstairs and opening the front door. The two men shook hands a second time before the doctor climbed into the front of the black van without a backward glance. The anonymous vehicle drove slowly round Smith Square then turned right and joined the heavy evening traffic.

Once the van was out of sight, Giles closed the door and ran back upstairs. He pulled up a chair and sat down by his sleeping wife.

◄o►

Giles must have fallen asleep because the next thing he knew Karin was sitting up in bed and staring at him. He blinked, smiled and took her in his arms.

'It's all over, my darling. You're safe now,' he said.

'I thought if you ever found out, you'd never forgive me,' she said, clinging on to him.

'There's nothing to forgive. Let's forget about the past and concentrate on the future.'

'But it's important I tell you everything,' said Karin. 'No more secrets.'

'Alan Redmayne has already fully briefed me,' said Giles, trying to reassure her.

'Not fully,' Karin said, releasing him. 'Even he doesn't know everything, and I can't go on living a lie.' Giles looked at her anxiously. 'The truth is, I used you to get out of Germany. Yes, I liked you, but once I was safely in England I intended to escape from both you and Pengelly and start a new life. And I would have, if I hadn't fallen in love with you.' Giles took her hand. 'But in order to keep you, I had to make sure Pengelly still believed I was working for him. It was Cynthia Forbes-Watson who came to my rescue.'

'Mine too,' said Giles. 'But in my case I fell in love with you after the night we spent together in Berlin. It wasn't my fault you took a little longer to realize just how lucky you were.' Karin burst out laughing and wrapped her arms around him. When she released him, Giles said, 'I'll go and make you a cup of tea.'

Only the British, thought Karin.

2

'WHAT TIME ARE WE commanded to attend Her Majesty's pleasure?' asked Emma, with a grin, unwilling to admit how proud she was of her husband, and how much she was looking forward to the occasion. Unlike the board meeting she would be chairing later that week, which was rarely far from her mind.

'Any time between ten and eleven,' said Harry, checking his invitation card.

'Did you remember to book the car?'

'Yesterday afternoon. And I double-checked first thing this morning,' he added as the front doorbell rang.

'That will be Seb,' said Emma. She looked at her watch. 'And he's on time for a change.'

'I don't think he was ever going to be late for this one,' Karin said.

Giles rose from his place at the breakfast table when Markham opened the door and stood aside to allow Jessica, Seb and a heavily pregnant Samantha to join them.

'Have you lot had breakfast?' Giles asked, as he kissed Samantha on the cheek.

'Yes, thank you,' said Seb, as Jessica plonked herself

down at the table, buttered a slice of toast and grabbed the marmalade.

'Clearly not all of you,' said Harry, grinning at his granddaughter.

'How much time have I got?' asked Jessica between mouthfuls.

'Five minutes at the most,' said Emma firmly. 'I don't want to arrive at the palace any later than ten thirty, young lady.' Jessica buttered another piece of toast.

'Giles,' said Emma, turning to her brother, 'it was kind of you to put us up for the night, and I'm only sorry you can't join us.'

'Immediate family only is the rule,' said Giles, 'and quite rightly, otherwise they'd need a football stadium to accommodate everyone who wanted to attend.'

There was a gentle tap on the front door.

'That will be our driver,' said Emma. Once again she checked that Harry's silk tie was straight and removed a grey hair from his morning suit before saying, 'Follow me.'

'Once a chairman, always a chairman,' whispered Giles, as he accompanied his brother-in-law to the front door. Seb and Samantha followed, with Jessica bringing up the rear, now munching her third piece of toast.

As Emma stepped out on to Smith Square, a chauffeur opened the back door of a black limousine. She ushered her flock inside before joining Harry and Jessica on the back seat. Samantha and Seb sat on the two tip-up seats facing them.

'Are you nervous, Grandpops?' asked Jessica, as the car moved off and joined the morning traffic.

'No,' said Harry. 'Unless you're planning to overthrow the state.'

'Don't put ideas into her head,' said Sebastian as they drove past the House of Commons and into Parliament Square.

Even Jessica fell silent when the car drove through Admiralty Arch and Buckingham Palace came into sight. The chauffeur proceeded slowly up the Mall, driving around the statue of Queen Victoria before stopping outside the palace gates. He wound down his window and said to the young Guards officer, 'Mr Harry Clifton and family.'

The lieutenant smiled and ticked off a name on his clipboard. 'Drive through the archway to your left and one of my colleagues will show you where to park.'

The driver followed his instructions and entered a large courtyard, where row upon row of cars were already parked.

'Please park next to the blue Ford on the far side,' said another officer, pointing across the yard, 'then your party can make their way into the palace.'

When Harry stepped out of the car, Emma gave him one final check.

'I know you're not going to believe this,' she whispered, 'but your flies are undone.'

Harry turned bright red as he zipped himself up before they made their way up the steps and into the palace. Two liveried footmen in the gold and red uniform of the royal household stood rigidly to attention at the bottom of a wide, red-carpeted staircase. Harry and Emma slowly climbed the steps, trying to take everything in. When they reached the top, they were greeted by two more gentlemen of the royal household. Harry noticed that the rank rose every time they were stopped.

'Harry Clifton,' he said before he was asked.

'Good morning, Mr Clifton,' said the senior of the two officers. 'Would you be kind enough to accompany me? My colleague will conduct your family to the Throne Room.'

'Good luck,' whispered Emma, as Harry was led away.

The family climbed another staircase, not quite as wide, which led into a long gallery. Emma paused as she entered the high-ceilinged room and stared at the rows of closely hung paintings that she'd only seen before in art books. She turned to Samantha. 'As we're unlikely to be invited a second time, I suspect Jessica would like to learn more about the Royal Collection.'

'Me too,' said Sebastian.

'Many of the kings and queens of England,' began Samantha, 'were art connoisseurs and collectors, so this is only a tiny selection from the Royal Collection, which is not actually owned by the monarch, but by the nation. You will notice that the focus of the picture gallery is on British artists from the early nineteenth century. A remarkable Turner of Venice hangs opposite an exquisite painting of Lincoln Cathedral by his old rival, Constable. But the gallery, as you can see, is dominated by a vast portrait of Charles I on horseback, painted by Van Dyck, who at the time was the court artist in residence.'

Jessica became so entranced she almost forgot why they were there. When they finally reached the Throne Room, Emma regretted not having set out earlier, as the first ten rows of chairs were already occupied. She walked quickly down the centre aisle, grabbed a place on the end of the first available row and waited for the family to join her. Once they were seated, Jessica began to study the room carefully.

Just over three hundred neat gold chairs were laid out

in rows of sixteen, with a wide aisle separating them down the centre. At the front of the room was a red-carpeted step that swept up to a large empty throne that awaited its rightful occupant. The buzz of nervous chatter ceased at six minutes to eleven when a tall, elegant man in morning dress entered the room, came to a halt at the foot of the step and turned to face the assembled gathering.

'Good morning, ladies and gentlemen,' he began, 'and welcome to Buckingham Palace. Today's investiture will begin in a few minutes' time. Can I remind you not to take photographs, and please do not leave before the ceremony is over.' Without another word, he departed as discreetly as he had entered.

Jessica opened her bag and took out a small pad and a pencil. 'He didn't say anything about drawing, Grandma,' she whispered.

As eleven o'clock struck, Her Majesty Queen Elizabeth II entered the throne room, and all the guests rose. She took her place on the step in front of the throne but did not speak. A nod from a gentleman usher, and the first recipient of an honour entered from the other side of the room. For the next hour, men and women from around the United Kingdom and Commonwealth received honours from their monarch, who held a short conversation with every one of them before the usher nodded once again and the next recipient took their place.

Jessica's pencil was poised and ready when Grandpops entered the room. As he walked towards the Queen, the gentleman usher placed a small stool in front of Her Majesty and then handed her a sword. Jessica's pencil didn't rest for even a moment, capturing the scene as Harry knelt down on one knee and bowed his head. The Queen touched the tip of the sword gently on his right shoulder, lifted it, then placed it on his left shoulder, before saying, 'Arise, Sir Harry.'

—◇—

'So what happened after you were marched off to the Tower?' demanded Jessica as they drove out of the palace and back down the Mall, to take Harry to his favourite restaurant a few hundred yards away for a celebration lunch.

'To begin with, we were all taken into an anteroom where a gentleman usher guided us through the ceremony. He was very polite, and suggested that when we met the Queen we should bow from the neck,' said Harry, giving a demonstration, 'and not from the waist like a page boy. He told us we shouldn't shake hands with her, should address her as Your Majesty, and should wait for her to begin the conversation. Under no circumstances were we to ask her any questions.'

'How boring,' said Jessica, 'because there are lots of questions I'd like to ask her.'

'And when replying to any question she might ask,' said Harry, ignoring his granddaughter, 'we should address her as ma'am, which rhymes with jam. Then once the audience is over, we should bow again.'

'From the neck,' said Jessica.

'And then take our leave.'

'But what would happen if you didn't leave,' asked Jessica, 'and began to ask her questions?'

'The gentleman usher assured us very politely that should we outstay our welcome, he had instructions to chop off our heads.' Everyone laughed except Jessica.

'I would refuse to bow or call her Your Majesty,' said Jessica firmly.

'Her Majesty is very tolerant of rebels,' said Sebastian, trying to guide the conversation back on to safer ground, 'and accepts that the Americans have been out of control since 1776.'

'So what did she talk about?' asked Emma.

'She told me how much she enjoyed my novels, and asked if there would be another William Warwick this Christmas. Yes, ma'am, I replied, but you might not enjoy my next book, as I'm thinking of killing William off.'

'What did she think of that idea?' asked Sebastian.

'She reminded me what her great-great-grandmother Queen Victoria had said to Lewis Carroll after she'd read *Alice in Wonderland*. However, I assured her that my next book will not be a mathematical thesis on Euclid.'

'How did she respond?' asked Samantha.

'She smiled, to show the conversation had come to an end.'

'So if you're going to kill off William Warwick, what will be the theme of your next book?' asked Sebastian, as the car pulled up outside the restaurant.

'I once promised your grandmother, Seb,' replied Harry, as he stepped out of the car, 'that I would try to write a more substantial work that would, in her words, outlast any bestseller list and stand the test of time. I'm not getting any younger, so once I've completed my present contract, I intend to try and find out if I'm capable of living up to her expectations.'

'Do you have an idea, a subject or even a title?' pressed Seb as they entered Le Caprice.

'Yes, yes, and yes,' said Harry, 'but that's all I'm willing to tell you at the moment.'

'But you'll tell me, won't you, Grandpops?' said

Jessica, as she produced a pencil drawing of Harry kneeling before the Queen, a sword touching his right shoulder.

Harry gasped as the rest of the family smiled and applauded. He was about to answer her question, when the maître d' stepped forward and rescued him.

'Your table is ready, Sir Harry.'

3

'NEVER, NEVER, NEVER,' said Emma. 'Do I have to remind you that Sir Joshua founded Barrington's Shipping in 1839, and in his first year made a profit of—'

'Thirty-three pounds, four shillings and tuppence, which you first told me when I was five years old,' said Sebastian. 'However, the truth is that although Barrington's managed a reasonable dividend for its shareholders last year, it's becoming more and more difficult for us to go on challenging the big boys like Cunard and P and O.'

'I wonder what your grandfather would have thought about Barrington's being taken over by one of his fiercest rivals?'

'After everything I've been told or read about the great man,' said Seb, looking up at the portrait of Sir Walter that hung on the wall behind his mother, 'he would have considered his options, and what would be best for the shareholders and employees, before coming to a final decision.'

'Without wishing to interrupt this family squabble,' said Admiral Summers, 'surely what we should be discussing is whether Cunard's offer is worth the biscuit.'

'It's a fair offer,' said Sebastian matter-of-factly, 'but I'm confident I can get them to raise their bid by at least ten per cent, possibly fifteen, which frankly is as much as we could hope for. So all we really have to decide is do we want to take their offer seriously, or reject it out of hand?'

'Then perhaps it's time to listen to the views of our fellow directors,' said Emma, looking around the board-room table.

'Of course, we can all express an opinion, chairman,' said Philip Webster, the company secretary, 'on what is unquestionably the most important decision in the company's history. However, as your family remain the majority shareholders, only you can decide the outcome.'

The other directors nodded in agreement but it didn't stop them offering their opinions for the next forty minutes, by which time Emma had discovered they were evenly divided.

'Right,' she said, after one or two directors began repeating themselves, 'Clive, as head of our public relations division, I suggest you prepare two press statements for the board's consideration. The first will be short and to the point, leaving Cunard in no doubt that while we are flattered by their offer, Barrington's Shipping is a family company, and is not for sale.'

The admiral looked pleased, while Sebastian remained impassive.

'And the second?' asked Clive Bingham, after writing down the chairman's words.

'The board rejects Cunard's offer as derisory and, as far as we're concerned, it's business as usual.'

'That will lead them to believe that you might just be interested if the price was right,' warned Seb.

'And then what would happen?' asked the admiral.

'The curtain will go up, and the pantomime will begin,' said Seb, 'because the chairman of Cunard will be well aware that the leading lady is doing no more than dropping her handkerchief on the floor in the expectation that the suitor will pick it up and begin an age-old courting process that just might end with a proposal she feels able to accept.'

'How much time have we got?' asked Emma.

'The City will be aware we're holding a board meeting to discuss the takeover bid, and will expect a response to Cunard's offer by close of business tonight. The market can handle almost anything, drought, famine, an unexpected election result, even a coup, but not indecision.'

Emma opened her handbag, removed a handkerchief and dropped it on the floor.

◄○►

'What did you think of the sermon?' asked Harry.

'Most interesting,' said Emma. 'But then, the Reverend Dodswell always preaches a good sermon,' she added as they left the churchyard and made their way back to the Manor House.

'I'd discuss his views on Doubting Thomas, if I thought you'd listened to a word.'

'I found his approach fascinating,' protested Emma.

'No, you didn't. He never once mentioned Doubting Thomas, and I won't embarrass you further by asking you what he did preach about. I only hope Our Lord will be understanding about your preoccupation with the possible takeover.'

They walked a few more yards in silence before Emma said, 'It's not the takeover that's worrying me.'

'Then what?' said Harry, sounding surprised. Emma took his hand. 'That bad?' he asked.

'The *Maple Leaf* has returned to Bristol and is docked in the breakers' yard.' She paused. 'Demolition work will begin on Tuesday.'

They continued walking for some time before Harry asked, 'What do you want to do about it?'

'I don't think we have a lot of choice, if we're not going to spend the rest of our lives wondering . . .'

'And it might finally answer the question that's be-devilled us for our entire lives. So why don't you try and find out if there's anything in the ship's double bottom as discreetly as possible.'

'Work could begin immediately,' admitted Emma. 'But I wasn't willing to give the final go-ahead until I had your blessing.'

—◁◦▷—

Clive Bingham had been delighted when Emma asked him to join the board of Barrington's Shipping, and although it hadn't been easy to take his father's place as a director, he felt the company had benefited from his experience and expertise in the public relations field, which it had been sadly lacking until his appointment. Even so, he had no doubt what Sir Walter Barrington would have thought about a PR man joining the board: like a tradesman being invited to dinner.

Clive headed up his own PR company in the City, with a staff of eleven who had experienced several takeover battles in the past. But he admitted to Seb that he'd been losing sleep over this one.

'Why? There's nothing particularly unusual about a

family company being taken over. It's been happening a lot recently.'

'I agree,' said Clive, 'but this time it's personal. Your mother had the confidence to invite me to join the board after my father resigned, and frankly it's not as if I'm briefing the trade press on a new shipping route to the Bahamas, or the latest loyalty scheme, or even the building of a third liner. If I get this one wrong—'

'So far your briefings have been pitch perfect,' said Seb, 'and Cunard's latest bid is almost there. We know it, and they know it, so you couldn't have done a more professional job.'

'It's kind of you to say so, Seb, but I feel like a runner in the home straight. I can see the tape but there's still one more hurdle to cross.'

'And you'll do it in style.'

Clive hesitated a moment before he spoke again. 'I'm not convinced your mother really wants to go ahead with the takeover.'

'You may well be right,' said Seb. 'However, there is a compensation for her that you might not have considered.'

'Namely?'

'She's becoming more and more involved with her work as chairman of the hospital, which, don't forget, employs more people and has an even bigger budget than Barrington's Shipping and, perhaps more important, no one can take it over.'

'But how do Giles and Grace feel? After all, they're the majority shareholders.'

'They've left the final decision to her, which is probably why she asked me how I felt. And I didn't leave her in any doubt that I'm a banker by nature, not a shipping man, and I'd rather be chairman of Farthings Kaufman than of Barrington's. It can't have been easy for her, but she's finally accepted that I couldn't do both. If only I had a younger brother.'

'Or sister,' said Clive.

'Shh . . . or Jessica might start getting ideas.'

'She's only thirteen.'

'I don't think that would worry her.'

'How's she settling down in her new school?'

'Her art teacher admitted she's letting it be known before it becomes too obvious that the school has a third-former who's already a better artist than she is.'

—◁○▷—

When Emma returned from the breakers' yard late on Monday evening, she knew she had to tell Harry what Frank Gibson and his team had found when they prised open the *Maple Leaf*'s double bottom.

'It turned out be exactly as we've always feared,' she said as she sat down opposite Harry. 'Even worse.'

'Worse?' repeated Harry.

She bowed her head. 'Arthur had scratched a message on the side of the double bottom.' She paused, but couldn't get the words out.

'You don't have to tell me,' said Harry, taking her hand.

'I do. Otherwise we'll just go on living a lie for the rest of our lives.' It was some time before she managed, 'He'd written, "Stan was right. Sir Hugo knew I was trapped down here" . . . So, my father murdered your father,' she said between sobs.

It was some time before Harry said, 'That's something

we can never be sure about, and perhaps, my darling, it's better we don't—'

'I no longer want to know. But the poor man should at least have a Christian burial. Your mother would have expected nothing less.'

'I'll have a quiet word with the vicar.'

'Who else should be there?'

'Just the two of us,' said Harry without hesitation. 'Nothing can be gained from putting Seb and Jessie through the pain we've had to suffer for so many years. And let's pray that's an end to the matter.'

Emma looked across at her husband. 'You clearly haven't heard about the Cambridge scientists who are working on something called DNA.'

-◄○►-

WE'RE ALMOST THERE, SAYS
BARRINGTON'S SPOKESMAN

'Damn,' said Clive when he had read the *Financial Times* headline. 'How can I have been so stupid?'

'Stop beating yourself up,' said Seb. 'The truth is, we *are* almost there.'

'We both know that,' said Clive. 'But we didn't need Cunard to find out.'

'They already knew,' said Seb, 'long before they saw that headline. Frankly, we'd be lucky to milk more than another percentage point out of this deal. I suspect they've already reached their limit.'

'Nevertheless,' said Clive, 'your mother won't exactly be pleased, and who could blame her?'

'She'll assume it's all part of the endgame, and I'm not going to be the one to disabuse her.'

'Thanks for the support, Seb. I appreciate it.'

'It's no more than you gave me when Sloane appointed himself chairman of Farthings and then sacked me the next day. Have you forgotten that Kaufman's was the only bank that offered me a job? And in any case, my mother might even be pleased by the headline.'

'What do you mean?'

'I'm still not convinced she wants this takeover to succeed.'

—◁○▷—

'Is this going to harm the takeover?' asked Emma after she'd read the article.

'We may have to sacrifice a point, possibly two,' said Seb. 'But don't forget Cedric Hardcastle's sage words on the subject of takeovers. If you end up with more than you expected, while the other side feel they've got the better of the deal, everyone leaves the table happy.'

'How do you think Giles and Grace will react?'

'Uncle Giles is spending most of his spare time running up and down the country visiting marginal seats in the hope that Labour can still win the next election. Because if Margaret Thatcher becomes our next prime minister, he may never hold office again.'

'And Grace?'

'I don't think she's ever read the *FT* in her life, and she certainly wouldn't know what to do if you handed her a cheque for twenty million pounds, remembering her present salary is about twenty thousand a year.'

'She'll need your help and advice, Seb.'

'Be assured, Mama, Farthings Kaufman will invest Dr Barrington's capital most judiciously, well aware that she'll be retiring in a few years and hoping for a regular income and somewhere to live.'

'She can come and live with us in Somerset,' said Emma. 'Maisie's old cottage would suit her perfectly.'

'She's far too proud for that,' said Seb, 'and you know it, Mama. In fact, she's already told me she's looking for somewhere in Cambridge so she can be near her friends.'

'But once the takeover goes through, she'll have enough to buy a castle.'

'My bet,' said Seb, 'is that she'll still end up in a small terraced house not far from her old college.'

'You're getting dangerously close to becoming wise,' said Emma, wondering if she should share her latest problem with her son.

4

'SIX MONTHS,' said Harry. 'The damn man should have been hanged, drawn and quartered.'

'What are you going on about?' asked Emma, calmly, as she poured herself a second cup of tea.

'The thug who punched an A and E nurse, and then assaulted a doctor, has only been sentenced to six months.'

'Dr Hands,' said Emma. 'While I agree with your sentiments, there were extenuating circumstances.'

'Like what?' demanded Harry.

'The nurse concerned wasn't willing to give evidence when the case came to court.'

'Why not?' asked Harry, putting down his paper.

'Several of my best nurses come from overseas and don't want to appear in the witness box for fear the authorities might discover that their immigration papers are not always, let's say, in apple-pie order.'

'That's no reason to turn a blind eye to this sort of thing,' said Harry.

'We don't have a lot of choice if the NHS isn't going to break down.'

'That doesn't alter the fact that this thug hit a nurse –'

Harry checked the article again – 'on a Saturday night when he was obviously drunk.'

'Saturday night is the clue,' said Emma, 'that William Warwick would have discovered once he'd interviewed the hospital matron and discovered why she turns on the radio every Saturday afternoon at five o'clock.' Harry raised an eyebrow. 'To hear the result of the Bristol City or Bristol Rovers match, depending on which of them is playing at home that day.' Harry didn't interrupt. 'If they've won, it will be a quiet night for A and E. If they've drawn, it will be bearable. But if they've lost, it will be a nightmare, because we simply don't have enough staff to cope.'

'Just because the home team lost a football match?'

'Yes, because you can guarantee the home fans will drown their sorrows and then end up getting into fights. Some, surprise, surprise, turn up in A and E, where they'll have to wait for hours before someone can attend to them. Result? Even more fights break out in the waiting room, and occasionally a nurse or doctor tries to intervene.'

'Don't you have security to handle that?'

'Not enough, I'm afraid. And the hospital doesn't have the resources while seventy per cent of its annual funding is spent on wages, and the government is insisting on cutbacks, not hand-outs. So you can be sure we'll face exactly the same problem next Saturday night should Rovers lose to Cardiff City.'

'Has Mrs Thatcher come up with any ideas for solving the problem?'

'I suspect she'd agree with you, my darling. Hanged, drawn and quartered would be too good for them. But I don't think you'll find that particular policy highlighted in the next Conservative Party manifesto.'

◄○►

Dr Richards listened to his patient's heartbeat, 72 bpm, and ticked another box.

'One final thing, Sir Harry,' said the doctor, pulling on a latex glove. 'I just want to check your prostate.'

'Hmm,' he said, a few moments later. 'There may be a very small lump there. We ought to keep an eye on it. You get dressed now, Sir Harry. All in all, you're in pretty good shape for a man approaching his sixties. An age when many of us are considering retirement.'

'Not me,' said Harry. 'I've still got to deliver another William Warwick before I can get down to my next novel, which could take me a couple of years. So I need to live until at least seventy. Is that understood, Dr Richards?'

'Three score years and ten. No more than the Maker's contract. I don't think that should be a problem,' he added, 'as long as you're still exercising.' He checked his patient's file. 'When I last saw you, Sir Harry, you were running three miles, twice a week, and walking five miles, three times a week. Is that still the case?'

'Yes, but I have to confess I've stopped timing myself.'

'Are you still keeping to that routine between your two-hour writing sessions?'

'Every morning, five days a week.'

'Excellent. In fact, that's more than many of my younger patients could manage. Just a couple more questions. I take it you still don't smoke?'

'Never.'

'And how much do you drink on an average day?'

'A glass of wine at dinner, but not at lunch. It would send me to sleep in the afternoon.'

'Then, frankly, seventy should be a doddle, as long as you don't get run over by a bus.'

'Not much risk of that, since our local bus only visits.

the village twice a day, despite Emma regularly writing to the council to complain.'

The doctor smiled. 'That sounds like our chairman.' Dr Richards closed the file, rose from behind his desk and accompanied Harry out of the consultation room.

'How's Lady Clifton?' he asked as they walked down the corridor.

Emma hated the courtesy title of 'lady' because she felt she hadn't earned it, and insisted everyone at the hospital still call her Mrs Clifton or 'chairman'. 'You tell me,' said Harry.

'I'm not her doctor,' said Richards, 'but I can tell you she's the best chairman we've ever had, and I'm not sure who'll be brave enough to replace her when she stands down in a year's time.'

Harry smiled. Whenever he visited the Bristol Royal Infirmary, he could sense the respect and affection the staff felt for Emma.

'If we win hospital of the year a second time,' Dr Richards added, 'she'll certainly have played her part.'

As they continued down the corridor, Harry passed two nurses who were taking a tea break. He noticed that one of them had a black eye and a swollen cheek which, despite heavy make-up, she hadn't been able to disguise. Dr Richards led Harry into a small cubicle that was empty apart from a bed and a couple of chairs.

'Take your jacket off. A nurse will be with you shortly.'

'Thank you,' said Harry. 'I look forward to seeing you again in a year's time.'

'Once we've got all the tests back from the labs, I'll drop you a line with the results. Not that I imagine they'll be much different from last year.'

Harry slipped off his jacket, hung it over the back of a

chair, took off his shoes and climbed on to the bed. He lay down, closed his eyes and began to think about the next chapter of *William Warwick and the Three Card Trick*. How could the suspect possibly have been in two places at once? Either he was in bed with his wife or he was driving up to Manchester. Which was it? The doctor had left the door open and Harry's thoughts were interrupted when he heard someone saying 'Dr Hands'. Where had he heard that name before?

'Will you report him to Matron?' the voice asked.

'Not if I want to keep my job,' said a second voice.

'So old wandering hands gets away with it again.'

'As long as it's just his word against mine, he has nothing to fear.'

'What did he get up to this time?'

Harry sat up, took a notebook and pen from his jacket pocket and listened carefully to the conversation that was taking place in the corridor.

'I was in the laundry room on the third floor picking up some fresh sheets when someone came in. When the door closed and I heard it lock, I knew it could only be one person. I pretended not to notice, picked up some sheets and made a beeline for the door. I tried to unlock it, but he grabbed me and pressed himself up against me. It was disgusting. I thought I'd throw up. No need for anyone to know about this, he said, just a bit of fun. I tried to elbow him in the groin but he had me pinned against the wall. Then he swung me round and started trying to kiss me.'

'What did you do?'

'Bit his tongue. He yelled, called me a bitch and slapped me across the face. But it gave me enough time to unlock the door and escape.'

'You have to report him. It's time the bastard was removed from this hospital.'

'Not much chance of that. When I saw him on ward rounds this morning, he warned me that I'd be looking for another job if I opened my mouth, and then added –' her voice dropped to a whisper – 'when a woman's got her mouth open, it's only good for one thing.'

'He's sick, and shouldn't be allowed to get away with it.'

'Don't forget how powerful he is. He got Mandy's boyfriend sacked by telling the police he'd seen him assaulting her, when Hands was the one who'd hit her. So what chance would I have after a grope in the laundry room? No, I've decided—'

'Good morning, Sir Harry,' said a staff nurse as she entered the room and closed the door behind her. 'Dr Richards has asked me to take a blood sample and send it to the labs. Just a routine check, so if you could roll up one of your sleeves.'

◄○►

'I suppose only one of us is qualified to be chairman,' said Giles, unable to hide a smirk.

'This is no laughing matter,' said Emma. 'I've already drawn up an agenda to make sure we cover all the topics that need to be discussed.' She handed Giles and Grace a copy each, and allowed them a few moments to consider the items before she spoke again.

'Perhaps I should bring you up to date before we move on to item one.' Her brother and sister nodded. 'The board accepted Cunard's final offer of three pounds forty-one pence a share, and the takeover was completed at midday on February the twenty-sixth.'

'That must have been quite a wrench,' said Giles, sounding genuinely sympathetic.

'I have to admit that while I was clearing out my office, I was still wondering if I'd done the right thing. And I was glad no one else was in the room when I took down Grandfather's portrait, because I couldn't look him in the eye.'

'I'd be happy to welcome Walter back to Barrington Hall,' said Giles. 'He can hang alongside Grandma in the library.'

'Actually, Giles, the chairman of Cunard asked if he could remain in the boardroom with all the other past chairmen.'

'I'm impressed,' said Giles. 'And even more convinced that I made the right decision about how I should invest some of my money,' he added without explanation.

'But what about you, Emma?' said Grace, turning to her sister. 'After all, you've also earned your right to a place in the boardroom.'

'Bryan Organ has been commissioned to paint my portrait,' said Emma. 'It will hang opposite dear Grandpa.'

'What did Jessica have to say about that?' asked Giles.

'She recommended him. Even asked if she might be allowed to attend the sittings.'

'She's growing up so fast,' said Grace.

'She's already a young lady,' said Emma. 'And I'm considering taking her advice on another matter,' she added before returning to the agenda. 'After the completion documents had been signed, a handover ceremony took place in the boardroom. Within twenty-four hours, the name of Barrington Shipping that had hung so proudly above the entrance gate for more than a century was replaced by Cunard.'

'I know it's only been a month,' said Giles, 'but have Cunard honoured their commitment to our staff, especially the long-serving ones?'

'To the letter,' said Emma. 'No one has been sacked, although quite a number of old-timers have taken advantage of the generous redundancy package Seb negotiated for them, along with a free trip on the *Buckingham* or the *Balmoral*, so no complaints on that front. However, we need to discuss our own position and where we go from here. As you both know, we've been offered a cash settlement of just over twenty million pounds each, with the alternative of taking Cunard shares, which has several advantages.'

'How many shares are they offering?' asked Grace.

'Seven hundred and ten thousand each, which last year yielded a dividend of £246,717. So have either of you made up your minds as to what you're going to do with the money?'

'I have,' said Giles. 'After seeking Seb's advice, I've decided to take half in cash, which Farthings Kaufman will invest across the board for me, and the other half in Cunard shares. They experienced a slight dip recently, which Seb tells me isn't unusual following a takeover. However, he assures me that Cunard's a well-run company with a proven record, and he expects their shares to continue yielding a three to four per cent dividend, while growing in value year on year by about the same amount.'

'That actually sounds very conservative,' said Emma, teasing her brother.

'With a small "c",' retorted Giles. 'I've also agreed to finance a research assistant for the Fabian Society.'

'What a bold gesture,' said Grace, not hiding her sarcasm.

'And you've done something more radical?' said Giles, returning the barb.

'I would hope so. Certainly more fun.'

Emma and Giles stared at their sister, like two students in her class awaiting an answer.

'I've already banked my cheque for the full amount. When I presented it to my bank manager, I thought he was going to faint. The following day, Sebastian came up to visit me in Cambridge, and on his advice I've put five million aside to cover any tax liability, and another ten into an investment account with Farthings Kaufman, to be spread across a wide range of well-established companies – his words. I've also left a million on deposit with the Midland, which will be more than enough for me to buy a small house near Cambridge, along with a guaranteed annual income of around £30,000. A lot more than I ever earned in all my years as a college don.'

'And the other four million?'

'I've donated a million to the Newnham College restoration fund, a further half million to the Fitzwilliam, and another half million to be divided among a dozen or so charities that I've taken an interest in over the years but have never been able to give more than a few hundred pounds in the past.'

'You make me feel quite guilty,' said Giles.

'I would hope so, Giles. But then I joined the Labour Party long before you did.'

'That still leaves another couple of million to be accounted for,' said Emma.

'I know it's out of character, but I went on a shopping spree with Jessica.'

'My God, what did she spend it on?' asked Emma. 'Diamonds and handbags?'

'Certainly not,' said Grace with some feeling. 'A Monet, a Manet, two Picassos, a Pissarro and a Lucian Freud, who she assures me is the coming man, as well as a Bacon of a *Screaming Pope* I wouldn't want to hear deliver a sermon. Plus a Henry Moore maquette entitled *King and Queen*, which I've long admired, along with a Barbara Hepworth and a Leon Underwood. However, I refused to buy an Eric Gill, after I was told that he'd slept with his daughters. It didn't seem to worry Jessica – you can't deny real talent, she kept reminding me – but I put my foot down. My final purchase was the artwork for a Beatles record cover by Peter Blake, which I gave to Jessica as a reward for her knowledge and expertise. She knew exactly which galleries to visit, and bargained with the dealers like an East End barrow boy. I wasn't sure whether to be proud or ashamed of her. And I must confess, I hadn't realized spending money could be quite so exhausting.'

Emma and Giles burst out laughing. 'You put us both to shame,' said Emma. 'I can't wait to see the collection. But where will you display it?'

'I think I've found an ideal house in Trumpington with enough wall space to hang all the paintings, and a large enough garden for the statues to be well displayed. So in future, it will be my turn to invite you to stay for the weekend. I haven't closed the deal yet, but I've set Sebastian on to the poor estate agents and left him to settle the price. Although I can't believe he'll do any better than Jessica – she's convinced that my art collection will turn out to be a more lucrative investment than stocks and shares, which she reminded her father you can't hang on a wall. He tried to explain to her the difference between "appreciation" and "appreciate", but he got nowhere.'

'Bravo,' said Emma. 'I only hope there's the odd Monet left over for me, because I'd also intended to ask Jessica's advice, although to tell you the truth I still haven't decided what to do with my windfall. I've had three meetings with Hakim Bishara and Seb, but I'm no nearer to making up my mind. Having lost one chairmanship, I've been concentrating on the government's new NHS reform package and its consequences for the Royal Infirmary.'

'That bill will never see the light of day if Margaret Thatcher wins the election,' said Giles.

'Amen to that,' said Emma. 'But it remains my responsibility to prepare my fellow board members for the consequences should Labour be returned to power. I don't intend to leave my successor, whoever he or she may be, to pick up the pieces.' She paused, before adding, 'Any other business?'

From under the table Giles produced magnificent models of the *Buckingham* and the *Balmoral*, along with a bottle of champagne. 'My dearest Emma,' he said, 'Grace and I will be forever in your debt. Without your leadership, dedication and commitment, we would not be in the privileged position we now find ourselves. We will be eternally grateful.'

Three tumblers that normally held water were filled to the brim with champagne by Giles, but Emma couldn't take her eyes off the two model ships.

'Thank you,' she said as they raised their glasses. 'But I confess I've enjoyed every moment and I'm already missing being chairman. I also have a surprise for you. Cunard have asked me to join their board, so I too would like to make a toast.' She rose from her place, and raised her glass.

'To Joshua Barrington, who founded the Barrington Shipping Line in 1839, and made a profit of thirty-three pounds, four shillings and tuppence in his first year as chairman, but promised the shareholders more.'

Giles and Grace raised their glasses.

'To Joshua Barrington.'

'Perhaps the time has come for us to celebrate the recent birth of my great-nephew, Jake,' said Giles, 'who Seb hopes will be the next chairman but one of Farthings Bank.'

'Would it be too much to hope that Jake might consider doing something more worthwhile than being a banker?' said Grace.

5

'How good was your source?'

'Unimpeachable. And he wrote down what he overheard, word for word.'

'Well, I can't pretend, chairman,' admitted Matron, 'that I haven't heard rumours of this kind before, but never anything that could be substantiated. The one nurse who did make an official complaint resigned a week later.'

'What options do we have?' asked Emma.

'Do you know anything about the nurse, other than the conversation that was overheard?'

'I can tell you that the alleged assault took place in the laundry room on the third floor.'

'That might cut it down to half a dozen nurses.'

'And she'd been on ward rounds with Dr Hands earlier that morning.'

'When was that?'

'Yesterday.'

'Then we're probably down to two or three nurses at most.'

'And she was West Indian.'

'Ah,' said Matron. 'I wondered why Beverley had a

black eye, and now I know. But she'd have to make an official complaint for us to consider opening an ethics enquiry.'

'How long would that take?'

'Six to nine months, and even then, as there were clearly no witnesses, I wouldn't give you much of a chance.'

'So it's back to square one and Dr Hands can continue on his merry way while we do nothing about it.'

'I'm afraid so, chairman, unless . . .'

—◦—

'Many congratulations on the successful takeover,' said Margaret Thatcher when Emma came on the line, 'although I can't imagine it was an easy decision.'

'I was torn in half,' admitted Emma. 'But the board, my family and all our professional advisors were unanimous in advising me to accept Cunard's offer.'

'So how are you filling your time, now you're no longer chairman of Barrington's?'

'I still have a few more months before I hand over the chairmanship of the Royal Infirmary, but after last night's vote of no confidence in the government, it looks as if I'll be spending most of my time running around the West Country trying to make sure you end up in Downing Street.'

'I'd rather you were running around the whole country doing the same job,' said Mrs Thatcher.

'I'm not sure I understand.'

'If you switch on your television, you'll see the Prime Minister being driven into Buckingham Palace for an appointment with the Queen. Mr Callaghan will be seeking her permission to prorogue Parliament so he can call a general election.'

'Has a date been fixed?'

'Thursday, May the third. And I want you to take on your brother head-on.'

'What do you have in mind?'

'As you probably know, he's once again in charge of Labour's marginal-seats campaign. Those fifty or sixty key constituencies that will determine the outcome of the election. I think you'd be the ideal person to do the same job for the Tory party.'

'But Giles has vast experience of election campaigns. He's a consummate politician—'

'—and no one knows him better than you.'

'There must be a dozen or more people who are far better qualified to take on such a responsibility.'

'You're my first choice. And I have a feeling your brother will not be pleased when he learns who he's up against.' A long silence followed, before Mrs Thatcher added, 'Come up to London and meet the party chairman, Peter Thorneycroft. He's already set everything up, so all I need now is a coordinator who will put the fear of God into our local chairmen in those marginal seats.'

This time Emma didn't hesitate. 'When do I start?'

'Tomorrow morning, ten o'clock, Central Office,' replied the leader of the opposition.

◄◦►

'You asked to see me, chairman.'

'I did, and I'll get straight to the point,' said Emma even before Hands had been given the chance to sit down. 'I've had several complaints from nurses concerning your unethical behaviour.'

'Several?' said Hands, who sat down in his chair, looking relaxed.

'During the past year, Matron has been collecting evidence, and she has asked me to set up an official enquiry.'

'Be my guest,' said Hands. 'You'll find nothing will stick, and I'll be completely exonerated.'

'Nothing will stick? An unfortunate choice of words, I would have thought, Dr Hands, unless of course . . .'

'You say another word, Lady Clifton, and I'll instruct my lawyers to issue a writ for libel.'

'I doubt it. Like you, I've made sure there are no witnesses, and while I accept that you may be cleared of all the charges, I intend to make sure that your reputation will be in tatters, and you'll never be able to find a job in this country again. So I suggest—'

'Are you threatening me? If you are, it could well be your reputation that ends up in tatters, once the enquiry proves to be a waste of time and money – and just when BRI has once again been shortlisted for hospital of the year.'

'Yes, I had considered that,' said Emma. 'In the past your strength has always been that it was your word against that of a young nurse. But this time you won't be dealing with a frightened young woman but the chairman of the hospital. And yes, I am willing to risk my reputation against yours.'

'You're bluffing,' said Hands. 'You've got less than a year to go, and you really wouldn't want this to be the one thing you're remembered for.'

'Wrong again, Dr Hands. When I expose you for what you are, I suspect your colleagues and the sixteen nurses who have provided written evidence –' Emma tapped a thick file on the desk in front of her, which was nothing more than a surveyor's report – 'will be only too grateful for my intervention, while you'll find it difficult to get a job in a minor African state.'

This time Hands hesitated before he spoke. 'I'll take my chances. I'm confident you don't have enough evidence to open an enquiry.'

Emma leant forward, dialled an outside number and switched the phone to speaker. A moment later they both heard the word, 'Editor.'

'Good morning, Reg. Emma Clifton.'

'Which one of my reporters do you want strung up this morning, Emma?'

'Not one of your reporters this time. One of my doctors.'

'Tell me more.'

'I'm about to instigate an enquiry into the behaviour of a doctor at the hospital, and I thought you'd want to hear about it before the nationals get hold of the story.'

'That's good of you, Emma.' Hands began waving at her frantically. 'But if the story is going to make the final edition, I'll need to send a reporter over to the hospital immediately.'

'I have an appointment at eleven,' said Emma, looking down at her diary, 'but I'll call you back in a few moments if I can rearrange it.'

As Emma hung up, she spotted beads of sweat appearing on Hands' forehead.

'If I'm to cancel my appointment with the reporter from the *Bristol Evening News*,' she said, once again tapping the file, 'I'll expect you to be off these premises by midday. Otherwise, I recommend you pick up today's final edition, in which you'll discover exactly what I think of doctors like you. Be sure to stay by your phone, as I have a feeling they'll want to hear your side of the story.'

Hands rose unsteadily from his seat and left the room without another word. Once the door had closed, Emma picked up the phone and re-dialled the number she had promised to call back.

'Thank you,' she said, when a voice came on the line.

'My pleasure,' said Harry. 'What time will you be home for dinner?'

—◦—

'If you're going to spend the next month in London,' said Harry after he'd heard Emma's news, 'where do you intend to stay?'

'With Giles. That way I'll be able to keep a close eye on his every move.'

'And he on yours. But I can't see him agreeing to such a cosy little arrangement.'

'He's not going to be given much choice,' said Emma. 'You've obviously forgotten I own the freehold of number twenty-three Smith Square. So if anyone's going to be looking for temporary accommodation, it will be Giles, not me.'

GILES BARRINGTON

1979–1981

6

'DO YOU WANT to hear the bad news?' said Giles as he strode into Griff Haskins's office and plonked himself down in the seat opposite a man who was lighting his fourth cigarette of the morning.

'Tony Benn's been found drunk in a brothel?'

'Worse. My sister is heading up the Conservatives' marginal-seat campaign.'

The veteran Labour agent collapsed in his chair and didn't speak for some time. 'A formidable opponent,' he eventually managed. 'And to think I taught her everything she knows. Not least how to fight a marginal seat.'

'It gets worse. She'll be staying with me in Smith Square for the duration of the campaign.'

'Then throw her out on the street,' said Griff, sounding as if he meant it.

'I can't. She actually owns the house. I've always been her tenant.'

This silenced Griff for a few moments, but he quickly recovered. 'Then we'll have to take advantage of it. If Karin can find out in the morning what she's up to that day, we'll always be one move ahead.'

'Nice idea,' said Giles, 'except I can't be sure whose side my wife is on.'

'Then throw her out on the street.'

'I don't think that would get the women's vote.'

'Then we'll have to rely on Markham. Get him to listen in on her phone calls, open her mail if necessary.'

'Markham votes Conservative. Always has.'

'Isn't there anyone in your house who supports the Labour party?'

'Silvina, my cleaner. But she doesn't speak very good English, and I'm not sure she has a vote.'

'Then you'll need to keep your eyes and ears open, because I want to know what your sister is up to every minute of every day. Which constituencies she's targeting, which leading Tories will be visiting those constituencies and anything else you can find out.'

'She'll be equally keen to find out what I'm up to,' said Giles.

'Then we must feed her with false information.'

'She'll have worked that out by the second day.'

'Possibly, but don't forget, you have much more ex-perience than her when it comes to fighting elections. She's going to be on a steep learning curve and relying a lot on my opposite number.'

'Do you know him?'

'John Lacy,' said Griff. 'I know him better than my own brother. I've played Cain to his Abel for over thirty years.' He stubbed out his cigarette before lighting another one. 'I first came across Lacy in 1945, Attlee versus Churchill, and like a Rottweiler he's been licking his wounds ever since.'

'Then let's take Clem Attlee as our inspiration, and do what he did to Churchill.'

'This is probably his last election,' said Griff, almost as if he was talking to himself.

'Ours too,' said Giles, 'if we lose.'

—◄○►—

'If you're living in the same house as your brother,' said Lacy, 'we must take advantage of it.'

Emma looked across the desk at her chief of staff and felt she was quickly getting to know how his mind worked. Lacy must have been around 5 foot 7 inches and, although he'd never participated in any sport other than baiting the Labour Party, there wasn't an ounce of spare flesh on him. A man who considered sleep a luxury he couldn't afford, didn't believe in lunch breaks, had never smoked nor drunk, and only deserted the party on Sunday mornings to worship the only being he considered superior to his leader. His thinning grey hair made him look older than he was, and his piercing blue eyes never left you.

'What do you have in mind?' asked Emma.

'The moment your brother leaves the house in the morning, I need to know which constituencies he plans to visit, and which senior Labour politicians will be accompanying him, so our workers can be waiting for them as they get off the train.'

'That's rather underhand, isn't it?'

'Be assured, Lady Clifton—'

'Emma.'

'Emma. We are not trying to win a baking competition at your local village fête, but a general election. The stakes couldn't be higher. You must look upon any socialists as the enemy because this is all-out war. It's our job to make sure that in four weeks' time, none of them are left standing – and that includes your brother.'

'That may take me a little time to get used to.'

'You've got twenty-four hours to get up to speed. And never forget, your brother is the best, and Griff Haskins is the worst, which makes them a formidable combination.'

'So where do I start?'

Lacy got up from behind his desk and walked across to a large chart pinned to the wall.

'These are the sixty-two marginal seats we have to win if we hope to form the next government,' he said, even before Emma had joined him. 'Each of them needs only a four per cent swing or less to change colour. If both the major parties end up with thirty-one of these seats' – he tapped the chart – 'it will be a hung parliament. If either can gain ten seats, they will have a majority of twenty in the House. That's how important our job is.'

'What about the other six hundred seats?'

'Most of them have already been decided long before a ballot box is opened. We're only interested in seats where they count the votes, not weigh them. Of course there will be one or two surprises, there always are, but we haven't the time to try to work out which ones they're going to be. Our job is to concentrate on the sixty-two marginals and try to make sure every one of them returns a Conservative Member of Parliament.'

Emma looked more carefully at the long list of seats, starting with the most marginal, Basildon, Labour majority of 22, swing needed 0.1 per cent.

'If we can't win that one,' said Lacy, 'we'll have to suffer another five years of Labour government.' His finger shot down to the bottom of the chart. 'Gravesend, which needs a 4.1 per cent swing. If that turned out to be the uniform swing across the country, it would guarantee the Conservatives a majority of thirty.'

'What are the seven little boxes alongside each constituency?'

'We need every one of them ticked off before election day.'

Emma studied the headings: Candidate, Swing Required, Agent, Chairman, Drivers, Adopted Constituency, AOP.

'There are three seats that still don't even have a candidate,' said Emma, staring at the list in disbelief.

'They will have by the end of the week, otherwise they could return a Labour member unopposed, and we're not going to let that happen.'

'But what if we can't find a suitable candidate at such short notice?'

'We'll find someone,' said Lacy, 'even if it's the village idiot, and there are one or two of those already sitting on our side of the House, some of them in safe seats.'

Emma laughed, as her eye moved on to 'Adopted Constituency'.

'A safe seat will adopt an adjoining marginal constituency,' explained Lacy, 'offering it the assistance of an experienced agent, canvassers, even money when it's needed. We have a reserve fund with enough cash to supply any marginal seat with ten thousand pounds at a moment's notice.'

'Yes, I became aware of that during the last election when I was working in the West Country,' said Emma. 'But I found some constituencies were more cooperative than others.'

'And you'll find that's the same right across the country. Local chairmen who think they know how to run a campaign better than we do, treasurers who would rather lose an election than part with a penny from their current account, Members of Parliament who claim they might lose their seats even when they have a twenty thousand majority. Whenever we come up against those sorts of problems, you'll be the one who has to call the constituency chairman and sort it out. Not least because they won't take any notice of an agent, however senior, and especially when everyone knows you have Mother's ear.'

'Mother?'

'Sorry,' said Lacy. 'It's agent shorthand for the leader.' Emma smiled.

'And "OAP"?' she asked, placing a finger on the bottom line.

'Not old age pensioners,' said Lacy, 'although they may well decide who wins the election because, assuming they can turn out, they're the most likely to vote. And even if they can't walk, we'll supply a car and driver to take them to the nearest polling station. When I was a young agent I even helped someone get to the poll on a stretcher. It was only when I dropped him back at his house he told me he'd voted Labour.'

Emma tried to keep a straight face.

'No,' said Lacy, 'it's AOP, which stands for Any Other Problems, of which there will be several every day. But I'll try to make sure you only have to deal with the really difficult ones because most of the time you'll be out on the road while I'm back here at base.'

'Is there any good news?' asked Emma, as she continued to study the chart.

'Yes. You can be sure that our opponents are facing exactly the same problems as we are, and just be thankful we don't have a box marked "Unions".' Lacy turned to his boss. 'I'm told you're well acquainted with the methods of Griff Haskins, your brother's right-hand. I've known him for years but really don't know him at all, so what's he like to work with?'

'Totally ruthless. Doesn't believe in giving anyone the benefit of the doubt, works untold hours, and considers all Tories were spawned by the devil.'

'But we both know he has one great weakness.'

'True,' said Emma, 'but he never drinks during a campaign. In fact, he won't touch a drop until the final vote has been cast in the last constituency, when, win or lose, he'll get plastered.'

◄○►

'I see the latest opinion poll gives Labour a two per cent lead,' said Karin, as she looked up from her paper.

'No politics at the breakfast table, please,' said Giles. 'And certainly not while Emma is in the room.'

Karin smiled across the table at her sister-in-law.

'Did you notice that your ex-wife is back in the headlines?' asked Emma.

'What's she been up to this time?'

'It appears that Lady Virginia will be withdrawing the Honourable Freddie from his posh prep school in Scotland. William Hickey is hinting that it's because she's once again short of cash.'

'I've never thought of you as an *Express* reader,' said Giles.

'Seventy-three per cent of its readers support Margaret Thatcher,' said Emma, 'which is why I don't bother with the *Mirror*.'

When the phone rang, Giles immediately left the table and, ignoring the phone on the sideboard, retreated into the corridor, closing the door firmly behind him.

'Where's he off to today?' whispered Emma.

'I plead the fifth,' said Karin, 'although I am willing to tell you his driver's taking him to Paddington.'

'Reading 3.7 per cent, Bath 2.9 per cent, Bristol Docklands 1.6 per cent, Exeter 2.7 per cent and Truro—'

'It can't be Truro,' said Karin. 'He's got a meeting at Transport House at eight o'clock this evening, so he couldn't be back in time.' She paused as Markham came into the room with a fresh supply of coffee.

'Who was my brother speaking to on the phone?' asked Emma casually.

'Mr Denis Healey.'

'Ah yes, and they're off to . . . ?'

'Reading, my lady,' said the butler, pouring Emma a cup of coffee.

'You would have made a good spy,' said Emma.

'Thank you, my lady,' said Markham, before clearing away the plates and leaving the room.

'How do you know he isn't one?' whispered Karin.

7

IF ANYONE HAD asked Emma to account for what took
place during the next twenty-eight days, she would have
described them as one long blur. Days that began with her
leaping into a car at six o'clock each morning continued
relentlessly until she fell asleep, usually in an empty train
carriage or the back of a plane, around one the following
morning.

Giles kept to roughly the same routine: same modes of
transport, same hours, different constituencies. Far from
them being able to spy continuously on each other, their
paths rarely crossed.

The polls consistently showed the Labour Party a
couple of points ahead, and John Lacy warned Emma
that during the last week of any campaign the electorate tended to move towards the government of the day.
Emma didn't get that feeling while she was out canvassing
on the high streets, but she did wonder if the voters were
just being polite when they spotted her blue rosette and
she asked if they'd be voting Conservative. Whenever
Mrs Thatcher was asked about the polls as she travelled
around the country, she would always reply, 'Straw polls

are for straw people. Only real people will be voting on May the third.'

Although she and Mrs Thatcher only had one conversation during the twenty-eight-day campaign, Emma concluded that her party leader was either a very accomplished actress, or really did believe the Conservatives were going to win.

'There are two factors the polls are unable to take into account,' she told Emma. 'How many people are unwilling to admit they will vote for a woman prime minister, and how many wives are not telling their husbands they will be voting Conservative for the first time.'

◄○►

Both Giles and Emma were in Bristol Docklands on the last day of the campaign, and when ten p.m. struck and the last vote had been cast, neither felt confident enough to predict the final outcome. They both hurried back to London by train, but didn't share the same carriage.

John Lacy had told Emma that the hierarchy of both parties would descend on their headquarters – Conservative Central Office and Labour's Transport House, political sentinels perched at different corners of Smith Square – where they would await the results.

'By two a.m.,' Lacy briefed her, 'the trend will have been set, and we'll probably know who's going to form the next government. By four a.m., the lights will be blazing in one building and celebrations will continue until daybreak.'

'And in the other building?' said Emma.

'The lights will begin to go out around three, when the vanquished will make their way home and decide who to blame as they prepare for opposition.'

'What do you think the result will be?' Emma had asked the chief agent on the eve of the poll.

'Predictions are for mugs and bookies,' Lacy had retorted. 'But whatever the result,' he added, 'it's been a privilege to work with the Boadicea of Bristol.'

When the train pulled into Paddington, Emma leapt off and grabbed the first available taxi. Arriving back in Smith Square, she was relieved to find that Giles hadn't yet appeared, but Harry was waiting for her. She quickly showered and changed her clothes before the two of them made their way across to the other side of the square.

She was surprised how many people recognized her. Some even applauded as she passed by, while others stared at her in sullen silence. Then a cheer went up, and Emma turned to see her brother getting out of a car and waving to his party's supporters before disappearing into Transport House.

Emma re-entered a building she had become all too familiar with during the past month, and was greeted by several leading party apparatchiks she'd come across while out on the campaign trail. People surrounded televisions in every room, as supporters, party workers and Central Office staff waited for the first result to come in. Not a politician in sight. They were all back in their constituencies, waiting to find out if they were still Members of Parliament.

Croydon Central was declared at 1.23 a.m., with a swing of 1.8 per cent to the Conservatives. Only muted cheers were offered up because everyone knew that suggested a hung parliament, with Jim Callaghan returning to the palace to be asked if he could form a government.

At 1.43 a.m. the cheers became louder when the Conservatives captured Basildon, which on Emma's chart suggested a Conservative majority of around 30. After that, the results began to come in thick and fast, including a recount in Bristol Docklands.

By the time Mrs Thatcher drove over from her Finchley constituency just after three a.m., the lights were already going out in Transport House. As she entered Central Office, the doubters were suddenly long-term supporters, and the long-term supporters were looking forward to joining her first administration.

The leader of the opposition paused halfway up the stairs and made a short speech of thanks. Emma was touched that hers was among the names mentioned in dispatches. After shaking several outstretched hands, Mrs Thatcher left the building a few minutes later, explaining that she had a busy day ahead of her. Emma wondered if she would even go to bed.

Just after four a.m., Emma dropped into John Lacy's office for the last time to find him standing by the chart and filling in the latest results.

'What's your prediction?' she asked as she stared at a sea of blue boxes.

'It's looking like a majority of over forty,' Lacy replied. 'More than enough to govern for the next five years.'

'And our sixty-two marginal seats?' Emma asked.

'We've won all except three, but they're on their third recount in Bristol Docklands, so it could be just two.'

'I think we can allow Giles that one,' Emma whispered.

'I always knew you were a closet wet,' said Lacy.

Emma thought about her brother, and how he must be feeling now.

'Goodnight, John,' she said. 'And thank you for everything. See you in five years' time,' she added before making her way out of the building and back across to her home on the other side of the square, where she planned to return to the real world.

◄○►

Emma woke a few hours later to find Harry seated on her side of the bed, holding a cup of tea.

'Will you be joining us for breakfast, my darling, now that you've done your job?'

She yawned and stretched her arms. 'Not a bad idea, Harry Clifton, because it's time I got back to work.'

'So what's the plot for today?'

'I have to get back to Bristol, sharpish. I've got a meeting with the newly appointed chairman of the hospital at three this afternoon, to discuss priorities for the next year.'

'Are you happy with your successor?'

'Couldn't be more pleased. Simon Dawkins is a first-class administrator and he was a loyal deputy, so I'm expecting the handover to be seamless.'

'Then I'll leave you to get dressed,' said Harry, before handing his wife her tea and heading back downstairs to join Giles for breakfast.

Giles was seated at the far end of the table surrounded by the morning papers, which didn't make good reading. He smiled for the first time that day when his brother-in-law entered the room.

'How are you feeling?' asked Harry, placing a consoling hand on the shoulder of his oldest friend.

'I've had better mornings,' admitted Giles, pushing the papers to one side. 'But I'm hardly in a position to complain. I've served as a minister for nine of the past fourteen years, and I must still have a chance of holding office in five years' time, because I can't believe that woman will last.'

Both men stood when Emma entered the room.

'Congratulations, sis,' said Giles. 'You were a worthy opponent, and it was a deserved victory.'

'Thank you, Giles,' she said, giving her brother a hug, something she hadn't done for the past twenty-eight days. 'So what are you up to today?' she asked as she sat in the chair beside him.

'Some time this morning I'll have to hand in my seals of office so that woman,' he said, stabbing a finger at the photograph on the front page of the *Daily Express*, 'can form her first, and I hope last, administration. Thatcher's due at the palace at ten, when she'll kiss hands before being driven to Downing Street in triumph. You'll be able to watch it on television, but I hope you'll forgive me if I don't join you.'

◄○►

After Emma had finished packing, Harry placed their suitcases by the front door before joining her in the drawing room, not surprised to find her glued to the television. She didn't even look up when he entered the room.

Three black Jaguars were emerging from Buckingham Palace. The crowds standing on the pavement outside the palace gates were waving and clapping as the convoy made its way up the Mall to Whitehall. Robin Day kept up a running commentary.

'The new Prime Minister will spend the morning appointing her first Cabinet. Lord Carrington is expected to be foreign secretary, Geoffrey Howe chancellor, and Leon Brittan home secretary. As for the other appointments, we will have to wait and see who is preferred. I don't suppose there will be many surprises, although you can be quite sure there will be several anxious politicians sitting by their phones hoping for a call from Number Ten,' he added as the three cars swept into Downing Street.

As the Prime Minister stepped out of her car, another cheer went up. She made a short speech quoting Saint Francis of Assisi before disappearing into No. 10.

'Better get moving,' said Harry, 'or we'll miss the train.'

◄○►

Emma spent the afternoon with Simon Dawkins, her successor at Bristol Royal Infirmary, before clearing out her second office that day. She filled the back seat of her car as well as the boot with all the personal possessions she had accumulated over the past decade. As she drove slowly out of the hospital grounds for the last time, she didn't look back. She was looking forward to a quiet supper at the Manor House with Harry, and later to placing her head on a pillow before midnight for the first time in weeks, while hoping for more than four hours' sleep.

◄○►

Emma was in her dressing gown enjoying a late breakfast when the call came.

Harry picked up the phone on the sideboard and listened for a moment, before covering the mouthpiece and whispering, 'It's Number Ten.'

Emma leapt up and took the phone, assuming it would be Mrs Thatcher on the other end of the line.

'This is Number Ten,' said a formal voice. 'The Prime

Minister wonders if you could see her at twelve thirty this afternoon.'

'Yes of course,' said Emma without thinking.

'When?' asked Harry as she put the phone down.

'Twelve thirty at Number Ten.'

'You'd better get dressed immediately while I bring the car round. We'll have to get a move on if you hope to catch the ten past ten.'

Emma ran upstairs and took longer than she intended deciding what to wear. A simple navy suit and a white silk blouse won the day.

Harry managed 'You look great,' as he accelerated down the driveway and out of the front gates, glad to have avoided the morning rush. He pulled up outside Temple Meads just after ten.

'Call me as soon as you've seen her,' he shouted at the departing figure, but couldn't be sure if Emma had heard him.

Emma couldn't help thinking as the train pulled out of the station, that if Margaret just wanted to thank her, she could have done it over the phone. She scanned the morning papers, which were covered with pictures of the new Prime Minister and details of her senior appointments. The cabinet were due to meet for the first time at ten o'clock that morning. She checked her watch: 10.15 a.m.

Emma was among the first off the train, and ran all the way to the taxi rank. When she reached the front of the queue and said, 'Number Ten Downing Street, and I have to be there by twelve thirty,' the cabbie looked at her as if to say, Pull the other one.

When the taxi drove into Whitehall and stopped at the bottom of Downing Street, a policeman glanced in the back, smiled and saluted. The taxi drove slowly up to the front door of No. 10. When Emma took out her purse, the driver said, 'No charge, miss. I voted Tory, so this one's on me. And by the way, good luck.'

Before Emma could knock on the door of No. 10, it swung open. She stepped inside to find a young woman waiting for her.

'Good morning, Lady Clifton. My name is Alison, and I'm one of the Prime Minister's personal secretaries. I know she's looking forward to seeing you.'

Emma followed the secretary silently up the stairs to the first floor where they came to a halt in front of a door. The secretary knocked, opened it and stood aside. Emma walked in to find Mrs Thatcher on the phone.

'We'll speak again later, Willy, when I'll let you know my decision.' The Prime Minister put the phone down. 'Emma,' she said, rising from behind her desk. 'So kind of you to return to London at such short notice. I'd assumed you were still in town.'

'Not a problem, Prime Minister.'

'First, my congratulations on winning fifty-nine of the sixty-two targeted marginal seats. A triumph! Although I expect your brother will tease you about failing to capture Bristol Docklands.'

'Next time, Prime Minister.'

'But that could be five years away and we've got rather a lot to do before then, which is why I wanted to see you. You probably know that I've invited Patrick Jenkin to be Secretary of State for Health, and of course he will need an undersecretary in the Lords to steer the new National Health Bill through the Upper House and safely on to the books. And I can't think of anyone better qualified to do that job. You have vast experience of the NHS, and your years as chairman of a public company make you the ideal candidate for the post. So I do hope you'll feel able to join the government as a life peer.'

Emma was speechless.

'One of the truly wonderful things about you, Emma, is that it hadn't even crossed your mind that was the reason I wanted to see you. Half my ministers assumed they got no more than they deserved, while the other half couldn't hide their disappointment. I suspect you're the only one who's genuinely surprised.'

Emma found herself nodding.

'So let me tell you what's going to happen now. When you leave here, there will be a car outside to take you to Alexander Fleming House, where the Secretary of State is expecting you. He will take you through your responsibilities in great detail. In particular, he will want to talk to you about the new National Health Bill, which I'd like to get through both Houses as quickly as possible, preferably within a year. Listen to Patrick Jenkin – he's a shrewd politician, as is the Department's Permanent Secretary. I would recommend you to also seek your brother's counsel. He was not only an able minister, but no one knows better how the House of Lords works.'

'But he's on the other side.'

'It doesn't work quite like that in the Lords, as you'll quickly find out. They are far more civilized at the other end of the House, and not just interested in scoring political points. And my final piece of advice is to make sure you enjoy it.'

'I'm flattered you even considered me, Prime Minister, and, I'm bound to admit, somewhat daunted by the challenge.'

'No need to be. You were my first choice for the

job,' said Mrs Thatcher. 'One final thing, Emma. You are among a handful of friends who I hope will still call me Margaret, because I won't have this job for ever.'

'Thank you, Prime Minister.'

Emma rose from her place and shook hands with her new boss. When she left the room, she found Alison standing in the corridor.

'Congratulations, minister. A car is waiting to take you to your department.'

As they walked back downstairs, past the photographs of former prime ministers, Emma tried to take in what had happened during the last few minutes. Just as she reached the hallway, the front door opened and a young man stepped inside, to be led up the stairs by another secretary. She wondered what position Norman was about to be offered.

'If you'd like to follow me,' said Alison, who opened a side door that led into a small room with a desk and telephone. Emma was puzzled until she closed the door and added, 'The Prime Minister thought you might like to call your husband before you begin your new job.'

8

GILES SPENT THE MORNING moving his papers, files and personal belongings from one end of the corridor to the other. He left behind a spacious, well-appointed office overlooking Parliament Square, just a few steps from the chamber, along with a retinue of staff whose only purpose was to carry out his every requirement.

In exchange, he moved into cramped quarters, manned by a single secretary, from which he was expected to carry out the same job in opposition. His downfall was both painful and immediate. No longer could he rely on a cadre of civil servants to advise him, organize his diary and draft his speeches. Those same servants now served a different master, who represented another party, in order that the process of government should continue seamlessly. Such is democracy.

When the phone rang, Giles answered it to find the leader of the opposition on the other end of the line.

'I'm chairing a meeting of the Shadow Cabinet at ten o'clock on Monday morning in my new office in the Commons, Giles. I hope you'll be able to attend.'

No longer able to call upon a private secretary to

summon Cabinet members to No. 10, Jim Callaghan was making his own phone calls for the first time in years.

—◁○▷—

To say that Giles's colleagues looked shell-shocked when they took their places around the table the following Monday would have been an understatement. All of them had considered the possibility of losing to the lady, but not by such a large majority.

Jim Callaghan chaired the meeting, having hastily scribbled out an agenda on the back of an envelope which a secretary had typed up and was now distributing to those colleagues who'd survived the electoral cull. The only subject that concentrated the minds of those seated around that table was when Jim would resign as leader of the Labour Party. It was the first item on the agenda. Once they had found their opposition feet, he told his colleagues, he intended to make way for a new leader. Feet that would, for the next few years, do little more than tramp through the Not Content's lobby to vote against the government, only to be defeated again and again.

When the meeting came to an end, Giles did something he hadn't done for years. He walked home – no ministerial car. He'd miss Bill, and dropped him a line to thank him, before joining Karin for lunch.

'Was it ghastly?' she asked him as he strolled into the kitchen.

'It was like attending a wake, because we all know we can't do anything about it for at least four years. And by then I'll be sixty-three,' he reminded her, 'and the new leader of the party, whoever that might be, will undoubtedly have his own candidate to replace me.'

'Unless you throw your support behind the man who

becomes the next leader,' said Karin, 'in which case you'll still have a place at the top table.'

'Denis Healey is the only credible candidate for the job in my opinion, and I'm pretty confident the party will get behind him.'

'Who's he likely to be up against?' Karin asked as she poured him a glass of wine.

'The unions will support Michael Foot, but most members will realize that with his left-wing credentials the party wouldn't have much hope of winning the next general election.' He drained his glass. 'But we don't have to worry about that possibility for some time, so let's talk about something more palatable, like where you'd like to spend your summer holiday.'

'There's something else we need to discuss before we decide that,' said Karin, as she mashed some potatoes. 'The electorate may have rejected you, but I know some-one who still needs your help.'

'What are you talking about?'

'Emma rang earlier this morning. She hopes you might be willing to advise her on her new job.'

'Her new job?'

'Hasn't anyone told you? She's been appointed Under Secretary of State for Health, and she'll be joining you in the Lords.' Karin waited to see how he would react.

'How proud our mother would have been,' were Giles's first words. 'So at least something good has come out of this election. I'll certainly be able to show her which potholes to avoid, which members to heed, which ones to ignore and how to gain the confidence of the House. Not an easy job at the best of times,' he said, already warming to the task. 'I'll call her straight after lunch and offer to take her round the Palace of Westminster while we're in recess.'

'And if we were to go to Scotland for our holiday this year,' said Karin, 'we could invite Harry and Emma to join us. It would be the first time in years you wouldn't be continually interrupted by civil servants claiming there's a crisis, or journalists who say sorry to disturb you on holiday, minister, but . . .'

'Good idea. By the time Emma is presented to the House in October, her new colleagues will think she's already spent a decade in the Lords.'

'And there's another thing we ought to discuss now you have so much more time on your hands,' said Karin as she placed a plate of stew on the table in front of him.

'You're quite right, my darling,' said Giles, picking up his knife and fork. 'But don't let's just talk about it this time, let's do something.'

◄○►

Lord Goodman heaved himself up from behind his desk as his secretary entered the office accompanied by a prospective client.

'What a pleasure to meet you at last, Mrs Grant,' the distinguished lawyer said as they shook hands. 'Do have a seat,' he added, ushering her to a comfortable chair.

'Is it correct that you were the Prime Minister's lawyer?' asked Ellie May, once she was seated.

'Yes, I was,' said Goodman. 'I now only serve Mr Wilson in a private capacity.'

'And have you found time to read the letter and enclosures I sent you recently?' Ellie May asked, well aware that small talk would be charged at the same rate as legal opinion.

'Every word,' said Goodman, tapping a file on the table in front of him. 'I only wish your husband had sought my advice at the time of this unfortunate incident. Had he done so, I would have recommended that he call the lady's bluff.'

'There would be far less need for lawyers, Lord Goodman, if we were all blessed with hindsight. But despite that, is it your opinion that Lady Virginia has a case to answer?'

'Most emphatically she does, madam. That is, assuming Mr and Mrs Morton will agree to sign an affidavit confirming that the Hon. Freddie Fenwick is their offspring, and that Lady Virginia was aware of that at the time of the child's birth.'

'Just put the necessary document in front of them, Lord Goodman, and they will sign. And once they've done so, can Cyrus claim back the full amount he's paid out to that charlatan over the years?'

'Every red cent, plus any interest or other charges set by the court, along with my fees, of course.'

'So your advice would be to sue the bitch?' Ellie May asked, leaning forward.

'With one proviso,' said Goodman, raising an eyebrow.

'Lawyers always come up with a proviso just in case they end up losing. So let's hear it.'

'There wouldn't be much point in suing Lady Virginia for such a large sum if she has no assets of any real value. One newspaper,' he said, opening a thick file, 'is claiming she's withdrawing young Freddie from his prep school because she can no longer afford the fees.'

'But she owns a house in Onslow Square, I'm reliably informed, and has half a dozen staff to run it.'

'Had,' said Goodman. 'Lady Virginia sold the house

some months ago and sacked all the staff.' He opened another file and checked some press cuttings before passing them across to his client.

Once Ellie May had finished reading them, she asked, 'Does this alter your opinion?'

'No, but to start with, I would recommend we send Lady Virginia a without prejudice letter, requesting that she pay back the full amount, and give her thirty days to respond. I find it hard to believe she won't want to make some sort of settlement rather than be declared bankrupt and even face the possibility of being arrested for fraud.'

'And if she doesn't . . . because I have a feeling she won't,' said Ellie May.

'You will have to decide whether or not to issue a writ, with the strong possibility that not one penny will be recovered, in which case you will still have to pay your own legal costs, which will not be insubstantial.' Goodman paused before adding, 'On balance, I would advise caution. Of course, the decision is yours. But as I have pointed out, Mrs Grant, that could end up costing you a great deal of money, with no guarantee of any return.'

'If that bitch ends up bankrupt, humiliated and having to face a spell in prison, it will have been worth every penny.'

◄○►

Harry and Emma joined Giles and Karin for a fortnight at Mulgelrie Castle, their maternal grandfather's family home in Scotland, and whenever the phone rang, it was almost always for Emma, and when red boxes arrived, Giles had to get used to not opening them.

Her brother was able to advise the fledgling minister on how to deal with civil servants who seemed to have forgotten she was on holiday, and political journalists who were desperate for an August story while the House wasn't sitting. And whenever they took a stroll on the grouse moors together, Giles answered all his sister's myriad questions, sharing with her his years of experience as a minister in the Lords, so that by the time she returned to London, Emma felt she hadn't so much had a holiday as attended several advanced seminars on government.

After Emma and Harry had departed, Giles and Karin stayed on for another couple of weeks. Giles had something else he needed to do before he attended the party conference in Brighton.

◂◦▸

'Thank you for agreeing to see me, Archie.'

'My pleasure,' said the tenth Earl of Fenwick. 'I will never forget your kindness when I took my father's seat in the House and made my maiden speech.'

'It was very well received,' said Giles. 'Even though you did attack the government.'

'And I intend to be equally critical of the Conservatives, if their farming policy is as antiquarian as yours. But tell me, Giles, to what do I owe this honour, because you've never struck me as a man who has time to waste.'

'I confess,' said Giles as Archie handed him a large glass of whisky, 'that I'm a seeker after information concerning a family matter.'

'It wouldn't be your ex-wife Virginia you're curious about, by any chance?'

'Got it in one. I was rather hoping you could bring me up to date on what your sister's been doing lately. I'll explain why later.'

'I only wish I could,' said Archie, 'but I can't pretend

we're that close. The only thing I know for sure is that Virginia's penniless once again, even though I have abided by the terms of my father's will, and continued to supply her with a monthly allowance. But it won't be nearly enough to deal with her present problems.'

Giles sipped his whisky. 'Could one of the problems be the Hon. Freddie Fenwick?'

Archie didn't reply immediately. 'One thing we now know for certain,' he eventually said, 'is that Freddie is not Virginia's son and, perhaps more interestingly, my father must have known that long before he left her only one bequest in his will.'

'The bottle of Maker's Mark,' said Giles.

'Yes. That had me puzzled for some time,' admitted Archie, 'until I had a visit from a Mrs Ellie May Grant of Baton Rouge, Louisiana, who explained that it was her husband Cyrus's favourite brand of whisky. She then told me in great detail what had taken place on her husband's visit to London when he had the misfortune to encounter Virginia. But I'm still in the dark as to how she got away with it for so long.'

'Then let me add what I know, courtesy of the Honorable Hayden Rankin, Governor of Louisiana, and an old friend of Cyrus T. Grant III. It seems that while Cyrus was on his first and last trip to London, Virginia set up an elaborate scam to convince him that he had proposed to her, despite the fact he already had plans to marry someone else – Ellie May, in fact. She then duped the foolish man into believing she was pregnant, and he was the father. That's about everything I know.'

'I can add a little more,' said Archie. 'Mrs Grant informed me she had recently employed Virginia's former butler and his wife, a Mr and Mrs Morton, who have signed an affidavit confirming that Freddie was their child, which is the reason Virginia's monthly payments from Cyrus suddenly dried up.'

'No wonder she's penniless. Is Freddie aware that the Mortons are in fact his parents?'

'No, he's never asked and I've never told him, as he clearly feels his parents abandoned him,' said Archie. 'And it gets worse. Mrs Grant has recently instructed Lord Goodman to represent her in an attempt to get back every penny Cyrus parted with. And having had the pleasure of meeting the formidable Ellie May Grant, I can tell you my sister has finally met her match.'

'But how can Virginia possibly—' Giles fell silent when the door swung open and a young boy burst in.

'What have I told you about knocking, Freddie, especially when I have a guest with me.'

'Sorry, sir,' said Freddie, and quickly turned to leave.

'Before you go, I'd like you to meet a great politician.' Freddie turned back. 'This is Lord Barrington, who until recently was leader of the House of Lords.'

'How do you do, sir,' said Freddie, thrusting out his hand. He stared at Giles for some time before he eventually said, 'Aren't you the man who was married to my mother?'

'Yes I am,' said Giles. 'And I'm delighted to meet you at last.'

'But you're not my father, are you?' said Freddie, after another long pause.

'No, I'm not.'

Freddie looked disappointed. 'My uncle says you are a great politician, but isn't it also true that you were once a great cricketer?'

'Never great,' said Giles, trying to lighten the mood. 'And that was a long time ago.'

'But you scored a century at Lord's.'

'Some still consider that my greatest achievement.'

'One day I'm going to score a century at Lord's,' said Freddie.

'I hope I'll be present to witness it.'

'You could come and watch me bat next Sunday. It's the local derby, Castle versus the Village, and I'm going to score the winning run.'

'Freddie, I don't think—'

'Sadly I have to be in Brighton for the Labour Party conference,' said Giles. Freddie looked disappointed. 'Though I must confess,' Giles continued, 'I'd far rather be watching you play cricket than listening to endless speeches by trade union leaders who'll be saying exactly the same thing as they said last year.'

'Do you still play cricket, sir?'

'Only when the Lords play the Commons and no one will notice how out of form I am.'

'Form is temporary, class is permanent, my cricket master told me.'

'That may be so,' said Giles, 'but I'm nearly sixty, and that's my age, not my batting average.'

'W. G. Grace played for England when he was over fifty, sir, so perhaps you'd consider turning out for us some time in the future?'

'Freddie, you must remember that Lord Barrington is a very busy man.'

'But not too busy to accept such a flattering offer.'

'Thank you, sir,' said Freddie. 'I'll send you the fixture list. Must leave you now,' he added. 'I have to work on the batting order with Mr Lawrie, our butler, who's also the Castle's captain.' Freddie dashed off before Giles had a chance to ask his next question.

'I'm sorry about that,' said Archie, after the door had closed, 'but Freddie doesn't seem to realize that other people just might have a life of their own.'

'Does he live here with you?' asked Giles.

'Only during the holidays, which I'm afraid isn't ideal, because now my girls have grown up and left home he's rather short of company. The nearest house is a couple of miles away, and they don't have any children. But despite Virginia abandoning the poor boy, he's no financial burden, because my father left Freddie the Glen Fenwick Distillery, which produces an annual income of just under a hundred thousand pounds, which he'll inherit on his twenty-fifth birthday. In fact, that's what you're drinking,' said Archie as he topped Giles's glass up, before adding, 'But I've recently been warned by our lawyers that Virginia has her eyes on the distillery, and is taking advice on whether she can break the terms of my father's will.'

'It wouldn't be the first time she's tried to do that,' said Giles.

9

'ARE YOU NERVOUS?'

'You bet I am,' admitted Emma. 'It reminds me of my first day at school,' she added, as she adjusted her long red robe.

'There's nothing to be nervous about,' said Giles. 'Just think of yourself as a Christian who's about to enter the Colosseum at the time of Diocletian, with several hundred starving lions waiting impatiently for their first meal in weeks.'

'That hardly fills me with confidence,' said Emma, as two doormen in court dress pulled open the west doors to allow the three peers to enter the chamber.

The Baroness Clifton of Chew Magna, in the county of Somerset, entered the chamber for the first time. On her right, also wearing a long red gown and carrying a tricorn hat, was Lord Belstead, the leader of the House of Lords. On her left, Lord Barrington of Bristol Docklands, a former leader of the House. The first time in the long history of the Lords that a new member had been supported by the leaders of the two main political parties.

As Emma walked on to the floor of the House, a thousand eyes stared at her, from both sides of the chamber.

The three of them doffed their tricorn hats and bowed to their peers. They then continued past the cross benches, packed with members who bore no allegiance to any political party, often referred to as the great and the good. They could be the deciding factor on any contentious issue once they decided which lobby to cast their vote in, Giles had told her.

They proceeded along the government front bench until Lord Belstead reached the despatch box. The table clerk gave the new peer a warm smile, and handed her a card on which was printed the oath of allegiance to the Crown.

Emma stared at the words she had already rehearsed in the bath that morning, during breakfast, in the car on the way to the Palace of Westminster and finally as she was being 'fitted up' in the robing room. But suddenly it was no longer a rehearsal.

'I, Emma, Baroness Clifton, swear by Almighty God, that I will be faithful, and bear allegiance to Her Majesty the Queen, her heirs and successors, according to the law, so help me God.'

The table clerk turned the page of a large parchment manuscript so the new member could add her name to the test roll. He offered her a pen which she politely declined in favour of one that had been given to her by her grandfather, Lord Harvey, at her christening almost sixty years ago.

Once Emma had signed the test roll, she glanced up at the Distinguished Strangers' Gallery, to see Harry, Karin, Sebastian, Samantha, Grace and Jessica smiling down at her with unmistakable pride. She smiled back, and when she lowered her eyes, saw a lady from the Commons standing at the bar of the House. The Prime

Minister gave her a slight bow, and Emma returned the compliment.

The Baroness Clifton followed her brother along the front bench, past the Woolsack on which sat the law lords, until she reached the Speaker's chair. The clerk of the house stepped forward and introduced the new peer to the Lord Speaker.

'Welcome to the House, Lady Clifton,' he said, shaking her warmly by the hand. This was followed by cries of 'Hear, hear' from all sides of the chamber as her fellow peers added their traditional welcome to a new member.

Giles then led his sister past the throne, where several members who were sitting on the steps smiled as she continued out of the east door and into the Prince's Chamber. Once they were outside the chamber, she removed her tricorn hat and breathed a long sigh of relief.

'It sounded as if the lions rather liked the look of you,' said Giles, as he bent down to kiss his sister on both cheeks, 'although I did notice one or two of my colleagues licking their lips in anticipation of your first appearance at the despatch box.'

'Don't be fooled by your brother,' said Belstead. 'He'll be among those licking his lips when the time comes for you to face the opposition.'

'But not until you've delivered your maiden speech, sis. However, after that, I'm bound to admit, you'll be fair game.'

'So what next?' asked Emma.

'Tea with the family on the terrace,' Giles reminded her.

'And once you're free,' said Belstead, 'may I suggest you slip back into the chamber and take your place on the end of the front bench. For the next few days, I would advise you to observe the workings of the House, accustom yourself to our strange ways and traditions, before you consider delivering your maiden speech.'

'The only speech you'll make when no members will even consider interrupting you, and whoever follows will praise your contribution as if you were Cicero.'

'And what then?'

'You must prepare for your first questions as Under Secretary of State for Health,' said Belstead, 'and try not to forget there will be several senior members of the medical profession in attendance.'

'When the gloves will be off,' said Giles. 'And you needn't expect any brotherly love, even from your kith and kin. The gentle smiles and "Hear, hear"s will only be coming from your side of the House.'

'And you won't always be able to rely on them,' said Belstead with a wry smile.

'Nevertheless, sis, welcome to the House. I confess, I feel a glow of pride whenever one of my fellow peers says, "Did you know, that's Lord Barrington's sister?"'

'Thank you, Giles,' said Emma. 'I look forward to the day when one of my fellow peers says, "Did you know, that's Lady Clifton's brother?"'

◄○►

Tap, tap, tap. Karin was the first to wake. She turned over, assuming she must be dreaming.

Tap, tap, tap. A little louder.

Suddenly she was wide awake. She climbed slowly out of bed and, not wanting to disturb Giles, tiptoed across to the window. Tap, tap, tap, even louder.

'Is that what I think it is?' said a sleepy voice.

'I'm about to find out,' said Karin as she pulled open the curtain and stared down at the pavement.

'Good God,' she said, and had disappeared out of the bedroom before Giles could ask her what was going on.

Karin ran down the stairs and quickly unlocked the front door to find a young boy hunched up on the doorstep, shivering.

'Come in,' she whispered. But he seemed reluctant to move until she put an arm around his shoulder and said, 'I don't know about you, Freddie, but I could do with a hot chocolate. Why don't you come inside and see what we can find?'

He took her hand as they walked along the hall and into the kitchen, just as Giles appeared on the landing.

'Do sit down, Freddie,' said Karin, pouring some milk into a saucepan. Giles joined them. 'How did you get here?' she added, casually.

'I took the train down from Edinburgh, but I hadn't realized how late it was by the time I arrived in London. I've been sitting on your doorstep for over an hour,' he explained. 'I didn't want to wake you, but it was getting rather cold.'

'Did you tell your headmaster or Lord Fenwick that you were coming to see us?' asked Giles, as Karin opened a tin of biscuits.

'No. I sneaked out of chapel during prayers,' he confessed. Karin placed a mug of hot chocolate and a plate of shortbread biscuits on the table in front of their unexpected guest.

'Did you let anyone know, even a friend, that you planned to visit us?'

'I don't have many friends,' admitted Freddie, sipping his chocolate. He looked up at Giles and added, 'Please don't tell me I have to go back.' Giles couldn't think of a suitable reply.

'Let's worry about that in the morning,' said Karin. 'Drink up, and then I'll take you to the guest bedroom so you can get some sleep.'

'Thank you, Lady Barrington,' said Freddie. He finished off his hot chocolate. 'I'm so sorry, I didn't mean to cause you any trouble.'

'You haven't,' said Karin. 'But now let's get you off to bed.' She took his hand once again and led him out of the room.

'Goodnight, Lord Barrington,' said a far more cheerful voice.

Giles switched on the kettle and took a teapot down from the shelf above him. While he waited for the kettle to boil, he picked up the phone, dialled directory enquiries and asked for the number of Freddie's prep school in Scotland. Once he'd made a note of it, he checked to make sure he had Archie Fenwick's home number in his phone book. He decided that seven a.m. would be a sensible hour to contact them both. The kettle began to whistle just as Karin reappeared.

'He fell asleep as soon as his head hit the pillow, poor fellow.'

Giles poured her a cup of tea. 'You were so calm and reassuring. Frankly I wasn't quite sure what to say or do.'

'How could you be?' said Karin. 'You've never experienced someone knocking on your door in the middle of the night.'

◄◦►

When the Baroness Clifton of Chew Magna rose to deliver her maiden speech in the House of Lords, the packed chamber fell silent. She looked up at the Distinguished Strangers' Gallery to see Harry, Sebastian, Samantha and Grace smiling down at her – but not Jessica. Emma wondered where she was. She turned her attention to the opposition front bench, where the shadow leader of the House sat, arms crossed. He winked.

'My lords,' she began, her voice trembling. 'You must be surprised to see this newly minted minister standing at the despatch box addressing you. But I can assure you, no one was more surprised than me.'

Laughter broke out on both sides of the House, which helped Emma to relax.

'Lord Harvey of Gloucester sat on these benches some fifty years ago, and Lord Barrington of Bristol Docklands sits on the other side of the House as the opposition leader. You see before you their inadequate granddaughter and sister.

'The Prime Minister has allowed me this opportunity to continue my work in the health service, not this time as a member of the board of a great hospital, its deputy chairman or even chairman, but as one of the government's undersecretaries of state. And I want members of this House to be in no doubt that I intend to carry out my duties as a minister with the same scrutiny and rigour that I have tried to bring to every position I have held, in both public office and private life.

'The National Health Service, my lords, is at a crossroads, although I know exactly in which direction I want it to go. In me, you will find a devoted champion of the surgeon, the doctor, the nurse and, most important of all, the patient. And as I look around this chamber, I can see one or two of you who might well be in need of the NHS in the not-too-distant future.'

Emma had considered the line added by her brother a little risky, but Giles had assured her that their lordships, unlike Queen Victoria, would be amused. He was right. They roared with laughter as she smiled across the despatch box at the leader of the opposition.

'And to that end, my lords, I shall continue to fight overweening bureaucracy, the fear of innovation, and overpaid and overrated special advisors who have never wielded a scalpel or emptied a bedpan.'

The House roared its approval.

'But just as important,' said Emma, lowering her voice, 'I will never forget the sage words of my grandfather, Lord Harvey, when as a young child I had the temerity to ask him, "What's the point of the House of Lords?" "To serve," he replied, "and keep those knaves in the Commons in check."'

This statement brought cheers from both sides of the House.

'So let me assure your lordships,' Emma concluded, 'that will always be my mantra whenever I take a decision on behalf of the government I serve. And finally, may I thank the House for its kindness and indulgence towards a woman who is painfully aware that she is not worthy to stand at the same despatch box as her grandfather or brother.'

Emma sat down to prolonged cheers and the waving of order papers, and those members who had wondered why this woman had been plucked out of obscurity were no longer in any doubt that Margaret Thatcher had made the right decision. Once the House had settled, Lord Barrington rose from his place on the opposition front bench and looked benignly across at his sister before he began his unscripted speech. Emma wondered when she would be able to do that, if ever.

'My lords, if I display a fraternal pride today, I can only hope the House will be indulgent. When the minister and I squabbled as children, I always won, but that was only because I was bigger and stronger. However, it was our mother who pointed out that once we both grew up, I would discover that I had won the battle, but not the argument.'

The opposition laughed while those seated on the government benches cried, 'Hear, hear!'

'But allow me to warn my noble kinswoman,' continued Giles, sounding serious for the first time, 'that her moment of triumph may be short-lived, because when the time comes for the government to present its new health bill, she should not expect to enjoy the same indulgence from this side of the House. We will scrutinize the bill line by line, clause for clause, and I do not have to remind the noble baroness that it was the Labour Party under Clement Attlee who founded the National Health Service, not this jumped-up bunch of bandwagon Tories, who are temporarily sitting on the government benches.'

The opposition cheered their leader.

'So I am happy to congratulate my noble kinswoman on a remarkable maiden speech, but advise her to savour the moment, because when she next returns to the despatch box, this side of the House will be sitting in wait for her, and let me assure the noble baroness that she will no longer be able to rely on any fraternal assistance. On that occasion she will have to win both the battle and the argument.'

The opposition benches looked as if they couldn't wait for the confrontation.

Emma smiled, and wondered how many people in the chamber would believe how much of her speech had been worked on by the same noble lord who was now jabbing an index finger at her. He had even listened to it being delivered in his kitchen in Smith Square the previous night. She only wished their mother could have been seated in the public gallery to watch them squabbling again.

<o>

Mr Sutcliffe, the headmaster of Grangemouth School, was grateful that Lady Barrington had accompanied Freddie back to Scotland, and once the boy had reluctantly returned to his house, asked if he might have a private word with her. Karin readily agreed, as she'd promised Giles she would try to find out the reason Freddie had run away.

Once they had settled down in his study, the headmaster didn't waste any time raising the subject that was on both their minds. 'I'm rather pleased that your husband isn't with you, Lady Barrington,' he began, 'because it will allow me to be more candid about Freddie. I'm afraid the boy's never really settled since the day he arrived, and I fear his mother is to blame for that.'

'If you're referring to Lady Virginia,' said Karin, 'I'm sure you know she isn't his mother.'

'I'd rather assumed that was the case,' said the headmaster, 'which would explain why she hasn't once visited Freddie while he's been here.'

'And she never will,' said Karin, 'because it doesn't serve her purpose.'

'And while Lord Fenwick does everything in his power to help,' continued Sutcliffe, 'he isn't the boy's father, and I'm afraid the situation became worse when Freddie met your husband for the first time.'

'But I thought that went rather well.'

'So did Freddie. He talked of nothing else for several days. In fact, after coming back at the beginning of term, he was a different child. No longer haunted by the other boys continually teasing him about his mother because he was now inspired by the man he wished was his father. From that day, he scoured the papers in search of any mention of Lord Barrington. When your husband called to say Freddie was with him in London, I can't pretend I was surprised.'

'But are you aware that Giles wrote to Freddie, wishing him every luck for the Castle versus Village cricket match, and asked him to let him know how it turned out but didn't get a reply?'

'He carries the letter around with him all the time,' said the headmaster, 'but unfortunately he scored a duck, and his side was soundly beaten, which might explain why he didn't reply.'

'How sad,' said Karin. 'I can assure you, Giles still scores far more ducks than centuries on and off the field.'

'But the boy couldn't know that, and his only other experience of reaching out was to Lady Virginia. Look where that got him.'

'Is there anything I can do to help? Because I'd be delighted to.'

'Yes, there is, Lady Barrington.' He paused. 'I know you come up to Scotland from time to time, and wondered if you'd consider taking Freddie out for the occasional exeat weekend?'

'Why only weekends? If Archie Fenwick will agree, he could also join us at Mulgelrie during the summer holidays.'

'I must confess it was Lord Fenwick's idea. He told me about the chance meeting with your husband.'

'I wonder if it was by chance?'

The headmaster didn't comment, simply adding, 'How do you think Lord Barrington will react to my request?'

'I'll let you into a little secret,' said Karin. 'He's already chosen the twenty-two yards on which to put up a cricket net.'

'Then you can tell your husband that Freddie is likely to be the youngest boy ever to play for the school's First Eleven.'

'Giles will be delighted. But can I make one small request, headmaster?'

'Of course, Lady Barrington.'

'May I be allowed to tell Freddie what we've decided before I return to London?'

10

WHEN JAMES CALLAGHAN made his final speech as leader of the Labour Party at the annual conference in Blackpool, Giles was well aware that if he backed the wrong candidate to succeed him, his political career was over.

When four former cabinet ministers from the Commons allowed their names to go forward, he wasn't in any doubt that there were only two serious candidates. In the right corner stood Denis Healey, who had served as Chancellor of the Exchequer under Callaghan and Harold Wilson, and like Giles had been decorated in the Second World War. In the left corner, Michael Foot, arguably the finest orator in the House of Commons since the death of Winston Churchill. Although his ministerial career did not compare to Healey's, he had the backing of most of the powerful trade unions, who had ninety-one paid-up members representing them in the House.

Giles tried to dismiss the thought that if he had chosen to stand in the by-election for Bristol Docklands ten years before, rather than accepting Harold Wilson's offer of a seat in the Upper House, he too could have been a serious contender to lead the party. However, he accepted that timing in politics is everything, and that there were at least a dozen of his contemporaries who could also come up with a credible scenario where they became leader of the party, and not long afterwards found themselves living in No. 10 Downing Street.

Giles believed there was only one candidate who could possibly beat Mrs Thatcher at the next general election and he could only hope that the majority of his colleagues in the Lower House had also worked that out. Having served in government and opposition for over thirty years, he knew you could only make a difference in politics when you were sitting on the government benches, not spending fruitless years in opposition, winning only the occasional unheralded victory.

The decision as to who should lead the party would be taken by the 269 Labour members who sat in the House of Commons. No one else would be allowed to vote. So once Callaghan had announced that he was stepping down, Giles rarely left the corridors of power until the lights were switched off each night following the final division. He spent countless hours roaming those corridors during the day, extolling the virtues of his candidate, while spending his evenings in Annie's Bar, buying pints as he tried to convince any wavering colleagues in the Lower House that the Conservatives were praying they would elect Michael Foot and not Denis Healey.

The Tories' prayers were answered when in the second ballot Foot beat Healey by 139 votes to 129. Some of Giles's colleagues in the Commons openly admitted they were quite happy to settle for a period in opposition as long as the new leader shared their left-wing ideology.

◄○►

Emma told Giles over breakfast the following day that when Margaret Thatcher had heard the news, she opened a bottle of champagne and toasted the 139 Labour members who'd guaranteed that she would remain in No. 10 Downing Street for the foreseeable future.

The long-held tradition in both parties is that when a new leader is chosen, every serving member of the front bench immediately tenders their resignation, then waits to be invited to join the new team. Once Giles had written his letter of resignation, he didn't waste any time waiting to hear which office of state he would be asked to shadow, because he knew the phone would never ring. The following Monday, he received a short, handwritten note from the new leader, thanking him for his long service to the party.

The following day, Giles moved out of the leader of the opposition's office in the Lords on the first floor to make way for his newly anointed successor. As he sat alone in an even smaller windowless room somewhere in the basement, he tried to come to terms with the fact that his front-bench career was over, and all he could look forward to was years in the wilderness on the back benches. Over dinner that night, he reminded Karin that just ten votes had sealed his fate.

'Five, if you think about it,' she replied.

SEBASTIAN CLIFTON

1981

11

'I'M SORRY.'

'Is that all you've got to say?' said Jessica, glaring at him.

Sebastian placed an arm around his daughter's shoulder. 'I promise I'll be back in time to take you and your mother for a celebration dinner.'

'I remember the last time you promised that, then flew off to another country. At least then it was to support an innocent man, not a crook.'

'Desmond Mellor is only allowed visitors on a Saturday afternoon between two and three o'clock, so I wasn't left with a lot of choice.'

'You could have told him to get lost.'

'I promise I'll be back by five. Six at the latest. And as it's your birthday, you can choose the restaurant.'

'And in the meantime I'm expected to babysit Jake, and when Mom gets back, explain to her why you're not around. I can think of more exciting ways of spending my birthday.'

'I'll make it up to you,' said Seb. 'I promise.'

'Just don't forget, Pops, he's a crook.'

◄○►

As Sebastian battled through the late morning traffic on his way out of London, he couldn't help thinking his daughter was right. Not only was it likely to be a wasted journey, but he probably shouldn't be having anything to do with the man in the first place.

He should have been taking Jessica to lunch at Ponte Vecchio to celebrate her sixteenth birthday, rather than heading for a prison in Kent to visit a man he despised. But he knew that if he didn't find out why Desmond Mellor wanted to see him so urgently, he would be forever curious. Only one thing was certain: Jessica would demand a blow-by-blow account of why the damned man had wanted to see him.

There were about ten miles to go before Seb spotted the first signposts to Ford Open. No mention of the word 'prison', which would have offended the locals. At the barrier an officer stepped out of the small kiosk and asked his name. After 'Clifton' had been ticked off on the inevitable clipboard, the barrier was raised and he was directed to a patch of barren land that on Saturdays acted as a car park.

Once he'd parked his car, Seb made his way to the reception area, where another officer asked for his name. But this time he was also requested to provide identification. He produced his driving licence – another tick on another clipboard – and was then instructed to place all his valuables, including his wallet, watch, wedding ring and some loose change, in a locker. He was told firmly by the duty officer that under no circumstances was he to take any cash to the meeting area. The officer pointed to a notice screwed to the wall warning visitors that anyone found in possession of cash inside the prison could end up with a six-month sentence.

'Forgive me for asking, sir,' said the officer, 'but is this the first time you've visited a prison?'

'No, it's not,' said Seb.

'Then you'll know about vouchers, should your friend want a cup of tea or a sandwich.' He's not my friend, Seb wanted to say, as he handed over a pound note in exchange for ten vouchers.

'We'll refund the difference when you return.'

Seb thanked him, closed the locker door and pocketed the key along with his vouchers. When he entered the waiting room, another officer handed him a small disc with the number 18 etched on it.

'Wait until your number is called,' said the officer.

Seb sat on a plastic seat in a room full of people who looked as if this was just part of their daily routine. He glanced around to see wives, girlfriends, parents, even young children, who had their own play area, all with nothing in common except a relation, a friend or a lover who was locked up. He suspected he was the only person visiting someone he didn't even like.

'Numbers one to five,' said a voice over the tannoy. Several of the regulars leapt up and hurried out of the room, clearly not wanting to waste a minute of their allocated hour. One of them left behind a copy of the *Daily Mail*, and Seb flicked through it to pass the time. Endless photographs of Prince Charles and Lady Diana Spencer chatting at a garden party in Norfolk; Diana looked extremely happy, while the Prince looked as if he was opening a power station.

'Numbers six to ten,' crackled the tannoy, and another group made their way quickly out of the waiting room. Seb turned the page. Margaret Thatcher was promising to bring in legislation to deal with wildcat strikes.

Michael Foot described the measures as draconian, and pronounced her policy as jobs for the boys, but not for the lads.

'Numbers eleven to fifteen.'

Seb looked up at the clock on the wall: 2.12 p.m. At this rate, he'd be lucky to get more than forty minutes with Mellor, although he suspected the man would have his pitch well prepared and wouldn't waste any time. He turned to the back page of the *Mail* to see an old photograph of Muhammad Ali jabbing his finger at reporters and saying, *His hands can't hit what his eyes can't see*. Seb wondered who came up with such brilliant lines – or was the ex-champ just brilliant?

'Numbers sixteen to twenty.'

Seb rose slowly from his place and joined a group of a dozen visitors who were already chasing after an officer as he headed into the bowels of the prison. They were stopped and searched before being allowed to enter the visitors' area.

Sebastian found himself in a large square room laid out with dozens of small tables, each surrounded by four chairs, one red, and three blue. He stared around the room but didn't spot Mellor until he raised a hand. He'd put on so much weight Seb hardly recognized him. Even before Seb had sat down, Mellor gestured towards the canteen at the other end of the room and said, 'Could you get me a cup of tea and a Kit Kat?'

Seb joined a small queue at the counter, where he handed over most of his vouchers in exchange for two cups of tea and two Kit Kats. When he returned to the table, he placed one of the cups and both chocolate bars in front of his old adversary.

'So, why did you want to see me?' Seb asked, not bothering with any small talk.

'It's a long story, but I don't expect any of it will surprise you.' Mellor took a sip of tea and removed the wrapper from a Kit Kat while he was speaking. 'After the police found out Sloane and I were responsible for having your friend Hakim Bishara arrested, Sloane turned Queen's evidence and stitched me up. I was sentenced to two years for perverting the course of justice, while he got away scot free. If that wasn't enough, once I was inside, he managed to take control of Mellor Travel. Claimed he was the only man who could rescue the company while the chairman was in jail, and the shareholders bought it.'

'But as the majority shareholder, you must still have overall control?'

'Not of a public company, as you will have discovered when Bishara was banged up. They don't even send me the minutes of the board meetings. But Sloane doesn't realize I've got someone on the inside who keeps me well informed.'

'Jim Knowles?'

'No. That bastard dropped me the moment I was arrested, and even proposed Sloane for chairman. In exchange, Knowles became his deputy on an inflated salary.'

'Cosy little arrangement,' said Seb. 'But you must have taken legal advice.'

'The best. But they'd been careful not to break the law, so there wasn't a whole lot I could do about it. But you can.'

Seb sipped his tea while Mellor tore the wrapper off the second Kit Kat.

'What do you have in mind?' asked Seb.

'As you pointed out, Mr Clifton, I am still the majority shareholder of Mellor Travel, but I suspect that by the time I get out, those shares won't be worth the paper they're written on. But if I were to sell them to you for one pound—'

'What's the catch?'

'No catch, although we've had our differences in the past. My sole interest is revenge – I want Adrian Sloane and Jim Knowles removed from the board and the company to be run properly, and I can't think of anyone better to do the job.'

'And what would you expect in return?' Seb paused and, looking him straight in the eye, added, 'When you get out of jail.'

A buzzer sounded, warning them they had ten minutes left.

'That might not be for some time,' said Mellor, snapping one of the chocolate fingers in half. 'I'm now facing a further charge you don't even know about.'

Seb didn't press him. Time was running out and he had several more questions that needed answering before he could consider Mellor's proposition. 'But you will get out eventually.'

'And when I do, I will expect my fifty-one per cent shareholding in Mellor Travel to be returned in full, also for one pound.'

'Then what's in it for Farthings?'

'This time you can appoint the chairman, the board, and run the company. Farthings can also charge a handsome retainer for their services, while collecting twenty per cent of Mellor Travel's annual profits, which I think you'll agree is more than fair. You'll also have the added pleasure of removing Adrian Sloane from the chair for a second time. All I'd ask in return is to receive a copy of the minutes following every board meeting, and to have a face to face meeting with you once a quarter.'

The buzzer sounded a second time. Five minutes.

'I'll give it some thought and when I've made up my mind, I'll call you.'

'You can't call me, Mr Clifton. Prisoners can't receive incoming calls. I'll ring you at the bank next Friday morning at ten, which should give you more than enough time to make up your mind.'

The buzzer sounded a third time.

—◀◦▶—

Jessica looked at the clock as her father walked into the hall and hung up his coat.

'You only just made it in time,' she said, giving him a reluctant kiss on the cheek.

Sebastian grinned. 'So where do you want to have dinner, young lady?'

'Harry's Bar.'

'In London or Venice?' he asked as they strolled into the drawing room.

'London this time.'

'I don't think I'll be able to get a table at such short notice.'

'I've already booked.'

'Of course you have. Anything else I should know about?' he asked, as he poured himself a stiff whisky.

'It's not what you should know,' scolded Jessica, 'it's what you've forgotten.'

'No, I haven't.' Like a magician, Seb produced a gift from an inside pocket.

'Is that what I think it is?' Jessica asked, smiling for the first time.

'Well, it's certainly what you've been hinting about for the past few weeks.'

Jessica threw her arms around her father. 'Thanks, Pops,' she said, ripping off the wrapping paper and opening a small, slim box.

'Am I back in favour?' asked Seb, as Jessica strapped the Warhol Swatch on to her wrist.

'Only if you've remembered Mom's present.'

'But it's not her birthday,' said Seb. 'At least, not for a couple of months.'

'I know that, Pops, but it is your wedding anniversary tomorrow, just in case you've forgotten.'

'Help! Yes, I had.'

'But luckily I hadn't,' said Jessica, pointing to a beautifully wrapped box on the table, with a card attached.

'What's inside?'

'A pair of Rayne shoes Mom spotted in the King's Road last week, but thought were a little too expensive. All you have to do is sign the card.'

They heard the front door open, and Seb quickly scribbled *An unforgettable year. Love Seb xxx* on the card. 'How did you manage to pay for them?' he whispered, as he placed the pen back in his pocket.

'On your credit card, of course.'

'God help your husband,' said Seb, as Samantha joined them.

'Look what Pops has given me for my birthday!' said Jessica, thrusting out her arm.

'What a lovely present,' said Samantha, admiring the Campbell's Soup watch.

'And I've got something for you too, my darling,' said

Seb, as he picked up the box from the table, just hoping the ink had dried. 'Happy anniversary,' he added, before taking her in his arms.

Samantha looked over her husband's shoulder and winked at her daughter.

◄◦►

Arnold Hardcastle joined Hakim and Sebastian in the chairman's office for the third time that week.

'Have you had enough time to consider Mellor's proposition?' asked Hakim, as the bank's legal advisor sat down opposite them.

'I most certainly have,' said Arnold, 'and there's no doubt it's a fair offer, but I have to ask, why is Mellor handing over the company to you of all people?'

'Because he hates Adrian Sloane even more than we do?' suggested Seb. 'Don't forget, Sloane was responsible for him failing to get his hands on the bank.'

'There are other banks in the City,' said Arnold.

'But none that know how Sloane operates as well as we do,' replied Hakim. 'Have you made contact with Mellor's lawyers to find out if they think this deal is for real?'

'It's real enough,' said Arnold. 'Although their senior partner confessed he was as puzzled by it as we are. I think he summed it up best when he suggested it might be a case of better the devil you know.'

'When's Mellor likely to be released?' asked Seb.

'It may not be for some time,' said Arnold, 'as he's facing further charges.'

'Further charges?' said Hakim.

'Dealing in counterfeit money. And there's another charge of entrapment.'

'I can't believe Mellor would do anything quite that stupid, especially when he was already in custody.'

'If you're locked in a prison cell all day,' said Arnold, 'I suspect your judgement might become clouded, especially if the only thought on your mind is how to get even with the man who's responsible for you being there.'

'I have to admit,' said Hakim, 'if I hadn't had you two watching over me when I was in prison, God knows what I might have got up to.'

'I'm still not convinced,' said Seb. 'It's all too easy. Don't forget that if Mellor swallowed a nail, it would come out as a corkscrew.'

'Then perhaps we should walk away from the deal,' said Arnold.

'And allow Sloane to go on taking advantage of his position, while growing richer by the minute?' Seb reminded them.

'Fair point,' said Hakim. 'And although I've never considered myself a vindictive man, I wouldn't be sorry to see Sloane finally destroyed. But perhaps Seb and I are taking this too personally and should simply look at the deal on its merits. What's your opinion, Arnold?'

'There's no doubt that under normal circumstances it would be a worthwhile deal for the bank, but after your past experiences with Mellor, perhaps it would be wise if I were to inform the Bank of England's Ethics Committee that we're considering entering into a business transaction with someone who's in jail. If they have no objection, who are we to disagree?'

'That's certainly the belt-and-braces solution,' said Hakim. 'Why don't you do that, Arnold, and report back to me once you've canvassed their opinion?'

'And I don't have to remind you,' said Seb, 'that Mellor will be phoning me at ten on Friday morning.'

'Just make sure he doesn't reverse the charges,' said Hakim.

◄○►

The two of them sat alone at the end of the bar to be sure they couldn't be overheard.

'When you think about it,' said Knowles, 'it's surprising that you ended up as the chairman of a travel company. After all, I've never known you to take a holiday.'

'I don't care for foreigners,' said Sloane. 'You can't trust them.' The barman refilled his glass with gin. 'And in any case, I can't swim, and lying on a beach getting burnt isn't my idea of fun. I prefer to stay in England and enjoy a few days' shooting, or walking in the hills on my own. Mind you, I don't think I'll be in the travel business for much longer.'

'Something I ought to know about?'

'I've had one or two offers for Mellor Travel that would make it possible for both of us to retire.'

'But Mellor still owns fifty-one per cent of the company, so he'd end up the main beneficiary.'

'I wasn't planning on selling the company,' said Sloane, 'just its assets. Asset-stripping is the new game in the City, and by the time Mellor's worked out what we're up to, there won't be a company left for him to chair, just a shell.'

'But when he comes out of jail—'

'I'll be long gone, and living somewhere that doesn't have an extradition treaty with Britain.'

'What about me? I'll be left carrying the can.'

'No, no – by then, you will have resigned from the

board in protest. But not before a large sum has been deposited in your Swiss bank account.'

'How much time will you need to close the deal?'

'I'm in no hurry. Our absentee chairman won't be going anywhere for the foreseeable future, by which time our pension plan should be in place.'

'There's a rumour Thomas Cook and Co. are interested in taking over the company.'

'Not while I'm chairman,' said Sloane.

—◦—

'There's a Mr Mellor on line one,' said Rachel, conscious that she was interrupting Sebastian's morning meeting with the bank's currency exchange director.

Seb glanced at his watch. Ten o'clock. 'Do you mind if I take this call?' he said, placing a hand over the mouthpiece.

'Go ahead,' said Victor Kaufman, well aware who was on the other end of the line.

'Put him through, Rachel. Good morning, Mr Mellor, it's Sebastian Clifton.'

'Have you come to a decision, Mr Clifton?'

'Yes, I have, and I can assure you that Farthings took your offer very seriously. However, after considerable deliberation, the board decided this was not the kind of business the bank wished to be involved in, and for that reason—'

The line went dead.

12

DESMOND MELLOR lay on the thin, horsehair mattress for hour upon hour, his head resting on a rock-hard pillow as he looked up at the ceiling and tried to work out what he should do now that Clifton had turned down his offer. The thought of Adrian Sloane ripping him off while at the same time destroying his company was making him ever more paranoid.

The cell door swung open and an officer yelled, 'Yard!' even though he was only a few feet away. It was that time every afternoon when prisoners were released from their cells for an hour and allowed to walk around the yard, get some exercise and be reunited with their mates so they could work on their next crime before they were released.

Mellor usually sought the company of first offenders who had no intention of returning to a life of crime. It amused him that he'd literally bumped into his first Etonian (marijuana) and his first Cambridge graduate (fraud) while circling the yard. But not today. He'd already decided who he needed to have a private word with.

Mellor had completed two circuits of the yard before he spotted Nash walking alone a few paces ahead of him.

But then, not many prisoners wanted to spend their hour's exercise break with a contract killer who looked likely to be spending the rest of his life in jail, and didn't seem to care that much if he spent a few days in solitary for roughing up any inmate who'd annoyed him. The last poor sod had been a hotplate server who'd failed to give Nash a large enough portion of fried potatoes and had ended up with a fried hand.

Mellor spent another circuit rehearsing his well-prepared script before he finally caught up with Nash, though the simple greeting 'Bugger off' almost caused him to think again. If he hadn't been desperate, Mellor would have quickly moved on.

'I need some advice.'

'Then get yourself a lawyer.'

'A lawyer would be useless for what I have in mind,' said Mellor.

Nash looked at him more closely. 'This had better be good, because if you're some fuckin' grass, you'll be spending the rest of your sentence in the prison hospital. Do I make myself clear?'

'Abundantly,' said Mellor, suddenly understanding the meaning of 'hard man', but it was too late now for him to turn back. 'Hypothetically speaking . . .' he added.

'What the fuck?'

'How much does a contract killer get paid?'

'If you're a copper's nark,' said Nash, 'I'll kill you myself for nothing.'

'I'm a businessman,' said Mellor. Although his heart was still beating overtime, he no longer felt afraid. 'And I need the services of a pro.'

Nash turned to face him. 'Depends what particular service you're lookin' for. Like any well-run business, our prices are competitive,' he added, with a thin smile that revealed three teeth. 'If you just want to put the frighteners on someone, broken arm, broken leg, it'll cost you a grand. A couple of grand if they're well connected, and a whole lot more if they've got protection.'

'He doesn't have any worthwhile connections, or protection.'

'That makes things easier. So what are you lookin' for?'

'I want you to break someone's neck,' said Mellor quietly. Nash looked interested for the first time. 'But it must never be traced back to me.'

'What do you take me for, a fucking amateur?'

'If you're that good,' said Mellor, taking his life in his hands, 'how did you end up in here?' Always bully a bully, his old man had taught him, and now he was about to find out if it was good advice.

'All right, all right,' said Nash. 'But it won't come cheap. The screws never take their fuckin' eyes off me. They read my letters before I see them and listen in on my calls,' he growled, 'though I've found a way round that. So my only chance is to set something up during a prison visit. Even then the surveillance cameras are on me the whole time, and now they've got a fuckin' lip-reading expert following my every word.'

'Are you saying it's impossible?'

'No. Expensive. And it's not going to happen tomorrow morning.'

'And the price?'

'Ten grand up front, another ten on the day of the funeral.'

Mellor was surprised how little a man's life was worth,

although he didn't care to think about the consequences if he failed to make the second payment.

'Get movin',' said Nash firmly, 'or the screws will get suspicious. If you do up your laces before you leave the yard, I'll know you're serious. Otherwise, don't bother me again.'

Mellor quickened his pace and joined a pickpocket who could remove your watch without you ever realizing it. A party trick inside, a profession outside. Sharp Johnny could make a hundred grand a year tax-free, and rarely ended up with a sentence of more than six months.

The siren sounded to warn the prisoners that it was time to return to their cells. Mellor dropped on one knee and retied a shoelace.

◄○►

Lady Virginia never enjoyed visiting Belmarsh high security prison. So different from the more relaxed atmosphere of Ford Open, where they had tea and biscuits on a Saturday afternoon. But since Mellor had been charged with a second, more serious offence, he'd been moved from the garden of England back to Hellmarsh, as it was known by the recidivists.

She particularly disliked being searched for drugs by a butch female officer, in places that would never have crossed her mind, and waiting while barred gates were locked and unlocked before being allowed to progress a few more yards. And the noise was incessant, as if half a dozen rock bands had been penned in together. When she was finally escorted into a large, white, windowless room, she looked up to see a number of officers peering down at the visitors from a circular balcony above them, while the surveillance cameras never stopped moving. But worst of all, she had to rub shoulders not only with the working classes, but with the criminal fraternity.

However, the possibility of earning some extra cash certainly helped to ease the humiliation, although even Mellor wouldn't be able to help with her latest problem.

That morning, Virginia had received a letter, a carefully worded letter, from the senior partner of Goodman Derrick. He had courteously but firmly requested the return, within thirty days, of some two million pounds obtained by false pretences, otherwise he would be left with no choice but to issue a writ on behalf of his client.

Virginia didn't have two thousand pounds, let alone two million. She immediately called her solicitor and asked him to make an appointment for her to see Sir Edward Makepeace QC in the hope that he might come up with a solution. She wasn't optimistic. The time may have come to finally accept an invitation from a distant cousin to visit his ranch in Argentina. He regularly reminded her of his offer during his annual visit to Cowdray Park, accompanied by a string of polo ponies and a bevy of handsome young men. Both changed with every visit. She could only think of one thing worse than having to spend a few years on a ranch in Argentina: having to spend a few years in a place like this.

Virginia parked her Morris Minor between a Rolls-Royce and an Austin A40 before making her way to reception.

◄○►

Mellor sat alone in the visitors' room, the precious minutes slipping away as he waited for Virginia to appear. She was never on time, but as he didn't have any other visitors, he was in no position to complain.

He looked around the room, his eyes settling on Nash, who was sitting opposite a peroxide blonde wearing thick red lipstick, a white T-shirt with no bra and a black leather miniskirt. It was a sign of just how desperate Mellor was that he fancied her.

He watched them carefully, as did several officers from the balcony above. They didn't appear to be speaking to each other, but then he realized that just because their lips weren't moving, it didn't mean they weren't having a conversation. Most people would have assumed they were man and wife, but as Nash was gay, this had to be strictly business. And Mellor knew whose business they were discussing.

He looked up as Virginia appeared at his table holding a cup of tea and a bar of chocolate. He remembered that Sebastian Clifton had bought him two bars.

'Any further news on your trial date?' Virginia asked, taking the seat opposite him.

'I've done a deal,' said Mellor. 'I've agreed to plead guilty to a lesser charge in exchange for a shorter sentence – another four years, making six in all. With good behaviour I could be out in three.'

'Not too long,' said Virginia, trying to sound optimistic.

'Long enough for Sloane to bleed my company dry. By the time I get out, I'll be left with nothing except the sign above the front door.'

'Is there anything I can do to help?'

'Yes, there is, which is why I wanted to see you. I have to get my hands on ten thousand pounds, sharpish. My mother's will has finally been settled, and although she left me everything, she only had one thing of any value, her semi-detached in Salford. The local estate agent has managed to sell it for twelve grand, and I've instructed them to make the cheque out to you. I need someone to pick it up as soon as possible.'

'I'll go up to Salford on Tuesday,' said Virginia, as she had an even more important meeting on Monday morning. 'But what do you want me to do with the money?'

Mellor waited for the camera to pass over him, before he spoke again.

'I need you to hand ten thousand in cash to a business associate. Anything left over will be yours.'

'How will I recognize him?'

'Her,' said Mellor. 'Look to my left, and you'll see a blonde talking to a guy who looks like a heavyweight boxer.' Virginia glanced to her right, and couldn't miss the two characters who looked as if they might be extras on *The Sweeney*. 'Can you see her?'

Virginia nodded.

'You're to meet her at the Science Museum. She'll be waiting by Stephenson's Rocket on the ground floor. I'll phone and let you know the details as soon as I have them.'

It would be Virginia's first visit to the Science Museum.

13

'ALLOW ME TO BEGIN, Lady Virginia, by reminding you that the relationship between a lawyer and his client is sacrosanct, so whatever you tell me concerning this case cannot, and will not, go beyond this room. However, it is equally important,' continued Sir Edward Makepeace, 'to stress that if you are not completely frank with me, I cannot advise you to the best of my ability.'

Nicely put, thought Virginia, sitting back and preparing herself for a series of questions she wouldn't want to answer.

'My first question is quite simple. Are you the mother of the Hon. Frederick Archibald Iain Bruce Fenwick?'

'No, I am not.'

'Are the parents of that child, as stated in Goodman Derrick's letter, a Mr and Mrs Morton, your former butler and his wife?'

'Yes.'

'And therefore the settlement and maintenance payments you received from Mr Cyrus T. Grant III –' the QC hesitated – 'were made erroneously?'

'Yes, they were.'

'So would it also be correct to suggest that Mr Grant's

demand,' Sir Edward checked the figure in Lord Goodman's letter, 'for two million pounds, is both fair and reasonable.'

'I'm afraid so.'

'With that in mind, Lady Virginia, I am bound to ask, do you have two million pounds available to pay Mr Grant, which would avoid him having to issue a writ and all the attendant publicity that would undoubtedly attract?'

'No, I do not, Sir Edward. That is the precise reason I am seeking your advice. I wanted to find out if there are any options left open to me.'

'Are you able to pay a large enough sum for me to attempt to make a settlement?'

'Out of the question, Sir Edward. I don't have two thousand pounds, let alone two million.'

'I'm grateful for your candid response to all my questions, Lady Virginia. But given the circumstances, it would be pointless for me to attempt to play for time and try to delay proceedings, because Lord Goodman is a wily old bird, and will realize exactly what I'm up to. In any case, you would then have the extra expense of both sides' legal costs to add to your misfortunes. And the judge would issue an order that all legal bills are paid first.'

'So what do you advise?'

'Sadly, madam, we have been left with only two choices. I can throw myself on their mercy, which I cannot believe will be met with any sympathy.'

'And the second option?'

'You can declare yourself bankrupt. That would make the other side realize that issuing a writ for two million pounds would be a complete waste of time and money, unless Mr Grant's sole purpose is to publicly humiliate you.' The lawyer remained silent as he waited for his client's response.

'Thank you for your advice, Sir Edward,' Virginia said eventually, 'and I am sure you will appreciate that I'll need a little time to consider my position.'

'Of course, my lady. However, it would be remiss of me not to remind you that the date on Goodman Derrick's letter is March thirteenth, and should we fail to respond before April thirteenth, you can be sure the other side will not hesitate to carry out their threat.'

'May I ask you one more question, Sir Edward?'

'Of course.'

'Am I right in thinking that a writ has to be served on the person named in the action?'

'That is correct, Lady Virginia, unless you instruct me to accept it on your behalf.'

◄○►

During her journey north the following morning, Virginia gave some considerable thought to her QC's advice. By the time the train pulled into Salford station, she had decided to invest some of the twelve thousand pounds she was about to collect in a one-way ticket to Buenos Aires.

When a taxi dropped her outside the estate agent's office, she switched her attention to the job in hand, and how much more money she could accumulate before departing for Argentina. Virginia was not surprised to be ushered into the senior partner's office within moments of telling the receptionist her name.

A man who had clearly put on his Sunday best suit for the occasion leapt up from behind his desk and introduced himself as Ron Wilks. He waited for her to be seated before resuming his place. Without another word, he opened a file in front of him, extracted a cheque for £11,400 and handed it across to her. Virginia folded it, placed it in her handbag and was about to leave when it became clear that Mr Wilks had something else to say.

'During the short conversation I was able to have with Mr Mellor over the phone,' he said, trying not to sound embarrassed, 'he didn't instruct me as to what I should do about his mother's goods and chattels, which we have removed from the house and placed in storage.'

'Are they worth anything?'

'A local second-hand scrap merchant has offered four hundred pounds for the lot.'

'I'll take it.'

The estate agent opened his cheque book and asked, 'Should this cheque also be made out to Lady Virginia Fenwick?'

'Yes.'

'Of course, this doesn't include the pictures,' said Wilks as he handed over the cheque.

'The pictures?'

'It seems Mr Mellor's mother had been collecting the works of a local artist for some years, and a London dealer has recently contacted me to say he would be interested in purchasing them. A Mr Kalman of the Crane Kalman gallery.'

'How interesting,' said Virginia, making a note of the name, only wondering if she still had enough time to contact him.

On the journey back to King's Cross, she went over her plans for the next few days. She would first have to dispose of any other valuables she still had and be on her way to Heathrow before any of her creditors were aware that she had, to quote her friend Bofie Bridgwater, done a bunk. As for Desmond Mellor, by the time he got out of prison, she would be the least of his problems, and Virginia was confident he wouldn't consider pursuing her halfway round the world for a few thousand pounds.

Virginia was grateful for Sir Edward's advice. After all, it would be difficult for anyone to serve her with a writ if they didn't know where she was. She'd already told Bofie she would be spending a few weeks in the South of France, to throw everyone off the scent. She didn't give a passing thought to what would become of Freddie. After all, he wasn't her child.

Soon after arriving back at her flat, Virginia was pleased to receive a telephone call from her distant cousin, confirming that a chauffeur would meet her at the airport and then drive her to his estate in the country. She liked the words chauffeur and estate.

◄○►

Once Virginia had cashed Mellor's cheques, cleared her bank account and purchased a one-way ticket to Buenos Aires, she set about the long process of packing. She quickly discovered just how many of her possessions, not least her shoes, she couldn't live without, and reluctantly accepted that she would have to buy another large suitcase. A short walk to Harrods usually solved most of her problems, and today was no exception. She managed to find a trunk with a dent in the side, and agreed to take it off their hands for half price. The young salesman hadn't noticed the dent before.

'Be sure to deliver it to my home in Chelsea,' she instructed the hapless assistant, 'later this morning.'

A green-coated doorman opened the door and

touched the peak of his cap as Virginia stepped out on to the Brompton Road.

'Taxi, madam?'

She was about to say yes when her gaze settled on an art gallery on the other side of the road. Crane Kalman. Why did she know that name? And then she remembered.

'No, thank you.' She raised a gloved hand to stop the traffic as she made her way across the Brompton Road, wondering if she could pick up another two or three hundred pounds for Mrs Mellor's old pictures. As she entered the gallery a bell rang and a short man with thick, wiry hair bustled up to her.

'Can I help you, madam?' he asked, unable to hide his mid-European accent.

'I was recently in Salford, and—'

'Ah, yes, you must be Lady Virginia Fenwick. Mr Wilks rang to say you might come in if you were interested in selling the late Mrs Mellor's art collection.'

'How much are you willing to offer?' asked Virginia, who didn't have a moment to waste.

'Over the years,' said Mr Kalman, who didn't appear to be in any hurry, 'Mrs Mellor acquired eleven oils, and twenty-three drawings from the local rent collector. Perhaps you were unaware that she was a close friend of the artist? And I have reason to believe—'

'How much?' Virginia repeated, aware of how little time she had before she needed to leave for Heathrow.

'I consider one eighty would be a fair price.'

'Two hundred, and you have a deal.'

Kalman hesitated for a moment before saying, 'I would agree to that, my lady, and even go to two thirty, if you were able to tell me where the missing painting was.'

'The missing painting?'

'I'm in possession of an inventory of all the works the artist sold or gave to Mrs Mellor, but I haven't been able to locate the *Mill Lane Industrial Estate*, which she gave to her son, and wondered if you had any idea where it is.'

Virginia knew exactly where it was but she didn't have the time to travel down to Bristol and pick it up from Mellor's office. However, one phone call to his secretary and it could be dispatched to the gallery immediately.

'I accept your offer of two hundred and thirty, and will make sure that the painting is delivered to you in the next few days.'

'Thank you, my lady,' said Kalman, who returned to his desk, wrote out a cheque and handed it over.

Virginia folded it, dropped it in her handbag and gave the gallery owner an ingratiating smile, before turning and walking back out on to the Brompton Road and hailing a taxi.

'Coutts in the Strand,' she instructed the driver.

She was considering how she would spend her last night in London – Bofie had suggested Annabel's – when the taxi drew up outside the bank.

'Wait here,' she said, 'this shouldn't take long.'

She entered the banking hall, hurried across to one of the tellers, took out the cheque and passed it across the counter.

'I'd like to cash this.'

'Certainly, madam,' said the cashier before catching his breath. 'I presume you mean you'd like to deposit the full amount in your account?'

'No, I'll take it in cash,' said Virginia, 'preferably fives.'

'I'm not sure that will be possible,' stammered the cashier.

'Why not?' demanded Virginia.

'I don't have two hundred and thirty thousand pounds in cash, my lady.'

—◦►—

'She's willing to make an offer?' said Ellie May. 'But I thought she was penniless?'

'So did I,' admitted Lord Goodman. 'I have it on good authority that she was cut out of her father's will and her only income is a modest monthly allowance supplied by her brother.'

'How much is she offering?'

'One million pounds, to be paid in ten equal instalments of one hundred thousand pounds over the next ten years.'

'But she stole two million from my husband!' said Ellie May. 'She can go to hell.'

'I sympathize with your feelings, Mrs Grant, but when I received the letter I decided to have an off-the-record conversation with Sir Edward Makepeace QC, who has represented the Fenwick family for many years. He made it clear that this offer represents a full and final settlement, and there is, to quote him, no wiggle room. He added that were you to turn it down, he has been instructed to receive the writ on Lady Virginia's behalf.'

'He's bluffing.'

'I can assure you, Mrs Grant, Sir Edward does not bluff.'

'So what do you think I should do?'

'I can appreciate why you would want to be repaid in full. However, if we were to go down that path, it might take several years to reach a settlement, and as we now know, Lady Virginia has enough money to cover her legal costs, so you might end up with nothing to show for it other than a large legal bill of your own. I'm not convinced it's her own money she's putting up – I suspect she's got her brother, the tenth earl, to bail her out. However, even Lord Fenwick will have his limits.' Goodman hesitated. 'And then we must consider all the other aspects of this case.'

'Like what?' asked Ellie May.

'Were the action to come to court, Lady Virginia would be ruined financially, and might possibly end up in prison.'

'Nothing would please me more.'

'At the same time, your husband's reputation would also suffer.'

'How could that be possible, when he's the innocent party?'

'Clearly, Mrs Grant, you have not experienced the British press on the rampage.'

'I have no idea what you're talking about.'

'Then let me assure you, this story would run and run in the tabloids and I fear your husband would not come out of it smelling of roses. The papers will paint him as a naive fool, and a cuckold.'

'Which is no more than the truth,' said Ellie May scornfully.

'Possibly, Mrs Grant, but is that something you want to share with the whole world?'

'What's the alternative?' she demanded.

'It's my considered opinion that you should settle, unpalatable as that may seem. I suggest you accept the offer of a million pounds, return to America and put this whole unpleasant experience behind you. I would, however, suggest one proviso: should Lady Virginia fail to honour any of the ten payments, she would still be liable for the full amount.' Lord Goodman waited for Ellie May's response but she remained silent. 'But you are the client, and naturally I will abide by your instructions, whatever they may be.'

'My late Scottish grandfather, Duncan Campbell, used to say, "Better a dollar in the bank, lass, than the promise of a dowry."'

'Was he a lawyer, by any chance?' asked Goodman.

—◄○►—

'It's a damn good offer,' said Knowles.

'Perhaps a little too good,' said Sloane.

'What are you getting at?'

'I am, as you know, Jim, suspicious by nature. Mellor might well be locked up in prison but that doesn't mean he's lying on his bunk all day feeling sorry for himself. Don't forget Belmarsh houses some of the top criminals in the country, and they'll be only too happy to advise a man they think has money.'

'But like him, they're all locked up.'

'True, but just remember Mellor's tried to stitch me up once before – and nearly succeeded.'

'But this guy Sorkin is sending his private jet to pick us up so we can spend the weekend on his yacht at Cap Ferrat. What more could you ask for?'

'I hate planes, and distrust people who own yachts. And what's more, no one in the City has ever come across Conrad Sorkin.'

'I could always go on my own.'

'Absolutely not,' said Sloane. 'We'll both go. But if I sense even for a second that Sorkin isn't what he claims to be, we'll be on the next flight back, and not in his private jet.'

━◇━

When Virginia received a letter from her solicitor to confirm that Mrs Ellie May Grant had accepted her offer, she wasn't sure how to react. After all, with £230,000 at her disposal, she could live a comfortable enough life swanning around Europe, staying with friends. But she admitted to Bofie that she would miss London, Ascot, Wimbledon, Glyndebourne, the royal garden party, the Proms, Annabel's and Harry's Bar, especially when all her continental buddies had migrated back to London for the season.

Although she had banked the cheque for £230,000 with Coutts, Virginia accepted that if she were to honour her agreement, the money would run out in a couple of years, and she wondered if she was simply postponing the inevitable trip to Argentina. But on the other hand, perhaps something else might turn up in the meantime, and she still had until 13 April before she had to make a final decision.

After changing her mind several times, Virginia reluctantly handed over the first £100,000 to her solicitor on April 13th, and at the same time cleared all her small debts, loans, and legal costs, leaving her with £114,000 in her current account. Her brother continued to supply her with an allowance of £2,000 a month, a sum that had dropped from £4,000 when she deserted Freddie. Virginia hadn't read the small print in her father's will. And if Archie ever found out about her windfall, she suspected he would cut her off without another penny.

The following morning, she returned to Coutts and

cashed a cheque for £10,000. She placed the money in a Swan and Edgar bag, as Mellor had instructed, walked back out on to the Strand and hailed a cab. She had no idea where the Science Museum was but was confident the cabbie would know. Twenty minutes later she was standing outside a magnificent Victorian building on Exhibition Road.

She entered the museum and walked across to the enquiry desk, where a young woman pointed her in the direction of Stephenson's Rocket. Virginia marched through the Energy Hall, the Space Gallery and into Making the Modern World without turning to look at any of the unique objects that surrounded her.

She spotted the peroxide blonde standing next to an old steam engine, surrounded by children. The two women didn't acknowledge each other. Virginia simply placed the bag on the floor by her side, turned around and left the museum as quickly as she had entered it.

Twenty minutes later she was sitting in Harry's Bar enjoying a dry Martini. A handsome young man sitting at the bar on his own smiled at her. She returned his smile.

–◇–

When Virginia visited Belmarsh the following Sunday, she was relieved to discover that Desmond Mellor didn't even know his mother had an art collection, and clearly had never heard of L. S. Lowry. He had supplied the old lady with a small monthly allowance, but confessed he hadn't visited Salford for some years.

'I sold her bits and pieces for four hundred pounds,' Virginia told him. 'What would you like me to do with the money?'

'Consider it a bonus. I heard this morning that the

pick-up went smoothly, for which I'm grateful.' He glanced across the room at Nash, who was having his monthly meeting with the peroxide blonde. They never once looked in his direction.

14

ADRIAN SLOANE reluctantly admitted that being flown to the South of France in a Learjet was something he could get used to. Jim Knowles agreed. A young hostess, who didn't look as if she knew a great deal about air safety, poured them another glass of champagne.

'Don't relax, even for a moment,' said Sloane, rejecting the drink. 'We still don't know what Sorkin expects for his money.'

'Why should we give a damn,' said Knowles, 'as long as the price is right?'

As the plane taxied to its stand at Nice Côte d'Azur airport, Sloane looked out of the window to see a Bentley Continental waiting for them on the tarmac. They climbed into the back seat – no passport checks, no queues, no customs. It was clear that Conrad Sorkin knew which palms to grease.

The harbour was packed cheek by jowl with gleaming yachts. Only one had its own dock, and that was where the Bentley came to a halt. A smartly dressed matelot opened the back door while two others collected the luggage from the boot. As Sloane walked up the wide gangway, he noticed a Panamanian flag fluttering gently in the breeze on the stern of the yacht. As they stepped on board, an officer in full whites saluted them and introduced himself as the purser.

'Welcome aboard,' he said in a clipped English accent. 'I'll show you to your cabins. Dinner will be served at eight on the upper deck, but do not hesitate to call me if there's anything you require before then.'

The first thing Sloane noticed when he entered his state room was a black attaché case in the middle of the double bed. He tentatively flicked it open to reveal row upon row of neatly stacked fifty-pound notes. He sat on the end of the bed and counted them slowly. Twenty thousand pounds – one per cent of the offer price in advance? He closed the lid and slid the case under the bed.

Sloane slipped out of his room and entered the next-door cabin without knocking. Knowles was counting his money.

'How much?' said Sloane.

'Ten thousand.'

Only half a per cent. Sloane smiled. Sorkin had done his research, and had already worked out which one of them would be closing the deal.

Sloane returned to his cabin, undressed and took a shower, then lay down on the bed and closed his eyes. He ignored the bottle of champagne in the ice bucket by the bedside. He needed to concentrate. After all, this could be the deal that would not only decide when he retired, but how much his pension would be.

◄○►

At five to eight, there was a light knock on the door. Sloane looked in the mirror and straightened his bow tie before opening the door to find a steward waiting for him.

'Mr Sorkin hopes you and Mr Knowles will join him for a drink,' he said, before leading them up a wide staircase.

Their host was standing on the upper deck waiting to greet his guests. Once he had introduced himself, he offered them a glass of champagne. Conrad Sorkin was not at all what Sloane had expected; tall, elegant, with a relaxed confidence that comes with success or breeding. He spoke with a slight South African accent and quickly put his guests at ease. Hard to guess his age, thought Sloane, possibly fifty, fifty-five. After some carefully worded questions, he discovered that Sorkin had been born in Cape Town and educated at Stanford. However, the small bronze bust of Napoleon that stood on the sideboard behind him revealed a possible weakness.

'So where do you live now?' asked Sloane, toying with his champagne.

'This ship is my home. It has everything I require, with the added advantage that I don't have to pay taxes.'

'Isn't that a little restricting?' asked Knowles.

'No, in fact the opposite. I quite literally enjoy the best of every world. I can visit any port I choose, and as long as I don't stay for more than thirty days the authorities take no interest in me. And I think it would be fair to say that this ship has everything a major city could offer, including a chef I stole from the Savoy. So, gentlemen, shall we go through to dinner?'

Sloane took a seat on the right of his host. He heard the engine turning over.

'I've asked the captain to sail slowly around the bay. I think you'll find the lights of Nice harbour make a stunning backdrop,' said Sorkin. A waiter filled their glasses with white wine, while another placed a plate of gravlax in front of them.

Sorkin boasted that the plaice and the Angus steak had been picked up from Grimsby and Aberdeen just hours before they boarded his jet that afternoon. Sloane had to admit that he might have been dining in one of the finest restaurants in London, and the quality of the wine made him want his glass to be constantly refilled. However, he restricted himself to a couple of glasses, as he waited for Sorkin to touch on the reason they were there.

After the last course had been cleared away, and brandy, port and cigars had been offered, the staff made a discreet withdrawal.

'Shall we get down to business?' said Sorkin, after he'd lit his cigar and taken a couple of puffs.

Sloane took a sip of port and Knowles poured himself a brandy.

'As I see it,' said Sorkin, 'you presently control a company that has some major assets, and although Mr Mellor still owns fifty-one per cent of the stock, while he remains in prison he cannot involve himself in any board decisions.'

'I can see you've done your homework,' said Sloane, before taking a puff on his cigar. 'But what particular assets are you interested in, Mr Sorkin?'

'Conrad, please. Let me make it clear that I have no interest in acquiring Mellor Travel. However, the company has forty-two travel agencies well placed in high streets throughout the UK. Those properties have a book value of less than two million pounds. But if we were to put them on the market individually, I estimate they have a real value of nearer six, possibly even seven million.'

'But,' interrupted Sloane, 'if we were to dispose of our

greatest asset, Mellor Travel would be little more than a shell company, unable to carry out its core business. I'm sure you're aware that Thomas Cook has already made us an offer of two million for the company, and made it clear that they wouldn't be sacking any staff or disposing of any of the properties.'

'And that two million would be paid to a company that will be run by Cook's until Desmond Mellor comes out of jail, so the best either of you could hope for is a decent redundancy package. That is why I am willing to equal Cook's offer, but with a subtle difference. My two million will be deposited in the bank of your choice, in the city of your choice.'

'But the Bank of England—' began Sloane.

'Adrian, the Bank of England is indeed a powerful body, but I can name twenty-three countries in which it has no jurisdiction, or even bilateral agreements. All you will have to do is convince your board to accept my offer, rather than Cook's. As the company only has five directors, and one of them can't attend board meetings, that shouldn't prove too difficult to achieve long before Mr Mellor is released – which I understand is not imminent.'

'You are well informed,' said Sloane.

'Let's just say we have contacts in all the right places, and inside information that keeps me ahead of my rivals.'

'If I was to accept your terms,' said Sloane, 'is the cash I found in my room a one per cent down payment against the two million you're offering?'

Knowles frowned.

'Certainly not,' said Sorkin. 'Consider that no more than a calling card to prove my credentials.'

Sloane drained his glass of port and waited for it to be refilled, before he said, 'We have a board meeting in a couple of weeks' time, Conrad, and you can be assured that I and my fellow directors will take your offer very seriously.'

The chairman of Mellor Travel leant back and relaxed for the first time, allowing himself to enjoy the port, confident he'd got the measure of Sorkin and that the two million could be treated as an opening bid. He'd already decided the figure he'd settle for, but would wait until breakfast before he made his next move.

Knowles looked disappointed, only too aware that Sloane was holding out for a larger sum. The same mistake he'd made when Hakim Bishara had bid for Farthings, and they'd ended up losing the deal. Knowles wasn't going to allow him to make the same error a second time. After all, he considered Sorkin's offer was more than enough, and there was no need to be greedy. Sloane's biggest weakness.

'I think I'll turn in,' Sloane said, rising slowly from his place, as he felt nothing more could be achieved that night. 'Goodnight, Conrad. I'll sleep on your offer. Perhaps we can talk again in the morning.'

'I'll look forward to that,' said Sorkin, as Sloane made his way unsteadily towards the door. Knowles made no attempt to join him, which annoyed Sloane, but he didn't comment.

Sloane had to hold on to the railing as he slowly descended the companionway. He was glad to see the purser waiting for him on the lower deck because he wasn't sure he'd be able to find his way back to his cabin. Perhaps he shouldn't have drunk so much port on top of such excellent wines. But when would he ever again be offered a third, or was it a fourth, glass of Taylor's 24?

He stumbled as his foot touched the bottom step, and

the purser quickly came to his rescue, placing an arm gently around his shoulder. Sloane swayed towards the ship's railing and leant over the side, hoping he wouldn't be sick, aware it would be reported back to Sorkin. After breathing in the fresh sea air he felt a little better. If he could just get back to his cabin and lie down, he was thinking, as two powerful arms circled his waist, and with one seamless movement he found himself being lifted into the air. He turned and tried to protest, only to see the purser smiling at him before unceremoniously dumping him overboard.

A moment later Sorkin appeared by the purser's side. Neither of them spoke as the chairman of Mellor Travel disappeared below the waves for a third time.

'How did you know he couldn't swim?'

'Inside information from the person who used to have your job,' Sorkin replied. As he turned away he added, 'You'll find your twenty thousand in Sloane's cabin, under the bed.'

◄○►

Nash bent down and tied up one of his shoelaces, the sign that Mellor should join him.

Mellor completed two more laps of the yard before he was by his side. He didn't need the watching screws to become suspicious.

'Job's done. No need to send any flowers to his funeral.'

'Why not?'

'He was buried at sea.' They walked a few more yards before Nash added, 'We've kept our side of the bargain, now I expect you to keep yours.'

'Not a problem,' said Mellor, hoping Nash hadn't

noticed that he'd broken out in a cold sweat. He'd called his estate agent in Bristol a couple of weeks before, and discovered that his old flat on Broad Street still hadn't been sold – not the easiest of markets, Mr Carter had explained, but if he were to lower the price, he felt confident a deal could be done. Mellor lowered the price, and an offer had been forthcoming, but the buyer wasn't willing to exchange until he'd seen the surveyor's report – which wouldn't be completed for another fortnight.

At least the Sloane problem had been dealt with. He would write to Knowles and ask him to make a prison visit as soon as possible. Surely he would fall in line now that Sloane was no longer around to call the tune.

A few more yards before he asked, 'When and where?' He hoped he sounded confident.

'Next Thursday. I'll let you know the details after Tracie's visit on Sunday. Just be sure that nice Lady Virginia doesn't forget to bring her Swan and Edgar bag with her.'

Mellor fell back and joined Sharp Johnny, who was as cheerful as ever, but then he only had nineteen days left to serve.

15

'I DON'T SUPPOSE you have ten thousand pounds you could spare?' said Mellor. Virginia wondered if he was joking until she saw the look of desperation in his eyes. 'I have a short-term cash-flow problem,' he explained, 'which can be resolved if only I'm given a little more time. But I need ten thousand quickly.' He glanced across the crowded room to where Nash was deep in conversation with his only ever guest. 'Very quickly.'

Virginia thought about the £111,000 she still had in her current account, and smiled sweetly. 'But no one knows better than you, Desmond, I'm as poor as a church mouse. My brother gives me an allowance of two thousand a month, which is barely enough to live on, and the only other income I've had recently was the small amount of money I received following the sale of your mother's house. I suppose I could let you have a thousand, and possibly another thousand in a month's time.'

'That's good of you, Virginia, but it will be too late by then.'

'Do you have any assets you could put up as collateral?' Virginia asked. Familiar words she'd heard her bank manager use whenever she was overdrawn.

'My ex-wife ended up with our house in the country as part of the divorce settlement. I've put my flat in Bristol on the market. It's worth about twenty thousand, and although someone has made an offer, contracts haven't been exchanged.'

'What about Adrian Sloane? After all, it wouldn't be a large amount to him.'

'That's no longer possible,' said Mellor, without explanation.

'And Jim Knowles?'

Mellor thought for a moment. 'I suppose Jim just might be willing to help if I put the flat up as collateral and there was something in it for him.'

'Like what?'

'To chair the company, cash, whatever he wants.'

'I'll get in touch with him the moment I get home, and find out if he's willing to help.'

'Thank you, Virginia. And of course there'll be something in it for you.'

Once again, Mellor looked across the room at Nash, who he knew would be taking instructions as to where the second instalment should be delivered. Never the same place twice, and never the same person, Nash had already explained.

'But I'll still need the ten thousand before Thursday,' Mellor said, turning back to Virginia. 'And I can't begin to tell you what the consequences could be if you fail.'

'How often are you allowed to make telephone calls?'

'Once a week, but I only get three minutes, and don't forget the screws are listening to every word.'

'Call me on Tuesday afternoon, around five o'clock. I

should have seen Knowles by then, and I'll do everything in my power to persuade him.'

—◦—

'It's all set up for Thursday,' said Nash, when Mellor joined him in the yard.

'Where and when?' asked Mellor, unwilling to admit he didn't have the money.

'Trafalgar Square, between the fountains, twelve o'clock.'

'Understood.'

'Will it be the same bag lady?'

'Yes,' said Mellor, hoping that Virginia had not only got the money, but would be willing to act as the intermediary once again.

Nash looked at him more closely. 'I hope you've given some thought to the consequences of not coming up with the second half of the payment.'

'Not a problem,' said Mellor, who had thought of little else for the past week. He fell back and walked alone, wondering, praying, hoping, that Virginia had convinced Knowles to lend him the ten thousand. He checked his watch. In another five hours he'd know.

—◦—

'Jim Knowles,' said a voice on the other end of the line.

'Jim, it's Virginia Fenwick.'

'Virginia, how are you? It's been a long time.'

'Too long. But I'm about to make up for it.'

'What do you have in mind?'

'I have a little proposition that you just might find interesting. I don't suppose you're free for lunch?'

—◦—

Virginia was sitting by the phone at five p.m. on Tuesday, well aware that she only had three minutes in which to deliver her well-prepared script. She had written out several bullet points to make sure she didn't miss anything of importance. When the phone rang, she picked it up immediately.

'7784.'

'Hello, my darling, it's Priscilla. I thought I'd give you a call and see if you're free for a spot of lunch on Thursday?'

'Not now,' said Virginia, slamming the receiver down. The phone rang again seconds later.

'7784,' she repeated.

'It's Desmond. Have you been able to—' He clearly didn't want to waste a second. She checked her first bullet point.

'Yes. Knowles has agreed to loan you ten thousand against the flat in Bristol.'

'Thank God,' said Mellor, breathing a deep sigh of relief that she could hear clearly.

'But if you fail to pay him back the full amount within thirty days, he's demanding extra collateral.'

'Like what?'

'Your shares in Mellor Travel.'

'But they're worth about a million and a half.'

'Take it or leave it, if I remember his exact words.'

Mellor paused for a moment, aware that his three minutes were fast running out.

'I don't have a lot of choice. Tell the bastard I accept his terms, and I'll pay him back the moment the flat is sold.'

'I'll pass on the message immediately, but he won't release the money until he's seen your signature on the document that will transfer ownership of the shares to him should you fail to pay him back within thirty days.'

'But how can I possibly sign it in time?' said Mellor, sounding desperate again.

'Don't worry. His lawyers have done all the paperwork, and it will be delivered to the prison later this evening. Just be sure you have someone looking out for it.'

'Address the envelope to Mr Graves. He's my floor officer, and he's already done me a couple of favours, so you can trust him. As long as he's on duty tonight, I should be able to turn it round immediately.'

Virginia made a note of the name, before checking her list again. 'Where and when do I deliver the money?'

'Thursday, twelve o'clock, Trafalgar Square. Your contact will be standing between the fountains. Just be sure you're not late.'

'Will it be the same woman?'

'No. Look for a bald middle-aged man wearing a navy blazer and jeans.' Virginia made another note. 'You're a diamond,' said Mellor. 'I owe you.'

'Anything else I can do?'

'No, but I'll be sending you a letter that I need you to—'

The line went dead.

◄O►

Mr Graves put down the phone in his office and waited for his instructions.

'You'll need to make sure you're on duty when the document arrives at the prison gate later this evening.'

'No problem. Not many officers volunteer for the night shift.'

'And make sure Mellor signs the agreement, and that you witness his signature.'

'What do I do then?'

'Take it out with you when you come off duty and deliver it to the address Mellor writes on the envelope. And don't forget, you've still got one more job to do before you can get paid.'

Graves frowned. 'You'd better get back to your cell before someone notices you're missing,' the prison officer said, trying to re-establish his authority.

'Whatever you say, guv,' said Nash, before slipping out of the office and making his way back to his cell.

◄O►

When Virginia woke the next morning, she found a large envelope lying on the doormat. She didn't want to know who'd delivered it, or when. She checked her watch: 9.14 a.m. Knowles wasn't due to pick it up until ten, giving her more than enough time.

She ripped open the envelope and extracted the document, quickly turning to the last page to check that Mellor had signed it. She smiled when she saw his friend, Mr Graves, had witnessed the signature. Virginia placed the agreement back in the envelope, left her little flat in Chelsea and headed for a shop in Pimlico that she'd checked out the previous day.

The young man behind the counter made two copies of the document and charged her £2.00 and another 20p for a large brown envelope. She was back in her flat twenty minutes later, reading the morning paper, when there was a knock at the door.

Knowles kissed her on both cheeks as if they were old friends, but once he'd exchanged one brown envelope for another, he left immediately. Virginia returned to the drawing room, ripped open the new envelope and counted the money. Fifteen thousand, as agreed. Not a bad morning's work. Now all she had to do was decide whether or not to deliver the ten thousand to the bald man in the navy blazer and jeans who would be waiting for her in Trafalgar Square.

◄o►

When Virginia arrived at the bank, she made her way straight to the manager's office. Mr Leigh stood up the moment she entered the room. Without a word, she extracted five cellophane packets and the copy of a three-page document from a Swan and Edgar bag, and placed them on his desk.

'Please credit my account with the five thousand pounds, and place this document among my personal papers.'

Mr Leigh gave her a slight bow and was about to ask . . . but she had already left the room.

Virginia walked out of the bank and on to the Strand, before making her way slowly towards Trafalgar Square. She had decided to carry out Mellor's instructions, not least because she recalled him saying how severe the consequences would be if he failed to repay the money, and she didn't want any harm to come to her only other source of income.

She paused opposite St Martin in the Fields and, clutching her Swan and Edgar bag tightly, waited for the traffic lights to turn red before she crossed the road. A flock of startled pigeons flew into the air as she stepped into the square and headed towards the fountains.

A child was jumping up and down in the water and

his mother was begging him to come out. Just beyond them was a bald-headed man wearing an open-neck shirt, dark blue blazer and jeans, whose eyes never left her. She walked across to him and handed over the shopping bag. He didn't even look inside, just turned his back and disappeared among a crowd of tourists.

Virginia breathed a sigh of relief. The operation had gone without a hitch, and she was already looking forward to having lunch with Priscilla. She made her way towards the National Gallery and hailed a taxi, while the bald man continued striding in the opposite direction. He couldn't miss the silver-grey Bentley that was parked outside South Africa House. As he approached the car a tinted window purred down and a hand appeared. He passed over the Swan and Edgar bag and waited.

Conrad Sorkin checked the ten cellophane packets before handing one of them back to the courier.

'Thank you, Mr Graves. Please let Mr Nash know that Lady Virginia failed to turn up.'

16

SIX MEN SAT opposite each other preparing for battle, although in truth they were all on the same side. Three of them represented Farthings Kaufman, and the other three Thomas Cook Ltd, one of the bank's oldest clients.

Hakim Bishara, chairman of Farthings Kaufman, sat on one side of the table, with Sebastian Clifton, his CEO, on his right, and the bank's in-house lawyer, Arnold Hardcastle, on his left. Opposite Hakim sat Ray Brook, the chairman of Cook's, on his right the company's MD, Brian Dawson, and on his left Naynesh Desai, his legal advisor.

'Allow me to open this meeting by welcoming all of you,' said Hakim. 'May I add how delighted we are to be representing Cook's in their attempt to take over Mellor Travel Ltd. Sadly, this is unlikely to be a mutually agreed takeover. In fact, it is more likely to be an all-out war, and a bloody one at that. But let me assure you, gentlemen, we will succeed. I will now ask Sebastian Clifton, who has been working on the project for some weeks, to bring us all up to speed.'

'Thank you, chairman,' said Seb as he opened a thick file in front of him. 'Allow me to begin by summing up our present position. Cook's have, for some time, expressed an interest in acquiring Mellor Travel, which has certain assets that would bring added value to their business. In particular, their forty-two high street shops, some in towns where Cook's do not have a presence, or where their present location is not as well placed as their rival's. Mellors also have a first-class, well-trained staff, although some of them have felt it necessary to leave the company during the past year.'

'One or two of them to join us,' interrupted Brook.

'Perhaps this is the time to mention the elephant in the room,' continued Seb. 'Namely Mr Desmond Mellor, who, although no longer chairman of the company, does retain fifty-one per cent of its shares. Therefore a take-over would be nigh on impossible without his blessing.'

'I understand that you've had dealings with Mr Mellor in the past,' said Dawson, removing his glasses. 'How is your present relationship?'

'I don't think it could be much worse,' admitted Seb. 'We both sat on the board of Barrington Shipping at a time when my mother was chairman. Not only did Mellor attempt to have her removed from the board, but after failing to do so, he tried to take over the company using tactics that were found to be unacceptable by the take-over panel. My mother prevailed, and continued to run Barrington's for several more years until the company was bought by Cunard.'

'I invited your mother to join our board,' said Brook, 'but unfortunately Margaret Thatcher trumped us.'

'I didn't know that,' said Seb.

'But you will recall that when Barrington's launched the *Buckingham*, and later the *Balmoral*, Mrs Clifton appointed Cook's as their preferred booking agent. We've never had a better partner, even if I did have to get used to her calling at six o'clock in the morning or ten at night.'

'You too?' said Seb with a grin. 'However, I have a confession to make. Before you approached us concerning this takeover, at his request I visited Desmond Mellor in prison.'

Jessica would have enjoyed drawing the expressions that appeared on the faces of the three men sitting opposite her father.

'Even worse, on that occasion Mellor offered to sell me fifty-one per cent of the company for one pound.'

'What did he want in exchange?' asked Brook.

'That once he was released from prison, we would return his fifty-one per cent, also for one pound.'

'Not a very seductive proposition,' suggested Dawson. 'Although it must have been tempting at the time.'

'But not tempting enough,' said Hakim, 'if as a result you have to rub shoulders with scumbags like Sloane and Knowles, who in my opinion should be locked up in the same cell as Mellor.'

'That was off the record,' interjected Arnold firmly, 'and does not represent the views of the bank.'

'I agree with you, Hakim,' said Brook. 'I only met Adrian Sloane once, and that was quite enough. However, let me ask you, Mr Clifton, do you think there's any chance that Mellor might consider reviving his offer?'

'It seems unlikely, although I'd be willing to give it a try, assuming he'd agree to see me.'

'Then let's find out as quickly as possible if that's a runner,' said Dawson.

'But even if Mellor did agree to see you,' said Arnold, 'I must warn you that the wheels of power grind even more slowly in the Prison Service than they do in White-hall.'

'But I remember you and Seb visiting me at Belmarsh at a moment's notice,' said Hakim.

'Those were legal visits,' said Arnold, 'and not subject to the usual prison restrictions – don't forget, you were my client.'

'So if Mellor were to agree to let you represent him,' said Hakim, 'we could cut through the red tape.'

'But why would he even consider doing that?' asked Dawson.

'Because Barry Hammond,' said Sebastian, 'a private detective employed by Farthings, discovered it was Sloane who stitched up Mellor. Which is why Mellor ended up in jail, and once he was safely out of the way, with the help of his friend Knowles, Sloane appointed himself chairman of Mellor Travel, which hasn't declared a profit or issued a dividend since. So it's just possible Mellor might be desperate enough to consider us the lesser of two evils.'

'If that's the home team,' said Brook, 'what have you managed to find out about our rivals?'

'That they're even worse,' replied Seb. 'Sorkin International is not an easy company to get to grips with. Their head office is registered in Panama, and although they have an office number, no one ever answers it.'

'Is Conrad Sorkin himself based in Panama?' asked Dawson.

'No. He spends most of his time on a yacht, constantly on the move. In fact, there are seven countries where he's currently persona non grata, but unfortunately the UK isn't one of them. And in any case, he seems to have access to bent lawyers, shell companies, even aliases to make sure he always stays one step ahead of the law.'

'An ideal bedfellow for Sloane and Knowles,' suggested Brook.

'Agreed,' said Seb, 'and as you know, Sorkin has recently matched our bid of two million for Mellor Travel. However, I think it's unlikely we'll be treated as an equal.'

'But surely Sorkin can't instigate a full-blooded takeover without Mellor's backing,' said Cook's lawyer.

'He doesn't need to,' said Hakim, 'because we're not convinced that's his purpose, as Seb will explain.'

'I'm pretty sure it's not the company that Sorkin is interested in,' said Seb. 'Just the forty-two shops and offices, which have a book value of under two million pounds, whereas my property analyst has valued them at over five million.'

'So that's his game,' said Dawson.

'I think he'll be happy to sell off the properties without consulting Mellor,' said Arnold, 'or even worrying about breaking the law, because I suspect Mr Sorkin will have long since disappeared before the police catch up with him.'

'Can we do anything to stop him?' asked Brook.

'Yes,' said Seb. 'Get hold of Mellor's fifty-one per cent, and sack Sloane.'

◄o►

When a letter landed on Virginia's doormat the following morning, she recognized the handwriting, and opened it to find another envelope inside addressed to Miss Kelly Mellor, but with no address attached, just a scribbled note:

Please be sure Kelly gets this. It's most important.
Desmond

Virginia immediately ripped open the second envelope and started to read a letter Desmond had written to his daughter.

Dear Kelly . . .

—◦—

Sebastian was just about to get in the lift, when Arnold Hardcastle came running down the corridor towards him.

'Haven't you got a wife and family to go home to?'

'Good news,' said Arnold, ignoring the comment. 'Mellor has not only agreed to see us, he wants a meeting as soon as possible.'

'Excellent. Hakim will be delighted.'

'I've already spoken to the prison governor, and he's agreed that a legal meeting can be held in the prison at twelve tomorrow.'

'Hakim will want to be there.'

'God forbid,' said Arnold. 'He'd probably end up strangling the man, and who could blame him? No, you should represent Farthings. After all, it was you he asked to see when he came up with his original proposal. I'd also suggest that Ray Brook be present, so Mellor realizes the bid's serious. One chairman to another. He'll be impressed by that.'

'That makes sense,' agreed Seb.

'Do you have anything scheduled for tomorrow morning?'

'If I do,' said Seb, opening his pocket diary, 'it's about to be cancelled.'

—◦—

Virginia had been in touch with Kelly Mellor's mother, but she wasn't at all cooperative. She probably thought Virginia was Mellor's latest girlfriend. However, she did reveal that the last time she'd heard from her daughter she was somewhere in Chicago, but admitted she'd lost touch with her.

—◦—

At eleven o'clock the following morning, Sebastian, Arnold and Ray Brook climbed into the back of a taxi, and Seb instructed the driver to take them to HMP Belmarsh. The cabbie didn't look pleased.

'Not much chance of a return fare,' Arnold explained.

'Why so early?' asked Brook.

'You'll find out why when you get there,' replied Arnold.

The three of them discussed tactics on their way to the prison, and agreed that their first priority was to put Mellor at ease and make him feel they were on his side.

'Keep mentioning Sloane and Knowles,' said Seb, 'because I'm confident he'd rather deal with us than them.'

'I don't think he would have agreed to see us,' said Brook as the cab left the city and headed east, 'unless we were in with a chance.'

By the time the cab drew up outside the vast forbidding green gates of HMP Belmarsh, they each knew the role they were expected to play. Arnold would open the proceedings and attempt to persuade Mellor that they were the good guys, and when Seb felt the moment was right, he would make him an offer of £1.5 million for his shares. Brook would confirm that the money would be deposited in his account the moment he signed the share transfer and that, as a bonus, Sloane and Knowles would be sacked before close of business that day. Seb was beginning to feel more confident.

When the three of them entered the prison they were escorted to the gatehouse and thoroughly searched. Brook's keyring pocket knife was immediately seized. The chairman of Cook Travel may have visited almost every country on earth, but it was clear he'd never entered a prison before. They left all their valuables, even their belts, with the desk sergeant, and, accompanied by two other officers, made their way across the square to A Block.

They passed through several barred gates, unlocked then locked behind them, before arriving at an interview room on the first floor. The clock on the wall showed five to twelve. Brook no longer needed to ask why they had set out so early.

One of the duty officers opened the door to allow the three men to enter a rectangular room with glass walls. Although they were left alone, two officers stationed themselves outside, looking in. They were there to make sure no one passed any drugs, weapons or money to the prisoner. Nothing gave the screws greater pleasure than arresting a lawyer.

The three visitors took their seats around a small square table in the centre of the room, leaving a vacant chair for Mellor. Arnold opened his briefcase and extracted a file. He took out a share-transfer certificate and a three-page agreement, the wording of which he checked once again before placing it on the table. If all went to plan, by the time they left the prison in an hour's time, there would be two signatures on the bottom line.

Seb couldn't stop staring at the clock on the wall,

aware that they would only be allowed an hour to close the deal and sign all the necessary legal documents. The moment the minute hand reached twelve, a man in a green bow tie, striped shirt and tweed jacket walked into the room. Arnold immediately stood and said, 'Good morning, governor.'

'Good morning, Mr Hardcastle. I'm sorry to have to inform you that this meeting is no longer able to take place.'

'Why?' demanded Seb, leaping to his feet.

'When the wing officer unlocked Mellor's cell at six o'clock this morning, he found his bed up-ended, and he'd hanged himself using a sheet as a noose.'

Seb collapsed back into his chair.

The governor paused to allow them all to take in the news, before adding matter-of-factly, 'Sadly, suicides are all too common at Belmarsh.'

—◁o▷—

When Virginia read the paragraph reporting Mellor's suicide on page eleven of the *Evening Standard*, her first thought was that another source of income had dried up. But then she had a second thought.

17

'IT'S SO RARE nowadays to have the family all together for the weekend,' said Emma, as they strolled into the drawing room after dinner.

'And we all know who's to blame for that,' said Sebastian. 'I only hope you're still enjoying the job.'

'Enjoying would be the wrong word. But not a day goes by when I don't think how lucky I am, and how a chance meeting with Margaret Thatcher changed my whole life.'

'What's it like working for the PM?' asked Samantha, pouring herself a coffee.

'To be honest, I don't get to see her that often, but whenever I do, she seems to know exactly what I've been up to.'

'And what have you been up to?' asked Seb as he joined his wife on the sofa.

'The new National Health Bill is about to leave the Commons and come to the Lords. It will be my job to steer it through the House clause by clause, before sending it back to the Commons, with I hope not too many opposition amendments attached.'

'That won't be easy with Giles trying to trip you up at

every turn,' said Grace, 'though I expect you'll catch him out on the detail.'

'Maybe, but he's still one of the finest debaters in either House, even though he's been relegated to the back benches.'

'Has he given up any hope of rejoining the shadow cabinet?' asked Samantha.

'I think the answer to that has to be yes, because Michael Foot can't have been pleased with his outspoken remarks following the donkey jacket incident.'

'Turning up at the Cenotaph on Remembrance Sunday wearing a donkey jacket revealed a certain lack of political nous,' suggested Seb.

'Just a pity Giles couldn't keep his mouth shut on the subject,' said Grace, as Emma handed her a coffee.

'The front bench's loss is our gain,' said Seb. 'Since Giles has rejoined the board of Farthings, he's opened doors we didn't have a key to.'

'Joining the board of a City bank is something else that won't have endeared him to Michael Foot,' said Emma. 'So I don't suppose we'll see him on the front bench again until the Labour Party has a new leader.'

'And possibly not even then,' suggested Seb. 'I'm afraid the next generation may well consider Giles a bit of a dinosaur, and, to quote Trotsky, consign him to the dustbin of history.'

'You couldn't get a dinosaur into a dustbin,' said Harry from a corner chair no one else would have dreamed of sitting in. The rest of the family burst out laughing.

'Enough of politics,' said Emma, turning to Samantha. 'I want to know what Jessica's been up to, and why she hasn't joined us for the weekend.'

'I think she's got a boyfriend,' said Sam.

'Isn't she a bit young?' said Harry.

'She's sixteen going on twenty,' Seb reminded his father.

'Have you met him?' asked Emma.

'No. In fact, we're not even meant to know about him,' said Sam. 'But when I was tidying her room the other day, I couldn't avoid seeing a drawing of a handsome young man on the wall beside her bed, where a poster of Duran Duran used to be.'

'I still miss my daughter,' said Harry wistfully.

'There are times when I'd be only too happy to give you mine,' said Seb. 'Last week I caught her trying to slip out of the house wearing a mini skirt, pink lipstick and high heels. I sent her back upstairs to remove the lipstick and change. She locked herself in her room and hasn't spoken to me since.'

'What do you know about the boy?' asked Harry.

'We think his name is Steve, and we know he's the captain of the school football team,' said Sam. 'So I suspect Jessica is waiting in a long queue.'

'I don't think Jessie does queues,' said Grace.

'And my other grandchild?' asked Emma.

'Jake's now walking without actually falling over,' said Sam, 'and spends most of his time heading for the nearest exit, so frankly he's a handful. I've put on hold any idea of going back to work for the time being, as I can't bear the thought of handing over the little fellow to a nanny.'

'I admire you for that,' said Emma. 'I sometimes wonder if I should have made the same decision.'

'I agree,' said Seb, leaning on the marble fireplace. 'I'm a classic example of someone who had a deprived upbringing, and ended up depraved.'

'Gee, Officer Krupke,' said Harry.

'I had no idea you were that with it, Dad,' said Seb.

'I took your mother to see *West Side Story* at the Bristol Old Vic on our wedding anniversary. And if you haven't seen it, you should.'

'Seen it,' said Seb. 'Farthings Kaufman is the show's biggest backer.'

'I'd never thought of you as an angel,' said Harry. 'And I certainly didn't see any mention of it in your latest portfolio report.'

'I put half a million of our clients' money into the show, but considered it too high a risk for the family, even though I had a dabble myself.'

'So we missed out,' said Grace.

'Mea culpa,' admitted Seb. 'You ended up with a 7.9 per cent annual return on your capital, while my other clients managed 8.4 per cent. *West Side Story* turned out to be a slam-dunker, to quote the American producer, who keeps sending me a cheque every quarter.'

'Perhaps you'll put us into your next show,' said Emma.

'There isn't going to be a next show, Mama. It didn't take much research to discover I'd been blessed with beginner's luck. Seven West End shows out of ten lose every penny for their investors. One in ten just about breaks even, one makes a worthwhile return, and only one in a hundred doubles its money, and they're usually the ones you can't get into. So I've decided to quit show business while I'm ahead.'

'Aaron Guinzburg tells me the next big hit will be something called *Little Shop of Horrors*,' said Harry.

'Farthings won't be investing in a horror show,' said Seb.

'Why not?' said Emma. 'After all, you tried to invest in Mellor Travel.'

'Still am,' admitted Sebastian.

'So what did you invest in?' asked Emma.

'ICI, Royal Dutch Shell, British Airways and Cunard. The only risk I took on your behalf was to buy a few shares in a fledgling bus company called Stagecoach, and you'll be pleased to know one of the founders is a woman.'

'And they've already shown a good return,' said Harry.

'I'm also considering picking up a sizeable holding in Thomas Cook, but only if we succeed in taking over Mellor Travel.'

'I never cared much for Desmond Mellor,' admitted Emma. 'But even I felt sorry for the man when I heard he'd committed suicide.'

'Barry Hammond isn't convinced it was suicide.'

'Neither am I,' said Harry. 'If William Warwick were on the case, he'd point out that there were far too many coincidences.'

'Like what?' asked Seb, always fascinated by how his father's mind worked.

'For a start, Mellor is found hanged in his cell during a takeover battle for his company. And at the same time, Adrian Sloane, the chairman of the company, disappears without trace.'

'I didn't know that,' said Emma.

'You've had more important things on your mind,' said Harry, 'than reading the *Bristol Evening Post*, and to be fair, I wouldn't have known about Mellor either if the local rags hadn't been obsessed with it. "Bristol businessman commits suicide in high-security prison" was a typical headline. And whenever the chairman of Mellor Travel is asked to make a statement on behalf of the company, all we get is that he's "unavailable for comment". Even more curious, Jim Knowles, who's described as the interim chairman, keeps trying to assure any anxious shareholders that it's business as usual, and that he'll be announcing some exciting news in the near future. Three unlikely coincidences, and certainly William Warwick would want to track down Adrian Sloane in case he could throw any light on the mystery of Mellor's death.'

'But the governor of Belmarsh was convinced it was suicide,' said Seb.

'Prison governors always say that whenever there's a death on their patch,' said Harry. 'So much more convenient than murder, which would mean setting up a Home Office enquiry that could take up to a year to report its findings. No, there's something missing in this case, although I haven't fathomed out yet what it is.'

'Not something,' said Seb, 'someone. Namely Mr Conrad Sorkin.'

'Who's he?' asked Grace.

'A shady international businessman, who until now I'd assumed was working with Sloane.'

'Does Sorkin run a travel company?' asked Emma. 'If he does, I've never come across him.'

'No, Sorkin isn't interested in Mellor Travel. He just wants to get his hands on the shops and offices the company owns so he can make a quick profit.'

'That's one piece of the jigsaw I wasn't aware of,' said Harry. 'But it might explain another coincidence that's been nagging away at me, namely the role played in this affair by a Mr Alan Carter.' Everyone in the room stared at Harry in rapt silence, not wanting to interrupt the storyteller. 'Alan Carter is a local estate agent, who up until now has only played a minor role in this whole saga.

But in my view, his evidence might well prove crucial.' Harry poured himself another cup of coffee and took a sip before he continued. 'So far Carter has only merited the occasional paragraph in the *Bristol Evening News*, for example when he told the paper's crime reporter that Mellor's Bristol flat was on the market. I assumed he'd done so simply to get some free publicity for his firm and a better price for his client's property. Nothing wrong with that. But it was his second statement, made a few days after Mellor's death, which I found far more intriguing.'

'Turn the page, turn the page,' demanded Seb.

'Carter told the press, without explanation, that Mellor's flat had been sold, but that he had been instructed by his client to hold back part of the sale money in escrow. What I'd like to know is how much he was asked to hold back, and why he didn't send the full amount to Mellor's executors and leave them to decide who was entitled to the money.'

'Do you think Carter will be working on a Saturday morning?' asked Seb.

'It's always the busiest morning of the week for an estate agent,' said Harry. 'But that wasn't the question you should have asked me, Seb.'

'You are maddening at times,' said Emma.

'Agreed,' said Seb.

'So what's the question Seb should have asked?' said Grace.

'Who is Desmond Mellor's next of kin?'

◄○►

Sebastian was standing outside Hudson and Jones on the Commercial Road at five to nine the following morning.

Three agents were already seated behind their desks waiting for the first customers.

When the doors opened, a neatly printed sign on one of the desks announced which agent was Mr Alan Carter. Seb sat down opposite a young man wearing a pinstriped suit, white shirt and green silk tie. He gave Seb a welcoming smile.

'Are you a buyer, a seller or possibly both, Mr—'

'Clifton.'

'You're not by any chance related to Lady Clifton?'

'She's my mother.'

'Then I hope you'll pass on my best wishes to her.'

'You know her?'

'Only as chairman of the Bristol Royal Infirmary. My wife had breast cancer, and they met when she was on one of her weekly ward rounds.'

'Every Wednesday morning, from ten to twelve,' said Seb. 'She said it gave her a chance to find out what the patients and staff were really thinking.'

'And I can tell you something else,' said Carter. 'When my son was knocked off his bike and twisted an ankle, there she was again, this time in A and E observing everything that was going on.'

'That would have been a Friday afternoon, between four and six.'

'That didn't surprise me, but what did was that she came over and had a word with my wife, and even remembered her name. So just tell me what you want, Mr Clifton, because I'm your man.'

'I'm afraid I'm neither a buyer nor a seller, Mr Carter, but a seeker of information.'

'If I can help, I will.'

'The bank I represent is currently involved in a take-over bid for Mellor Travel, and I was interested by a statement you made to the local press concerning the sale of Mr Desmond Mellor's flat in Broad Street.'

'Which one of the many statements I made?' asked Carter, clearly enjoying the attention.

'You told a reporter from the *Evening News* that you had held back part of the proceeds from the sale of the flat rather than pass over the full amount to the executors of Mr Mellor's will, which puzzled my father.'

'Clever man, your father. Which is more than can be said for the reporter, who failed to follow it up.'

'Well, I'd like to follow it up.'

'And if I were to assist you, Mr Clifton, would it be of any benefit to your mother?'

'Indirectly, yes. If my bank is successful in taking over Mellor Travel, my parents will benefit from the trans-action, because I manage their share portfolio.'

'So one of them can get on with the writing, while the other runs the NHS?'

'Something like that.'

'Between you and me,' whispered Carter, leaning conspiratorially across his desk, 'I thought it was a strange business from the start. A client who can only phone you once a week and is restricted to three minutes because he's calling from prison was a challenge in itself.'

'Yes, I can believe that.'

'Mind you, his first instruction was straightforward enough. He wanted to put his flat on the market, with the proviso that the whole transaction had to be completed within thirty days.'

Seb took out a cheque book from an inside pocket, and wrote on the back '30 days'.

'He called a week later and made another request that puzzled me, because I'd assumed he was a rich man.' Seb kept his pen poised. 'He asked if I could advance him a short-term loan of ten thousand pounds against the property, as he needed the cash urgently. I began to explain to him that it was against company policy, when the line went dead.'

Seb wrote down '£10,000', and underlined it.

'A fortnight later, I was able to tell him I'd found a buyer for the flat, who'd deposited ten per cent of the asking price with his solicitor, but wouldn't complete until he'd seen the surveyor's report. Mr Mellor then made an even stranger request.'

Seb continued to look enthralled by every word Carter had to say.

'Once the sale had gone through, I was to hand over the first ten thousand to a friend of his from London, but not until they had produced a legal document that had been signed by him, witnessed by a Mr Graves, and dated May twelfth 1981.'

Seb wrote down 'friend, £10,000, legal doc signed by Mellor/Graves' and the date.

'Whatever sum was left over,' continued Carter, 'after we'd deducted our fees, was to be deposited in his personal account at Nat West on Queen Street.'

Seb added, 'Nat West Queen Street' to his ever-growing list.

'I finally managed to get rid of the flat, but not before we'd lowered the price considerably. Once I had, I carried out Mr Mellor's instructions to the letter.'

'Are you still in possession of the document?' asked Seb, who could feel his heart pounding.

'No. But a lady rang this office, and when I confirmed

I was holding ten thousand in escrow, she sounded very interested, until I added that I couldn't release the money unless she could produce the document signed by Mr Mellor. She asked if a copy would suffice, but I told her I'd need sight of the original document before I would be willing to release the ten thousand.'

'What did she say to that?'

'Frankly, she lost her cool, and started to threaten me. Said I'd be hearing from her solicitor if I didn't hand over the money. But I stood firm, Mr Clifton, and I haven't heard from her since.'

'Quite right.'

'I'm glad you agree, Mr Clifton, because a few days later the strangest thing happened.' Seb raised an eyebrow. 'A local businessman turned up late one afternoon, just as we were about to close, and produced the original document, so I had no choice but to hand over the ten thousand to him.'

Seb wrote down 'local businessman'. He now had to agree with his father – Carter was in possession of several pieces of the jigsaw. However, he still needed one more question answered.

'And the woman's name?'

'No, Mr Clifton,' said Carter after a slight hesitation. 'I think I've gone quite far enough. But I can tell you that she was a lady like your mother, but not like your mother, because I doubt if she would remember my name.'

Seb wrote down the word 'lady' on the back of his cheque book before rising from his place. 'Thank you,' he said as he shook hands with Mr Carter. 'You've been most helpful, and I'll pass on your kind comments to my mother.'

'My pleasure. I'm only sorry I can't give you the lady's name.'

'Not to worry,' said Seb. 'But if Lady Virginia should call you again, do give her my best wishes.'

18

SEBASTIAN PLACED HIS cheque book on the table in front of him. Hakim Bishara, Arnold Hardcastle and Giles Barrington were clearly intrigued, but said nothing.

'I've just spent the weekend in Somerset with my parents,' said Seb, 'and I discovered that my father has been taking an inordinate amount of interest in the death of Desmond Mellor. Like Barry Hammond, he's not convinced it was suicide, and once you accept that as a possibility, several options arise.'

The three men seated around the table were listening intently.

'My father advised me to visit a local estate agent on Saturday morning and have a chat with the man who was responsible for selling Mellor's Bristol flat.' Seb looked at the long list of bullet points he'd written on the back of his cheque book during his meeting with Carter. Twenty minutes later he had explained to his attentive audience why he thought the lady in question was Lady Virginia Fenwick, and the local businessman none other than Jim Knowles.

'But how could those two have met?' asked Giles. 'They hardly mix in the same circles.'

'Mellor has to be the common factor,' suggested Arnold.

'And money the glue,' added Hakim, 'because that woman wouldn't waste her time on either of them unless she could see a profit in it for herself.'

'But that still doesn't explain why Mellor needed ten thousand in cash so quickly,' said Giles. 'After all, he was a very rich man.'

'In assets,' said Hakim, 'but not necessarily cash.'

'I've spent the last couple of days trying to fathom that one out,' said Seb, 'but of course it was my father who came up with the most likely scenario. He thought that if Mellor needed that amount of cash urgently, you should look no further than the prison. He also wondered if the mysterious disappearance of Adrian Sloane had something to do with it.'

'Maybe Mellor was being threatened,' said Arnold. 'That's not uncommon when it's thought a prisoner has money.'

'Possibly,' said Hakim, 'but if he urgently needed a loan of ten thousand pounds, he would have had to come up with something as security.'

'Like his flat in Bristol,' suggested Arnold.

'But it wasn't sold in time to solve his cash-flow problem, so he must have found something else.'

'His shares in Mellor Travel, perhaps?' suggested Giles.

'Seems unlikely,' said Hakim. 'They're worth at least a million and a half, and he only needed ten thousand.'

'It depends how desperate he was,' said Giles.

'Which is why I'm convinced he was being threatened by another inmate,' said Arnold.

'But why would he turn to Virginia for help,' said

Giles, 'when it was her who relied on him for an income, not the other way round?'

'She must have been the intermediary,' said Seb, 'and my father suggests that's how Knowles became involved.'

'And once he realized he could end up with fifty-one per cent of Mellor Travel if Mellor wasn't around to pay the ten thousand back within thirty days . . .'

'Which is why my father is convinced it wasn't suicide, but murder,' said Seb.

'Jim Knowles may be a nasty piece of work,' said Arnold, 'but I can't believe he'd involve himself in murder.'

'I suspect that's where Sorkin comes in,' said Seb.

'And there's something else I can tell you from past experience,' said Arnold. 'Contract killers usually charge around ten thousand, and there are sure to be one or two of them in Belmarsh.'

A long silence followed, until Hakim said, 'So once Sorkin got his hands on the shares, if Mellor was no longer around, the company would fall into his lap. And there's certainly no chance of us getting anything out of Knowles or Sloane.'

'That's another mystery,' said Seb. 'There's been no sign of Sloane for over a month. I can't believe he'd have done a runner only days before he had the chance of hitting the jackpot.'

'I agree,' said Hakim. 'However, I suspect there is one other person who could probably answer all our questions.'

'The Lady Virginia Fenwick,' said Sebastian. 'All we have to decide is who will approach her?'

'We could always draw straws to see who should bell the cat?'

'No need,' said Hakim. 'There's only one person who can pull this off.' He turned and smiled at Giles.

'But I haven't spoken to Virginia for almost thirty years,' protested Giles, 'and there's no reason to believe she'd even be willing to see me.'

'Unless you were able to offer her something she couldn't resist,' said Seb. 'After all, we know Mellor was willing to pay ten thousand pounds to get that document back, so all you have to do is find out how much Virginia wants to supply you with a copy.'

'How do we even know she's got a copy?' asked Arnold.

'Another piece of information kindly supplied by Mr Carter,' said Seb.

'Which raises the question,' said Hakim, 'who's got the original?'

'Knowles,' said Seb without hesitation. 'Don't forget, it was he who collected the ten thousand from Carter.'

'But on whose behalf?' asked Arnold.

'We're going round in circles,' said Hakim, 'which I'm sure Lady Virginia can square.' Once again he turned and smiled at Giles.

◄○►

Giles spent some considerable time trying to work out how he should approach Virginia. A letter suggesting a meeting would be a waste of time, as he knew from past experience that it was often days before she opened her mail, and even when she did, it was most unlikely she would bother to reply to anything that came from him. The last time he'd rung her, she had slammed the phone down before he'd had a chance to deliver the second sentence. And if he turned up on her doorstop unannounced,

179

he could end up with a slapped face or a slammed door, and possibly both. It was Karin who came up with the solution. 'That woman is only interested in one thing,' she said, 'so you'll have to bribe her.'

—◦—

A DHL messenger delivered an envelope marked 'Urgent & Personal' to Virginia's home in Chelsea the following morning, and didn't leave until she'd signed for it. She phoned Giles within an hour.

'Is this some kind of joke?' she demanded.

'Not at all. I just wanted to be sure I caught your attention.'

'Well, you've succeeded. So what do I have to do to get you to sign the cheque?'

'Supply me with a copy of the document Mr Carter wanted to see before he was willing to hand over ten thousand pounds.'

There was a long pause before Virginia spoke again. 'Ten thousand won't be enough for that, because I know exactly why you're so desperate to get your hands on it.'

'How much?'

'Twenty thousand.'

'I've been authorized to go up to fifteen,' said Giles, hoping he sounded convincing.

Another long pause. 'Once I'm in possession of a cheque for fifteen thousand pounds, I'll send you a copy of the document.'

'I don't think so, Virginia. I'll hand over the cheque when you give me a copy of the document.'

Virginia fell silent once again, before she said, 'When and where?'

—◦—

Giles pushed his way through the revolving doors into the Ritz Hotel just after 2.45 the following afternoon. He made his way straight to the Palm Court and selected a table from which he would be able to see Virginia the moment she appeared.

He flicked through the pages of the *Evening Standard* to pass the time, but still found himself looking up every few moments and repeatedly checking his watch. He knew Virginia wouldn't be on time, especially after he'd provoked her, but he was equally confident that she wouldn't be too late, because Coutts closed their doors at five o'clock, and she would want to bank the cheque before going home.

When Virginia entered the tea room at eleven minutes past three, Giles gasped. No one would have thought it possible that this elegant woman was over sixty. In fact, several men stole a second glance as 'the most classy broad in the joint', to quote Bogart, walked slowly across to join her ex-husband.

Giles stood up to greet her. As he bent down to kiss her on both cheeks, the slight fragrance of gardenia brought back many memories.

'It's been too long, my darling,' purred Virginia as she sat down opposite him. After the slightest of pauses, she added, 'And you've put on so much weight.'

The spell was broken, and Giles was quickly reminded why he didn't miss her.

'Shall we get the business out of the way,' she continued, opening her handbag and extracting an envelope. 'I'll give you what you came for, but not before you hand over my cheque.'

'I need to see the document before I'm willing to part with any money.'

'You're just going to have to trust me, my darling.' Giles stifled a smile. 'Because if I let you read it, you may feel you no longer need to pay me.'

Giles couldn't fault her logic. 'Perhaps we can agree on a compromise,' he suggested. 'You turn to the last page of the document and show me Mellor's signature and the date, and I'll show you the cheque.'

Virginia thought for a moment before she said, 'First I want to see the money.'

Giles produced a cheque for £15,000 from an inside pocket and held it up for her to see.

'You haven't signed it.'

'I will, as soon as I see Mellor's signature.'

Virginia slowly unsealed the envelope, extracted a thin legal document and turned to the third page. Giles leant forward and studied Mellor's signature, which had been witnessed by a Mr Colin Graves, senior prison officer, and dated May 12th, 1981.

He placed the cheque on the table, signed it and passed it across to Virginia. She hesitated for a moment, then smiled mischievously before slipping the document back into the envelope and handing it to Giles. He placed it in his briefcase, before saying casually, 'If you only got the copy, who has the original?'

'That will cost you another five thousand.'

Giles wrote out a second cheque and handed it across.

'But it's only for one thousand,' Virginia protested.

'That's because I think I already know who it is. The only mystery is how he got his hands on it.'

'Tell me the name, and if you're wrong, I'll tear up this cheque and you can write out another one for five thousand.'

'Jim Knowles collected it from Carter on behalf of Conrad Sorkin.'

The second cheque joined the first in Virginia's handbag, and although Giles pressed her, it was clear she wasn't going to let him know how Sorkin had got his hands on the original, not least because, like him, she suspected that Desmond hadn't committed suicide, and she didn't want to become involved.

'Tea?' suggested Giles, hoping she would decline so he could get back to the bank where the other three were waiting for him.

'What a nice idea,' said Virginia. 'Quite like old times.'

Giles hailed a waiter and ordered tea for two, but no cakes. He was wondering what they could possibly talk about, until Virginia solved that problem. 'I think I've got something else you might want,' she said, displaying the same mischievous smile.

Giles hadn't been prepared for this. He sat back, trying to appear relaxed, as he waited to find out if Virginia was just enjoying herself at his expense, or if she really did have something worthwhile to offer.

The waiter reappeared and placed a pot of tea and a selection of wafer-thin sandwiches in the centre of the table.

Virginia picked up the teapot. 'Shall I be Mother? Milk and no sugar, if I remember correctly.'

'Thank you,' said Giles.

She poured them both a cup of tea. Giles waited impatiently while she added a splash of milk and two sugar lumps before she spoke again.

'Such a pity the coroner concluded that poor Desmond died intestate.' She took a sip of her tea. 'Earl Grey,' she remarked, before adding, 'It's going to be difficult for anyone to prove otherwise before June twelfth, when the company will fall so conveniently into that nice Mr Sorkin's hands, and for a mere ten thousand pounds he'll be entitled to fifty-one per cent of Mellor Travel, which I estimate to be worth at least a million and a half, possibly more.'

'The board of Farthings has already considered that problem,' said Giles, 'and the question of who might be judged by the court to be Mellor's next of kin. Arnold Hardcastle concluded that with two ex-wives, one daughter he's lost touch with and two stepchildren, the legal battle alone could take years to be resolved.'

'I agree,' said Virginia, taking another sip of tea. 'Unless, of course, someone came across a will.'

Giles stared at her in disbelief as she returned to her handbag and extracted a slim manila envelope, which she held up for Giles to see. He studied the neat copperplate handwriting that proclaimed, *The last will and testament of Desmond Mellor*, dated May 12th, 1981.

'How much?' asked Giles.

19

SEBASTIAN STEPPED OFF the plane and joined the other passengers making their way into the busiest terminal on earth. As he only had an overnight bag, he headed straight for customs. An officer stamped his passport, smiled and said, 'Welcome to America, Mr Clifton.'

He made his way out of the airport and joined a long taxi queue. He had already decided to go straight to Kelly Mellor's last known address on the South Side of Chicago, which had been supplied by Virginia, but not before she'd extracted another £5,000 from Giles. If Kelly was there, the chairman considered it would have been worth every penny, because he wanted Desmond Mellor's heir back in England as quickly as possible. They needed to have everything in place for the crucial board meeting in ten days' time, when it would be decided whether it was Thomas Cook or Sorkin International that would take over Mellor Travel, and Kelly Mellor could be the deciding factor.

He climbed into the back of a yellow cab and handed the driver the address. The cabbie gave Seb a second look. He only visited that district about once a month, and that was once too often.

Seb sat back and thought about what had taken place during the past twenty-four hours. Giles had arrived back at the bank just after five, armed not only with a copy of the legal agreement showing that Mellor had risked losing 51 per cent of his company to Sorkin for a mere £10,000, but with the bonus of the only letter Mellor had ever written to his daughter, supplied by Virginia. No doubt acquired after the threat that if Giles didn't pay up, she would burn the letter in front of him. The singed bottom right-hand edge suggested that Giles hadn't given up bargaining until the match was struck.

'We're going to have to move quickly,' Hakim had said. 'We only have eleven days left before Mellor Travel's next board meeting, when it will be decided who takes over the company.'

This time it was Sebastian the chairman selected for the unenviable task of flying to Chicago and bringing back to London the only person who could stop Sorkin taking over Mellor Travel, although there was a Plan B.

Seb had boarded the first available flight from Heathrow to Chicago, and by the time the plane touched down at O'Hare, he felt he'd covered every possible scenario – except one. He couldn't actually be certain that Mellor's daughter was living at 1532 Taft Road, because he'd had no way of contacting her to warn her he was coming, although he was confident that if she was, what he had to offer would make her feel like a lottery winner.

He glanced out of the taxi window as they drove into Taft, and was immediately aware why this wasn't an area taxis would choose to hang around at night looking for fares. Row upon row of dilapidated wooden houses, none of which had seen a lick of paint for years, and no one would have bothered with a double lock because there wouldn't have been anything worth stealing.

When the cab dropped him outside 1532, his confidence grew. One and a half million pounds was certainly going to change Kelly Mellor's life for ever. He checked his watch; just after six p.m. Now he could only hope she was at home. The taxi had sped away even before he'd been given a chance to offer the driver a tip.

Seb walked up the short path between two scrubby patches of grass that couldn't have been described as a garden by even the most creative estate agent. He knocked on the door, took a step back and waited. A moment later the door was opened by someone who couldn't have been Kelly Mellor, because she only looked about five or six years old.

'Hello, I'm Sebastian. Who are you?'

'Who wants to know?' said a deep, gruff voice.

Seb turned his attention to a squat, muscle-bound man who stepped out of the shadows. He was wearing a grubby T-shirt with 'Marciano's' printed on it, and a pair of Levi's that looked as if they hadn't been taken off for a month. A snake tattoo slithered down each well-exercised arm.

'My name's Sebastian Clifton. I wondered if Kelly Mellor lives here.'

'You from the IRS?'

'No,' said Seb, suppressing a desire to laugh.

'Or that fuckin' Child Protective Services?'

'No.' Seb no longer wanted to laugh, as he had noticed a fading bruise on the little girl's arm. 'I've flown over from England to let Kelly know her father has died and left her some money in his will.'

'How much?'

'I'm only authorized to disclose the details to Mr Mellor's next of kin.'

'If this is some kind of scam,' the man said, clenching his fist, 'this will end up in the middle of your pretty face.' Seb didn't budge. Without another word the man turned and said, 'Follow me.'

It was the smell that first hit Seb as he entered the house: half-empty fast-food trays, cigarette ends and empty beer cans littered a small room furnished with two unrelated chairs, a sofa and the latest VCR player. He didn't sit down, but smiled at the young girl who was now standing in a corner staring up at him.

'Kelly!' the man bellowed at the top of his voice without looking round. He hadn't taken his eyes off Seb.

A few moments later a woman appeared in a dressing gown embroidered with the words *The Majestic Hotel*. She looked worn out, although Seb knew she was only in her early twenties. But she was unquestionably the young girl's mother, and she had something else in common with the child – several bruises and, in her case, a black eye that heavy make-up couldn't disguise.

'This guy says your old man's died and left you some money, but he won't tell me how much.'

Seb noticed the man's right fist was still clenched. He could see that Kelly was too frightened to speak. She kept glancing towards the door, as if trying to let him know that he ought to leave as quickly as possible.

'How much?' the man repeated.

'Fifty thousand dollars,' said Seb, having decided that the suggestion of £1.5 million would have been greeted with incredulity and would mean he'd never be rid of the man.

'Fifty grand? Hand it over.'

'It's not quite that easy.'

'If this is a con,' said the man, 'you'll wish you'd never got off the plane.'

Seb was surprised that he felt no fear. As long as this thug thought there was a chance of picking up some easy money, Seb was confident he had the upper hand.

'It's not a con,' said Seb quietly. 'But because it's such a large sum of money, Kelly will have to accompany me to England and sign some legal documents before we can hand over her inheritance.'

In truth, Seb had all the necessary paperwork in his overnight bag should Kelly be unwilling to return to England – Plan B. He only needed a signature and a witness, and then he could have handed over a banker's draft for the full amount in exchange for 51 per cent of Mellor Travel. But now he'd met her partner, that was never going to happen. He had moved way beyond Plan A, B or C, and his mind was now working overtime.

'She ain't goin' nowhere without me,' the man said.

'Fine by me,' said Seb. 'But you'll have to pay your own plane fare to London.'

'I don't believe a fuckin' word you're saying,' the man said, picking up a steak knife and advancing towards Seb. For the first time Seb felt frightened, but he stood his ground, and even decided to take a risk.

'Makes no difference to me,' he said, looking directly at Kelly. 'If she doesn't want the money, it will automatically go to her younger sister.' He hesitated for a moment. 'Maureen.' Seb's eyes never left hers.

'I didn't know you had a sister,' said the man, swinging round to glare at Kelly.

Seb gave her a slight, almost undetectable nod.

'I, I haven't seen her for years, Richie. I didn't even know she was still alive.'

She had told him everything he needed to know.

'Maureen is very much alive,' said Seb. 'And she rather hopes Kelly won't be returning to England.'

'Then she can think again,' said Richie. 'Just make sure that bitch comes back with my money,' he said, squeezing the little girl's arm until she burst into tears, 'otherwise she won't be seein' Cindy again. So what happens now?'

'My flight leaves for London at ten o'clock tomorrow morning, so I could pick Kelly up around eight.'

'Five hundred dollars would help convince me you'll be back,' said Richie, brandishing the knife in front of him.

'I don't have that much on me,' said Seb, taking out his wallet. 'But I can give you everything I do have.' He handed over $345, which quickly disappeared into the back pocket of Richie's jeans.

'I'll pick you up at eight tomorrow morning,' said Seb. Kelly nodded, but didn't speak. Seb smiled at the little girl, and left without saying goodbye.

Once he was back on the street, he began the long walk to his hotel in the centre of town, aware that it would be some time before he came across a cab. He cursed. If only he'd known Kelly had a daughter.

<><>

Sebastian woke at two o'clock the next morning, eight o'clock in London. Despite closing his eyes, he knew he wouldn't get back to sleep, because his body clock was ticking and he was wide awake on another continent. In any case, his mind was buzzing with thoughts about how

Kelly Mellor could possibly have ended up living in such circumstances and with a man like that. It had to be the child.

When three o'clock struck on a nearby church tower, Seb phoned Hakim at the bank, and told him in great detail about his encounter with Richie, Kelly and Cindy.

'It's sad that she'll have to go back to Chicago if she wants to be with her daughter,' were Hakim's first words.

'No mother would be willing to leave her child with a monster like that,' said Seb. 'In fact, I'm not even certain she won't have changed her mind about leaving her by the time I get back.'

'I wonder if you gave him a thousand dollars in cash, he might let the girl go too?'

'I don't think so. But twenty-five thousand might do it.'

'I'll leave you to decide what Plan C is,' said Hakim. 'But make sure you've got a thousand dollars on you, just in case,' he added before putting the phone down.

Seb took a long hot shower, shaved, dressed, then went downstairs to join the other early risers for breakfast. Looking at the menu, he realized he'd forgotten just how much an American could eat first thing in the morning. He politely declined an offer of waffles and maple syrup, fried eggs, sausage, bacon and hash browns, in favour of a bowl of muesli and a boiled egg.

He checked out of the hotel just after seven thirty. The doorman hailed a cab, and once again the driver looked surprised when Seb gave him the address.

'I'm picking someone up,' he explained, 'and then we'll need to go on to O'Hare.'

The cab pulled up outside 1532 Taft a few minutes early and, after taking one look at the house, the driver kept the engine running. Seb decided to stay put until just before eight o'clock, not wanting to antagonize Richie any more than was necessary. But he hadn't noticed two pairs of eyes staring expectantly out of the window, and a moment later the front door eased open and a little girl came scampering down the path towards him. Her mother closed the door quietly behind her and then also began to run.

Seb leant across and quickly opened the back door of the taxi to allow them to jump in beside him. Kelly pulled it closed and screamed, 'Go, go, for God's sake, go,' her eyes never leaving the front door of the house even for a moment. The driver happily obeyed her command.

Once they'd turned the corner and were heading towards the airport, Kelly breathed a deep sigh of relief, but didn't stop clinging on to her daughter. It was some time before she had recovered enough to say, 'Richie didn't get back until after two this morning, and he was so drunk he could barely stand. He collapsed on the bed and fell asleep straight away. He probably won't stir before midday.'

'By which time you and Cindy will be halfway across the Atlantic.'

'And one thing's for sure, Mr Clifton, we won't be coming back,' she said, still clinging on to her daughter. 'I can't wait to see Bristol again. Fifty thousand dollars will be more than enough to buy a little place of my own, find a job and get Cindy settled into a decent school.'

'It isn't fifty thousand,' said Seb quietly.

Kelly looked alarmed, her expression revealing her fear at the thought that she might have to return to 1532 empty-handed. Seb took an envelope out of his briefcase addressed to Miss Kelly Mellor and handed it to her.

She ripped it open and pulled out the letter. As she read it, her eyes widened in disbelief.

HMP Belmarsh
London
May 12, 1981

Dear Kelly,

This is the first letter I've written to you, and I fear it may be the last. The thought of death has caused me to finally come to my senses. It's far too late for me to make up for being an abject failure as a father, but at least allow me the chance to make it possible for you to enjoy a better life than I've led.

With that in mind, I have decided to leave you all my worldly goods, in the hope that you might, in time, feel able to forgive me. I would be the first to admit I have not led a blameless life, far from it, but at least this tiny gesture will allow me to leave this world feeling I have done something worthwhile for a change. If you have any children, Kelly, be sure to give them the opportunities I failed to give you.

Yours,

Desmond Mellor (AZ2178)

Witnessed by Colin Graves, SPO

P.S. You may find it strange that when writing a letter to my daughter, I have signed it with my full name, and had it witnessed by a prison officer. It's simply to show that this letter is to be considered my last will and testament.

The letter fell to the floor of the taxi, but only because Kelly had fainted.

20

'TODAY THE BOARD must decide,' said the chairman, 'who will lead Mellor Travel into the twenty-first century. Two highly respected companies, Sorkin International and Thomas Cook, have each made a bid of two million pounds for the company, but it is for us to decide which we feel is best suited to our present needs. I should point out at this juncture,' continued Knowles, 'that I wrote to both Mr Sorkin and Mr Brook of Thomas Cook inviting them to address the board so we could assess the merits of both their offers. Mr Brook failed to reply to my invitation. Make of that what you will.' Knowles didn't add that although he'd signed the letter to Brook a week ago, he'd only posted it the previous day. 'Mr Sorkin, however, not only replied immediately, but interrupted his busy schedule to be with us today, and this morning deposited two million pounds with our bank to prove his intent.'

Knowles smiled, but then he'd already been promised that a further million would be transferred to his numbered account at Pieter & Cie in Geneva, to be cleared the moment Conrad Sorkin took control of the company. What Knowles didn't know was that Sorkin never had any intention of paying two million for the company. In a few hours' time he would own 51 per cent of Mellor Travel, and everyone sitting around that boardroom table would be out of a job, Knowles included, and he could whistle for his million, because he would no longer be the chairman.

'And so,' continued Knowles, 'I would now like to invite Mr Sorkin to address the board, so he can tell you how he sees the future of Mellor Travel were we to accept his takeover bid.'

Sorkin, dressed in an elegantly tailored dark grey suit, white shirt and a crimson-and-yellow-striped MCC tie that he didn't have the right to wear, rose from his place at the other end of the table.

'Mr Chairman, may I begin by telling you a little about the philosophy of my company. First and foremost, Sorkin International believes in people, and therefore its first priority is to its employees, from the tea lady to the managing director. I believe in loyalty and continuity above all things, and can assure the board that no one currently employed by Mellor Travel need fear being made redundant. I consider myself to be no more than a guardian of the company, who will work tirelessly on behalf of its shareholders. So let me assure you from the outset that if Sorkin International is fortunate enough to take over Mellor Travel you can look forward to a rapid expansion of the workforce, because I intend to employ more staff, not fewer, and in the fullness of time, I would hope it will be Mellor Travel that is making a bid for Thomas Cook, and not the other way round. This of course will require a large capital investment, which I can promise the board I'm happy to commit to. But my company will also require a firm and reliable hand at the tiller, following the distressing circumstances of the past few months. To misquote Oscar Wilde, *To lose one chairman is unfortunate, but to lose two . . .'*

Knowles was pleased to see one or two members of the board smiling.

'With that in mind,' continued Sorkin, 'I think it's important to show my confidence not only in your chairman, but in the entire board. So let me say unequivocally, if my company is chosen today to take over Mellor Travel, I would invite Jim Knowles to stay on as chairman, and would ask each and every one of you to remain on the board.'

This time only one director wasn't smiling.

'Let's work together and quickly rebuild this company to where it used to be, and then look forward to expanding, so that Mellor International will be the envy of the travel business throughout the world. Let me finish by saying I hope you will consider me the right person to take the company into the next century.'

Sorkin sat down to cries of 'Hear, hear!' and one director even patted him on the back.

'Gentlemen,' said Knowles, 'as the chairman of Thomas Cook has failed to make an appearance, perhaps we should move on and decide which company should take over Mellor Travel, Sorkin International or Thomas Cook? I will now ask the company secretary to conduct the vote.'

Mr Arkwright rose slowly from his place and said, 'Would those members of the board who wish to cast their vote in favour of Sorkin International raise their—'

The boardroom door burst open, and three men and a woman entered the room.

'What is the meaning of this intrusion?' demanded

Knowles, leaping to his feet. 'This is a private board meeting and you have no right to be here.'

'I think you'll find we do,' said Arnold Hardcastle, speaking first. 'As you know, Mr Knowles, I am the legal representative of Farthings Kaufman, and I am accompanied today by Mr Sebastian Clifton, the bank's managing director, and Mr Ray Brook, the chairman of Thomas Cook, who only received an invitation to attend this meeting earlier this morning.'

'And the young lady?' said Knowles, not attempting to hide his sarcasm. 'Who invited her?'

'She didn't receive an invitation,' said Hardcastle. 'But I will leave it to Miss Mellor to explain to the board why she is here.'

Knowles collapsed back into his chair, as if floored by a heavyweight boxer.

Sebastian gave Kelly a reassuring smile. For countless hours during the past week, he had prepared his protégée for this moment. She had turned out to be a quick study. No longer shabbily dressed and with a fading black eye, the young woman standing before them displayed the confidence of someone well aware of the power she now possessed as the majority shareholder of Mellor Travel. Few would have recognized her as the same woman Sebastian had first met in Chicago only a few days earlier.

Seb had quickly discovered just how intelligent Kelly was, and once she had been released from the shackles of 1532 Taft Road, she had immediately grasped the significance of owning 51 per cent of her father's company. By the day of the board meeting, she was more than ready to play her part in reclaiming her birthright.

Conrad Sorkin rose slowly from his place, and certainly didn't appear intimidated. But then Seb suspected he'd been in far tighter spots than this in the past. He was staring directly at Kelly, as if daring her to open her mouth.

'Mr Sorkin,' she said, giving him a warm smile, 'my name is Kelly Mellor, and I am the daughter of the late Desmond Kevin Mellor, who in his last will and testament left me all his worldly goods.'

'Miss Mellor,' said Sorkin, 'I have to point out that I am still in possession of fifty-one per cent of the company's shares, which I purchased quite legally from your father.'

'Even if that were true, Mr Sorkin,' said Kelly, not needing to be prompted by Seb, 'if I repay you your ten thousand pounds before close of business today, those shares automatically revert to me.'

Hardcastle stepped forward, opened his briefcase and took out his client's passport, Mellor's will and a banker's order for £10,000. He placed them on the table in front of Sorkin, who ignored them.

'Before close of business today, if I may be allowed to repeat your words, Miss Mellor,' said Sorkin. 'And as the banks close their doors in twelve minutes' time,' he said, checking his watch, 'I think you'll find that your cheque cannot be cleared until Monday morning, by which time the contract will be null and void, and it is I who will own Mellor Travel, not you.'

'If you take the trouble to look more closely,' said Arnold, coming in on cue, 'you will see that it's not a cheque we're presenting you with, Mr Sorkin, but a banker's order, and therefore legal tender, which allows Miss Mellor, as her father's heir, to claim back her rightful inheritance.'

One or two members of the board were looking distinctly uneasy.

Sorkin counter-punched immediately. 'Clearly you are not aware, Mr Hardcastle, that I have already received the board's approval to take over the company, as Mr Knowles will confirm.'

'Is that correct?' asked Seb, turning to face the chairman.

Knowles glanced nervously at Sorkin. 'Yes, the vote has already been taken, and Sorkin International now controls Mellor Travel.'

'Perhaps it's time for you to leave, Mr Clifton,' said Sorkin, 'before you make an even bigger fool of yourself.'

Seb was about to protest, but he knew that if the board had voted in favour of Sorkin International taking over the company, he would have to abide by their decision, and although Kelly still held 51 per cent of the shares, once Sorkin had sold off the company's assets, they would be worthless.

Arnold was placing his files back in his briefcase when a lone voice declared, 'No vote was taken.'

Everyone turned to look at one of the directors who had not spoken until then. Sebastian recalled Mellor telling him when he'd visited him in prison that he still had one friend on the inside. 'We were just about to take the vote when you arrived,' said Andy Dobbs. 'And I can assure you, Mr Clifton, I may have been the only one, but I would have thrown my support behind Thomas Cook.'

'As would I,' said another director.

Knowles looked desperately around the table for support, but it was clear that even his carefully selected placemen were deserting him.

'Thank you, gentlemen,' said Sebastian. 'Perhaps the

time has come for you to take your leave, Mr Sorkin. Or would you like me to put that to a vote?'

'Piss off, you patronizing git,' said Sorkin. 'I'm not that easily threatened.'

'I wasn't threatening anyone,' said Seb. 'On the contrary. I was trying to be helpful. As you are no doubt aware, it's June the twelfth, which means you've been resident in this country for the past twenty-nine days. So if you have not left these shores by midnight tonight, you will be subject to British taxation, which I'm pretty sure is something you would want to avoid.'

'You don't frighten me, Clifton. My lawyers will be more than able to deal with a pipsqueak like you.'

'Perhaps. But it might be wise to warn them that I felt it was my duty to inform the tax authorities of your presence in Bristol, so don't be surprised if the police board your yacht at one minute past midnight and seize it.'

'They wouldn't dare.'

'I don't think that's a risk you'll be willing to take, as I also understand Scotland Yard has opened an enquiry into the suspicious death of Desmond Mellor, while the French authorities, who recently recovered a body washed up off the coast of Nice, which they have reason to believe is that of Adrian Sloane, have issued a warrant for your arrest.'

'They won't be able to pin anything on me.'

'Possibly not. But I have a feeling Mr Knowles may want to assist Interpol with their enquiries. That is, if he doesn't wish to spend the rest of his life in the same cell as you.'

Knowles, visibly turning pale, slumped back in his chair.

'I'd worry about your own life, if I were you, Clifton,' said Sorkin.

'That was a foolish threat to make in front of so many witnesses,' said Seb, 'especially as one of them is a QC, who you will observe is writing down your every word.'

Sorkin stared at Arnold Hardcastle, and fell silent.

'Frankly, I think it's time for you, like your hero Napoleon, to beat a hasty retreat.'

The two men continued to stare at each other, until Sorkin threw the contract on to the table, picked up the banker's order and was about to leave the room when Kelly stepped forward once again and said, 'Before you go, Mr Sorkin, can I ask how much you would be willing to offer for my fifty-one per cent of Mellor Travel?'

Everyone turned to face the new head of the company, and Sebastian couldn't hide his surprise. This wasn't part of their well-rehearsed script. She was staring directly at Sorkin, waiting for his reply.

'I would be willing to pay three million pounds for your shares,' said Sorkin calmly, aware that he could still make a handsome profit now that Knowles wouldn't be getting his million.

Kelly appeared to consider his proposition before finally saying, 'I'm grateful for the offer, Mr Sorkin, but on balance, I think I'd prefer to deal with Farthings Kaufman.'

Sebastian smiled at Kelly and breathed a sigh of relief.

'And as you'll have to be outside territorial waters before midnight, Mr Sorkin, I won't detain you any longer.'

'Bitch,' said Sorkin as he passed her on the way out of the boardroom.

Kelly's smile revealed that she was flattered by the insult.

Knowles waited until Sorkin had slammed the door behind him before saying, 'We were just about to take a vote, Miss Mellor. So can I ask the company secretary to—'

'That will no longer be necessary,' said Kelly, picking up the agreement Sorkin had left on the table. 'As I am now the majority shareholder, it is I who will decide the company's future.'

Word perfect, thought Sebastian. Couldn't have put it better myself.

'My first decision as the new owner is to fire you, Mr Knowles, along with the rest of the board. I suggest you all leave immediately.'

Seb couldn't resist a smile as Knowles and the rest of the board gathered up their papers and quietly left the room.

'Well done,' he said, when the last board member had departed.

'Thank you, Mr Clifton,' said Kelly. 'And allow me to say how much I appreciate all you and your team at Farthings Kaufman have done to make this possible.'

'My pleasure.'

'I'm bound to ask,' she continued, 'as Mr Sorkin was willing to offer me three million for my shares, can I assume that Thomas Cook will match that price?'

She'd turned another page of the script Seb hadn't read. Before he could respond, Ray Brook chuckled, and said, 'You've got yourself a deal, young lady.'

'Thank you,' said Kelly, who turned to the bank's lawyer and added, 'I'll leave you to draw up the paperwork, Mr Hardcastle, and do let me know the moment you receive the three million.'

'I think that's our cue to leave,' said the chairman of Cook's, unable to resist a grin. The three men left the boardroom, closing the door behind them.

Kelly sat down at the head of the table for a few moments before she picked up the phone in front of her and dialled a number she had called every evening for the past two weeks.

As soon as she heard the familiar voice on the other end of the line, she said, 'It all went to plan, Virginia.'

LADY VIRGINIA FENWICK

1981–1982

21

'I DON'T KNOW HOW to begin to thank you,' said Kelly. 'If you hadn't written to warn me that Mr Clifton was on his way, I would never have known he was no friend of my father's.'

'It was the least I could do,' said Virginia.

'And then those endless reverse-charge calls. They must have cost you a fortune . . .'

'I felt it was important that you knew the truth about Farthings, and particularly how Sebastian Clifton had treated your father in the past.'

'But he's always seemed so nice.'

'Are you surprised, when so many millions were involved? And you have to remember his first interest was always Thomas Cook, not you.'

'And what a brilliant idea of yours to find out how much Mr Sorkin would have paid for my shares and then get Thomas Cook to match it.'

'Your father was not only a close friend, but taught me a great deal about business over the years.'

'But you didn't have to lend me twenty thousand pounds until the deal went through.'

'I thought it would help tide you over.'

'It will do more than that, so much more,' said Kelly. 'I must pay you back every penny I owe you.'

'There's no hurry,' said Virginia, who still had over two hundred thousand pounds in her current account, and was already looking forward to another windfall. 'More important, Kelly my dear, how is little Cindy settling down?'

'I've never seen her so happy. She loves her new school, and already has several best friends.'

'I do envy you. I've always wanted a child of my own, and now it's too late. Perhaps you'll allow me to be an honorary grandmother.'

'I can't think of anyone more appropriate to guide Cindy through her formative years,' said Kelly, who hesitated for a moment before adding, 'but there's something else I need to discuss with you, Virginia, that I've been feeling a little guilty about.'

'You have nothing to feel guilty about, my dear. On the contrary. I'll never be able to repay your father for his kindness to me over the years.'

'And I must now repay you for your kindness, because I know you and my father were not only close friends, but business partners, and I therefore have to ask you an embarrassing question.' Kelly hesitated again, and this time Virginia didn't come to her rescue. 'What percentage did he pay after you'd closed a deal?'

A question Virginia was well prepared for. 'Desmond was a generous man,' she said, 'and always paid me a fee of twenty-five thousand pounds, and ten per cent of the final settlement plus any expenses I had incurred on his behalf. But there's no need for you to—'

'There most certainly is. I shall treat you the same way

my father did, and you'll be paid in full just as soon as the deal with Thomas Cook goes through.'

'No hurry, my darling,' said Virginia. 'Your friendship is far more important to me.'

—◦—

Five weeks later Kelly received a cheque from Thomas Cook for three million pounds, and immediately sent a cheque to Virginia for £345,000 to cover her loan, her fee and 10 per cent of the three million.

Virginia didn't press Kelly for any expenses. After all, she hadn't invested a great deal to find her quarry. A few phone calls and, once Kelly was back in England, a couple of meals in restaurants where no one was likely to recognize them. The only real cost had been hiring a private detective in Chicago to track down the missing Kelly Mellor. Well, to be accurate, he first caught up with Cindy Mellor at her school, where he handed over two letters to Cindy's mother when she came to pick up her daughter. Once she'd read the two letters, Kelly made a reverse-charge call from a phone box that afternoon. So when Giles got in touch with Virginia, she knew exactly what he was really after.

The detective's bill of $2,000 had been more than covered by Farthings in return for a copy of Desmond Mellor's will and an address that would lead them to his next of kin. Sebastian Clifton also saved her the expense of travelling to Chicago, bringing Kelly Mellor back to England and preparing her for the encounter with Sorkin, only to end up having to pay double for Kelly's 51 per cent of the company. Virginia decided she could afford to be magnanimous about expenses this time, confident that

Kelly was about to replace her father as an alternative source of income.

◄o►

'Let me try to understand what you are proposing, Lady Virginia,' said Sir Edward Makepeace. 'You want me to approach Cyrus T. Grant's solicitors, and suggest that instead of paying £100,000 a year for the next nine years, you would be willing to settle the action with a one-off payment of £500,000?'

'In full and final settlement.'

'I'll get in touch with Lord Goodman and let you know what he thinks of your proposal.'

◄o►

It took Cyrus T. Grant III a month before he agreed to settle his action with Virginia for £500,000 in full and final settlement, and only after being nagged constantly by Ellie May.

'As my grandfather used to say,' she reminded him, 'better a dollar in the bank than the promise of a dowry.'

◄o►

Another month passed before Virginia received a bill from Sir Edward Makepeace, for £2,300, which she settled immediately, as she could never be sure when she might need his services again.

One of the few letters she did open during the following weeks was from Coutts, informing her that her current account was still £41,000 in credit. Desmond Mellor was proving to be far more lucrative dead than alive.

When the clocks went back an hour, and the temperature began to drop, Virginia's thoughts turned to a winter vacation. She was finding it difficult to decide between a villa in the South of France, or the royal suite at the Sandy Lane hotel in Barbados. Perhaps she'd let the young man she'd recently met in Annabel's decide which he would prefer. She was thinking about Alberto, when she opened another letter which quickly removed any thought of holidays from her mind. After Virginia had recovered from the shock, she looked up the number of her bank manager and made an appointment to see Mr Leigh the following day.

◄○►

'One hundred and eighty-five thousand pounds?' protested Virginia.

'That is correct, my lady,' said Mr Leigh, once he'd read the letter from HM Inspector of Taxes.

'But how can that be possible?'

'I presume you're familiar with capital gains tax, my lady?'

'Familiar, yes, but we've never been introduced.'

'Well, I fear you are about to be,' said Leigh, 'because the taxman is demanding thirty per cent of the £230,000 profit you made from the sale of the Lowrys, the £300,000 commission, and the £25,000 fee you were paid following the successful takeover of Mellor Travel.'

'But doesn't the taxman realize I haven't got £185,000? I parted with almost every penny to clear my debt with Cyrus.'

'HM's Inspector of Taxes is blind to any personal problems you might have,' Mr Leigh pointed out unhelpfully. 'They are only aware of your earnings, not how much you spend.'

'What will happen if I don't reply to their letter?'

'If you fail to respond within thirty days, they will start charging you a punitive interest rate until you do.'

'And if I can't?'

'They will take you to court, have you declared bankrupt and confiscate all your assets.'

'Who would have thought,' said Virginia, 'the taxman would turn out to be an even worse bitch than Ellie May Grant.'

◄○►

Virginia knew the one person who could be relied on to solve her problem with the taxman, and although she hadn't been in touch with her for several months – 'Pressure of work,' she would explain – she didn't think it would be difficult to convince Kelly to invest a couple of hundred thousand in a deal that couldn't fail.

Once she had arrived home following her meeting with Mr Leigh, Virginia spent some time searching for the letter Kelly had sent some weeks earlier, which she now regretted not replying to. Still, she thought, looking at the address on top of the notepaper, all the more reason to pay a surprise visit to The Little Gables, Lodge Lane, Nailsea, near Bristol.

The following morning Virginia rose before the sun, an unusual occurrence, but in truth she hadn't been able to sleep. She set off for the West Country just after nine a.m., and used the long drive to rehearse the lines about a once-in-a-lifetime investment opportunity that Kelly would be foolish not to take advantage of.

She passed a sign for Nailsea just before midday, and stopped to ask an elderly gentleman the way to Lodge Lane. As she drew up outside The Little Gables her heart sank when she spotted a For Sale sign on the front lawn. Virginia assumed Kelly must be moving to a bigger house. She walked up the driveway and knocked on the front door. A few moments later it was opened by a young man who gave her an expectant smile.

'Mrs Campion?'

'No, I am not Mrs Campion. I'm the Lady Virginia Fenwick.'

'I apologize, Lady Fenwick.'

'I'm also not Lady Fenwick. I am the daughter of an earl, not the wife of a life peer. You may address me as Lady Virginia.'

'Of course,' he said, and apologized a second time. 'How can I help you, Lady Virginia?'

'You can start by telling me who you are.'

'My name is Neil Osborne and I'm the estate agent in charge of the sale of this property. Are you an interested party?'

'Certainly not. I am simply visiting my old friend Kelly Mellor. Does she still live here?'

'No, she moved out soon after instructing us to put the house back on the market.'

'Has she moved somewhere locally?'

'Perth.'

'In Scotland?'

'No, Australia.' That silenced Virginia for a moment, and allowed the young man to complete a second sentence. 'All I can tell you, Lady Virginia, is that Kelly instructed us to send the proceeds of the sale to a joint bank account in Perth.'

'A joint bank account?'

'Yes, I only met Barry once, quite soon after they became engaged. He seemed a nice enough fellow,'

Osborne added as he looked over Virginia's shoulder. 'Are you Mr and Mrs Campion?' he asked a young couple who were walking up the driveway.

—◄o►—

When Virginia received a second letter from HM Inspector of Taxes, she realized there was only one person left she could turn to, although he wasn't someone who would believe a story about an investment that couldn't fail.

She chose a weekend when the Hon. Freddie Fenwick would be at boarding school, and her sister-in-law, a woman Virginia had never much cared for, and she suspected the feeling was mutual, would be visiting an elderly aunt in Dumfries.

Virginia didn't take the sleeper, a misnomer in her opinion, because she could never manage more than an hour's sleep while the carriage rattled over the points. Instead, she opted to travel up to Scotland during the day, which would give her more than enough time to go over her plan, and prepare for any awkward questions her brother might come up with. After all, when she'd rung him to say she wanted his advice and needed to see him urgently, she knew he would assume that 'advice' was another misnomer, although she accepted that he might consider £185,000 a bit steep, unless he was willing to support her claim that . . .

Archie sent the car, if you could call a clapped-out 1975 Vauxhall estate a car, to pick her up when she arrived at Edinburgh Waverley. Her ladyship was driven to Fenwick Hall accompanied only by the smell of Labradors and spent cartridges, without once addressing the chauffeur.

As the butler accompanied Lady Virginia to the guest

bedroom, he informed her that his lordship was out shooting but was expected back in time for dinner. Virginia took her time unpacking, something that would have been done by a lady's maid in her father's day, followed by a soak in a warm bath that she'd had to run herself. After dressing for dinner, she sharpened her nails in preparation for the encounter.

Dinner passed smoothly enough, but then they didn't discuss anything consequential until after coffee had been served and the servants had retired.

'I'm pretty sure you didn't come all this way simply to find out how the family are, Virginia,' said Archie after pouring himself a brandy. 'So tell me, what's the real reason for your visit?'

Virginia put down her coffee cup, took a deep breath, and said, 'I'm giving serious consideration to challenging father's will.' After she had delivered her well-prepared opening salvo, it was clear from the expression on her brother's face that he wasn't surprised.

'On what grounds?' he asked calmly.

'On the grounds that father had promised to leave the Glen Fenwick Distillery to me, along with its annual profits of around £100,000 a year, which would have allowed me to live comfortably for the rest of my days.'

'But as you well know, Virginia, in his will Father left the distillery to Freddie, whom you abandoned several years ago, leaving me with the responsibility of bringing your son up.'

'He isn't my son, as you well know. He's no more than the offspring of my former butler and his wife. So he has absolutely no claim on father's estate.'

Virginia eyed her brother, waiting to see how he

would react to this bombshell, but once again, not a flicker of surprise furrowed his brow.

Archie bent down and stroked Wellington, who was sleeping by his side. 'Not only am I well aware that Freddie isn't your son, but it was confirmed beyond doubt following a visit from Mrs Ellie May Grant, who told me in great detail about the charade you set up when her fiancé was staying at the Ritz some years ago, and your subsequent claim that you were pregnant and that Cyrus was Freddie's father.'

'Why did that woman want to see you?' demanded Virginia, somewhat thrown off course.

'To find out if I was willing to pay back any of the money you'd fraudulently claimed from her husband over the past decade.'

'You could have offered her the income from the distillery until the debt was cleared, which would have solved all my problems.'

'As you are well aware, Virginia, it isn't mine to offer. Father left the distillery to Freddie and stipulated that it should be managed by me until the boy reaches his twenty-fifth birthday, when it will automatically become his.'

'But now you know Freddie isn't my son, surely you'll support my claim that in an earlier will, which both of us saw, Father left the distillery to me.'

'But he later changed his mind. And it wasn't until Mrs Grant told me what her husband's favourite whisky was that I realized the significance of father only leaving you a bottle of Maker's Mark in his will, which rather suggests that he also knew Freddie wasn't your son.'

'I've received a tax bill for £185,000,' blurted out Virginia, 'that I can't afford to pay.'

'I'm sorry to hear that,' said Archie. 'But from my experience, the taxman doesn't send out demands for £185,000 unless the person concerned has made a capital gain of –' he hesitated for a moment – 'around half a million.'

'I've spent every penny I made settling Cyrus's claim, and now there's nothing left.'

'Well, I certainly don't have that kind of money at my disposal, Virginia, even if I was willing to help you. Every penny I earn is ploughed back into the estate, which incidentally just about broke even last year, and as you can see, we're not exactly living high on the hog. In fact, if I'm forced to make any more cutbacks, the next one will have to be your monthly allowance. The irony is that Freddie did better out of Father's will than any of us.'

'But all that would change if only I could get my hands on the distillery.' Virginia leant forward and looked hopefully at her brother. 'If you back me, Archie, I'd be willing to split fifty-fifty.'

'Not a chance, Virginia. Those were clearly Father's wishes, and in that same will, he instructed me to see that they were carried out. And that's exactly what I intend to do.'

'But surely blood comes before—'

'Keeping your word? No, it doesn't, Virginia, and I must warn you that if you were reckless enough to challenge Father's will and the matter were to come to court, I wouldn't hesitate to back Freddie's claim, because that is no more than Father would have expected of me.'

On her return journey to London, Virginia concluded that once again, she would have to get in touch with her distant cousin in Argentina – and fairly urgently.

◄◦►

The following morning Virginia received a final reminder from HM Inspector of Taxes, which she screwed up and dropped into the nearest waste-paper basket. By the afternoon, she was reluctantly considering booking an economy class ticket to Buenos Aires, and had even started to pack, while thinking about the things she would miss if she were exiled, including Annabel's, her friend Priscilla, Bofie and even the *Daily Mail*. She somehow doubted that the *Buenos Aires Herald* would have quite the same appeal.

She turned to Nigel Dempster to find out what her friends were up to. A photograph of a woman she didn't care for dominated his column, although the news of her death didn't cause Virginia's heart to miss a beat.

It is with great sadness, Dempster reported, *that I learned of the death of Lavinia, Duchess of Hertford, who was so admired for her beauty, charm and wit.* That wasn't how you described her when she was alive, thought Virginia. *She will be sadly missed by her many friends* – who could all have joined her for tea in a telephone box. But because she was so rich and powerful, everyone had always bowed and scraped to her. *The funeral will be held at St Albans Abbey, and will be attended by Princess Margaret, one of the Duchess's oldest friends. The Duchess leaves behind a son, Lord Clarence, two daughters, Lady Alice and Lady Camilla, and her devoted husband, the thirteenth Duke of Hertford. The funeral will take place on . . .*

Virginia opened her diary, pencilled in the date and unpacked again.

22

VIRGINIA MAY HAVE been penniless but no one who saw her walk into St Albans Abbey that morning would have believed it. She was wearing a black silk dress with a pearl brooch her grandmother had left her, and carried a black Hermès handbag she still hadn't paid for.

She entered the west door a few minutes before the service was due to begin, only to find the abbey was already full. She was looking around the packed congregation, anxious not to be relegated to a place near the back, unnoticed, when she spotted a tall, elegant man in a tailcoat carrying an usher's rod. She gave him a warm smile, but he clearly didn't recognize her.

'I'm the Lady Virginia Fenwick,' she whispered. 'A close family friend.'

'Of course, m'lady, please follow me.'

Virginia accompanied him down the aisle, past rows of mourners who knew their place. She was delighted when the usher found her a seat in the fifth row, directly behind the family, which fitted in neatly with the first part of her plan. While pretending to study the order of service, she glanced around to see who was seated nearby. She recognized the dukes of Norfolk, Westminster and

Marlborough, along with several hereditary peers who had all been friends of her late father. She glanced back to see Bofie Bridgwater seated several rows behind her, but she didn't acknowledge his exaggerated bow.

The organ struck up to announce a parade of the great and good who were led sedately down the aisle by the chief usher. The Mayor of Hertford was followed by the sheriff and the lord lieutenant of the county, all of whom were shown to their places in the third row. A moment later they were followed by the Lord Barrington of Bristol Docklands, the former leader of the House of Lords.

As Giles passed Virginia, she turned away. She didn't want her ex-husband to know she was there. Not part of her well-choreographed plan. Giles took his reserved seat in the second row.

A moment later the congregation rose as one when the coffin, bedecked in white lilies, began its slow passage down the aisle towards the chancel. It was borne on the shoulders of six guardsmen from the First Battalion of the Coldstream Guards, the regiment the duke had served in as a major during the Second World War, and of which he was now honorary colonel.

The thirteenth Duke of Hertford, followed by his son and two daughters, walked behind the coffin, and took their places in the front row, while the coffin was placed on a bier in the chancel. The funeral service was conducted by the Bishop of Hertford, whose eulogy reminded those present what a saintly person the late duchess had been, emphasizing her tireless work as patron of Dr Barnardo's and as chairman of the Mothers' Union. The bishop concluded by expressing his heartfelt condolences to the duke and his family, finally adding that he hoped with the help of the Almighty they would come to terms with their loss.

Along with a little assistance from me, thought Virginia.

When the service was over, Virginia joined a select group of mourners who attended the burial, and then cadged a lift back to the castle for a reception she hadn't been invited to. When she arrived she paused at the bottom of the steps, taking a moment to admire the Jacobean building as if she were a prospective buyer.

During the funeral service and the burial, Virginia had remained still, but once she entered the castle and the butler announced 'The Lady Virginia Fenwick', she never stopped moving.

'How kind of you to take the trouble to travel up to Hertfordshire, Virginia,' said the duke, bending down to kiss her on both cheeks. 'I know Lavinia would have appreciated it.'

I wouldn't have missed it for the world, she wanted to tell him, but restricted herself to, 'Such a dear, kind lady. We'll all miss her.'

'How sweet of you to say so, Virginia,' said the duke, not letting go of her hand. 'I do hope you'll keep in touch.'

You need have no fear about that, thought Virginia. 'Nothing would give me greater pleasure, your grace,' she said, giving him a slight curtsey.

'His grace, the Duke of Westminster,' announced the butler.

Virginia moved on into the great hall, and while the elks and boars stared down from the walls above, her eyes swept the room in search of the three people she needed to see, and the one person she hoped to avoid.

She declined several offers of canapés and wine, well aware that her time was restricted and she had a job to do.

She stopped to chat to Miles Norfolk, although he was only a pit stop on her progress to the chequered flag. And then she saw him, leaning against the Adam fireplace, chatting to an elderly man she didn't recognize. She left Miles and began to drift in his direction, and the moment the elderly gentleman turned to talk to another guest, she moved in like a laser beam on her target.

'Clarence. You may not remember me.'

'You are not easily forgettable, Lady Virginia,' he ventured. 'Father always speaks so warmly of you.'

'How kind of him,' gushed Virginia. 'Are you still serving with the Blues and Royals?'

'I am indeed, but unfortunately I'm about to be posted overseas. I'm sorry to be going abroad so soon after my mother's death.'

'But the duke will have the support of your sisters.'

'Sadly not. Camilla is married to a sheep farmer in New Zealand. A hundred thousand acres, can you believe it? They'll be returning to Christchurch in a few days' time.'

'That is unfortunate, and must place quite a responsibility on Alice's shoulders.'

'And there's the rub. Alice has been offered a senior position with L'Oréal in New York. I know she's thinking of turning it down, but Papa insists she shouldn't miss such a golden opportunity.'

'How typical of your father. But if you think it might help, Clarence, I'd be only too happy to drop in and see him from time to time.'

'That would take a weight off my mind, Lady Virginia.

But I must warn you, the old man can be quite a handful. Sometimes I think he's nearer seven than seventy.'

'That's a challenge I'd relish,' said Virginia. 'I don't exactly have a lot going on in my life at the moment, and I've always enjoyed your father's company. Perhaps I could drop you a line from time to time and let you know how he's getting on.'

'How considerate, Lady Virginia. I just hope you won't find him too much of a burden.'

'A bloody good show you've put on, Clarence,' declared a portly man who joined them. 'You've done the old girl proud.'

'Thank you, Uncle Percy,' said Clarence, as Virginia slipped away to continue her three-pronged attack. The missile changed direction and headed towards its second target.

'Congratulations on your new job, Alice, and I'm bound to say, I agree with your father. You shouldn't turn down such a wonderful opportunity.'

'How kind of you to say so,' said Alice, not altogether sure who she was talking to. 'But I still haven't made up my mind whether or not to take up the offer.'

'But why not, my dear? After all, you may never get another chance like this again.'

'I suppose you're right. But I'm already feeling guilty about leaving Papa to fend for himself.'

'No need to, my dear, believe me. In any case, there will be more than enough of us to make sure he's well occupied. So off you go, and show those Yanks what we British are made of.'

'I know that's what he wants,' said Alice, 'but I just can't bear the idea of him being on his own so soon after dear Mama's death.'

'You needn't worry yourself on that count,' said Virginia, who was pleased to see Giles paying his respects to the duke before he left.

Virginia gave Alice a warm hug before heading off in search of her final prey. A mother, a father and three small children were not difficult to locate, but this time she wasn't greeted with quite the same enthusiasm.

'Hello, I'm—' began Virginia.

'I know exactly who you are,' said Lady Camilla, and before Virginia could deliver her next well-prepared sentence, she turned her back on her and started chatting to an old school friend, making no attempt to include Virginia in the conversation. Virginia quickly took her leave before anyone could notice the slight. Two out of three wasn't a bad return, especially as the one failure lived on the other side of the world. Virginia saw no purpose in hanging around any longer, so she made her way across to the duke to bid him farewell . . . for now.

'I've had the most enjoyable time renewing my acquaintance with your delightful children,' she said. She wondered if he knew how little she'd seen of them during the past twenty years, not least because of the late duchess's attempts to keep them apart.

'And I'm sure they enjoyed seeing you again,' said the duke. 'I hope I will too, and in the not-too-distant future,' he added, 'if you have nothing better to do.'

'Nothing would give me greater pleasure. I'll wait for you to be in touch,' she said, as a small queue began to form behind her.

'My family are only able to be with me for a few more days,' whispered the duke. 'Once they've all gone their separate ways, may I give you a call?'

'I'll look forward to that, Perry,' a name only the late

duchess and the duke's oldest friends ever used when addressing his grace, the Duke of Hertford.

Once Camilla had seen Virginia depart, she didn't waste any time before joining her brother.

'Did I see you talking to that frightful woman, Virginia Fenwick?'

'You did,' said Clarence. 'She seems a nice enough lady, and she promised to keep an eye on Pa while we're all away.'

'I'll bet she did. If anything would stop me going back to New Zealand, it's the thought of that woman getting her hands on Pa.'

'But she couldn't have been more considerate.'

'Don't allow that consummate actress to fool you for one moment.'

'Why are you so set against her, Camilla, when all she wants to do is help?'

'Because dear Mama always had a good word for everyone, and she had two for the Lady Virginia Fenwick. Scheming bitch.'

◄○►

'How long have I got?' asked Virginia.

'The Revenue will grant you no more than ninety days before they begin proceedings, my lady,' replied the bank manager.

'So how long have I got?' repeated Virginia.

Mr Leigh turned over several pages of his diary before he responded. 'The final day for payment, unless you wish to be saddled with extortionate interest, is December twenty-first.'

'Thank you,' said Virginia, before leaving the bank manager's office without another word.

She could only wonder how long it would be before the duke got in touch, because if he didn't call soon, she would be spending Christmas Day in Buenos Aires.

23

VIRGINIA DIDN'T HAVE TO wait long before the duke called and invited her out on their first date. And that was certainly how she regarded their evening at Mosimann's. She was coy, flattering and flirtatious, and made him feel twenty years younger, or at least that's what he told her when he dropped her back at her flat in Chelsea, with a kiss on both cheeks. Appropriate for a first date, thought Virginia. She didn't invite her paramour in for coffee for several reasons, not least because he couldn't have failed to notice that there were only hooks where paintings had once hung.

The duke rang the following morning and invited Virginia out on a second date.

'I've got tickets for *Noises Off* starring Paul Eddington, and I thought we might have supper afterwards.'

'How sweet of you, Perry. But unfortunately I have to attend a charity gala this evening,' she said, looking down at an empty page in her diary. 'But I'm free on Thursday evening.'

After that, her dance card had only one name on it.

Virginia was surprised how much she enjoyed her role as the duke's companion, confidante and friend, and quickly grew used to a style of life she had always assumed was hers by right. However, she had to accept that the taxman was still demanding his pound of flesh, 185,000 pounds of flesh to be exact, and that if she didn't pay up, this idyllic existence would stop as abruptly as a train hitting the buffers.

She considered asking Perry for a loan to cover her tax bill, but felt it was a little too soon, and if he thought that was the only reason she'd shown any interest in him, the relationship would surely end as quickly as it had begun.

◄◦►

Over the next few weeks, the duke showered her with gifts of flowers, clothes, even jewellery, and although she considered returning them to some of the more fashionable establishments on Bond Street in exchange for cash, it wouldn't have even made a dent in the taxman's demand. In any case, it would only be a matter of time before the duke found out what she had been up to.

However, when the weather changed from a chilly November to a freezing December, Virginia began to despair, and decided that she had no choice but to tell Perry the truth, whatever the consequences.

She selected his seventieth birthday as the day of revelation, during a celebration dinner at Le Gavroche. She was well prepared, having spent most of her monthly allowance on a gift for Perry that she could ill afford. Cartier had crafted a pair of gold cufflinks, engraved with the Hertford crest. She would need to choose the right moment to present them, and then explain why she would be leaving for Buenos Aires early in the New Year.

During the meal, which consisted mostly of vintage champagne, the duke became a little maudlin and began talking about 'crossing the finishing line', his euphemism for death.

'Don't be silly, Perry,' Virginia reprimanded him. 'You have many years ahead of you before you need to think about anything quite so depressing, especially if I've got anything to do with it. And don't forget, I promised the children I'd keep you going.'

'And you've more than kept your end of the bargain, old gal. In fact, I don't know how I would have survived without you,' he added as he took her hand.

Virginia had become accustomed to the duke's little signs of affection, even a hand reaching under the table and ending up on her thigh. But tonight, it remained there while the maître d' opened another bottle of champagne. Virginia had drunk very little that evening, as she needed to be as sober as a judge when she delivered her plea in mitigation. She chose that moment to present him with his birthday present.

He slowly unwrapped it, before opening the leather box.

'My darling Virginia, how kind of you. I've never had a more thoughtful present in my life.' He leant across and kissed her gently on the lips.

'I'm so glad you like it, Perry. Because it's almost impossible to find something for a man who has everything.'

'Not quite everything, my darling,' he replied, still clutching her hand.

Virginia decided there was never going to be a better moment to tell him about her problem with the taxman.

'Perry, there's something I need to ask you.'

'I know,' he said. Virginia looked surprised. 'You were going to ask, your place or mine?'

Virginia giggled like a schoolgirl, but didn't lose her concentration, although she suddenly realized she should perhaps delay telling him about her imminent departure, as there might be an even better opportunity to plead her case a little later.

The duke raised his other hand, and a moment later the maître d' appeared by his side bearing a silver tray on which there lay a single slip of paper. Virginia had become used to checking the details of every bill before allowing the duke to write out a cheque. It was not unknown for a restaurant to add an extra dish, even another bottle of wine, after a guest had consumed a little too much.

It was when she opened the bill and saw the figure £18.50, that the idea first crossed her mind. But could she risk it? She had to admit such a gift-wrapped opportunity was unlikely to present itself again. She waited for the sommelier to pour him a second glass of Taylor's before she declared, 'The bill's fine, Perry. Shall I write out a cheque while you enjoy your port?'

'Good idea, old gal,' said the duke, taking out his cheque book and handing it to her. 'Be sure to add a generous tip,' he said as he drained his glass. 'It's been a memorable evening.'

Virginia wrote out the figure 185,000, having moved the comma and added two noughts. She dated the cheque December 3rd 1982, before placing it in front of him. He signed unsteadily, just below where Virginia's finger covered the noughts. When he disappeared to 'spend a penny', another of his oft-used euphemisms, Virginia deposited the cheque in her handbag, took out her own cheque book and wrote out the correct figure. She handed it to the maître d' just before Perry returned.

'It's the duke's birthday,' she explained, 'so it's my treat.'

Marco didn't comment that she'd forgotten to add the generous tip the duke had suggested.

Once they were seated in the back of the duke's Rolls-Royce, he immediately leant across, took Virginia in his arms and kissed her; the kiss of a man who was hoping for more.

When the car stopped outside the duke's home in Eaton Square, the chauffeur rushed around to open the back door, giving Virginia enough time to straighten her dress while the duke buttoned up his jacket. The duke led Virginia into the house, where they found the butler waiting for them, as if it was midday, not midnight.

'Good evening, your grace,' he said, before taking their coats. 'Will you require your usual brandy and cigar?'

'Not tonight, Lomax,' the duke replied, as he took Virginia by the hand and led her up the sweeping staircase and into a room she'd never entered before. The bed-room was about the same size as her flat, and dominated by an antique oak four-poster, adorned with the family crest and motto, *Ever Vigilant*.

Virginia was about to comment on the Constable hanging above the Adam fireplace, when she felt the zip on the back of her dress being clumsily pulled down. She made no attempt to stop it falling to the floor, and began to unbuckle the duke's belt as they edged unsteadily towards the bed. She couldn't remember when she'd last made love, and could only hope that the same was true for the duke.

He was like a schoolboy on a first date, petting and

fumbling, clearly needing her to take the lead, which she was happy to do.

'That's the best birthday present I could have hoped for,' he said once his heartbeat had returned to normal.

'Me too,' said Virginia, but he didn't hear her, because he'd fallen asleep.

When Virginia woke the following morning, it took her a few moments to remember where she was. She began to consider the consequences of everything that had taken place the previous evening. She had already decided not to present the cheque for £185,000 until December 23rd, confident that it wouldn't be cleared before Christmas, possibly even the New Year.

However, there was an outside chance that someone along the line would consider it their duty to alert the duke about such a large withdrawal. There was also the possibility – although it seemed unlikely to Virginia – that the cheque might bounce. If either of these catastrophes occurred, she'd be on her way to Heathrow not Castle Hertford, because it wouldn't be HM Inspector of Taxes pursuing her but an ever-vigilant duke, and she suspected his daughter Camilla wouldn't be far behind.

The duke had already invited Virginia to spend Christmas on his estate in Hertford. But she had only accepted when she learned that Camilla and her family wouldn't be travelling over from New Zealand, as they felt two trips to England within a few months was an unnecessary extravagance.

Virginia had written to Clarence and Alice regularly during the past few weeks, to keep them up to date on everything their father was up to, or at least her version of it. In their replies, both of them made it clear how delighted they were that she would be joining them at Castle Hertford for Christmas. The idea that at the last moment she might have to beat a hasty retreat and spend the New Year in Buenos Aires with a distant cousin wasn't that appealing.

When the duke finally awoke, he knew exactly where he was. He turned over, delighted to find that Virginia hadn't already left. He took her in his arms, and spent considerably longer making love a second time. She began to feel confident that this wasn't going to be a one-night stand.

◄O►

'Why don't you move in with me?' the duke suggested as Virginia straightened his tie.

'I'm not sure that would be wise, Perry, especially if the children are staying at the castle over Christmas. Perhaps early in the New Year, once they've gone?'

'Well, at least stay with me until they arrive?'

Virginia happily agreed to his request, but only ever left one change of clothes at Eaton Square, aware that she might be sent packing at a moment's notice. The morning Clarence landed at Heathrow she reluctantly returned to her little flat in Chelsea, where she soon realized how much she missed not only her new way of life, but also Perry.

JESSICA CLIFTON

1982–1984

24

'I'M SURPRISED YOU didn't see that one coming, Pops,' said Jessica as she joined her father for breakfast.

'And of course you did,' said Sebastian. Jake began tapping a spoon on his high chair to gain attention. 'And I don't need your opinion, young man.'

'He's just preparing to take over as chairman of Farthings Kaufman.'

'I was rather hoping I might be the next chairman.'

'Not if Lady Virginia continues to run circles around you.'

'You seem to forget, young lady, that Virginia had the inside track. She was regularly visiting Mellor in prison, and we now know she'd not only read the letter he wrote to his daughter, but had been in touch with her long before my plane touched down in Chicago.'

'But you had a chance to get control of the company for a pound before that, and you turned it down.'

'At the time, if I remember correctly, you were against me even visiting Mellor in prison, and made your position very clear.'

'Touché,' said Samantha, picking up the spoon Jake had cast on the kitchen floor.

'You should have realized that if there was even a chance of Virginia making some money on the side,' pressed Jessica, ignoring her mother, 'she wasn't to be trusted.'

'And may I ask when you worked all this out? During one of your O level economics classes, no doubt?'

'She didn't have to,' said Samantha, placing a rack of toast on the table. 'She's been eavesdropping on our breakfast conversations for the past six months. It's nothing more than hindsight, so don't rise, Seb.'

'Plus a little female intuition,' insisted Jessica.

'Well, in case you didn't notice, young lady, Thomas Cook did take over Mellor Travel, and their shares continue to rise, despite your misgivings.'

'But they had to pay far more than you'd originally intended. And what I'd like to know,' continued Jessica, 'is how much of the extra money ended up in Virginia's pocket.'

Sebastian didn't know, though he suspected it was more than the bank was paid, but he took Samantha's advice and didn't rise to the bait.

'Not a bad return for half a dozen prison visits,' were Jessica's parting words, after giving Jake a huge hug.

Samantha smiled as her daughter left the room. She had told Seb soon after Jake's birth that she was anxious that Jessica might respond negatively to the new arrival, having been the centre of attention for so long. But the exact opposite turned out to be the case, because Jake immediately became the centre of Jessica's life. She was happy to babysit whenever her parents wanted to go out in the evening, and at weekends she would wheel him around St James's park in his pram, before putting him to bed. Elderly matrons cooed over him, not sure if

Jessica was an attentive older sister or a young unmarried mother.

Jessica had settled down quickly in her adopted country, after finally bringing her parents to their senses, and now she rejoiced not only in their happiness, but in the joy of having a baby brother. She adored her new extended family. Pops, who was tolerant, kind and amusing, Grandpops who was wise, thoughtful and inspiring, and Grandma who the press often dubbed 'the Boadicea of Bristol', which made Jessica feel Boadicea must have been one hell of a woman.

However, settling into her new school hadn't proved quite as easy. While some of the girls called her the Yank, others less generously described her as a stick insect. Jessica concluded that the Mafia and the Ku Klux Klan combined could have learnt a great deal about intimidation from the pupils of St Paul's Girls' School, and by the end of her first year, she only had one close friend, Claire Taylor, who shared most of her interests, including boys.

◄○►

During her final year at St Paul's, Jessica hovered around the middle of the class, regularly beaten by Claire in every subject except art, where she remained unassailable. While most of her classmates were anxious about being offered a university place, no one doubted where Jessica was heading.

Jessica did, however, confide in Claire a fear that if she was offered a place at the Slade, she might discover that Avril Perkins, who came second in art, was right when she remarked within Jessica's hearing that she was just a big fish in a small pool, who was about to be cast into the ocean where she would undoubtedly sink without trace.

Claire told her to dismiss Avril for the little creep she was, but Jessica still spent her final term at St Paul's wondering if she might be right.

When the high mistress announced at prize-giving that Jessica Clifton had been awarded the Gainsborough Scholarship to the Slade School of Fine Art, Jessica seemed to be the only person in the hall who was surprised. In fact, she took as much pleasure in Claire being offered a place at University College to read English as she did in her own triumph. However, she wasn't pleased to learn that Avril Perkins would be joining her at the Slade.

—◦—

'The chairman would like a word with you, Mr Clifton.'

Sebastian stopped signing letters and looked up to see the boss's secretary standing in the doorway. 'I thought he was in Copenhagen?'

'He came back on the first flight this morning,' said Angela, 'and asked to see you the moment he walked into his office.'

'Sounds serious,' said Seb, raising an eyebrow, but receiving no response.

'All I can tell you, Mr Clifton, is that he's cleared his diary for the rest of the morning.'

'Perhaps he's going to sack me,' said Seb, hoping to tempt Angela into an indiscretion.

'I don't think so, because that usually only takes him a couple of minutes.'

'Not even a clue?' whispered Sebastian as they left his office and walked along the corridor together.

'All I'm willing to say,' said Angela, 'is that you can't have missed the fact that Mr Bishara has travelled to

Copenhagen six times in the last month. Perhaps you're about to find out why,' she added before knocking on the chairman's door.

'Has he taken over Lego or Carlsberg?' said Seb as Angela opened the door and stood aside to allow him to enter.

'Good morning, chairman,' said Seb. But he couldn't work out from the sphinx-like expression on Hakim Bishara's face if it was good news or bad.

'Good morning, Sebastian.' First clue, thought Seb. The chairman only ever called him Sebastian when he was about to discuss something serious. 'Have a seat.' Second clue, this wasn't going to be a short meeting.

'Sebastian, I wanted you to be the first to know that I got married on Saturday.'

Seb had considered half a dozen possible reasons the chairman would want to see him, but marriage wasn't among them, and to say he was taken by surprise would have been an understatement. For a moment he couldn't think of what to say. Hakim leant back in his chair and enjoyed the unusual experience of a silent CEO.

'Do I know the lady in question?' Seb eventually managed.

'No, but you've seen her from a distance.'

Sebastian decided to join in the game. 'In London?'

'Yes.'

'In the City?'

'Yes,' Hakim repeated, 'but you're heading down the wrong road.'

'Is she a banker?'

'No, a landscape architect.'

'So she must have worked on one of our projects,' suggested Seb.

'Yes and no.'

'Was she for or against us?'

'Neither,' said Hakim. 'I would describe her as neutral, but not helpful.'

Another long silence followed before Sebastian said, 'Oh my God, it's the woman who gave evidence in your trial. Mrs, um, Mrs . . .'

'Bergström.'

'But she was the Crown's key witness, and she certainly didn't help our cause. I remember everyone regretting that Mr Carman had tracked her down.'

'Everyone except me,' said Hakim. 'I spent endless nights in prison regretting that I hadn't spoken to her when we sat next to each other on that flight back from Lagos. So a few days after I was released, I flew to Copenhagen.'

'I've never thought of you as the romantic type, Hakim, and I suspect most of our colleagues in the City would agree with me. May I ask what Mr Bergström had to say about your proposed takeover bid?'

'I wouldn't have boarded the plane if there'd been a Mr Bergström. It only took Barry Hammond a couple of days to discover that Kristina's husband died of a heart attack at the age of fifty-two.'

'Don't tell me, he was a banker.'

'Head of the loans division at the Royal Bank of Copenhagen.'

'They nearly went under a couple of years ago.'

'On his watch, I'm afraid,' said Hakim quietly.

'So will Mrs Bergström—'

'Mrs Bishara.'

'Be moving to London?'

'Not immediately. She has two children who are still

at school, and she doesn't want their lives disrupted, so I had to make a deal.'

'Which you're usually very good at.'

'Not when it's personal. Something I've always warned you about. We plan to live in Copenhagen for the next couple of years, until Inge and Aksel are settled at university. After that, Kristina has agreed to come to England.'

'In the meantime, you'll be living on an aeroplane.'

'Not a chance. Kristina has made it abundantly clear that she doesn't need a second husband to die of a heart attack. Which is why I needed to see you, Sebastian. I want you to take over as chairman of the bank.'

This time Seb was stunned into a far longer silence, which Hakim again took advantage of.

'I intend to call a board meeting early next week so I can brief the directors on my decision. I shall propose that you replace me as chairman, while I become president of the bank. All you'll need to decide is who will be your CEO.'

Seb didn't need to spend much time thinking about that, but he waited to hear Hakim's opinion.

'I assume you'll want Victor Kaufman to take your place,' said Hakim. 'After all, he's one of your oldest friends, and owns twenty-five per cent of the bank's stock.'

'That doesn't qualify him to be in charge of the day-to-day operations of a major financial institution. We're running a bank, Hakim, not a local sports club.'

'Does that mean you have another candidate in mind?'

'John Ashley would be my first choice,' said Seb without hesitation.

'But he's only been with the bank a couple of years. He's hardly got his feet under the table.'

'But what a pedigree,' Seb reminded him. 'Manchester Grammar School, the London School of Economics, and a scholarship to Harvard Business School. And let's not forget how much we had to pay to tempt him away from Chase Manhattan. And how long will it be before one of our rivals offers him a golden hello? Sooner rather than later, would be my guess, especially if Victor ends up as CEO of Farthings. No. If you want me to be chairman, Hakim, appointing John Ashley to that position is the deal-maker.'

◄○►

'Congratulations,' said Jessica.

'What's a chairman?' demanded Jake.

'Someone who's in charge of everything and everybody, rather like a high mistress.'

'I'd never thought of it quite like that,' admitted Sebastian, as Samantha burst out laughing.

Jessica walked around the table and gave her father a hug. 'Congratulations,' she repeated.

'Hakim seems far too young to retire,' said Samantha, as she sliced the top off Jake's egg.

'I agree,' said Seb, 'but he's fallen in love.'

'I hadn't realized that if you were the chairman of a bank and fell in love, you were expected to resign.'

'It's not compulsory,' said Seb, laughing, 'but banks generally prefer their chairman to reside in the same country, and the lady in question lives in Copenhagen.'

'Why doesn't she come and live in England?' asked Jessica.

'Kristina Bergström is a very successful landscape architect with an international reputation but she has two children by her first marriage and she doesn't want to move them while they're still at school.'

'But how will Hakim occupy his time, given he has the energy of ten men?'

'He plans to open a new branch of Farthings in Copenhagen, and Kristina's company will be his first client. She's already agreed that once the children leave school, she'll set up a practice in London.'

'And when Hakim returns, will he resume the role of chairman?'

'No. He couldn't have made his position clearer. On September first, Hakim will become president of Farthings Kaufman, before I take over as chairman in the new year, with John Ashley as my CEO.'

'Have you told Victor?' asked Samantha.

'No, I thought I'd wait until it's official.'

'I'd like to be a fly on the wall for that meeting,' said Samantha. 'Have you ever met Ms Bergström?'

'No, I only saw her in the witness box when she gave evidence at Hakim's trial. As he was in custody at the time, it must have been love at first sight.'

'Men often fall in love at first sight,' declared Jessica, who had remained silent until then. 'Women rarely do.'

'I'm sure we are both grateful, Jessica, for your considerable insight on the subject of love,' said Seb, 'as we were for your grasp of macroeconomics.'

'It's not my opinion,' said Jessica, 'but D. H. Lawrence's. It's a quote from *Lady Chatterley's Lover*, which although it wasn't one of the English set texts at St Paul's, Claire thought I ought to read anyway.'

Sebastian and Samantha glanced at each other.

'Perhaps this is as good a time as any,' said Jessica, 'to tell you I'm planning to move out.'

'No, no, no,' said Jake.

While Seb might have agreed with his son, he didn't interrupt his daughter.

'Claire and I have found a small flat just off Gower Street, only half a mile from the Slade.'

'Sounds ideal,' said Samantha. 'When will you be leaving us?'

'In about a fortnight's time. If that's all right with you, Pops.'

'Of course it's fine,' said Samantha.

'No, no, no,' repeated Jake, pointing his spoon at Jessica.

'Don't point, Jake,' said his mother.

25

'TODAY'S LIFE DRAWING class has been cancelled,' said Professor Howard. A groan went up around the room when the professor added, 'Our model has once again failed to turn up.'

The twelve students were beginning to gather up their equipment, when a young man Jessica had never seen before rose from his seat, strolled into the middle of the room, stripped off and sat down on the dais. A round of applause followed, as the first-year students returned to their easels and set about their work.

Paulo Reinaldo was the first man Jessica had ever seen naked, and she couldn't take her eyes off him. He was like a Greek god, she thought. Well, a Brazilian god. She sketched a charcoal outline of his body with a few sweeping movements, an exercise that would take her fellow students considerably longer, and without the same results. Next, she concentrated on his head, which she began to capture in greater detail. Long curly dark hair that she wanted to run her hands through. Her eyes travelled down his body and she began to wish she was a sculptor. His torso rippled, and his legs looked as if they were built to run a marathon. She tried to concentrate as her tutor looked over her shoulder.

'You've caught him,' said Professor Howard. 'Most impressive. But I need you to think about shadow and perspective, and never forget, less is more. Have you ever seen the drawings Bonnard did of his wife climbing out of a bath?'

'No.'

'You'll find some excellent examples in the academy library. They are the proof, if proof is needed, that if you want to know just how great an artist is, you should study their preliminary drawings before you even consider their masterpieces. By the way, try not to make it quite so obvious how much you fancy him.'

◄○►

During the next week, Jessica didn't come across Paulo again. He was never to be found in the library and didn't seem to attend lectures. After Professor Howard's remarks, she made no attempt to find out more about him from her fellow students. But whenever his name came up, she stopped talking and started listening.

'He's the son of a Brazilian industrialist,' said a student from the year above her. 'His father wanted him to come to London and brush up on his English, among other things.'

'I think he only intends to hang around for a couple of years, then go back to Rio and open a nightclub,' offered another, while a third said, somewhat testily, 'He only comes to figurative drawing to scout out his next victim.'

'You seem well informed,' said Avril Perkins.

'I ought to be, I slept with him half a dozen times

before he dumped me,' the girl said casually. 'That's how he spends most of his time, except the evenings.'

'What does he do in the evenings?' asked Jessica, unable to remain silent any longer.

'Makes a close study of English nightclubs, rather than English watercolours. He claims that's the real reason he's over here. But he did tell me he plans to have slept with every female student at the Slade by the end of his first year.'

They all laughed except Jessica, who was rather hoping to be his next victim.

◄o►

When Jessica turned up for life drawing the following Thursday, two other girls were already seated on either side of Paulo. One of them was Avril Perkins. Jessica sat opposite him on the other side of the semi-circle of students, trying to concentrate on the model, a middle-aged woman who looked bored and cold, unlike Avril.

Her eyes eventually returned to Paulo, to find he only needed one hand for drawing, while the other rested on Avril's thigh.

When Professor Howard suggested a mid-morning break, Jessica waited for Avril to leave before she strolled around the circle of drawings, pretending to study her fellow students' efforts. Paulo's wasn't bad, it was dreadful. She wondered how he could ever have been offered a place at the Slade.

'Not bad,' said Jessica as she continued to look at his drawing.

'I agree,' said Paulo. 'It's awful, and you know it, because you're so much better than any of us.'

Was he flirting, or did he really believe what he'd just said? Jessica didn't care.

'Would you like to come out for a drink tonight?' he asked.

'Yes please,' she said, immediately regretting the 'please'.

'I'll pick you up around ten and we can go clubbing.'

Jessica didn't mention that by that time she was normally in bed with a book, not out clubbing.

She rushed home straight after her final class, and spent over an hour deciding what she would wear for her 'losing her virginity date', constantly seeking Claire's opinion. She ended up with a short pink leather skirt, Claire's, a leopard-print top, hers, black patterned stockings and gold high heels.

'I look like a tart!' Jessica exclaimed when she looked in the mirror.

'Believe me,' said Claire, 'if you're hoping to finally get laid, that's the perfect outfit.'

Jessica gave in to Claire's superior knowledge on the subject.

◄o►

When Paulo turned up at the flat thirty minutes late (evidently that was also fashionable), two things happened that Jessica hadn't been prepared for. Could anyone be that good-looking and own a Ferrari?

'Tell him I'm available tomorrow night,' Claire whispered as they left the flat.

The third surprise was just how charming and sophisticated Paulo was. He didn't immediately jump on her, as her fellow students had claimed he would. In fact, he couldn't have been more solicitous. He even opened the car door for her, and on their way into the West End, chatted about the impact she was making at the Slade. She was already regretting her choice of clothes, and kept trying to pull down her skirt.

When he parked his Ferrari outside Annabel's, a doorman took the keys and drove the car away. They descended the stairs to a dimly lit nightclub, where it quickly became clear that Paulo was a regular, as the maître d' stepped forward and greeted him by name, before guiding them to a discreet corner table.

Once they had selected two courses from the largest menu Jessica had ever seen – it was almost a book – Paulo seemed keen to find out all about her. Although she didn't raise the subject herself, he seemed well aware who her grandparents were, and said he always saved the latest William Warwick for the long flight back to Rio.

The moment he'd finished his meal, Paulo lit a cigarette and offered her one. She declined but took an occasional puff of his. It didn't taste like any cigarette she'd ever smoked before. After coffee, he led her on to the crowded dance floor where dimly lit became black. She quickly realized that, unlike drawing, dancing was a skill Paulo had mastered, and she also noticed that several other women were no longer paying much attention to their partners. However, it wasn't until Chaka Khan was replaced by Lionel Richie's 'Hello', that Paulo's hands strayed below her waist. She made no attempt to resist.

Their first kiss was a little clumsy, but after the second, all she wanted to do was go home with him, even though she had already accepted that she probably wouldn't still be on the menu the following evening. They didn't leave Annabel's until just after one a.m., and once they were back in the car, Jessica was impressed by Paulo's ability to steer a Ferrari with one hand, while the other moved up her stockinged thigh. The car never moved out of first gear.

It continued to be a night of surprises. His Knightsbridge apartment was stylish and elegant, filled with pictures and antiques she would have liked to spend more time admiring, had he not taken her by the hand and led her straight to the bedroom, where she was greeted by the largest bed she'd ever seen. The black silk cover was already folded back.

Paulo took her in his arms, and Jessica discovered another of his skills, undressing a woman while he was kissing her.

'You're so beautiful,' he said, after her top and skirt had been deftly removed. She would have replied, but he'd already fallen to his knees and was kissing her again, this time on her thighs, not her lips. They fell back on to the bed, and when she opened her eyes, he was already naked. How had he managed that, she wondered. She lay back, and waited for what Claire had told her would happen next. When Paulo entered her, Jessica wanted to cry out, not from pleasure, but pain. A few moments later he withdrew, slumped back on his side of the bed and mumbled, 'You were fantastic,' which made her wonder if anything else he'd whispered to her that evening could be believed.

She waited for him to put his arms around her and tell her some more lies, but instead he turned his back on her, and within moments he was fast asleep. Jessica waited until she heard steady breathing, before she slipped out from under the sheet, tiptoed across to the bathroom and didn't turn the light on until she'd closed the door. She took some time tidying herself up, noticing she was still wearing her black stockings. Claire would no doubt explain the significance of that when she got home. She returned to the bedroom, wondering if he was actually wide awake and just hoping she would go home. She picked up her discarded clothes and got dressed quickly, crept out of the bedroom and closed the door quietly behind her.

Jessica didn't even stop to admire the paintings, as she couldn't wait to get out of the apartment, fearing that Paulo might wake up and expect her to repeat the whole dreadful experience. She tiptoed along the corridor and took the lift to the ground floor.

'Would you like a taxi, miss?' asked the doorman politely. He was clearly not surprised to see a scantily dressed young woman appearing in the lobby at three in the morning.

'No, thank you,' said Jessica, giving the Ferrari one last look before she took off her high heels and set out on the long walk back to her little flat.

26

NO ONE WAS MORE surprised than Jessica when Paulo asked her out on a second date. She had assumed he would have already moved on, but then she remembered the girl who claimed to have slept with him half a dozen times before he dumped her.

She told Claire that she liked being driven around in a Ferrari, dining at Annabel's and sampling the finest premier cru champagnes, and even admitted to her friend that she rather enjoyed Paulo's company, and was grateful to him for solving her 'virgo intacta' problem, even if she hadn't been overwhelmed by the experience.

'It gets better,' Claire assured her, 'and let's face it, not all of us are wined and dined by a Brazilian god before we lose our virginity. I'm sure you remember my experience behind the school pavilion with Brian, the second eleven wicket keeper?' she added. 'It might have been more enjoyable if he hadn't left his pads on.'

The only thing that changed on the second date was the nightclub. Annabel's was replaced by Tramp, and Jessica felt far more relaxed mixing with a younger crowd. She and Paulo went back to his flat around two in the morning, and this time she didn't leave the moment he fell asleep.

She was woken in the morning to find Paulo gently kissing her breast, and he continued to hold her in his arms long after they'd made love. When she saw the clock on the bedside table, she shouted, 'Help!', jumped out of bed and took a hot shower. Paulo clearly didn't believe in breakfast, so she gave him a kiss and left him in bed. During her still-life class, Jessica found she wasn't able to concentrate, her mind continually returning to Paulo. Was she falling in love?

Professor Howard frowned when he took a closer look at her drawing of a bowl of oranges, and even checked to make sure it was Jessica sitting there. Although her drawing was still superior to those of her fellow students, her tutor continued to frown.

During the week, Jessica visited three other night-clubs, where each time, Paulo was welcomed as a regular. Over the next few weeks she began to develop a craving for his favourite brand of cigarettes, which didn't seem to come from a packet, and to enjoy the brandy Alexanders that always appeared moments after they'd drained their second bottle of wine.

As the months went by, Jessica started to turn up later and later at the Slade, occasionally missing classes and lectures, and then whole days. She didn't notice herself drifting out of her old world and becoming a part of Paulo's.

◄○►

When the first letter came towards the end of term, it should have been a wake-up call, but Paulo convinced her to ignore it.

'I had three of those in my first term,' he said. 'After a while they just stop sending them.'

Jessica decided that once he became bored with her, which she feared couldn't be too long now, as she'd already passed the statutory half-dozen dates, she would return to the real world, although she was beginning to wonder if that would now be possible. It so nearly did end after she'd attended a lecture on the art of the English watercolour, and found herself falling asleep. When she woke, the other students were already leaving the lecture theatre. She had decided that rather than head back to the flat, she would go straight to Paulo's apartment.

She took a bus to Knightsbridge, then ran all the way to Lancelot Place. The doorman opened the door with one hand and saluted with the other as she got into the lift. When she reached the fourth floor, she tapped lightly on Paulo's door, which was opened by his Brazilian maid. She looked as if she was about to say something, but Jessica brushed past her and headed for the bedroom. She began to tear off her clothes, leaving them in a trail on the floor behind her, but when she entered the room she stopped in her tracks. Paulo was in bed, smoking hash with Avril Perkins.

Jessica knew that was the moment she should have turned around, marched out and never looked back, but instead she found herself walking slowly towards them. Paulo grinned as she crawled up on to the bed. He pushed Avril aside, took Jessica in his arms and pulled off the only garment she was still wearing.

◄○►

The next letter Jessica received from the Slade was signed by the principal, and had the words 'second warning' boldly underlined.

Mr Knight pointed out that she had missed her last six drawing classes, and had also failed to attend any lectures for over a month. If this continued, he wrote, the board would have to consider withdrawing her scholarship. When Paulo set fire to the letter, Jessica burst out laughing.

During the following term, Jessica began sleeping at Paulo's apartment during the day and spending most of her waking life accompanying him to nightclubs. On the rare occasions she and Paulo dropped into the Slade, few people recognized them. She became used to a string of different girls coming and going during the day, but she was the only one who spent the night with him.

The third letter, which Professor Howard handed to Jessica personally on one of the rare occasions she did get up in time to attend a morning drawing class, could not be ignored. The principal informed her that as she had been caught smoking marijuana on the college's premises, her scholarship had been rescinded and would be awarded to another student. He added that she would be allowed to remain as a pupil for the present, but only if she attended classes and her work greatly improved.

Professor Howard warned her that if she still hoped to graduate and be offered a place at the Royal Academy to study for an MA, she would have to build a portfolio of work for the examiners to consider, and time was slipping away.

When Jessica went home that afternoon, she didn't show the letter to Claire, who rarely missed a lecture, and had a steady boyfriend called Darren, who considered a visit to Pizza Express a treat.

◄◊►

Jessica made sure that whenever she visited her parents or grandparents, which was becoming less and less frequent, she was always soberly dressed and never smoked or drank in their presence.

She made no mention of her lover, or the double life she was leading, and was relieved that Paulo had never once suggested he would like to meet her family. Whenever one of her parents raised the subject of the Royal Academy, she assured them that Professor Howard was delighted with her progress, and remained confident that the academy would offer her a place the following year.

◄◊►

By the beginning of her second year at art school, Jessica was conducting two lives. Neither of them in the real world. This might well have continued if she hadn't bumped into Lady Virginia Fenwick.

Jessica was standing at the bar of Annabel's when she turned at the same moment as an elderly lady with her back to her and spilled some champagne on her sleeve.

'What are the young coming to?' said Virginia, when Jessica didn't even bother to apologize.

'And it's not just the young,' said the duke. 'One of those new life peers Thatcher has just appointed had the nerve to address me by my Christian name.'

'Whatever next, Perry?' said Virginia as the maître d' guided them to their usual table. 'Mario, do you by any chance know who that young lady is standing at the bar?'

'Her name is Jessica Clifton, my lady.'

'Is it indeed? And the young man she's with?'

'Mr Paulo Reinaldo, one of our regular customers.'

For the next few minutes Virginia made only mono-syllabic replies to anything the duke said. Her gaze rarely left a table on the far side of the room.

Eventually she got up, telling the duke she needed to go to the loo, then took Mario to one side and slipped him a ten-pound note. As Lady Virginia wasn't known for her generosity, Mario assumed this could not be for services rendered, but for services about to be rendered. By the time her ladyship returned to the duke and suggested it was time to go home, she knew everything she needed to know about Paulo Reinaldo, and the only thing she needed to know about Jessica Clifton.

◄o►

When Paulo took Jessica to Annabel's to celebrate her nineteenth birthday, neither of them noticed the elderly couple seated in an alcove.

Virginia and the duke usually left the club around eleven, but not tonight. In fact the duke dozed off after a third Courvoisier even though he had suggested on more than one occasion that perhaps they should go home.

'Not yet, darling,' Virginia kept saying, without ex-planation.

The moment Paulo called for the bill, Virginia shot out of the stalls and made her way quickly across to the private phone booth discreetly located in the corridor. She already had a telephone number and the name of an officer she had been assured would be on duty. She dialled the number slowly and the phone was answered almost immediately.

'Chief Inspector Mullins.'

'Chief inspector, my name is Lady Virginia Fenwick, and I wish to report a dangerous driving incident. I think the driver must be drunk, because he almost hit our Rolls-Royce as he overtook us on the inside.'

'Can you describe the car, madam?'

'It was a yellow Ferrari, and I'm fairly sure the driver wasn't English.'

'You didn't by any chance get the registration number?'

Virginia checked a slip of paper in her hand. 'A786 CLC.'

'And where did the incident take place?'

'My chauffeur was driving around Berkeley Square when the Ferrari turned right down Piccadilly and drove off towards Chelsea.'

'Thank you, madam. I'll look into it immediately.'

Virginia put the phone down just as Paulo and Jessica passed her in the corridor. She remained in the shadows as the young couple made their way up the stairs and out on to Berkeley Square. A liveried doorman handed Paulo his car key in exchange for a five-pound note. Paulo jumped into the driver's seat, eased the gear lever into first and accelerated away as if he was in pole position on the starting grid at Monte Carlo. He'd only gone a few hundred yards when he spotted a police car in his rear-view mirror.

'Lose them,' said Jessica. 'It's only a clapped-out Sierra.'

Paulo moved into third and began to dodge in and out of slow-moving traffic. Jessica was screaming obscenities and cheering him on, until she heard the siren. She looked back to see the traffic moving aside to allow the police car through.

Paulo glanced in his rear-view mirror as the traffic

light in front of him turned red. He shot through it, turned right and narrowly missed a bus as he careered down Piccadilly. By the time he reached Hyde Park Corner, two police cars were in pursuit and Jessica was clinging on to the dashboard, wishing she'd never encouraged him.

As he swerved around Hyde Park Corner and on to the Brompton Road, he ran another red light, only to see a third police car heading towards him. He threw on the brakes and skidded to a halt, but was too late to avoid crashing head on into the squad car.

Jessica didn't spend her nineteenth birthday in the arms of her lover in his luxury Knightsbridge apartment, but alone on a thin, urine-stained foam mattress in cell number three of Savile Row police station.

27

SAMANTHA WAS WOKEN just before seven the following morning by a telephone call from Chief Inspector Mullins. She didn't need to wake Seb, who was in the bathroom shaving. When he heard his wife's anxious voice, he put down his razor and walked quickly back into the bedroom. He couldn't remember when he'd last seen Sam crying.

A cab pulled up outside Savile Row police station just after 7.30 a.m. Sebastian and Sam stepped out, to be met by flashing bulbs and shouted questions, which reminded Seb of when Hakim was on trial at the Old Bailey. What he couldn't understand was who could have alerted the press at that time in the morning.

'Is your daughter a drug addict?' shouted one.

'Was she driving?' Another.

'Did she take part in an orgy?' Yet another.

Seb recalled Giles's golden rule when facing a pack of hacks: if you've got nothing to say, say nothing.

Inside the police station, Seb gave the duty sergeant at the front desk his name.

'Take Mr and Mrs Clifton down to cell number three,'

the sergeant instructed a young constable, 'and I'll let the chief inspector know they've arrived.'

The constable led them along a corridor and down some steep steps into the basement. He inserted a large key into a heavy door and pulled it open, then stepped aside to allow them to enter the cell.

Sebastian stared at the dishevelled girl hunched up on the corner of the bed, her face smeared with mascara from crying. It took him a few moments to realize it was his daughter. Samantha crossed the room quickly, sat down beside Jessica and wrapped her arms around her.

'It's all right, my darling, we're both here.'

Although Jessica had sobered up, the smell of stale alcohol and marijuana still lingered on her breath. A few moments later they were joined by the case officer, who introduced himself as Chief Inspector Mullins and explained why their daughter had spent the night in a police cell. He then asked if either of them knew a Mr Paulo Reinaldo.

'No,' they both said without hesitation.

'Your daughter was with Mr Reinaldo when we arrested him this morning. We've already charged him with drink-driving, and possession of three ounces of marijuana.'

Seb tried to remain calm. 'And my daughter, chief inspector, has she also been charged?'

'No, sir, although she was drunk at the time and we suspect had been smoking marijuana and later assaulted a police officer, we will not be pressing charges.' He paused. 'On this occasion.'

'I'm most grateful,' said Samantha.

'Where is the young man?' asked Sebastian.

'He will appear before Bow Street magistrates later this morning.'

'Is my daughter free to leave, chief inspector?' Samantha asked quietly.

'Yes she is, Mrs Clifton. I'm sorry about the press. Someone must have tipped them off, but I can assure you it wasn't us.'

Seb took Jessica gently by the arm and led her from the cell, up a well-trodden staircase and out of the police station into Savile Row, where they were once again greeted by flashing bulbs and hollered questions. He bundled his wife and daughter into the back of a taxi, pulled the door closed and told the cabbie to get moving.

Jessica sat cowering between her parents, and didn't raise her head even after the cab had turned the corner and the press were no longer to be seen.

◄O►

When they arrived back home in Lennox Gardens, they were met by another group of photographers and journalists. The same questions, but still no answers. Once they were safely inside, Seb accompanied Jessica into the living room, and before she had a chance to sit down, he demanded the truth, and nothing less.

'And don't spare us, because I've no doubt we'll read every lurid detail in the *Evening Standard* later today.'

The self-assured young woman who'd left Annabel's after celebrating her birthday had been replaced by a stammering, tearful nineteen-year-old, who replied to their questions in a quivering, uncertain voice that neither of her parents had ever experienced before. Between embarrassed silences, Jessica described how she'd first met Paulo and became infatuated by his charm, his sophistication and, most of all, she admitted, the endless flow of cash. Although she told her parents everything, she never placed any blame on her lover, and even asked if she might be allowed to see him one more time.

'For what purpose?' asked Sebastian.

'To say goodbye.' She hesitated. 'And to thank him.'

'I don't think that would be wise, while the press will be dogging his every step and hoping you'll do just that. But if you write him a letter, I'll make sure he gets it.'

'Thank you.'

'Jessie, you have to face the fact that you've let us both down badly. However, one thing's for sure, nothing will be gained by raking over it. It's now in the past, and only you can decide what you want to do about your future.'

Jessica looked up at her parents, but didn't speak.

'In my opinion, you have two choices,' said Seb. 'You can come back home and find out if it's possible to pick up the pieces, or you can leave, and return to your other life.'

'I'm so sorry,' said Jessica, tears streaming down her cheeks. 'I know what I did was unforgivable. I don't want to go back, and I promise I'll do everything I can to make it up to both of you if you'll just give me another chance.'

'Of course we will,' said Samantha, 'but I can't speak for the Slade.'

—◦—

Sebastian left the flat a couple of hours later to pick up an early edition of the *Evening Standard*. The headline screamed out at him from a poster long before he'd reached the newsagent:

**HEALTH MINISTER'S GRANDDAUGHTER
INVOLVED IN DRUGS SCANDAL**

He read the article as he walked slowly back home. It included almost all of the details Jessie had volunteered earlier. A night spent in a police cell, champagne, marijuana, two bottles of expensive wine followed by brandy Alexanders consumed at Annabel's in Mayfair. A police chase that ended up with a £100,000 Ferrari crashing head on into a squad car, and even the suggestion of four in a bed.

Mr Paulo Reinaldo warranted only a passing mention, but then the reporter was far more interested in making sure the Baroness Emma Clifton, Under Secretary of State for Health, Sir Harry Clifton, popular author and civil rights campaigner, Lord Barrington, former leader of the House of Lords, and Sebastian Clifton, chairman of a leading city bank, all got a mention, despite the fact that they were all fast asleep at the time Jessica Clifton was arrested.

Sebastian let out a deep sigh. He could only hope that his beloved daughter would eventually be able to chalk this down to experience and, given time, not only fully recover but be stronger for it. It wasn't until he reached the last paragraph that he realized that wasn't going to be possible.

◄о►

Virginia also purchased an early edition of the *Evening Standard*, and couldn't stop smiling as she read the 'exclusive' word for word. Ten pounds well spent, she thought to herself. Her only disappointment was that Paulo Reinaldo had pleaded guilty, and received a fine of £500 after assuring the judge he would be returning to Brazil in the next few days.

However, the smile reappeared on Virginia's face

when she came to the last paragraph of the article. Mr Gerald Knight, the principal of the Slade School of Fine Art, told the reporter he had been left with no choice but to expel both Mr Reinaldo and Miss Jessica Clifton from the college. He added that he had done so reluctantly in the case of Miss Clifton, as she was an extremely gifted student.

◄o►

'It's a great pleasure to finally meet you, Dr Barrington. I've long been an admirer of yours.'

'That's kind of you, Sir James, but I had no idea you'd even heard of me.'

'You taught my wife Helen when she was up at Cambridge,' said Sir James as they sat down by the fire.

'Remind me of her maiden name, Sir James?'

'Helen Prentice. We met when I was reading Law at Trinity.'

'Ah, yes, I remember Helen. She played the cello in the college orchestra. Does she still play?'

'Only at weekends when no one is listening.' They both laughed.

'Well, do pass on my best wishes to her.'

'I will indeed, Dr Barrington. But I confess, neither of us could work out why you would want to see me, unless you're on one of your well-known fund-raising drives, in which case I should remind you that British Petroleum has recently increased its annual grant to the Newnham College scholarship fund.'

Grace smiled. 'You're wearing the wrong hat, Sir James. I didn't come to see the chairman of BP but the president of the Slade School of Fine Art.'

'I'm still none the wiser.'

'Try not to think of me as a Barrington, but as being related to several Cliftons, and one in particular, my great-niece Jessica, whose case I come to plead on her behalf.'

Sir James Neville's warm and relaxed demeanour was quickly replaced with a sullen frown.

'Even if you were Portia, I'm afraid your pleas would fall on deaf ears, Dr Barrington. The board voted unanimously to expel Miss Clifton from the Slade. Not only was she drunk, and possibly under the influence of drugs, when she was arrested, but she assaulted a police officer while in custody. I personally felt she was most fortunate not to have been charged, and even given a custodial sentence.'

'But that's the whole point, Sir James. She wasn't charged, or sentenced.'

'The young man who was driving the car at the time, if I remember correctly, was charged, given a heavy fine and deported.'

'An older and much more sophisticated individual, with whom Jessica was unfortunately besotted.'

'Quite possibly, Dr Barrington. But are you also aware that Miss Clifton's scholarship was rescinded earlier this year after she was caught smoking marijuana on college premises?'

'Yes, I am, Sir James. Jessica has told me everything that happened during the past year, and I can assure you she deeply regrets her actions, but if you reinstate her, she will not let you down a second time.'

'Whose word do we have for that?'

'Mine.'

Sir James hesitated, before saying, 'I'm afraid it's out of the question, Dr Barrington. Did Miss Clifton also mention that she only attended three lectures and seven classes last term, and during that time her work went from excellent to unacceptable?'

'Yes, she did.'

'And when her supervisor, Professor Howard, raised the matter with her, she told him, and I apologize for my language, to fuck off?'

'And you've never resorted to such language, Sir James?'

'Not when addressing my tutor, and I doubt if your great-niece has resorted to such language in front of you, Dr Barrington, or any other members of your family.'

'So you've never known a student to rebel against what you and I would consider acceptable behaviour? After all, you have a son and two daughters of your own.' Sir James was silenced for a moment, which allowed Grace to continue. 'I've had the privilege of teaching many talented young women over the years, but rarely have I encountered one as gifted as my great-niece.'

'Talent is not an excuse to flout college rules, while expecting everyone else to behave properly, as the principal clearly spelt out in his report on this unhappy state of affairs.'

'In that same report, Sir James, Professor Howard addressed the board on Jessica's behalf, and if I recall his words correctly, he said that she possessed a rare talent that should be nurtured, not stamped out.'

'The board considered Professor Howard's words most carefully before we came to our decision, and I'm afraid the attendant publicity left us with no choice but to—'

'The attendant publicity, Sir James, was not caused

by Jessica, but my sister Emma, my brother-in-law Harry, and even my brother, Giles Barrington.'

'That is possibly the case, Dr Barrington, but the privilege of being brought up in such a remarkable family gives one added responsibility.'

'So if Jessica had been the daughter of a single mother, whose father had deserted her, your whole attitude might have been different?'

Sir James rose angrily from his place. 'I apologize, Dr Barrington, but I can see no purpose in prolonging this discussion. The board has made its decision, and I do not have the authority to overturn it.'

'I'm loath to correct you, Sir James,' said Grace, not rising from her seat, 'but I think you'll find, if you check the statutes of the Slade carefully, that rule 73b allows you to do just that.'

'I don't recall rule 73b,' said Sir James, sinking back into his chair, 'but I have a feeling you're about to enlighten me.'

'It is the president's prerogative,' said Grace calmly, 'to overrule a board decision if he believes that there were extenuating circumstances that had not been taken into consideration at the time.'

'Such as?' said Sir James, barely able to disguise his irritation.

'Perhaps it's time to remind you about another student, who didn't have the same privileges as Jessica Clifton. A young man who, when he was an undergraduate at Cambridge, took his tutor's motorbike without permission and in the middle of the night went on a joyride. When he was pulled over by the police for speeding, he claimed he had the owner's permission.'

'That was just a harmless prank.'

'And when he appeared in front of the magistrate the following morning, he wasn't charged, but was told to return the bike to its owner and apologize. And fortunately, because the young man was not the son of a government minister, the incident didn't even manage a paragraph in the *Cambridge Evening News*.'

'That's not altogether fair, Dr Barrington.'

'And when he returned the bike to his tutor and apologized, the undergraduate was not sent down or even rusticated, because his tutor was a civilized fellow, and was well aware that the young man was only a few weeks away from his finals.'

'That's below the belt, Dr Barrington.'

'I cannot disagree,' said Grace. 'But I think it worthy of mention that the young man in question graduated with a first-class honours degree, and later became chairman of BP, president of the Slade School of Art, and a knight of the realm.'

Sir James bowed his head.

'I apologize for resorting to such tactics, Sir James, and can only hope you will forgive me when Dame Jessica Clifton RA is appointed president of the Royal Academy.'

◄○►

'Tell me, Grandpops,' said Jessica, 'have you ever made a complete fool of yourself?'

'Do you mean this week, or last week?' asked Harry.

'I'm serious. I mean when you were young.'

'That's so long ago, I can't even remember,' said Harry. Jessica remained silent as she waited for him to answer her question. 'What about being arrested for murder?' he finally managed. 'Does that count?'

'But you were innocent and it was all a terrible mistake.'

'The judge didn't seem to think so, because he sentenced me to four years in jail, and if I remember correctly, you only managed one night.' Jessica frowned, and didn't respond. 'And then there was the time I disobeyed orders and advised a German general to lay down his arms and surrender, when all I had at my disposal was a pistol and an Irish corporal.'

'And the Americans decorated you for that action.'

'But that's the point, Jessie. Often in war you're hailed as a hero for something that had you done in peacetime, you would have been arrested for and possibly shot.'

'Do you think my father will ever forgive me?'

'There's no reason why he shouldn't. He did something far worse at your age, which was the reason your mother left him and returned to America.'

'She told me they drifted apart.'

'True, but what she didn't tell you was why. And they have you to thank for bringing them back together.'

'And whom do I have to thank?'

'Your great-aunt Grace, if you're asking who made it possible for you to return to the Slade in September.'

'I assumed it was you or Grandmama who intervened.'

'No. Although she won't thank me for telling you, Grace joined forces with Professor Howard, proving that when two people work together, they can become an army.'

'How can I ever begin to thank them?'

'By proving they were right. Which leads me to ask how your work's coming on.'

'I don't know, is the honest answer. Can you ever be sure how one of your books is shaping up?'

'No. In the end I leave it to the critics and the public to make that decision.'

'Then I guess it will be the same for me. So would you be willing to offer an honest opinion on my latest work?'

'I could try,' said Harry, hoping he wouldn't have to dissemble.

'Then no better time than now,' said Jessica, grabbing him by the hand and leading him out of the library. 'It was kind of you to allow me to come down for the summer and see if I could pick up the pieces,' she added as they climbed the stairs.

'And have you?'

'That's exactly what I'm hoping you'll tell me,' said Jessica, as she opened the door to the old playroom and stood aside.

Harry walked tentatively in and looked at row upon row of preliminary drawings scattered across the floor. They didn't begin to prepare him for the huge canvas that stood on an easel in the centre of the room. He stared at a painting of the Manor House, which he had thought he knew so well. The lawn, the rose garden, the lake, the folly, the vast oaks that led your eye to the horizon. Every colour was wrong, but when put together . . .

When Jessica could bear it no longer she said, 'Well? Say something, Grandpops.'

'I only hope my latest book is half as good.'

28

'BUT IT'S A FAMILY TRADITION,' insisted Emma.

'Couldn't we have a year off?' mocked Sebastian.

'Certainly not. I promised your great-grandfather that the family would always spend Christmas together, and on New Year's Eve we would tell each other our New Year's resolutions. So who would like to start this year?'

'My father was even worse,' said Samantha. 'He made us write down our resolutions, and a year later we had to read them out to remind everyone what we'd foolishly promised.'

'I've always liked your father,' said Emma. 'So why don't you begin?'

'By this time next year,' said Samantha, 'I will have a job.'

'But you already have a job,' said Emma. 'You're bringing up the next but one chairman of Farthings Kaufman.'

'I don't think so,' said Seb, looking down at his son, who was landing a model of Concorde on the floor. 'I think he plans to be a test pilot.'

'Then he'll have to become chairman of British Airways,' said Emma.

'Perhaps he won't want to be chairman of anything,' suggested Grace.

'If you had a choice, Sam,' said Harry, 'what job would you like?'

'I've applied for a position at the Courtauld Institute, in their research department. The hours are flexible, and now Jake is going to nursery school, it would be ideal.'

'For the more practical members of our family,' said Sebastian, 'it may interest them to know that employing a nanny will cost more than Sam can hope to earn as a researcher at the Courtauld.'

'A sensible distribution of wealth,' said Grace. 'Two people each doing a job they want to do, and both being rewarded accordingly.'

'What's your New Year's resolution, Aunt Grace?' asked Sebastian.

'I've decided to take early retirement, and will be leaving the university at the end of the academic year.'

'Come and join us in the House of Lords,' said Giles. 'We could do with your wisdom and common sense.'

'Thank you,' said Grace, 'but two Barringtons in the Upper House is quite enough. In any case, like Samantha, I'm also looking for another job.'

'Dare one ask what?' asked Harry.

'I've applied for a teaching post at a local comprehensive, in the hope that I can help some bright young girls get into Cambridge, who might not otherwise have considered it possible.'

'Why not boys?' demanded Giles.

'There are quite enough of them at Cambridge already.'

'You put us all to shame, Aunt Grace,' said Sebastian. 'So what do you have planned for this year, Seb?'

retorted Grace. 'Other than making more and more money?'

'Let's hope you're right, because frankly that's what my customers, of which you're one, will be expecting me to do.'

'Touché,' said Emma.

'Your turn, Jessica,' said Grace. 'I hope you plan to do something more worthwhile than chairing a bank.'

No one needed to be reminded of Jessica's resolution a year ago: *to be worthy of my great-aunt's belief in me, and to make the best of being given a second chance.*

'I'm determined to win a scholarship to the Royal Academy Schools.'

'Bravo,' said Emma.

'Not good enough,' said Grace. 'We all know you're going to achieve that. Raise the bar, young lady.'

Jessica hesitated for a moment, before she said, 'I'll win the Founder's Prize.'

'That's more like it,' said Grace. 'And we'll all be present when you accept the award.'

'Your turn, Mama,' said Sebastian, coming to the rescue of his daughter.

'I'm going to join a gym and lose half a stone.'

'But that was your resolution last year!'

'I know,' said Emma, 'and now I need to lose a stone.'

'Me too,' said Giles, 'but unlike Emma at least I've achieved last year's resolution.'

'Remind us?' said Harry.

'I swore I'd get back on the front bench and be offered a challenging portfolio now that Michael Foot had finally resigned and made way for someone who actually wants to live in Number Ten.'

'Which portfolio has Mr Kinnock asked you to shadow?' asked Grace.

Giles couldn't help grinning.

'No,' said Emma, 'you wouldn't dare! I presume you turned him down?'

'I couldn't resist it,' said Giles. 'So my New Year's resolution is to frustrate, harass and cause as many problems as possible for the government, and in particular its minister for health.'

'You're a rat!' said Emma.

'No, to be fair, sis, I'm a rat catcher.'

'Time out,' said Harry, laughing. 'Before you two come to blows, who's next?'

'Freddie, perhaps?' suggested Karin.

It had been Freddie's first Christmas at the Manor House, and Jessica had mothered him like an only child, while Jake never seemed to be more than a few steps behind his new friend.

'My New Year's resolution,' said Freddie, 'will be the same this year, and every year, until I have achieved it.' Freddie may not have intended to, but he'd caught everyone's attention. 'I shall score a century at Lord's, and emulate my father.'

Giles turned away, not wishing to embarrass the boy.

'And once you've done that, what next?' asked Harry, when he saw his oldest friend close to tears.

'A double century, Sir Harry,' said Freddie without hesitation.

'It won't be difficult to work out what you'll want the following year, once you've achieved that,' said Grace.

Everyone laughed.

'Now it's your turn, Karin,' said Emma.

'I've decided to run the London Marathon, and to raise money for immigrants who want to go to university.'

'How far is a marathon?' asked Samantha.

'Just over twenty-six miles.'

'Rather you than me. But put me down for five pounds a mile.'

'That's very generous, Sam,' said Karin.

'Me too,' said Sebastian.

'And me,' added Giles.

'Thank you, but no thank you,' said Karin, taking a notebook from her pocket. 'I already had Samantha down for five pounds a mile, and the rest of you will be expected to give the same proportion of your income.'

'Help,' said Sebastian.

'I'll be coming to you last,' said Karin, smiling at Seb before consulting her list. 'Grace is down for twenty-five pounds a mile, Emma and Harry fifty pounds each, and Giles one hundred. And Sebastian, as you're chairman of the bank, I've got you down for a thousand pounds a mile. That adds up to –' she once again consulted her notebook – 'thirty-one thousand, nine hundred and eighty pounds.'

'Can I put in a plea on behalf of an immigrant art student from the new world, who isn't at all sure who her parents are, and has unfortunately lost her scholarship?' Everyone laughed. 'And what's more, Freddie, Jake and I would each like to give ten pounds a mile.'

'But that would cost you seven hundred and eighty pounds,' said her father. 'So I have to ask, how do you intend to pay?'

'The bank will be requiring a portrait of its chairman to hang in the boardroom,' said Jessica. 'Guess who they're about to commission, and what her fee will be?'

Harry smiled, delighted that his granddaughter had

regained her irreverent streak, along with her acerbic sense of humour.

'Do I have any say in this?' asked Seb.

'Certainly not,' said Jessica. 'Otherwise what's the point of being a father?'

'Bravo, Karin,' said Grace, 'we all applaud you.'

'Wait, wait, wait,' said Seb. 'There will be a sub-clause attached to the contract. Not a penny will be paid if Karin fails to finish.'

'Fair enough,' said Karin, 'and my thanks to you all.'

'Who's left?' asked Emma.

Everyone turned their attention to Harry, who couldn't resist making them all wait for a few more moments.

'Once upon a time there was a remarkable old lady, who, just before she died, wrote a letter to her son suggesting that perhaps the time had come for him to write that novel he had so often told her about.' He paused. 'Well, Mother,' he said, looking towards the heavens, 'that time has come. I no longer have any excuse not to fulfil your wish, as I've just completed the final book in the William Warwick series.'

'Unless of course your wicked publisher,' suggested Emma, warming to the theme, 'were to offer his susceptible author an even larger advance that he found impossible to resist.'

'I'm happy to tell you that won't be possible,' said Harry.

'How come?' asked Seb.

'I've just sent the final draft to Aaron Guinzburg, and he's about to discover that I've killed off William Warwick.'

Everyone was stunned into silence, except Giles, who

said, 'That didn't stop Sir Arthur Conan Doyle bringing Sherlock Holmes back to life after his loyal readers thought Moriarty had thrown him off a clifftop.'

'The same thought did cross my mind,' said Harry, 'so I ended the book with William Warwick's funeral, and his wife and children standing by the graveside watching his coffin being lowered into the ground. As far as I can recall, only one person has ever risen from the dead.'

That silenced even Giles.

'Are you able to tell us anything about the next novel?' asked Karin, who, like everyone else, was hearing about the death of William Warwick for the first time.

Once again Harry waited until he had everyone's attention, even Jake's.

'It will be set in one of the Russian satellites, probably Ukraine. The first chapter will open in a suburb of Kiev, where a family, mother, father and child, will be having supper together.'

'A boy or a girl?' asked Jessica.

'Boy.'

'Age?'

'Haven't decided yet. Fifteen, possibly sixteen. All I know for certain is that the family are celebrating the boy's birthday, and during the meal, not exactly a feast, the reader will learn about the problems they face living under an oppressive regime when the father, a trade union leader, is considered to be a trouble-maker, a dissident, someone who dares to challenge the state's authority.'

'If he'd been born in this country,' said Giles, 'he would have been the leader of the opposition.'

'But in his own country,' continued Harry, 'he's treated like an outlaw, a common criminal.'

'What happens next?' asked Jessica.

'The boy is about to open his only present, when an army truck comes to a screeching halt outside the house, and a dozen soldiers break down the door, drag the father out on to the street and shoot him in front of his wife and child.'

'You kill the hero in the first chapter?' said Emma in disbelief.

'This is going to be a story about the child,' said Grace, 'not the father.'

'And the mother,' said Harry, 'because she's an intelligent, resourceful woman, who's already worked out that if they don't escape from the country, it won't be long before her rebellious son will seek revenge, and inevitably end up suffering the same fate as his father.'

'So where do they escape to?' demanded Jessica.

'The mother can't decide between America and England.'

'How do they decide?' asked Karin.

'On the toss of a coin.'

The rest of the family continued to stare at the storyteller.

'And what's the twist?' asked Seb.

'We follow what happens to the mother and child, chapter by chapter. In chapter one, they escape to America. In chapter two, England. So you have two parallel and very different stories taking place at the same time.'

'Wow,' said Jessica. 'Then what happens?'

'I wish I knew,' said Harry. 'But it's my New Year's resolution to find out.'

29

'TEN MINUTES TO GO,' said a voice over the loud-speaker. Karin kept jogging on the spot, attempting to get into what the seasoned runners called 'the zone'. She'd put in hours of training, even run a half marathon, but suddenly she felt very alone on the starting line.

'Five minutes,' said the voice of doom.

Karin checked her stopwatch, a recent gift from Giles. 0.00. Get as close to the front as you can, Freddie had told her. Why add unnecessary time or distance to the race? Karin had never considered the marathon to be a race, she just hoped to finish in under four hours. Right now, she just hoped to finish.

'One minute,' boomed the starter's voice.

Karin was about eleven rows back, but as there were over 8,000 runners, she considered that was near enough to the front.

'Ten, nine, eight, seven, six, five, four, three, two, one!' the runners all shouted in unison, before a klaxon blared ominously. Karin pressed the button on her stopwatch and set off, swept along by an enthusiastic tide of runners.

Each mile was marked with a thick blue line stretching across the road, and Karin completed the first mile in under eight minutes. As she settled into a steady rhythm, she became more aware of the crowds lining both sides of the course, some cheering, some clapping, while others just stared in disbelief at the mass of human flesh, of all shapes and sizes, which was passing them at different speeds.

Her mind began to drift. She thought about Giles, who'd driven her to the little village of tents earlier that morning to register, and who would now be out there somewhere standing in the cold, waiting for her to appear among the also-rans. Her thoughts turned next to her recent visit to the House of Lords to hear the health minister answering questions from the despatch box. Emma had coped well, and in Giles's opinion had quickly got into her stride. As Karin passed the halfway mark, she hoped she was also in her stride, although she accepted the winner would already be crossing the finishing line.

◄○►

Giles had warned them that Karin was unlikely to complete the course in under four hours, so the family had all risen early that morning to make sure they could find a spot where she was certain to see them. The previous evening Freddie had been on his knees preparing a placard that he hoped would make Karin laugh as she staggered past them.

Once Giles had returned to Smith Square after dropping his wife off at the A–D registration tent in Greenwich Park, he led her little band of supporters to the back of the Treasury building and found a front-row place behind the barriers on Parliament Square, opposite the statue of Winston Churchill.

◄○►

Karin was now approaching what was known by all marathon runners as the wall. It usually came at around 17 to 20 miles, and she'd heard so often about the temptation to try and convince yourself that if you dropped out, no one would notice. Everyone would notice. They might not say anything, but Sebastian had made it clear that he wouldn't be parting with a penny unless she crossed the finishing line. A deal's a deal, he'd reminded her. But she seemed to be going slower and slower, and it didn't help when she spotted a 30 miles per hour road sign ahead of her.

But something, possibly the fear of failure, kept her going, and she pretended not to notice when she was overtaken by a letter box, and a few minutes later by a camel. Go, go, go, she told herself. Stop, stop, stop, her legs insisted. As she passed the 20-mile mark, the crowd cheered loudly, not for her, but for a caterpillar who strolled past her.

When Karin spotted the Tower of London in the distance, she began to believe she just might make it. She checked her watch: 3 hours 32 minutes. Could she still complete the course in under four hours?

As she turned off the Embankment and passed Big Ben, a loud, sustained cheer went up. She looked across to see Giles, Harry and Emma waving frantically. Jessica never stopped drawing, while Freddie held up a placard that declared KEEP GOING, I THINK YOU'RE IN THIRD PLACE!

Karin somehow managed to raise an arm in acknowledgement, but by the time she turned into the Mall, she could barely place one foot in front of the other. With a quarter of a mile to go, she became aware of the packed stands on both sides of the road, the crowds cheering more loudly than ever and a BBC television crew who were filming her while running backwards faster than she was running forwards.

She looked up to see the digital clock above the finishing line ticking relentlessly away. Three hours 57 minutes, and she suddenly began to take an interest in the seconds, 31, 32, 33 . . . With one last herculean effort, she tried to speed up. When she finally crossed the line, she raised her arms high in the air as if she were an Olympic champion. After a few more strides, she collapsed in a heap on the ground.

Within a moment, a race official in a Red Cross smock was kneeling beside her, a bottle of water in one hand, a shiny silver cape in the other.

'Try to keep moving,' he said as he placed a medal round her neck.

Karin began walking slowly, very slowly, but her spirits were lifted when in the distance she spotted Freddie running towards her, arms outstretched, with Giles only a few paces behind.

'Congratulations!' Freddie shouted, even before he'd reached her. 'Three hours, fifty-nine minutes and eleven seconds. I'm sure you'll do better next year.'

'There isn't going to be a next year,' said Karin with considerable feeling. 'Even if Sebastian offers me a million pounds.'

LADY VIRGINIA FENWICK

1983–1986

30

VIRGINIA HAD MOVED OUT of her flat in Chelsea and into the duke's Eaton Square townhouse the day after his chauffeur drove Clarence and Alice to Heathrow to go their separate ways; one flying east, the other west.

Although still a little apprehensive, she became more and more confident that she'd got away with it, until they travelled up to the country together to spend a long weekend at Castle Hertford.

It was while the duke was out shooting that Mr Moxton, the estate manager, had dropped her a hand-written note requesting a private meeting with her.

'I apologize for raising the subject,' he said after Virginia had summoned him to join her in the drawing room, 'but may I ask if the £185,000 the duke gave you was a gift or a loan?'

'Does it make any difference?' asked Virginia sharply.

'Only for tax purposes, my lady.'

'Which would be more convenient?' she asked, her tone softening.

'A loan,' said Moxton, who Virginia hadn't suggested should sit, 'because then there are no tax implications. If it was a gift, you would be liable for a tax bill of around one hundred thousand pounds.'

'And we wouldn't want that,' said Virginia. 'But when would I be expected to repay the loan?'

'Shall we say five years? At which time of course it could be rolled over.'

'Of course.'

'However, in the unlikely possibility that his grace should pass away before then, you would be liable to return the full amount.'

'Then I shall have to do everything in my power to make sure his grace lives for at least another five years.'

'I think that would be best for everyone, my lady,' said Moxton, not sure if he was meant to laugh. 'May I also ask if there are likely to be any further loans of this kind in the future?'

'Certainly not, Moxton. This was a one-off, and I know the duke would much prefer the matter was not referred to again.'

'Of course, my lady. I will draw up the necessary loan document for you to sign and then everything will be settled.'

As the weeks had drifted by, and then the months, Virginia became more and more confident the duke wasn't aware of what she and Moxton had agreed, but even if he was, he certainly never referred to it. When the time came to celebrate the duke's seventy-first birthday, Virginia was ready to move on to the next stage of her plan.

◄○►

If 1983 had been a leap year, the problem might have solved itself. But it wasn't, and Virginia was unwilling to wait.

She had been living at Eaton Square with the duke for almost a year, and once the official mourning period was over, her next purpose was quite simply to become her grace, the Duchess of Hertford. There was only one obstacle in her path, namely the duke, who seemed to be quite satisfied with the present arrangement, and had never once raised the subject of marriage. That state of affairs would have to be brought to a head. But how?

Virginia considered the alternatives that were open to her. She could move out of Eaton Square and return to Chelsea, starving Perry of her company and, more important, sex, which was no longer quite as regular as it had once been, and hope that would do the trick. However, with only her two thousand pounds a month allowance from her brother to live on, Virginia feared she would give in long before he did. She could propose herself, but she didn't care for the humiliation of being turned down. Or she could simply leave him, which didn't bear thinking about.

When she discussed the problem over lunch with Bofie Bridgwater and Priscilla Bingham, it was Bofie who came up with a simple solution which would undoubtedly force the duke to make a decision one way or the other.

'But it might backfire,' said Virginia, 'and then I'd be back on Queer Street.'

'You could be right,' admitted Bofie. 'But frankly you haven't been left with a lot of choice, old gal, unless you're happy to drift along until the time comes to attend the duke's funeral as an old friend.'

'No, I assure you that isn't part of my plan. If I were to let that happen, the Lady Camilla Hertford would come after me, all guns blazing, demanding the £185,000 loan be repaid in full. No, if I'm going to risk everything on one throw of the dice, it's going to have to be before Christmas.'

'Why is Christmas so important?' asked Priscilla.

'Because Camilla will be flying over from New Zealand, and she's already written to Perry warning him that if "that woman" is among the house guests, then neither she nor her husband nor Perry's grandchildren, whom he adores, will be boarding the plane.'

'She dislikes you that much?'

'Even more than her late mother did, if that were possible. So if we're going to do anything about it, time isn't on my side.'

'Then I'd better make that call,' said Bofie.

—<o>—

'*Daily Mail*.'

'Could you put me through to Nigel Dempster.'

'Who's calling?'

'Lord Bridgwater.'

'Bofie, good to hear from you,' said the next voice on the line. 'What's cooking?'

'I've had a call from William Hickey at the *Express*, Nigel. Of course, I refused to speak to them.'

'I'm grateful for that, Bofie.'

'Well, if the story has to come out, I'd much rather it was in your column.'

'Fire away.'

Dempster wrote down every word Bofie had to say, and was somewhat surprised because he'd always described Lord Bridgwater in his column as a 'confirmed bachelor'. But there wasn't any question that this exclusive was coming straight from the horse's mouth.

—<o>—

As soon as the *Daily Mail* dropped on her doormat the following morning, Virginia immediately grabbed it. She ignored the front page headline 'Divorce?' above a photo of Rod and Alana Stewart, and quickly turned to Dempster's column, to see the headline 'Marriage?' above a not very flattering photo of the Lady Virginia Fenwick in Monte Carlo with Bofie.

As Virginia read Dempster's lead story, she regretted ever letting Bofie loose. *A close family friend* (code for the subject of the story) *tells me that Lord Bridgwater is hoping shortly to announce his engagement to the Lady Virginia Fenwick, the only daughter of the late Earl Fenwick. This might come as a surprise to my regular readers, because as recently as last week, Lady Virginia was seen at a point-to-point on the arm of the Duke of Hertford. Watch this space.*

Virginia read the article a second time, fearing that Bofie had over-egged the pudding, because you didn't need to read between the lines to realize that Dempster didn't believe a word of it. She would have to call Perry and tell him it was all complete rubbish. After all, everyone knew Bofie was gay.

After several cups of coffee and even more false starts, Virginia finally picked up the phone and dialled Perry's number in Eaton Square. It had just begun to ring when there was a knock on her front door.

'The Duke of Hertford's residence,' said a voice on the other end of the line that she immediately recognized.

'It's Lady Virginia, Lomax. I wondered if I might speak to—'

The knocking at the door continued.

'I'm afraid his grace is not at home, my lady,' said the butler.

'Do you know when he'll be back?'

'No, my lady. He left in a hurry this morning, and gave no instructions. Would you like me to let him know you called?'

'No thank you,' said Virginia, putting down the phone. The knocking persisted like the hammering of a rent collector who knew you were inside.

She walked to the door in a daze, imagining Perry must have left for the country without her, for the first time in over a year. She needed time to think, but first she must get rid of whoever it was at the door.

She opened it and was about to let loose on the intruder, only to find Perry, down on one knee. 'Don't tell me I'm too late, old gal,' he said, looking up at her forlornly.

'Of course you're not, Perry, but do get up.'

'Not until you say you'll marry me.'

'Of course I will, my darling. I've already told Bofie you're the only man in my life, but he won't take no for an answer,' she said as she helped the duke back on to his feet.

'I don't want to hang about, old gal,' he said. 'I can see the finishing line, so we'd better get on with it.'

'I understand exactly how you feel,' said Virginia, 'but don't you think you should talk it over with your children before you make such an important decision?'

'Certainly not. Fathers don't ask their children's permission to marry. In any case, I'm sure they'll be delighted.'

Three weeks later, thanks to a tip from a family friend, Nigel Dempster printed an exclusive photograph of the Duke and Duchess of Hertford leaving Chelsea Register Office in the pouring rain. *And the happy couple*, wrote

Dempster, *will be enjoying their honeymoon on the duke's estate near Cortona, and plan to return to Castle Hertford to spend Christmas with the family.*

31

CHRISTMAS WITH THE Hertfords was frosty inside as well as outside the castle. Even Clarence and Alice were clearly dismayed that their father had married without informing them, while Camilla left no one – family or staff – in any doubt as to how she felt about the usurper.

Whenever Virginia entered a room, Camilla would leave with her husband and their two children trailing behind her. However, Virginia still had an advantage over the rest of the family: there was one room none of them could enter, and where she had complete domain for eight hours in every twenty-four.

While Virginia worked on her husband by night, she concentrated on Clarence and Alice by day, accepting that Camilla was not for turning, although she hadn't altogether given up on her husband and children.

Virginia made sure that whenever any member of the family saw her with the duke, she appeared to be caring, solicitous and genuinely devoted to him, taking care of his every need. By the end of the first week some of the frost had begun to thaw, and to her delight, on Christmas Eve Clarence and Alice accompanied them on their morning walk around the grounds. They were surprised to discover what an interest Virginia was taking in the upkeep of the estate.

'After all,' she told Clarence, 'when you eventually leave the army, we must make sure you take over a flourishing enterprise, and not a moribund estate.'

'Then I'll need to find a wife as conscientious as you, Virginia,' he replied.

One down, two to go.

Alice was the next to fall in line. When she opened her Christmas present to find the latest Graham Greene novel, *The Tenth Man*, she asked, 'How did you know he's my favourite author?'

'Mine too,' said Virginia, who had quickly read three of Greene's novels after she'd spotted a well-thumbed paperback on Alice's bedside table. 'I'm not surprised to find we have that in common, and although *The End of the Affair* is quite excellent, *Brighton Rock* is still my favourite.'

'That's hardly surprising,' said Camilla. 'After all, you and Pinkie Brown have so much in common.'

Alice frowned, although it was clear that the duke had no idea what they were talking about. Two down, one to go.

When the grandchildren opened their Christmas presents, they yelped with joy. A Star Trek watch for Tristan, and a Barbie doll for Kitty, which Virginia had purchased soon after she discovered that Camilla had refused to consider them in favour of a Shorter Oxford Dictionary and a sewing kit.

Camilla's gift had been the most difficult of all to decide on, until Virginia came across a photograph of her playing the flute in her school orchestra, and Cook told her that she'd heard her ladyship was thinking of taking up the instrument again. After all, you have quite a lot of spare time when the nearest town is over a hundred miles away.

When Camilla opened her present and saw the gleaming instrument, she was speechless. Virginia considered her monthly allowance had been well spent. This was confirmed when Tristan walked over to her and said, 'Thank you, Grandmama,' and gave her a kiss.

By the end of the second week, both Clarence and Alice had agreed that Papa was a fortunate man to have found such a gem, and although Camilla didn't agree with her siblings, she no longer left the room whenever Virginia entered it.

On the day of the family's departure, Virginia organized packed lunches and lemonade for the children to take on the plane, and before they all climbed into the waiting car, everyone kissed her goodbye, except Camilla, who shook hands with her. As the chauffeur-driven Rolls-Royce headed down the long drive on its way to Heathrow, Virginia didn't stop waving until the car was out of sight.

'What an absolute triumph for you,' said the duke as they walked back into the castle. 'You were magnificent, old gal. I think towards the end even Camilla was beginning to come around.'

'Thank you, Perry,' said Virginia, linking her arm through his. 'But I can understand Camilla's feelings. After all, I would feel the same way if someone tried to take the place of my mother.'

'You have such a generous heart, Virginia. But I fear there's a subject Camilla raised with me that I can't put off discussing with you any longer.'

Virginia froze. How had Camilla found out about the

loan, when she'd arranged for Moxton to leave for his Christmas holiday the day before the family arrived, and not to return until the day after they'd departed?

'I'm sorry to have to raise such a painful subject,' said the duke, 'but I'm not getting any younger, and I have to consider the future, and yours in particular, old gal.'

Virginia made no attempt to speak because this was something she had already thought about. Also, Desmond Mellor had taught her that whenever you hope to strike a bargain, be sure the other side makes the opening bid.

'The old finishing line and all that,' added the duke. 'So I've decided to draw up a codicil to be added to my will, so you'll have nothing to worry about after I've gone.'

'My only worry,' said Virginia, 'is that after you've gone, I'll be all alone. I know it's selfish of me, Perry, but if I could have my way, I would die before you. I just can't bear the thought of having to live without you.' She even managed to manufacture a tear.

'How did I get so lucky?' said the duke.

'It was me who got lucky,' purred Virginia.

'Before I call my solicitor and get the ball rolling, old gal, I want you to give some thought to what I might leave you. Of course you'll have the Dower House on the estate, and an allowance of five thousand a month, but if there's anything else in particular you'd like, just let me know.'

'That's so thoughtful of you, Perry. I can't think of anything at the moment. Perhaps just a little memento to remind me of you.'

The truth was that Virginia had already given the matter a great deal of thought, as it was all part of her retirement plan. She didn't need reminding that she'd already missed out on two wills and she didn't intend to do so a third time.

However, she needed to carry out some more research before briefing Perry on which little memento she had in mind. She knew exactly the right person to advise her on the subject, but she couldn't invite him to the castle while the duke was in residence. No matter, that problem would be solved in a couple of weeks' time when Perry went up to London for his annual regimental reunion, an event he never missed because, as the regiment's honorary colonel, he would be expected to chair the dinner.

32

VIRGINIA JOINED PERRY for the short journey to the local station.

'I wish I was going with you,' she said as they walked out on to the platform together.

'Not much point, old gal, I'm only staying in town overnight, and I'll be back by tomorrow afternoon.'

'When you'll find me standing on the platform waiting for you.'

'You don't have to,' he said as the train pulled in.

'I want to be here when you return,' she said as the duke climbed into a first-class carriage.

'That's good of you, old gal.'

'Goodbye,' Virginia called out, and waved as the train set off on its journey to London. She then quickly left the station in search of another man.

'Are you Poltimore?' she asked a young man standing on the pavement and looking a little lost. His fair hair almost reached his shoulders, and he was wearing a duffle coat and carrying a small suitcase.

'I am indeed, your grace,' he said, giving her a slight bow. 'I wasn't expecting you to come and pick me up.'

'My pleasure,' said Virginia, as the chauffeur opened the back door of the car for them.

On the drive back to the castle, Virginia explained why she'd invited an art historian from Sotheby's to come and view the Hertford collection.

'For some time the duke has been concerned that he might have overlooked something of real value that ought to be insured. We keep a full inventory, of course, but as my husband doesn't take a great deal of interest in his family heirlooms, I thought it would be sensible to bring it up to date. After all, none of us are getting any younger.'

'I've been looking forward to seeing the collection,' Poltimore replied. 'It's always a bit special to be allowed to view a collection that hasn't been seen by the public. I am, of course, aware of the Constable of Castle Hertford, and the Turner masterpiece of St Mark's Square, but I can't wait to find out what other treasures you have.'

Me too, thought Virginia, but didn't interrupt the young man's enthusiastic flow.

'It didn't take a lot of research to discover that it was the third duke, who travelled extensively around the continent during the eighteenth century,' continued Poltimore, 'who was responsible for putting together such a fine collection.'

'But he can't have been responsible for purchasing the Turner or the Constable,' said Virginia.

'No, that would have been the seventh duke. He also commissioned Gainsborough's portrait of Catherine, Duchess of Hertford.'

'You'll find her hanging in the hall,' said Virginia, who had already studied the inventory in great detail, before coming to the conclusion that the duke would never agree to part with any of the Hertford family heirlooms.

However, she was rather hoping that during the past three hundred years, something just might have escaped their notice.

On arrival back at the castle, Virginia didn't waste any time, but took the man from Sotheby's straight to the library, where she presented him with three thick, leather-bound volumes entitled *The Hertford Collection*.

'I'll leave you to get on with your work, Mr Poltimore. Do feel free to roam around the house, remembering that your main purpose is to try to find anything we might have missed.'

'I can't wait,' said Poltimore, as he opened the first volume.

As she turned to leave, Virginia said, 'We dress for dinner, Mr Poltimore, which will be served promptly at eight.'

◄○►

'I've been able to check almost everything listed in the inventory,' said Poltimore over a glass of sherry before dinner, 'and I can confirm that it all appears to be in order. However, I do think the current estimates for insurance purposes are well below the collection's true value.'

'That's hardly surprising,' said Virginia. 'I doubt if many of the aristocracy could afford to insure their possessions at their current value. I remember my father once telling me that if the family pictures were to come on the market, he would no longer be able to buy them. Did you come across anything of significance that wasn't accounted for?'

'Not so far. But I haven't had the chance to check the two upper floors, which I'll do first thing tomorrow morning.'

'Those are mainly the staff quarters,' said Virginia, trying to mask her disappointment. 'I don't think you'll find anything worthwhile up there. But you may as well look, as you're here.'

A gong sounded and she led her guest through to the dining room.

◄◌►

'Where's Mr Poltimore, Lomax?' Virginia asked the butler when she came down for breakfast the following morning.

'He took an early breakfast, your grace, and when I last saw him he was on the top floor making notes of the pictures hanging on the landing.'

Virginia retired to the library after breakfast and began to double-check the inventory, wondering if there just might be a minor masterpiece somewhere that the duke wasn't particularly attached to and would be willing to part with. However, when she looked through Poltimore's revised valuations, there was nothing that would make it possible for her to continue to live in the style she considered worthy of a duchess. She would just have to make sure that her monthly allowance was raised from £5,000 to £10,000 so she didn't starve. Her mood didn't improve when Poltimore told her over lunch that he had found nothing of any real significance on the top two floors.

'Hardly surprising, bearing in mind they're the staff quarters,' Virginia replied.

'But I did come across a drawing by Tiepolo, and a watercolour by Sir William Russell Flint that should be added to the inventory.'

'I'm most grateful,' said Virginia. 'I only hope you don't feel your visit has been a waste of time.'

'Not at all, your grace. It's been a most enjoyable experience, and if the duke were ever to consider selling anything from his collection, we would be honoured to represent him.'

'I can't imagine the circumstances in which that would happen,' said Virginia, 'but if it should arise, I will be in touch immediately.'

'Thank you. I still have time,' he said, looking at his watch, 'to check the lower ground floor before I leave.'

'I can't imagine you'll find anything below stairs,' said Virginia, 'other than a few ancient pots and pans, and an antique Aga that I've been telling the duke should have been replaced years ago.'

Poltimore laughed dutifully, before finishing the last mouthful of his bread and butter pudding.

'The car will be ready to take you to the station at two forty,' said Virginia, 'which should give you plenty of time to catch the five past three back to London.'

◄○►

Virginia was talking to the gardener about planting a new bed of fuchsias when she looked up to see Poltimore running towards her. She waited for him to catch his breath, before he said, 'I think I may have found something quite remarkable, but I'll need to check with the head of our Chinese department before I can be absolutely certain.'

'Your Chinese department?'

'I nearly missed them, hidden away in a corner of the downstairs corridor, near the pantry.'

'Missed what?' said Virginia, trying not to display her impatience.

'Two large blue and white vases. I checked the markings on the base, and I think they just might be Ming Dynasty.'

Virginia kept her tone casual. 'Are they valuable enough to be added to the inventory?'

'Without question, if they turn out to be originals. A similar pair, but much smaller than yours, came up at auction in New York a couple of years ago, and the hammer price was over a million dollars. I've taken some photographs of them,' Poltimore continued, 'in particular the distinctive markings on the base, which I'll show to our Chinese expert as soon as I get back to Bond Street. I'll write to let you know his opinion.'

'I would prefer you to telephone me,' said Virginia. 'I wouldn't want to get the duke's hopes up, only to find it was a false alarm.'

'I'll call you some time tomorrow,' Poltimore promised.

'Good, then that's settled,' said Virginia, as a footman came out carrying a suitcase which he placed in the boot of the car.

'I'll say goodbye now, your grace.'

'Not quite yet, Mr Poltimore,' said Virginia, who joined him in the back. She waited until they had set off down the drive before whispering, 'If the duke were to decide to sell the vases, how would you recommend he go about it?'

'If our expert confirms they are Ming Dynasty, we would advise you which sale would be most appropriate for a piece of such historic importance.'

'If possible, I'd like to sell them with the minimum of fuss and the maximum discretion.'

'Of course, your grace,' said Poltimore. 'But I should

point out that if the Hertford name were attached to the vases, one could expect them to fetch a far higher price. I'm sure you're aware that two things really matter when a discovery of this potential importance comes up for auction: provenance, and when the piece last appeared on the market. So if you can combine the name of Hertford with three hundred years of history, frankly it would be an auctioneer's dream.'

'Yes, I can see that would make a difference,' said Virginia, 'but for personal reasons, the duke might want to remain anonymous.'

'Whatever you decided we would, of course, abide by your wishes,' said Poltimore as the car drew up outside the station.

The chauffeur opened the door to allow the duchess to get out.

'I look forward to hearing from you, Mr Poltimore,' she said, as the train pulled into the station.

'I'll call you as soon as I have any news, and whatever decision you make, be assured that Sotheby's will be proud to serve you with the utmost discretion.' He gave a slight nod before climbing aboard.

Virginia didn't return to the car, but crossed the foot-bridge to platform number two, and only had to wait for a few minutes before the London train pulled in. When she waved to the duke, he rewarded her with a huge smile.

'Good of you to come and meet me, old gal,' he said, bending down to kiss her.

'Don't be silly, Perry, I couldn't wait to see you.'

'Has anything interesting happened while I was away?' the duke asked as he handed the stationmaster his ticket.

'I've planted a bed of fuchsia, which should flower in

the summer, but frankly I'm more interested in hearing everything that happened at your regimental dinner.'

◄o►

Poltimore was as good as his word, and rang the following afternoon to let Virginia know that Mr Li Wong, Sotheby's Chinese expert, had studied the photographs of the vases, and in particular the distinctive markings on their bases, and was fairly confident that they were Ming Dynasty. However, he stressed that he would need to examine them in person before he could give his final imprimatur.

Li appeared a fortnight later, when the duke was visiting his doctor in Harley Street for his annual check-up. He didn't need to stay overnight, as a few minutes was quite enough to convince him that the two vases were works of genius which would ignite global interest among the leading Chinese collectors. He was also able to add one corroborative piece of scholarship.

After spending a day at the British Museum, he had come across a reference which suggested that the fourth Duke of Hertford had led a diplomatic mission to Peking some time in the early nineteenth century, on behalf of His Majesty's government, and the two vases were probably a gift from the Emperor Jiaqing to mark the occasion. Li went on to remind the duchess, more than once, that this historical evidence would add considerable value to the pieces. A gift of two Ming vases from an emperor to a duke who was representing a king would have the auction world buzzing.

Li was clearly disappointed when Virginia told him that if the duke were to part with the vases, it was most unlikely that he would want the world to know he was selling off a family heirloom.

'Perhaps his grace would agree to the simple nomen-clature, "the property of a nobleman"?' suggested the Chinese expert.

'A most satisfactory compromise,' agreed the duchess, who didn't accompany Li to the station, as he would be safely back in London long before the duke boarded his train for Hertford.

—◦—

As Virginia knocked on the door of the duke's study, it brought back memories of being summoned by her father to be given a lecture on her shortcomings. But not today. She was about to be told the finer details of Perry's will.

He had asked her during breakfast to join him in his study around eleven, as he was seeing the family solicitor at ten to discuss the contents of his will, and in particular the wording of the proposed codicil. He reminded Virginia that she still hadn't told him if there was anything she would particularly like as a keepsake.

As she entered her husband's study, Perry and the solicitor immediately rose from their places and remained standing until she had taken the seat between them.

'Your timing couldn't be better,' said Perry, 'because I've just agreed the wording of a new codicil that concerns you, and which Mr Blatchford will attach to my will.'

Virginia bowed her head.

'I fear, Mr Blatchford,' said the duke, 'that my wife finds this whole experience a little distressing, but I have managed to convince her that one has to deal with such matters if the taxman is not to become your next of kin.' Blatchford nodded sagely. 'Perhaps you would be kind enough to take the duchess through the details of the codicil, so we need never refer to the subject again.'

'Certainly, your grace,' said the elderly solicitor, who looked as if he might die before Perry. 'On the duke's demise,' he continued, 'you will be given a house on the estate along with the appropriate staff to assist you. You will also receive a monthly stipend of five thousand pounds.'

'Will that be enough, old gal?' interrupted the duke.

'More than enough, my darling,' said Virginia quietly. 'Don't forget that my dear brother still provides me with a monthly allowance, which I never manage to spend.'

'I understand,' continued Blatchford, 'that the duke has asked you to choose some personal memento to remember him by. I wonder if you have decided what that might be?'

It was some time before Virginia raised her head and said, 'Perry has a walking stick that would remind me of him whenever I take my evening stroll around the garden.'

'Surely you'd like something a little more substantial than that, old gal?'

'No, that will be quite enough, my darling.' Virginia was quiet for some time before she added, 'Although I confess there are a couple of old vases gathering dust below stairs that I've always admired, but only if you could bear to part with them.' Virginia held her breath.

'There's no mention of them in the family inventory,' said Blatchford, 'so with your permission, your grace, I'll add the walking stick along with the pair of vases to the codicil, and then you can engross the final copy.'

'Of course, of course,' said the duke, who hadn't been below stairs since he was a boy.

'Thank you, Perry,' said Virginia, 'that's so very generous of you. While you're here, Mr Blatchford, could I ask for your guidance on another matter?'

'Of course, your grace.'

'Perhaps I should also be thinking about making a will.'

'Very wise, if I may say so, your grace. I'll be happy to draw one up for you. Perhaps I can make an appointment to see you on some other occasion?'

'That won't be necessary, Mr Blatchford. I intend to leave everything I possess to my beloved husband.'

33

Twenty minutes later an ambulance, siren blaring, pulled up outside the castle gates.

Two orderlies, under the direction of Virginia, followed her quickly up to the duke's bedroom. They lifted him gently on to the stretcher and then proceeded slowly back downstairs. She held Perry's hand and he managed a weak smile as they lifted him into the ambulance.

Virginia climbed in and sat on the bench beside her husband, never letting go of his hand as the ambulance sped through the countryside. After another twenty minutes they arrived at the local cottage hospital.

A doctor, two nurses and three orderlies were waiting for them. The duke was lifted on to a trolley which was wheeled through the open doors to a private room that had been hastily prepared.

All three doctors who examined him came to the same conclusion, a minor heart attack. Despite their diagnosis, the senior registrar insisted that he remain in the hospital for further tests.

◄○►

Virginia visited Perry in hospital every morning, and although he repeatedly told her he was right as rain, the doctors wouldn't agree to release him until they were convinced he had fully recovered, and Virginia made it clear, in Matron's hearing, that he must carry out the doctors' orders to the letter.

The following day she telephoned each of the duke's children, repeating the doctors' diagnosis of a minor heart attack, and as long as he took some exercise and was careful with his diet, there was no reason to believe he wouldn't live for many more years. Virginia emphasized that the doctors didn't feel it was necessary for them to rush home, and looked forward to seeing them all at Christmas.

A diet of watermelon, boiled fish and green salads with no dressing didn't improve the duke's temper, and when he was finally released after a week, Matron presented Virginia with a list of 'dos and don'ts': no sugar, no carbohydrates, no fried food, and only one glass of wine at dinner – which was not to be followed by brandy or a cigar. Just as important, she explained, was that he should take a walk in the fresh air for an hour a day. Matron gave Virginia a copy of the hospital's recommended diet, which Virginia promised she would give to Cook the moment they got home.

Cook never caught sight of Matron's diet sheet, and allowed the duke to start the day as he always had, with a bowl of porridge and brown sugar, followed by fried eggs, sausages, two rashers of bacon and baked beans (his favourite), smothered in HP Sauce. This was accompanied by white toast with butter and marmalade and piping hot coffee with two spoonfuls of sugar. He would then retire to read *The Times* in his study, where a packet of Silk Cut had been left on the armrest of his chair. At around eleven thirty, the butler would bring him a mug of hot chocolate and a slice of coffee cake, just in case he felt a little peckish, which kept him going until lunch.

Lunch consisted of fish, just as Matron had recommended. However, it wasn't boiled but fried in batter, with a large bowl of chips near at hand. Chocolate pudding – Matron had made no mention of chocolate – was rarely turned down by the duke, followed by more coffee and his first cigar of the day.

Virginia allowed him an afternoon siesta, before waking him for a long walk around the estate so he could work up an appetite for his next meal. After he'd changed for dinner, the duke would enjoy a sherry, perhaps two, before going through to the dining room, where Virginia took a particular interest in selecting the wines that would accompany their meal. Cook was well aware that the duke liked nothing better than a rare sirloin steak with roast potatoes and all the trimmings. Cook felt it was nothing less than her duty to keep his grace happy, and hadn't he always had second helpings of everything?

After dinner, the butler would dutifully pour a balloon of brandy and clip the duke's Havana cigar before lighting it. When they eventually retired to bed, Virginia did everything in her power to arouse the duke, and although she rarely succeeded, he always fell asleep exhausted.

Virginia kept to her routine slavishly, indulging her husband's slightest whim, while appearing to any onlooker to be caring, attentive and devoted. She made no comment when he could no longer do up the buttons on his trousers, or dozed off for long spells during the afternoon, and told anyone who asked, 'I've never seen him fitter, and it wouldn't surprise me if he lived to a hundred,' although that wasn't quite what she had in mind.

◄○►

Virginia spent some considerable time preparing for Perry's seventy-second birthday. A special occasion, was how she described it to all and sundry, on which the duke should be allowed, just for once, to indulge himself.

After enjoying a hearty breakfast, Perry went off to shoot pheasants with his pals, carrying his favourite Purdey shotgun under his arm, and a flask of whisky in his hip pocket. He was on top form that morning and bagged twenty-one birds before returning to the castle, exhausted.

His spirits were lifted by the sight of guinea fowl, sausages, onions, fried potatoes and a jug of thick gravy. Could a man ask for more, he demanded of his chums. They agreed wholeheartedly, and continually raised their glasses to toast his health. The last of them didn't depart until dusk, by which time he had fallen asleep.

'You take such good care of me, old gal,' he said when Virginia woke him in time to change for dinner. 'I'm a remarkably lucky man.'

'Well, it is a special occasion, my darling,' said Virginia, presenting him with her birthday present. His eyes lit up when he tore off the wrapping paper to discover a box of Romeo y Julieta cigars.

'Churchill's favourites,' he declared.

'And he lived to over ninety,' Virginia reminded him.

During dinner, the duke looked a little tired. However, he managed to finish his blancmange before enjoying a glass of brandy and the first of the Churchill cigars. When they finally climbed the stairs just after midnight, he had

315

to cling on to the bannister as he struggled to mount each step, his other arm firmly around Virginia's shoulders.

When they finally reached the bedroom, he only managed a few more paces before collapsing on to the bed. Virginia began to slowly undress him, but he'd fallen asleep before she'd taken off his shoes.

By the time she had undressed and joined him in bed, he was snoring peacefully. Virginia had never seen him looking so contented. She switched off the light.

◄o►

When Virginia woke the following morning, she turned over to find the duke still had a smile on his face. She pulled back the curtains, returned to the bedside and took a closer look. She thought he looked a little pale. She checked his pulse, but couldn't find it. She sat on the end of the bed and thought carefully about what she should do next.

First, she removed any signs of the cigar and the brandy, replacing them with a bowl of nuts and a carafe of water with a slice of lemon. She opened the window to allow in some fresh air, and once she had checked the room a second time, she sat down at her dressing table, checked her make-up and composed herself.

Virginia allowed a few moments to go by before she took a deep breath and let out a piercing scream. She then rushed to the door and, for the first time since she'd married Perry, left the bedroom wearing a dressing gown. She ran down the wide staircase and the moment she saw Lomax, her voice breaking, she said, 'Call an ambulance. The duke has had another heart attack.'

The butler immediately picked up the phone in the hall.

Dr Ainsley arrived thirty minutes later, by which time Virginia had dressed and was waiting for him in the hall. She accompanied him to the bedroom. It didn't take a long examination before he told the dowager duchess something she already knew.

Virginia broke down in tears and no one was able to console her. However, she did manage to send telegrams to Clarence, Alice and Camilla, after ordering the butler to move the two blue and white vases from the servants' corridor and place them in the duke's bedroom. Lomax was puzzled by the request, and later that evening he said to the housekeeper, 'She's not herself, poor thing.'

The chauffeur was even more puzzled when he was instructed to take the vases down to London and drop them off at Sotheby's before going on to Heathrow to pick up Clarence and bring him back to Castle Hertford.

The dowager duchess wore black, a colour that suited her, and over a light breakfast she read the duke's obituary in *The Times*, which was long on compliments, while being short on accomplishments. However, there was one sentence that brought a smile to her face: *The thirteenth Duke of Hertford died peacefully in his sleep.*

34

VIRGINIA HAD GIVEN considerable thought to how she should conduct herself during the next few days. Once the family had gone their separate ways after the funeral, she intended to make some fairly radical changes at Castle Hertford.

The fourteenth duke was the first member of the family to arrive, and Virginia was standing on the top step waiting to greet him. As he walked up the steps, she gave a slight curtsey, to acknowledge the new order.

'Virginia, what a sad occasion for all of us,' said Clarence. 'But it's at least a comfort for me to know that you were by his side to the last.'

'It's so kind of you to say so, Clarence. What a blessed relief it is that my dear Perry suffered no pain when he passed away.'

'Yes, I was relieved to hear that Papa died peacefully in his sleep. Let's be thankful for small mercies.'

'I hope it won't be too long before I join him,' said Virginia, 'because, like Queen Victoria, I will mourn my dear husband until the day I die.' The butler and two footmen appeared and began to unload the car. 'I've put you in your old room for the time being,' said Virginia.

'But of course I will move out to the Dower House, just as soon as my dear Perry has been buried.'

'There's no hurry,' said Clarence. 'I'll be returning to my regiment after the funeral, and in any case we're going to have to rely on you to keep things ticking over in my absence.'

'I'll be happy to do whatever I can. Why don't we discuss what you have in mind once you've unpacked and had something to eat?'

The duke was a few minutes late for lunch, and apologized, explaining that several people had telephoned, requesting to see him urgently.

Virginia could only wonder who had called, but satisfied herself with saying, 'I thought we should hold the funeral on Thursday, but only if that meets with your approval.'

'I'm happy to abide by your wishes,' said the duke. 'Perhaps you could also give some thought to the order of service, and suggest who you think should be invited to the reception afterwards?'

'I've already begun working on a list. I'll let you have it later today.'

'Thank you, Virginia. I knew I could rely on you. I have some meetings to attend this afternoon, so I hope you'll be around when Alice arrives.'

'Of course. And when are you expecting Camilla and her family?'

'Later this evening, but as I'll be in Father's study—'

'Your study,' said Virginia quietly.

'It may take me a little time to get used to that. Would you be kind enough to let me know when Alice arrives?'

◄○►

Virginia was working on the list of guests she wanted to attend the private reception following the funeral, as well as those she didn't, when a taxi drew up outside the castle and Alice stepped out. Once again, she took her place at the top of the steps.

'Poor Virginia,' were Alice's first words as she greeted her. 'How are you bearing up?'

'Not well. But everyone's been so kind and understanding, which has been a great comfort.'

'Of course they have,' said Alice. 'After all, you were his rock and soulmate.'

'It's so kind of you to say so,' said Virginia, as she led Alice up the staircase to the guest bedroom she had chosen for her. 'I'll let Clarence know you're here.'

She strolled downstairs and went into the duke's study without knocking, to find Clarence deep in conversation with Mr Moxton, the estate manager. Both men immediately stood as she entered.

'You asked me to let you know when Alice arrived. I've put her in the Carlyle Room. I hope you'll be able to join us for tea in about half an hour.'

'That may not be possible,' said the duke, giving her a curt nod, clearly not pleased to have been interrupted, which Virginia found somewhat disconcerting. She left without another word and retreated to the drawing room, where Montgomery, Perry's old Labrador, sat up and began wagging his tail. She took a seat near the open door, which allowed her to keep an eye on the comings and goings in the corridor outside. She intended to have a word with Clarence about replacing Moxton in the not-too-distant future.

The next person to enter the duke's study was the butler, who didn't come out for another forty minutes.

He then disappeared below stairs, only to return a few moments later accompanied by the cook, who Virginia couldn't recall ever seeing on the ground floor.

Another twenty minutes passed before Cook reappeared and scurried back downstairs. Virginia could only wonder what had taken them so long, unless they'd been discussing the menu for the reception, a responsibility she had rather assumed the duke would leave to her.

Virginia was distracted by a loud knock on the front door, but before she could answer it, Lomax appeared and opened the door.

'Good afternoon, Dr Ainsley,' he said. 'His grace is expecting you.'

As they crossed the hall, Moxton came out of the study, shook hands with Dr Ainsley and quickly left the house. Although he couldn't have missed Virginia standing in the doorway of the drawing room, he made no attempt to acknowledge her. She would get rid of him as soon as the duke returned to his regiment.

Virginia was pleased to see Alice coming down the stairs and hurried out of the drawing room to join her. 'Shall we go and see your brother?' she said, without waiting for a reply. 'I know he's been looking forward to seeing you,' she added as she opened the study door and entered without knocking. Once again both men rose.

'Alice has just come down and I remembered you wanted to see her immediately.'

'Of course,' said Clarence, giving his sister a hug. 'It's wonderful to see you, my dear.'

'I thought we might all have tea together in the drawing room.'

'That's very thoughtful of you, Virginia,' said Clarence, 'but I'd like a few moments alone with my sister, if you don't mind.'

Alice looked surprised by her brother's waspish tone of voice, and Virginia hesitated for a moment before she said, 'Yes, of course,' and retreated to the drawing room. This time Montgomery didn't even raise his head.

Dr Ainsley came out of the study twenty minutes later, and also departed without making any effort to pay his respects to the grieving widow. Virginia waited patiently for the duke to summon her to the study, but no such call came, and when a maid, whose name she could never remember, began to turn on the lights all over the house, she decided it was time to change for dinner. She had just stepped out of the bath when she heard a car coming down the drive. She went over to the window and peered out to see Camilla and her family being greeted by Clarence. She dressed quickly, and when she opened her bedroom door a few minutes later she saw the butler and the two children heading towards the corner suite, which she hadn't allocated to them.

'Where is your mother?' asked Virginia.

The children swung round, but it was Lomax who responded. 'His grace asked Lady Camilla and her husband to join him in the study and requested that they should not be disturbed.'

Virginia closed the door behind her. She had never known Lomax to address her in that offhand manner. She tried to concentrate on her make-up, but couldn't help wondering what they were discussing in the duke's old study. She assumed all would be revealed over dinner.

Half an hour later, Virginia walked slowly down the wide staircase, across the hall and into the drawing room, only to find nobody else was there. She sat and waited, but no one joined her. When the gong was struck at eight o'clock, she made her way through to the dining room, to find the table had been laid for one.

'Where are the rest of the family?' she demanded when Lomax appeared carrying a small tureen of soup.

'His grace, Lady Camilla and Lady Alice are having a light supper in the library,' he said without further explanation.

Virginia shivered, although the fire was crackling in the hearth. 'And the children?'

'They have already eaten, and as they were tired following their long journey they went straight to bed.'

A feeling of foreboding gripped her and she tried to convince herself that there was nothing to worry about, but without a great deal of conviction. She waited until the clock in the hall struck nine before leaving the dining room and making her way slowly upstairs to her room. She undressed and went to bed, but she didn't sleep. She had never felt more alone.

◄○►

Virginia was relieved when Clarence and Alice joined her for breakfast the following morning, only to find that the conversation was stilted and formal as if she were a stranger in her own home.

'I've almost completed the order of service,' volunteered Virginia, 'and I thought perhaps—'

'No need to waste any more of your time on that,' interrupted Clarence. 'I have an appointment with the bishop at ten this morning, and he told me he agreed all the details of the ceremony with my father some time ago.'

'And does he agree with me that Thursday—'

'No,' said Clarence equally firmly. 'He recommends Friday, which will be more convenient for my father's friends who will be travelling up from London.'

Virginia hesitated before saying, 'And the guest list, would you like to see my recommendations?'

'We settled on the final list last night,' said Alice. 'But if there are one or two names you'd like to be added, do let me know.'

'Isn't there anything I can do to help?' asked Virginia, trying not to sound desperate.

'No, thank you,' said Clarence. 'You've done quite enough already.' He folded his napkin and rose from his place. 'Please excuse me. I don't want to be late for the bishop.' He left without another word.

'And I ought to be getting on,' said Alice. 'I've rather a lot to do if everything is to be in place by Friday.'

After breakfast, Virginia took a stroll around the grounds as she tried to fathom what had caused such a sudden change of attitude. She derived some comfort from the fact that she still had the Dower House, five thousand pounds a month, and two Ming vases that Li Wong had confirmed were worth at least a million. Her smile disappeared when she saw Camilla and her husband coming out of the estate manager's office.

Virginia had lunch on her own, and decided to go into town and buy some new clothes, as she intended to shed her widow's weeds the moment they had all departed. When she got back to the castle that evening, there was light coming from under the study door, and she thought she could hear Camilla's strident voice.

Virginia had supper alone in her room, one thought

continually returning to her mind. She was beginning to wish Perry was still alive.

◄○►

St Albans Abbey was already packed by the time Virginia made her entrance. The senior usher accompanied the dowager duchess down the aisle to a place in the second row. She didn't feel able to protest while a thousand eyes were on her.

As the first chimes of eleven sounded on the cathedral clock, the organ struck up and the congregation rose as one. The coffin, draped in decorations and honours, processed slowly down the aisle, borne on the shoulders of six Coldstream Guards, followed by the immediate family. Once it had been placed on the bier in the chancery, the duke, his two sisters and the grandchildren took their places in the front row. They didn't look back.

The service was a blur to Virginia, who was still trying to work out why they were sending her to Coventry. During the burial ceremony, held in the grounds of the cathedral, she was only allowed to step forward and cast a spadeful of earth on to the coffin before she got back in line. Once the family and a few close friends had left the graveside, she had to cadge a lift back to the castle with Percy, the duke's uncle, who accepted her explanation that there must have been an oversight, but then they've all been under a great deal of pressure.

During the reception, Virginia mingled with the guests, many of whom were kind and offered words of sympathy, while others turned away the moment she approached them. However, the greatest slight was saved until after the last guest had departed, when Clarence spoke to her for the first time that day.

'While you were at the service,' he said, 'all your possessions were packed and moved into the Dower House. A car is waiting to take you there immediately. There will be a family meeting in my study at eleven tomorrow morning, which I hope you will attend. There are some serious matters I wish to discuss with you,' he added, reminding Virginia of her father.

Without another word, the duke walked to the front door, opened it and waited for Virginia to leave, so she could begin her first day of banishment.

35

Virginia rose early the following morning and took her time inspecting the Dower House, which turned out to be quite large enough for someone living on her own. Her staff consisted of an under-butler, a maid and a cook, no more and no less than Perry had specified in his will.

At ten to eleven a car arrived to take her to the castle, which only a few days ago had been her sole domain.

The front door of the castle opened as the car drew up, and after a perfunctory 'Good morning, your grace,' the butler accompanied her to her husband's old study. Lomax knocked quietly on the door, opened it and stood aside to allow the dowager duchess to enter.

'Good morning,' said Clarence as he rose from his place behind the desk. He waited until Virginia had taken the only available chair. She smiled at his sisters, but they didn't return the compliment.

'Thank you for coming,' began Clarence, as if she'd had any choice. 'We felt it would be useful to let you know what we have planned for the future.'

Virginia had a feeling he meant 'your future'. 'That's considerate of you,' she said.

'I intend to report back to my regiment in a few days'

time, and I won't be returning before Christmas. Alice will be flying back to New York on Monday.'

'Then who will run the estate?' asked Virginia, hoping they had at last come to their senses.

'I have entrusted that responsibility to Shane and Camilla – with my father's blessing, I might add, as he accepted that I'd always wanted to be a soldier and was never cut out to be a farmer. Shane, Camilla and the children will live at the castle, fulfilling another of my father's wishes.'

'How very sensible,' said Virginia. 'I hope you'll allow me to help out, at least during the transition?'

'That won't be necessary,' said Camilla, speaking for the first time. 'We've received a good offer for our farm in New Zealand, and my husband will be flying back to finalize the sale and deal with any other personal matters that need attending to, after which he'll return to take over the management of the estate. With the help of Mr Moxton, I will keep things ticking over until he's back.'

'It's just that I thought—'

'No need to,' said Camilla. 'We've thought of everything.'

'And I fear, Virginia, there is another matter I have to raise with you,' said Clarence. Virginia shifted uneasily in her seat. 'It has been brought to my attention by Mr Moxton that my father, without my knowledge, made you a loan of £185,000. Fortunately, Moxton had the good sense to formalize the arrangement,' said Clarence, as he turned to the third page of a document Virginia remembered signing. She suddenly wished she'd spent a little more time reading the first two pages.

'The loan was made for a period of five years, with a compound interest rate of five per cent. If my father died before then, the full amount was to be repaid within twenty-eight days. I have consulted my accountant, and he has written to let me know –' he turned his attention to a letter lying on the desk – 'that with accumulated interest, the exact amount you currently owe the estate is £209,145. So I have to ask you, Virginia, if you have sufficient funds to cover that amount.'

'But Perry told me that if he died before me – and I remember his exact words – the slate would be wiped clean.'

'Do you have any proof of that?' asked Camilla.

'No. But he gave me his word, which surely should be enough.'

'It's not his words we're discussing,' said Camilla, 'but yours.'

'And if he did,' said Clarence, 'he certainly didn't let Moxton know of any such arrangement. There's no mention of it in the original agreement, which my father also signed.' Clarence swivelled it around so Virginia could see a signature she recognized well.

'I will have to consult my lawyers,' she stammered, unable to think of anything else to say.

'We have already consulted ours,' said Alice, 'and Mr Blatchford has confirmed that there is no mention in Father's will of any such gift, just an allowance of five thousand pounds a month, a briar walking stick and two porcelain vases.'

Virginia suppressed a smile.

'If you are unable to repay the loan,' continued Clarence, 'our accountant has come up with a compromise which I hope you will find acceptable.' He returned to the letter. 'If we were to withhold your monthly allowance of five thousand pounds, the full amount would be paid off in approximately four years, at which time your allowance would be restored.'

'However, should you die at some time during the next four years,' interjected Camilla, 'let me assure you, the slate would be wiped clean.'

Virginia remained silent for some time before blurting out, 'But how can I be expected to survive in the meantime?'

'My father told me, on more than one occasion,' said Clarence, 'that your brother gives you a generous monthly allowance which you once said you were never able to spend, so I rather assumed . . .'

'He stopped those payments the day I married your father.'

'Then we must hope that once he has been acquainted with your present circumstances, he will be willing to restore your allowance, otherwise you will have to rely on your substantial assets, which you also mentioned to my father. Of course, if you are able to repay the full amount of the loan within twenty-eight days that will solve the whole problem.'

Virginia bowed her head and burst into tears, but when she eventually looked up, it was clear that none of them was moved.

'Perhaps this would be a good opportunity for us to discuss some domestic matters,' said Camilla. 'As my brother has explained, my husband will be taking over the management of the estate, and our family will be living here in the castle. Clarence and Alice will be returning from time to time, but in my brother's absence, I will be mistress of Castle Hertford.' Camilla waited for her words to sink in before she continued. 'I wish to make it clear, so there can be no misunderstanding in the future, that you will not be welcome here at any time, and that includes Christmas or any other holidays. You will also make no attempt to contact either of my children, or any members of the castle staff. I have made my wishes clear to Mr Lomax.'

Virginia looked at Clarence and then at Alice, but it was obvious the family were acting as one.

'Unless you have anything to ask concerning your future arrangements,' said Clarence, 'we have nothing more to discuss with you.'

Virginia rose from her place and left the room with as much dignity as she could muster. She walked slowly across the hall to the front door, which the butler was holding open. He didn't address her as she walked out of the castle for the last time. All she heard was the door closing behind her.

Another door was already open so she could be driven back to the Dower House. Once Virginia had been dropped off, she went straight to her study, picked up the phone and dialled a London number, to be greeted with the first friendly voice she had heard that day.

'How nice to hear from you, your grace. How can I help?'

'I need to make an appointment to see you as quickly as possible, Mr Poltimore, because I've changed my mind.'

36

'I HAVE NO DOUBT,' said Poltimore, 'that you've made a wise decision. But can I ask what caused you to change your mind?'

'My late husband wouldn't have wanted anyone to think he was selling off the family heirlooms.'

'And the new duke?' asked Poltimore. 'How does he feel?'

'Frankly, Clarence wouldn't know the difference between Ming and Tupperware.'

Poltimore wasn't sure whether to laugh, and simply said, 'Before you agree to allow the vases to go under the hammer, your grace, you might like to know that I've had an offer of seven hundred thousand pounds for them from a private dealer in Chicago, and I'm confident I can push him over the million mark. And perhaps it could be done without anyone even knowing the transaction had taken place.'

'But surely a dealer will simply be selling my vases on to one of his customers?'

'While at the same time making a handsome profit for himself, which is why I'm confident they will fetch a far higher price at auction.'

'But there must be an outside chance that if the vases do come up for auction, the same dealer might pick them up for less than a million.'

'That's most unlikely, your grace, with a piece of this importance. And despite that possibility, I still consider it a risk worth taking, because I've already approached half a dozen leading collectors in the field, and they all showed considerable interest, including the director of the National Museum of China in Beijing.'

'You've convinced me,' said Virginia. 'So what should I do next?'

'Once you've signed a release form, you can leave the rest to us. You're well in time to catch the autumn sale, which is always one of the most popular of the year, and I have already suggested that we feature the Hertford vases on the cover of the catalogue. Be assured, our customers won't be in any doubt how important we consider these pieces to be.'

'Can I mention something in the strictest confidence, Mr Poltimore?'

'Of course, your grace.'

'I am most keen that there should be the minimum of publicity before the auction, but the maximum amount possible afterwards.'

'That shouldn't be a problem, especially as the arts correspondents from all the national newspapers will be attending the sale. And if the vases fetch the sort of price we anticipate, it will generate considerable interest in the press, so you can be sure that the following morning, everyone will be aware of your triumph.'

'I'm not interested in everyone,' said Virginia, 'just one member of one particular family.'

◄○►

'A gold-plated bitch,' said Virginia.

'That bad?' asked Priscilla Bingham, once their dessert plates had been whisked away.

'Worse. She has the airs and graces of a duchess, but she's nothing more than the wife of a jumped-up antipodean sheep farmer.'

'And you said she's the second daughter?'

'That's right. But she behaves as if she's the mistress of Castle Hertford.'

'Wouldn't all that change if the duke were to get married and decide to reclaim his family seat?'

'That's unlikely. Clarence is married to the army, and hopes to be the next colonel of the regiment.'

'Like his father before him.'

'He's nothing like his father,' said Virginia. 'If Perry were still alive, he would never have allowed them to humiliate me in this way. But I intend to have the last laugh.' She extracted a newly minted auction catalogue from her bag and handed it to her friend.

'Are these the two vases you told me about?' asked Priscilla, looking admiringly at the cover.

'They are indeed. And you'll see just how much I'm going to make if you turn to lot forty-three.'

Priscilla flicked through the pages and when she reached Lot 43, Two Ming Vases, circa 1462, her eyes settled on the estimate. Her mouth opened, but no words came out.

'How very generous of the duke,' she eventually managed.

'He had no idea how much they were worth,' said Virginia, 'otherwise he would never have let them go.'

'But surely the family will find out long before the sale takes place.'

'Seems unlikely. Clarence is holed up somewhere in Borneo, Alice is in New York peddling bottles of perfume and Camilla never leaves the castle unless she has to.'

'But I thought you wanted them to find out?'

'Not until after the sale, by which time I will have banked the cheque.'

'But even then, they may not hear about it.'

'Mr Poltimore, who's conducting the auction, tells me he's already had calls from several of the leading arts correspondents, so we can expect extensive coverage in the press the following morning. That's when they'll find out, and by then it will be too late because I will have banked the money. I do hope you'll be able to come to the auction next Thursday evening, Priscilla, and then you can join me for dinner afterwards at Annabel's to celebrate. I've even booked Perry's favourite table. It will be just like old times.'

'Old times,' repeated Priscilla, as a waiter appeared and served coffee. 'Which reminds me, do you ever hear from your ex, following your little coup with Mellor Travel?'

'If you mean Giles, he sent me a Christmas card for the first time in years, but I didn't return the compliment.'

'I see he's back on the front bench.'

'Yes, he's been pitched against his sister. But he's so wet, I expect he regularly lets her off the hook,' Virginia added as she took a sip of coffee.

'And now she's a baroness.'

'She's a life peer,' said Virginia. 'Anyway, she only got her place in the Lords because she backed Margaret Thatcher when she stood for the leadership of the Tory party. It's almost enough to make one consider voting Labour.'

'To be fair, Virginia, the press all seem to agree that she's doing a rather good job as a health minister.'

'She'd be better off spending her time worrying about the health of her own family. Drink, drugs, three in a bed, assaulting the police, and her granddaughter ending up in jail.'

'It was only for one night,' Priscilla reminded her. 'And she was back at the Slade the following term.'

'Someone must have pulled some very long strings to make that possible,' said Virginia.

'Probably your ex-husband,' suggested Priscilla. 'He may be in opposition, but I suspect he still has a lot of clout.'

'And what about your husband?' asked Virginia, wanting to change the subject. 'I hope all's well with him,' she added, hoping to hear otherwise.

'He's still producing a hundred thousand jars of fish paste a week, which allows me to live like a duchess, even if I'm not one.'

'And is your son still doing the PR for Farthings Kaufman?' asked Virginia, ignoring the barb.

'Yes, he is. In fact, Clive's hoping it won't be long before they ask him to join the main board.'

'It must help with Robert being an old friend of the chairman.'

'And how's your son?' asked Priscilla, trading blow for blow.

'Freddie is not my son, as you well know, Priscilla. And when I last heard, he'd run away from school, which would have solved all my problems, but unfortunately he returned a few days later.'

'So who takes care of him during the holidays?'

'My brother Archie, who lives off the income from the family distillery, which Father promised to me.'

'You haven't done too badly, duchess,' said Priscilla, looking back down at the Sotheby's catalogue.

'You may well be right, but I'm still going to make certain it's me who has the last laugh,' said Virginia as a waiter appeared by their side, unsure who he should present the bill to. Although Virginia had invited Priscilla to join her for lunch, she was painfully aware that if she wrote a cheque it would bounce. Still, all that was about to change.

'My turn next time,' said Virginia. 'Annabel's on Thursday night?' she added, looking the other way.

◄○►

When Priscilla Bingham returned to her home in the Boltons, she left the Sotheby's catalogue on the hall table.

'Quite magnificent,' said Bob when he spotted the cover. 'Are you considering bidding for them?'

'Nice idea,' said Priscilla, 'but you'd have to sell an awful lot more fish paste before we could consider that.'

'Then why are you interested?'

'They belong to Virginia, and she's having to put them up for sale because the Hertford family have found a way of cheating her out of her monthly allowance.'

'I'd like to hear the Hertfords' side of the story before I make a judgement on that,' said Bob, as he flicked through the catalogue looking for Lot 43. He let out a low whistle when he read the estimate. 'I'm surprised the family were willing to part with them.'

'They weren't. The duke left them to Virginia in his will without the slightest idea what they were worth.'

Bob pursed his lips, but said nothing.

'By the way,' said Priscilla, 'are we still going to the theatre tonight?'

'Yes,' replied Bob. 'We've got tickets for *The Phantom of the Opera*, and the curtain goes up at seven thirty.'

'Then I still have time to change,' said Priscilla as she headed upstairs.

Bob waited for her to disappear into the bedroom before he picked up the catalogue and slipped into his study. Once he was seated at his desk, he turned his attention to Lot 43 and took his time studying the provenance of the two vases. He began to understand why they were considered so important. He pulled open the bottom drawer of his desk, took out a large brown envelope and slipped the catalogue inside. He wrote on it in bold capitals:

THE DUKE OF HERTFORD
CASTLE HERTFORD
HERTFORDSHIRE

Bob had dropped it into the postbox on the corner and returned home before Priscilla got out of the bath.

37

'SOLD! FOR ONE HUNDRED and twenty thousand pounds,' said Poltimore as he brought down the hammer with a thud. 'Lot thirty-nine,' he said, turning to the next page of the catalogue. 'A white jade marriage bowl of the Qianlong period. Shall I open the bidding at ten thousand pounds?'

Poltimore looked up to see the Dowager Duchess of Hertford making an entrance, accompanied by another lady he didn't recognize. They were led down the central aisle by an assistant and, although the sale room was packed, they were shown to two vacant seats near the front, whose reserved signs were quickly removed before the two ladies sat down.

Virginia enjoyed the murmurs around her, to show that she had arrived. Although the sale had begun at seven o'clock, Mr Poltimore had advised her there was no need to turn up before 7.45, as he didn't anticipate Lot 43 would be coming under the hammer much before 8.15, possibly 8.30.

She and Priscilla were seated in the fifth row, which Poltimore had assured her were the best seats in the room, not unlike house seats in a West End theatre. As

Virginia had no interest in a jade marriage bowl of the Qianlong period, she tried to take in what was going on around her, and hoped it wasn't too obvious that this was the first time she'd attended a major auction.

'It's so exciting,' she said, as she gripped Priscilla's hand, admiring the men in the audience who were dressed in dinner jackets, obviously going on to another function once the sale was over, while the rest were wearing smart suits and colourful ties. But it was the women she was most fascinated by, dressed in their designer outfits with the latest accessories. For them, this was more of a fashion show than an auction, each one trying to outdo the other, as if it were the opening night of a new play. Priscilla had told her that sometimes the final price could be decided by these women, who often had plans to make sure a particular item went home with them that evening, while some of the men would bid higher and higher simply to impress the woman they were with – and sometimes a woman they weren't with.

The room was large and square and Virginia couldn't see an empty seat. She calculated there must be around four hundred potential customers in a room crammed with collectors, dealers and the simply curious. In fact, several of the audience were having to stand at the back.

Directly in front of her stood Mr Poltimore, on a raised semi-circular dais that offered him a perfect view of his victims. Behind the dais stood another, smaller group of senior staff, experts in their own fields, who were there to assist and advise the auctioneer, while others took a note of the successful bidder and the hammer price. To Poltimore's right, reined in behind a loose rope, were a group of men and women, notepads open, pens poised, who Virginia assumed were the press.

'Sold! For twenty-two thousand pounds,' said Polti-more. 'Lot forty, an important polychrome decorated carved wood figure of a seated Luohan, circa 1400. I have an opening bid of one hundred thousand.'

The sale was clearly warming up, and Virginia was delighted when the Luohan sold for £240,000 – forty thousand above its high estimate.

'Lot forty-one, a rare celadon jade model of a lion.'

Virginia had no interest in the lion, which was being held up by a porter for all to see. She looked to her right and noticed for the first time a long table, slightly raised, on which stood a dozen white phones, each manned by a member of Sotheby's staff. Poltimore had explained to her that they represented overseas clients, or those who simply didn't want to be seen in the sale room, although they would sometimes be seated discreetly among the audience. Three of the staff were on the phone, hands cupped, whispering to their clients, while the other nine phones lay idle because, like her, those clients were not interested in the little jade lion. Virginia wondered how many of the phones would be ringing when Poltimore opened the bidding for Lot 43.

'Lot forty-two. An extremely rare, enamelled, im-perial yellow-ground floral Yuhuchunping vase. I have an opening bid of one hundred thousand.'

Virginia could feel her heart beating, aware that the next lot to be announced would be her two Ming vases. When the hammer came down on Lot 42 at £260,000, a buzz of anticipation swept around the room. Poltimore looked down at the duchess and gave her a benign smile as two porters placed the magnificent vases on separate stands each side of him.

'Lot number forty-three. A unique pair of Ming

Dynasty vases, circa 1462, that were a gift from the Emperor Jiaqing to the fourth Duke of Hertford in the early nineteenth century. These vases are in perfect condition and are the property of an English lady of title.' Virginia beamed as the journalists scribbled away. 'I have an opening bid –' a silence descended that had not been experienced before – 'of three hundred thousand pounds.' The silence was replaced with a gasp, as Poltimore leant back casually and looked around the room. 'Am I bid three hundred and fifty?'

Virginia felt an eternity had passed, although it was only a few seconds before Poltimore said, 'Thank you, sir,' as he gestured to a bidder seated near the back of the room. Virginia wanted to look round, but somehow managed to restrain herself.

'Four hundred thousand,' said Poltimore, turning his attention to the long row of phones on his left, where eight members of staff were keeping their clients informed on how the sale was progressing.

'Four hundred thousand,' he repeated, when a smartly dressed young woman at one of the phones raised a hand, while continuing to talk to her client. 'The bid is on the phone at four hundred thousand,' said Poltimore, immediately switching his attention to the gentleman at the back of the room. 'Four hundred and fifty thousand,' he murmured, before returning to the phones. The young woman's hand shot up immediately. Poltimore nodded. 'I have five hundred thousand,' he declared, returning to the man at the back of the room, who shook his head. 'I'm looking for five fifty,' said Poltimore, his eyes once again sweeping the room. 'Five hundred and fifty thousand pounds,' he repeated. Virginia was beginning to wish she'd taken the offer from the dealer in Chicago until Poltimore announced, 'Five fifty,' his voice rising. 'I have a new bidder.' He looked down at the director of the National Museum of China.

When he swung back to the phones, the young woman's hand was already raised. 'Six hundred thousand,' he said, before switching his attention back to the director, who was talking animatedly to the man seated on his right before he eventually looked up and gave Poltimore a slight nod.

'Six hundred and fifty thousand,' said Poltimore, his eye fixed once again on the young woman on the phone. This time her response took a little longer, but eventually a hand was raised. 'Seven hundred thousand pounds,' demanded Poltimore, aware that this would be a world record for a Chinese piece sold at auction.

The journalists were scribbling more furiously than ever, aware that their readers liked world records.

'Seven hundred thousand,' whispered Poltimore in a reverential tone, trying to tempt the director, but making no attempt to hurry him, as he continued his conversation with his colleague. 'Seven hundred thousand?' he offered, as if it were a mere bagatelle. A disturbance at the back of the room caught his eye. He tried to ignore it, but became distracted by two people pushing their way through the crowd as the museum director raised his hand.

'I have seven hundred thousand,' Poltimore said, glancing in the direction of the phones, but he could no longer ignore the man and woman striding down the aisle towards him. A pointless exercise, he could have told them, because every seat was taken. 'Seven hundred and fifty thousand,' he suggested to the director, assuming the pair would turn back, but they didn't stop.

'I have seven hundred and fifty thousand,' Poltimore

said, and following another nod from the director, he turned back to the young woman on the telephone. He tried not to lose his concentration, assuming that a security guard would appear and politely escort the tiresome couple out. He was staring hopefully at the woman on the phone when an authoritative voice announced firmly, 'I am presenting you with a court order to prevent the sale of the Hertford Ming vases.'

The man handed an engrossed document to Poltimore, just as the young woman on the phone raised her hand.

'I have eight hundred thousand,' said Poltimore, almost in a whisper, as a smartly dressed man stepped forward from the small group of experts behind the rostrum, took the document, removed the red tape and studied the contents.

'Eight hundred and fifty thousand?' suggested Poltimore, as some of those seated in the front row began chattering among themselves about what they had just overheard. By the time the Chinese whispers had reached the director, almost everyone in the room except Virginia was talking. She simply stared in silence at the man and woman standing by the rostrum.

'Mark,' said a voice from behind Poltimore. He turned, bent down and listened carefully to the advice of a Sotheby's in-house lawyer, then nodded, raised himself to his full height and declared, with as much gravitas as he could muster, 'Ladies and gentlemen, I am sorry to have to inform you that lot number forty-three has been withdrawn from the sale.' His words were greeted with gasps of disbelief and an outbreak of noisy chattering.

'Lot forty-four,' said Poltimore, not missing a beat. 'A black glazed mottled bowl of the Song Dynasty . . .'

but no one was showing the slightest interest in the Song Dynasty.

The penned-in journalists were trying desperately to escape and discover why Lot 43 had been withdrawn, aware that an article they had hoped might stretch to a couple of columns in the arts section was now destined for the front page. Unfortunately for them, the Sotheby's experts had become like Chinese mandarins, lips sealed and non-communicative.

A posse of photographers broke loose and quickly surrounded the duchess. As their bulbs began to flash she turned to Priscilla for solace, but her friend was no longer there. The Lady Virginia swung back to face the Lady Camilla; two queens on a chess board. One of them about to be toppled, while the other, a woman who never left the castle unless she had to, gave her adversary a disarming smile and whispered, 'Checkmate.'

38

'THE ARISTOCRATS' CLAUSE.'

'I have no idea what you're talking about,' said Virginia as she looked across the desk at her QC.

'It's a common enough clause,' said Sir Edward, 'often inserted as a safeguard in the wills of members of wealthy families to protect their assets from generation to generation.'

'But my husband left the vases to me,' protested Virginia.

'He did indeed. But only, and I quote the relevant clause in his will, as a gift to be enjoyed during your lifetime, after which they will revert to being part of the current duke's estate.'

'But they were thought to be of no value,' said Virginia. 'After all, they'd been languishing below stairs for generations.'

'That may well be so, your grace, but this particular aristocrats' clause goes on to stipulate that this applies to any gift deemed to have a value of more than ten thousand pounds.'

'I still don't know what you're talking about,' said Virginia, sounding even more exasperated than before.

'Then allow me to explain. A clause of this type is often inserted to ensure that aristocratic estates cannot be broken up by females who are not of the bloodline. The most common example is when a member of the family is divorced and the former wife tries to lay claim to valuable pieces of jewellery, works of art or even property. For example, in your particular case, you are permitted to live in the Dower House on the Hertford estate for the rest of your life. However, the deeds of that property remain in the duke's name, and on your demise the house will automatically revert to the family estate.'

'And that also applies to my two vases?'

'I'm afraid it does,' said the elderly silk, 'because they are without question worth more than ten thousand pounds.'

'If only I'd disposed of them privately,' said Virginia ruefully, 'without the duke's knowledge, no one would have been any the wiser.'

'If that had been the case,' said Sir Edward, 'you would have been committing a criminal offence, as it would be assumed that you knew the true value of the vases.'

'But they would never have found out if . . .' said Virginia, almost as if she were talking to herself. 'So how did they find out?'

'A fair question,' said Sir Edward, 'and indeed I asked the Hertfords' legal representatives why they hadn't alerted you to the relevant clause in the late duke's will as soon as they became aware that the sale was taking place. Had they done so, it would have avoided any unnecessary embarrassment for either side, not to mention the lurid headlines that appeared in the national press the following day.'

'And why didn't they?'

'It seems that someone sent the family a copy of the Sotheby's catalogue, which aroused no interest at the time as none of them recognized the vases, even though they were displayed on the cover.'

'Then how did they find out?' repeated Virginia.

'It was evidently the duke's nephew, Tristan, who raised the alarm. He is apparently in the habit of sneaking down to the kitchen during the school holidays. He thought he recognized the vases on the cover of the catalogue and told his mother where he'd last seen them. Lady Camilla contacted the family solicitor, Mr Blatchford, who wasted no time in obtaining a court order to prevent the sale. Having done so, they took the next train to London, and arrived, to quote Mr Blatchford, in the nick of time.'

'What would have happened if they had arrived after the hammer had come down?'

'That would have caused the family an interesting dilemma. The duke would have been left with two choices. He could either have allowed the sale to proceed and collected the money, or sued you for the full amount, in which case I'm bound to say that, in my opinion, a judge would have had no choice but to come down in favour of the Hertford estate, and might even have referred the case to the DPP to decide if you had committed a criminal offence.'

'But I didn't know about the aristocrats' clause,' protested Virginia.

'Ignorance of the law is not a defence,' said Sir Edward firmly. 'And in any case, I suspect a judge would find it hard to believe that you hadn't selected the vases most carefully, and knew only too well what they were worth. I should warn you, that is also Mr Blatchford's opinion.'

'So will the vases have to be returned to the duke?'

'Ironically, no. The Hertfords must also abide by the letter of the law, as well as the spirit of your late husband's will, so the vases will be sent back to you to enjoy for the rest of your life. However, Mr Blatchford has informed me that if you return them within twenty-eight days, the family will take no further legal action, which I consider is generous in the circumstances.'

'But why would they want the vases now, when they'll get them back anyway in the fullness of time?'

'I would suggest that the possibility of them banking a million pounds might well be the answer to that question, your grace. I understand Mr Poltimore has already been in touch with the duke and informed him that he has a private buyer in Chicago lined up.'

'Has the man no morals?'

'However, I would still advise you to return them by October nineteenth if you don't want to face another lengthy and expensive court case.'

'I will, of course, take your advice, Sir Edward,' said Virginia, accepting she had been left with no choice. 'Please assure Mr Blatchford that I will return the vases to Clarence by October nineteenth.'

◄o►

An agreement was struck between Sir Edward and Mr Blatchford that the two Ming Dynasty vases would be returned to the fourteenth Duke of Hertford at his home in Eaton Square, on or before October 19th. In exchange, Clarence had signed a legally binding agreement that no further action would be taken against Virginia, Dowager

Duchess of Hertford, and he also agreed to cover her legal costs for the transaction.

Virginia had a long liquid lunch with Bofie Bridgwater at Mark's Club on October 19th and didn't get back home to Chelsea until nearly four, by which time the lights in the square had already been turned on.

She sat alone in the front room of her little flat and stared at the two vases. Although she had only possessed them for a few months, as each day passed, she had come to appreciate why they were regarded as works of genius. She had to admit, if only to herself, that she was going to miss them. However, the thought of another legal battle and Sir Edward's exorbitant fee, catapulted her back into the real world.

It was Bofie who had pointed out, just after they'd opened their second bottle of Merlot, the significance of the words 'on or before', and it amused Virginia to think she could at least have a little fun at Clarence's expense.

After a light supper, she ran herself a bath, and lay among the bubbles giving considerable thought to what she should wear for the occasion, as this was clearly going to be a closing-night performance. She settled on black, a colour her late husband had always favoured, especially after escorting her back to Eaton Square following an evening at Annabel's.

Virginia didn't hurry herself, aware that her timing had to be perfect, before the curtain could come down. At 11.40 p.m., she stepped out of the flat and hailed a taxi. She explained to the driver that she would require some help in putting two large vases in the back. He couldn't have been more obliging, and once Virginia had settled herself on the back seat, he asked, 'Where to, madam?'

'Thirty-two Eaton Square. And could you drive slowly, as I wouldn't want the vases to be damaged.'

'Of course, madam.'

Virginia sat on the edge of the seat, a hand placed firmly on the rim of each vase while the cabbie drove the short distance from Chelsea to Eaton Square, never moving out of first gear.

When the cab finally pulled up outside No. 32, memories of her time with Perry came flooding back, reminding Virginia once again just how much she missed him. The driver climbed out and opened the back door for her.

'Would you be kind enough to put the vases on the top step,' she said as she climbed out of the cab. She waited until the driver had done so before adding, 'If you could wait, I'll only be a few moments, then you can drive me back home.'

'Of course, madam.'

Virginia checked her watch: nine minutes to twelve. She had kept her side of the bargain. She pressed the doorbell and waited until she saw a light on the third floor go on. A few moments later a familiar face appeared at the window. She smiled up at Clarence, who opened the window and peered down at her.

'Is that you, Virginia?' he asked, trying not to sound exasperated.

'It most certainly is, my darling. I'm just returning the vases.' She looked again at her watch. 'I think you'll find it's seven minutes to midnight, so I've kept my side of the bargain.' A second light came on and Camilla leant out of another window and said, 'And only just in time.'

Virginia smiled sweetly up at her stepdaughter. She was about to walk back to the taxi, but paused for a moment to give the two vases one last look. She then bent down, and with all the strength she could muster, lifted one of them high above her head like an Olympic weight-lifter. After holding it there for a moment, she allowed it to slip from her fingers. The exquisite five-hundred-year-old national treasure bounced down the stone steps, before finally shattering into a hundred pieces.

Lights began to go on all over the house, and the words 'fucking bitch' were among the more restrained of Camilla's opinions.

Warming to her task, Virginia stepped forward as if to take a curtain call. She picked up the second vase and, like the first, raised it high above her head. She heard the door open behind her.

'Please, no!' shouted Clarence, as he leapt forward, arms outstretched, but Virginia had already let go of the vase and, if anything, the second irreplaceable Chinese masterpiece broke into even more pieces than the first.

Virginia walked slowly down the steps, making her way carefully through a mosaic of blue and white broken porcelain, before climbing into the waiting taxi.

As the driver began the journey back to Chelsea, he looked in his rear-view mirror to see his passenger had a smile on her face. Virginia didn't once look back to survey the carnage, because this time she'd read the legal document clause by clause, and there was no mention of what condition the two Ming vases should be in when they were returned 'on or before October 19th'.

As the cab turned right out of Eaton Square, the clock on a nearby church struck twelve.

SEBASTIAN CLIFTON

1984–1986

39

'You asked to see me, chairman.'

'Can you hang on for a moment, Victor, while I sign this cheque? In fact, you can be the second signatory.'

'Who's it for?'

'Karin Barrington, following her triumph in the London Marathon.'

'Quite right,' said Victor, taking out his pen and signing with a flourish. 'A fantastic effort. I don't think I could have done it in a week, let alone in under four hours.'

'And I'm not even going to try,' said Seb. 'But that wasn't why I needed to see you.' His tone changed, once the small talk the English so delight in before getting to the point had been dispensed with. 'I need you to step up to the plate and take on more responsibility.'

Victor smiled, almost as if he knew what the chairman was about to suggest.

'I want you to become deputy chairman of the bank, and my right hand.'

Victor didn't attempt to hide his disappointment. Seb wasn't surprised, and only hoped he would come round, if not immediately, at least in the long term.

'So who'll be your chief executive?'

'I intend to offer that job to John Ashley.'

'But he's only been with the bank for a couple of years, and rumour has it that Barclays are about to invite him to head up their Middle East office.'

'I've heard those rumours too, which only convinced me we couldn't afford to lose him.'

'Then offer him the deputy chairmanship,' said Victor, his voice rising. Sebastian couldn't think of a convincing reply. 'Not that there would be much point,' continued Victor, 'because you know only too well he would see that role as nothing more than window dressing, and rightly turn it down.'

'That isn't how I see it,' said Seb. 'I consider it to be not only a promotion, but an announcement that you are my natural successor.'

'Balls. Have you forgotten we're the same age? No, if you make Ashley the CEO, everyone will assume you've decided he's your natural successor, not me.'

'But you'd still be in charge of foreign exchange, which is one of the bank's most lucrative departments.'

'And reports directly to the CEO, in case you've forgotten.'

'Then I'll make it clear that in future you report directly to me.'

'That's nothing more than a sop, and everyone will know it. No, if you don't feel I'm up to being managing director, you've left me with no choice but to resign.'

'That's the last thing I want,' said Sebastian, as his oldest friend gathered his papers and left the room without another word. Victor closed the door quietly behind him.

'That went well,' said Seb.

'You've been putting it off for years,' said Karin after she'd read the letter.

'But I'm over sixty,' protested Giles.

'It's the Castle versus the Village,' she reminded him, 'not England against the West Indies. In any case, you're always telling me how much you wished I'd seen your cover drive.'

'In my prime, not in my dotage.'

'And,' continued Karin, ignoring the outburst, 'you gave your word to Freddie.' Giles couldn't think of a suitable reply. 'And let's face it, if I can run a marathon, you can certainly turn out for a village cricket match.' Words that finally silenced her husband.

Giles read the letter once more and groaned as he sat down at his desk. He extracted a sheet of paper from the rack, removed the top from his pen and began to write.

Dear Freddie,
  I would be delighted to join your team for . . .

◄○►

'Aren't they magnificent?' the young man said as he admired the seven drawings that had been awarded the Founder's Prize.

'Do you think so?' replied the young woman.

'Oh yes! And such a clever idea to take the seven ages of woman as her theme.'

'Oh, I missed that,' she said, looking at him more closely. The young man's clothes rather suggested he hadn't looked in a mirror before leaving for work that morning. Nothing matched. A smart Harris Tweed jacket paired with a blue shirt, green tie, grey trousers and brown shoes. But he displayed a warmth and enthusiasm for the artist's work that was quite infectious.

'As you can see,' he said, warming to the task, 'the artist has taken as her subject a woman running a marathon, and has depicted the seven stages of the race. The first drawing is on the starting line, when she's warming up, apprehensive but alert. In the next,' he said, pointing to the second drawing, 'she's reached the five-mile mark, and is still full of confidence. But by the time she's reached ten miles,' he said, moving on to the third drawing, 'she's clearly beginning to feel the pain.'

'And the fourth?' she asked, looking more carefully at the drawing, which the artist had described as 'the wall'.

'Just look at the expression on the runner's face, which leaves you in no doubt that she's beginning to wonder if she'll be able to finish the course.' She nodded. 'And the fifth shows her just clinging on as she passes what I assume must be her family cheering. She's raised an arm to acknowledge them, but even in the raising of that arm, with a single delicate line the artist leaves you in no doubt what a supreme effort it must have been.' Pointing to the sixth drawing, he continued effusively, 'Here we see her crossing the finishing line, arms raised in triumph. And then moments later, in the final drawing, she collapses on the ground exhausted, having given everything, and is rewarded with a medal hung around her neck. Notice that the artist has added the yellow and green of the ribbon, the only hint of colour in all seven drawings. Quite brilliant.'

'You must be an artist yourself.'

'I wish,' he said, giving her a warm smile. 'The nearest I ever got was when I won an art prize at school and decided to apply for a place at the Slade, but they turned me down.'

'There are other art colleges.'

'Yes, and I applied to most of them – Goldsmiths, Chelsea, Manchester. I even went up to Glasgow for an interview, but always with the same result.'

'I'm so sorry.'

'No need to be, because I finally asked a member of one of the interviewing panels why they kept rejecting me.'

'And what did they say?'

'Your A-level results were impressive enough,' the young man said, holding the lapels of his jacket and sounding twenty years older, 'and you are clearly passionate about the subject and have buckets of energy and enthusiasm, but sadly something is missing. "What's that?" I asked. "Talent," he replied.'

'Oh, how cruel!'

'No, not really. Just realistic. He went on to ask if I'd considered teaching, which only added salt to the wound, because it reminded me of George Bernard Shaw's words, *those who can, do, those who can't, teach.* But then I went away and thought about it, and realized he was right.'

'So now you're a teacher?'

'I am. I read Art History at King's, and I'm now teaching at a grammar school in Peckham, where at least I think I can say I'm a better artist than my pupils. Well, most of them,' he added with a grin.

She laughed. 'So what brings you back to the Slade?'

'I go to most of the student exhibitions in the hope of spotting someone with real talent whose work I can add to my collection. Over the years I've picked up a Craigie Aitchison, a Mary Fedden and even a small pencil sketch by Hockney, but I'd love to add these seven drawings to my collection.'

'What's stopping you?'

'I haven't had the courage to ask how much they are, and as she's just won the Founder's Prize, I'm sure I won't be able to afford them.'

'How much do you think they're worth?'

'I don't know, but I'd give everything I have to own them.'

'How much do you have?'

'When I last checked my bank balance, just over three hundred pounds.'

'Then you're in luck, because I think you'll find they're priced at two hundred and fifty pounds.'

'Let's go and find out if you're right, before someone else snaps them up. By the way,' he added as they turned to walk towards the sales counter, 'my name's Richard Langley, but my friends call me Rick.'

'Hi,' she said as they shook hands. 'My name's Jessica Clifton, but my friends call me Jessie.'

40

'IF YOU PULL YOUR sweater down,' said Karin, 'no one will notice that you can't do up the top button.'

'It's twenty years since I last played,' Giles reminded her, as he pulled in his stomach and made one final attempt to do up the top button of a pair of Archie Fenwick's cricket trousers.

Karin burst out laughing when the button popped off and landed at her feet. 'I'm sure you'll be fine, my darling. Just remember not to run after the ball, because it could end in disaster.' Giles was about to retaliate when there was a knock at the door.

'Come in,' he said, quickly placing a foot on the rebellious button.

The door opened and Freddie, dressed neatly in crisp whites, entered the room. 'I'm sorry to bother you, sir, but there's been a change of plan.'

Giles looked relieved, as he assumed he was about to be dropped.

'The butler, our skipper, has cried off at the last minute, a pulled hamstring. As you played for Oxford against Cambridge, I thought you'd be the obvious choice to take his place.'

'But I don't even know the other members of the team,' protested Giles.

'Don't worry, sir. I'll keep you briefed. I'd do the job myself, but I'm not sure how to set a field. Could you be available to take the toss in about ten minutes? Sorry to have disturbed you, Lady Barrington,' he said before rushing back out.

'Do you think he'll ever call me Karin?' she said after the door closed.

'One step at a time,' said Giles.

◄◦►

When Giles first saw the large oval plot of land set like a jewel in the castle's grounds, he doubted if there could be a more idyllic setting for a game of cricket. Rugged forest covered the hills which surrounded a couple of acres of flat green land that God had clearly meant to be a cricket pitch, if only for a few weeks a year.

Freddie introduced Giles to Hamish Munro, the local bobby and the Village captain. At forty, he looked in good shape, and certainly would not have had any trouble buttoning up his trousers.

The two captains walked out on to the pitch together just before two o'clock. Giles carried out a routine he hadn't done for years. He sniffed the air, before looking up at the sky. A warm day by Scottish standards, a few stray clouds decorated an otherwise blue horizon, no rain and, thankfully, no harbingers of rain. He inspected the pitch – a tinge of green on the surface, good for fast bowlers – and finally he glanced at the crowd. Much larger than he'd expected, but then it was a local derby. About a couple of hundred spectators were sprinkled around the boundary rope waiting for battle to commence.

Giles shook hands with the opposing captain.

'Your call, Mr Munro,' he said before spinning a pound coin high into the air.

'Heads,' declared Munro, and they both bent down to study the coin as it landed on the ground.

'Your choice, sir,' said Giles, staring at the Queen.

'We'll bat,' said Munro without hesitation, and quickly returned to the pavilion to brief his team. A few minutes later a bell rang and two umpires in long white coats emerged from the pavilion and made their way slowly on to the field. Archie Fenwick and the Rev. Sandy McDonald were there to guarantee fair play.

A few moments later, Giles led his unfamiliar band of warriors out on to the pitch. He set an attacking field, with sotto voce advice from Freddie, then tossed the ball to Hector Brice, the Castle's second footman, who was already scratching out his mark some twenty yards behind the stumps.

The Village's opening batsmen strolled out on to the pitch, rotating their arms, and running on the spot, affecting a nonchalant air. The local postman asked for middle and leg, and once he'd made his mark, the vicar declared, 'Play!'

The Village openers made a brisk start, scoring 32 before the first wicket fell to Ben Atkins, the farm manager – a sharp catch in the slips. Hector then followed up with two quick wickets and it was 64 for 3 after fifteen overs had been bowled. A fourth wicket partnership was beginning to take hold between the publican Finn Reedie and Hamish Munro, when Freddie suggested that Giles should turn his arm over. A call to arms the captain hadn't seriously considered. Even in his youth, Giles had rarely been asked to bowl.

His first over went for eleven, which included two wides, and he was going to take himself off but Freddie wouldn't hear of it. Giles's second over went for seven, but at least there were no wides and, to his surprise, in his third, he captured the important wicket of the publican. An LBW appeal to which the tenth Earl of Fenwick pronounced 'Out!' Giles thought he'd been a little fortunate, and so did Reedie.

'Leg before pavilion more like,' muttered the publican as he passed the earl.

One hundred and sixteen for 4. The first footman continued with his slow leg cutters from one end, accompanied by Giles's attempt at military medium from the other. The Village went in to tea at 4.30 p.m., having scored 237 for 8, which Hamish Munro clearly felt was enough to win the match, because he declared.

Tea was held in a large tent. Egg and cress sandwiches, sausage rolls, jam tarts and scones topped with clotted cream were scoffed by all, accompanied by cups of hot tea and glasses of cold lime cordial. Freddie ate nothing, as he pencilled the Castle team's batting order into the scorebook. Giles looked over his shoulder and was horrified to see his name at the top of the list.

'Are you sure you want me to open?'

'Yes, of course, sir. After all, you opened for Oxford and the MCC.'

As Giles padded up he wished he hadn't eaten quite so many scones. A few moments later, he and Ben Atkins made their way out on to the pitch. Giles took guard, leg stump, then looked around the field, displaying an air of confidence that belied his true feelings. He settled down and waited for the first delivery from Ross Walker, the local butcher. The ball fizzed through the air and hit Giles firmly on the pad, plum in front of the middle stump.

'Howzat!' screamed the butcher confidently, as he leapt in the air.

Humiliation, thought Giles, as he prepared to return to the pavilion with a golden duck.

'Not out,' responded the tenth Earl of Fenwick, saving his blushes.

The bowler didn't hide his disbelief and began to shine the ball furiously on his trousers before preparing to deliver the next ball. He charged up and hurled the missile at Giles a second time. Giles played forward, and the ball nicked the outside edge of his bat, missing the stump by inches before running between first and second slip to the boundary. Giles was off the mark with a scratchy four, and the butcher looked even angrier. His next ball was well wide of the stumps, and somehow Giles survived the rest of the over.

The farm manager turned out to be a competent if somewhat slow-scoring batsman, and the two of them had mustered 28 runs before Mr Atkins was caught behind the wicket off the butcher's slower ball. Giles was then joined by a cow-hand who, although he had a range of shots worthy of his calling, still managed to notch up 30 in a very short time before being caught on the boundary. Seventy-nine for 2. The cow-hand was followed by the head gardener, who clearly only played once a year. Seventy-nine for 3.

Three more wickets fell during the next half hour, but somehow Giles prospered, and with the score on 136 for 6, the Hon. Freddie came out to join him at the crease, greeted by warm applause.

'We still need another hundred,' said Giles, glancing

at the scoreboard. 'But we have more than enough time, so be patient, and only try to score off any loose balls. Reedie and Walker are both tiring, so bide your time, and make sure you don't give your wicket away.'

After Freddie had taken guard, he followed his captain's instructions to the letter. It quickly became clear to Giles that the boy had been well coached at his prep school and, fortunately, had a natural flair, known in the trade as 'an eye'. Together they passed the 200 mark to rapturous applause from one section of the crowd, who were beginning to believe that Castle might win the local derby for the first time in years.

Giles felt equally confident as he steered a ball through the covers to the far boundary, which took him into the seventies. A couple of overs later, the butcher came back on to bowl, no longer displaying his earlier cockiness. He charged up to the wicket and released the ball with all the venom he possessed. Giles played forward, misjudged the pace and heard the unforgiving sound of falling timber behind him. This time the umpire wouldn't be able to come to his rescue. Giles made his way back to the pavilion to rapturous applause, having scored 74. But, as he explained to Karin as he sat down on the grass beside her and unbuckled his pads, they still needed 28 runs to win, with only three wickets in hand.

Freddie was joined in the middle by his lordship's chauffeur, a man who rarely moved out of first gear. He was aware of the chauffeur's record and did everything in his power to retain the strike and leave his partner at the non-striking end. Freddie managed to keep the scoreboard ticking over until the chauffeur took a pace back to a bouncer and trod on his stumps. He walked back to the pavilion without the umpire's verdict needing to be called upon.

Fifteen runs were still needed for victory when the second gardener (part-time) walked out to join Freddie in the middle. He survived the butcher's first delivery, but only because he couldn't get bat on ball. No such luck with the fifth delivery of the over, which he scooped up into the hands of the Village captain at mid-off. The fielding side jumped in the air with joy, well aware they only needed one more wicket to win the match and retain the trophy.

They couldn't have looked more pleased when Hector Brice walked out and took his guard before facing the last ball of the over. They all recalled how long he'd lasted the previous year.

'Don't take a single, whatever you do,' was Freddie's only instruction.

But the Village captain, a wily old bird, set a field to make a single tempting. His troops couldn't wait for the footman to quickly return to the line of fire. The butcher hurled the missile at Hector, but somehow the second footman managed to get bat on ball, and he watched it trickling towards backward short leg. Hector wanted to take a single, but Freddie remained resolutely in his place.

Freddie was quite happy to face the Village spinner for the penultimate over of the match, and hit him for 4 off his first ball, 2 off the third, and 1 off the fifth. Hector only needed to survive one more ball, leaving Freddie to face the butcher for the final over. The last ball of the over was slow and straight and beat Hector all ends up, but just passed over the top of the stumps before ending up in the wicket-keeper's gloves. A sigh of relief came from those seated in the deckchairs, while groans erupted from the Village supporters.

'Final over,' declared the vicar.

Giles checked the scoreboard. 'Only eight more needed, and victory is ours,' he said, but Karin didn't reply because she had her head in her hands, no longer able to watch what was taking place in the middle.

The butcher shone the ragged ball on his red-stained trousers as he prepared for one final effort. He charged up and hurled the missile at Freddie, who played back and nicked it to first slip, who dropped it.

'Butter fingers,' were the only words the butcher muttered that were repeatable in front of the vicar.

Freddie now had only five balls from which to score the eight runs needed for victory.

'Relax,' said Giles under his breath. 'There's bound to be a loose ball you can put away. Just stay calm and concentrate.'

The second ball took a thick outside edge and shot down to third man for two. Six still required, but only four balls left. The third might have been called a wide, making the task easier, but the vicar kept his hands in his pockets.

Freddie struck the fourth ball confidently to deep mid-on, thought about a single, but decided he couldn't risk the footman being left with the responsibility of scoring the winning runs. He tapped his bat nervously on the crease as he waited for the fifth ball, never taking his eyes off the butcher as he advanced menacingly towards his quarry. The delivery was fast but just a little short, which allowed Freddie to lean back and hook it high into the air over square leg, where it landed inches in front of the rope before crossing the boundary for four. The

Castle's supporters cheered even louder, but then fell into an expectant hush as they waited for the final delivery.

All four results were possible: a win, a loss, a tie, a draw.

Freddie didn't need to look at the scoreboard to know they needed one for a tie and two for a win off the final ball. He looked around the field before he settled. The butcher glared at him before charging up for the last time, to release the ball with every ounce of energy he possessed. It was short again, and Freddie played confidently forward, intending to hit the ball firmly through the covers, but it was faster than he anticipated and passed his bat, rapping him on the back pad.

The whole of the Village team and half of the crowd jumped in the air and screamed, 'Howzat!' Freddie looked hopefully up at the vicar, who hesitated only for a moment before raising his finger in the air.

Freddie, head bowed, began the long walk back to the pavilion, applauded all the way by an appreciative crowd. Eighty-seven to his name, but Castle had lost the match.

'What a cruel game cricket can be,' said Karin.

'But character-forming,' said Giles, 'and I have a feeling this is a match young Freddie will never forget.'

Freddie disappeared into the pavilion and slumped down on a bench in the far corner of the dressing room, head still bowed, unmoved by the cries of 'Well played, lad', 'Bad luck, sir', and 'A fine effort, my boy', because all he could hear were the cheers coming from the adjoining room, assisted by pints being drawn from a beer barrel supplied by the publican.

Giles joined Freddie in the home dressing room and sat down on the bench beside the desolate young man.

'One more duty to perform,' said Giles, when Freddie

eventually looked up. 'We must go next door and congratulate the Village captain on his victory.'

Freddie hesitated for a moment, before he stood up and followed Giles. As they entered the opposition's changing room, the Village team fell silent. Freddie went up to the policeman and shook him warmly by the hand.

'A magnificent victory, Mr Munro. We'll have to try harder next year.'

◄○►

Later that evening, as Giles and Hamish Munro were enjoying a pint of the local bitter in the Fenwick Arms, the Village skipper remarked, 'Your boy played a remarkable innings. Far finer teams than ours will suffer at his hand, and I suspect in the not-too-distant future.'

'He's not my boy,' said Giles. 'I only wish he was.'

41

'DID YOU KNOW that Jessica has a new boyfriend?' said Samantha.

Sebastian always booked the same corner table at Le Caprice where his conversation wouldn't be overheard and he had a good view of the other guests. It always amused him that the long glass mirrors attached to the four pillars in the centre of the room allowed him to observe other diners, while they were unable to see him.

He had no interest in film stars he barely recognized, or politicians who were hoping to be recognized, or even Princess Diana, whom everyone recognized. His only interest was in keeping an eye on other bankers and businessmen to see who they were dining with. Deals that it was useful for him to know about were often closed over dinner.

'Who are you staring at?' asked Samantha, after he didn't respond.

'Victor,' he whispered.

Sam looked around, but couldn't spot Seb's oldest friend. 'You're a peeping Tom,' she said after finishing her coffee.

'And what's more, they can't see us,' said Seb.

'They? Is he having dinner with Ruth?'

'Not unless she's lost a couple of inches around her waist and put them on her chest.'

'Behave yourself, Seb. She's probably a client.'

'No, I think you'll find he's the client.'

'You've inherited your father's vivid imagination. It's probably quite innocent.'

'You're the only person in the room who'd believe that.'

'Now you have got me intrigued,' said Sam. She turned round once again, but still couldn't see Victor. 'I repeat, you're a peeping Tom.'

'And if I'm right,' said Seb, ignoring his wife's remonstration, 'we have a problem.'

'Surely Victor's got the problem, not you.'

'Possibly. But I'd still like to get out of here without being seen,' he said, taking out his wallet.

'How do you plan to do that?'

'Timing.'

'Are you going to cause some kind of diversion?' she teased.

'Nothing as dramatic as that. We'll stay put until one of them goes to the loo. If it's Victor, we can slip out unnoticed. If it's the woman, we'll leave discreetly, not giving him any reason to believe we've spotted them.'

'But if he does acknowledge us, you'll know it's quite innocent,' said Sam.

'That would be a relief on more than one level.'

'You're rather good at this,' said Sam. 'Experience possibly?'

'Not exactly. But you'll find a similar plot in one of Dad's novels, when William Warwick realizes the witness to a murder must have been lying, and has to get out of a restaurant unnoticed if he's going to prove it.'

'What if neither of them goes to the loo?'

'We could be stuck here for a very long time. I'll get the bill,' said Seb, raising a hand, 'just in case we have to make a dash for it. And I'm sorry, Sam, but did you ask me something just before I became distracted?'

'Yes, I wondered if you knew Jessica's got a new boy-friend.'

'What gives you that idea?' said Seb, as he checked the bill before handing over his credit card.

'She never used to care how she looked.'

'Isn't that par for the course for an art student? She always looks to me as if she's been dressed by Oxfam, and I can't say I've noticed any change.'

'That's because you don't see her in the evening, when she stops being an art student and becomes a young woman, and doesn't look half bad.'

'The daughter of her mother,' said Seb, taking his wife's hand. 'Let's just hope the new guy is an improve-ment on the Brazilian playboy, because I can't see the Slade being quite so understanding a second time,' he said as he signed the credit slip.

'I don't think that will be a problem this time. When he came to pick her up, he was driving a Polo, not a Ferrari.'

'And you have the nerve to call me a peeping Tom? So when do I get the chance to meet him?'

'That might not be for some time because so far she hasn't even admitted she has a boyfriend. However, I'm planning—'

'Action stations. She's heading towards us.'

Seb and Sam went on chatting as a tall, elegant young woman passed their table.

'Well, I like her style,' said Sam.

'What do you mean?'

'Men are all the same. They just look at a woman's legs, figure and face, as if they're in a meat market.'

'And what does a woman look for?' asked Seb defensively.

'The first thing I noticed was her dress, which was simple and elegant, and definitely not off the peg. Her bag was stylish without screaming a designer label, and her shoes completed a perfect ensemble. So I hate to disabuse you, Seb, but as we say in the States, that's one classy dame.'

'Then what's she doing with Victor?'

'I have no idea. But like most men, if you see a friend with a beautiful woman, you immediately assume the worst.'

'I still think it would be best if we slip out unnoticed.'

'I'd much rather go over and say hello to Victor, but if you—'

'There's something I haven't told you. Victor and I aren't exactly on speaking terms at the moment. I'll explain why once we're back in the car.'

Seb stood up and navigated a circuitous route around the restaurant, avoiding Victor's table. When the maître d' opened the front door for Samantha, Seb slipped him a five-pound note.

'So what is it I ought to know about?' asked Sam, once she'd climbed into the car and taken the seat next to him.

'Victor's angry because I didn't make him chief executive.'

'I'm sorry to hear that,' said Sam, 'but I can understand how he felt. Who did you appoint as CEO?'

'John Ashley,' said Seb, as he turned into Piccadilly and joined the late-night traffic.

'Why?'

'Because he's the right man for the job.'

'But Victor's always been a good and loyal friend, especially when you were down.'

'I know, but that's not a good enough reason to appoint someone as the CEO of a major bank. I invited him to be my deputy chairman, but he took umbrage and resigned.'

'I can understand that too,' said Sam. 'So what are you doing to keep him on the board?'

'Hakim flew over from Copenhagen to try and get him to change his mind.'

'Did he succeed?' asked Sam as Seb halted at a red light.

◄o►

Giles was dashing out of the chamber to keep an appointment when he saw Archie Fenwick standing outside his office. He didn't slow down.

'If it's about the government's proposed grain subsidies, Archie, could you make an appointment? I'm already late for the chief whip.'

'No, it isn't,' said Archie. 'I came down from Scotland this morning in the hope you might have time to discuss a personal matter.' Code for Freddie.

'Of course,' said Giles, who continued on into his office and said to his secretary, 'Make sure I'm not disturbed while I'm with Lord Fenwick.' He closed the door behind him. 'Can I get you a whisky, Archie? I even have your own label,' he said, holding up a bottle of Glen Fenwick. 'Freddie gave me a case at Christmas.'

'No, thank you. Although you won't be surprised that it's Freddie I've come to talk to you about,' said Archie, sitting down on the other side of the desk. 'But remembering how busy you are, I'll try not to take too much of your time.'

'If you had wanted to discuss the problems facing the Scottish agricultural industry, I can spare you five minutes. If it concerns Freddie, take your time.'

'Thank you. But I'll get straight to the point. Freddie's headmaster called me yesterday evening to say the boy failed his common entrance exam to Fettes.'

'But when I read his most recent end-of-term report, I even wondered if he might win a scholarship.'

'So did the headmaster,' said Archie, 'which is why he called for his papers. It quickly became clear he'd made no effort to pass.'

'But why? Fettes is one of the best schools in Scotland.'

'In Scotland may be the answer to your question,' said Archie, 'because he sat a similar exam for Westminster a week later, and came out in the top half dozen.'

'I don't think we need to call on the assistance of Freud to fathom that one out,' said Giles. 'So all I need to know is whether he wants to be a day boy or a boarder.'

'He put a cross in the box marked day boy.'

'It's a long way for him to commute to Fenwick Hall and back every day, and as Westminster is a stone's throw from our front door, I think he might have been trying to tell us something.' Archie nodded. 'In any case, he's already selected his bedroom,' Giles added as the phone on his desk began to ring.

He grabbed it and listened for a moment before he said, 'Sorry, chief, something came up, but I'll be with you in a moment.' He put the phone down and said, 'Why don't you join Karin and me for dinner in Smith Square this evening, and we can thrash out the details.'

'I don't know how to thank you,' said Archie.

'It's me who should be thanking you.' Giles stood up and headed for the door. 'It's the only piece of good news I've had all day. I'll see you around eight.'

'Any hope of discussing the government's proposed grain subsidy at some time?' Archie asked, but Giles didn't reply as he quickly left the office.

—◦—

'What's Cunard's spot price this morning?' asked Seb.

'Four pounds twelve. Up two pence on yesterday,' replied John Ashley.

'That's good news all round.'

'Do you think your mother ever regrets selling Barrington's?'

'Daily. But luckily she's so overworked at the Department of Health that she doesn't have much time to think about it.'

'And Giles?'

'I know he's extremely grateful for the way you've handled the family portfolio, because it allows him to pursue his first love.'

'Battling against your mother?'

'Something like that.'

'What about your aunt Grace?'

'She thinks you're a vulgar capitalist, or at least that's how she describes me, so I can't believe she'd consider you any better.'

'But I've made her a multi-millionaire,' protested Ashley.

'Indeed you have, but that won't stop her marking her pupils' homework tonight while nibbling on a cheese sandwich. But on her behalf, John, well done. Is there anything else we need to discuss?'

'Yes, I'm sorry to say there is, chairman, and I'm not quite sure how to handle it.' Ashley opened a file marked private and shuffled through some papers. Seb was surprised to see that a man who'd played front row for the Harlequins, and never hesitated to face any member of the board head on, was now clearly embarrassed.

'Spit it out, John.'

'A Miss Candice Lombardo has recently opened an account with the bank, and her guarantor is the deputy chairman.'

'So that's her name,' said Seb.

'You know her?'

'Let's just say I've come across her. So what's the problem?'

'She withdrew five thousand pounds yesterday, without having a penny in her account, to purchase a mink coat from Harrods.'

'Why did you clear the cheque?'

'Because Victor has guaranteed her overdraft and I don't have the authority to put a stop on it without consulting him.'

'Cedric Hardcastle will be turning in his grave,' said Seb, looking up at the portrait of the bank's founding chairman. 'He used to be fond of saying never say never, unless you're asked to sign a personal guarantee.'

'Should I have a word with Victor?'

Seb leant back and thought about the suggestion for a

few moments. Hakim had managed to convince Victor to remain on the board, and even take up the post of deputy chairman, so the last thing Seb needed was to give him any reason to change his mind.

'Do nothing,' he eventually said. 'But keep me briefed if Miss Lombardo presents any more cheques.'

Ashley nodded, but didn't make a note in his file.

'I thought you'd also want to know,' he continued, 'that your daughter's account is overdrawn by £104.60. Not a large amount, I know, but you did ask me to brief you, following—'

'I did indeed,' said Seb. 'But to be fair, John, I've just paid her a thousand pounds for seven of her drawings.'

Ashley opened a second file and checked another bank statement. 'She hasn't presented that cheque, chairman. In fact, her only recent deposit was for two hundred and fifty pounds from a Richard Langley.'

'The name doesn't mean anything to me,' said Seb. 'But keep me informed.' Ashley frowned. 'What does that look mean?'

'Just that on balance, I'd prefer to deal with the chairman of Cunard than your daughter.'

42

THE FOUR OF THEM sat in the drawing room looking distinctly uncomfortable.

'It's so nice to meet you at last,' said Samantha, pouring Richard a cup of tea.

'You too, Mrs Clifton,' said the young man who sat nervously opposite her.

'How did you two meet?' asked Seb.

'We bumped into each other at the Slade Founder's Prize exhibition,' said Jessica.

'I go to all the college art shows,' said Richard, 'in the hope of spotting a new talent before they're snapped up by a West End dealer, when I'll no longer be able to afford them.'

'How very sensible,' said Samantha, as she offered her guest a cucumber sandwich.

'Picked up anything worthwhile recently?' asked Sebastian.

'A coup,' said Richard, 'a veritable coup. A set of remarkable line drawings by an unknown artist, entitled *The Seven Ages of Woman*, that won the Founder's Prize. I couldn't believe my luck when I heard the price.'

'Forgive me for mentioning it,' said Seb, 'but I'm surprised you can afford a thousand pounds on a teacher's salary.'

'I didn't pay a thousand pounds, sir, just two hundred and fifty. And I only just had enough left in my account to take the artist out to supper.'

'But I thought—' Seb didn't complete the sentence when he noticed Samantha glaring at him and his daughter looking embarrassed. He decided to change tack. 'I'd be willing to offer you a couple of thousand for those drawings. Then you can take the artist out for supper regularly.'

'They're not for sale,' said Richard, 'and they never will be.'

'Three thousand?'

'No, thank you, sir.'

'Perhaps you'd consider a deal, Richard. If you were ever to give up my daughter, you'd sell the drawings back to me for two thousand pounds.'

'Sebastian!' said Samantha sharply. 'Richard is Jessica's friend, not a client, and in any case it's outside banking hours.'

'Not a hope, sir,' said Richard. 'I don't intend to part with either your daughter or the drawings.'

'You can't win them all, Pops,' said Jessica with a grin.

'But if Jessie were to give you up,' said Seb, as if he was chasing a million-pound deal, 'would you reconsider then?'

'Forget it, Pops. That's not going to happen. You've lost the drawings, and you're about to lose your daughter, because I'm planning to move in with Richard,' she said, taking his hand.

Sebastian was about to suggest that perhaps . . . when Samantha jumped in.

'That's wonderful news. Where will you be living?'

'I have a flat in Peckham,' said Richard, 'quite near where I work.'

'But we're looking for something bigger,' said Jessica.

'To rent, or buy?' asked Seb. 'Because in current market conditions, I would recommend—'

'I would recommend,' said Samantha, 'that they should be allowed to make up their own minds.'

'Much more sensible to buy,' said Seb, ignoring his wife, 'and with my two thousand, you'd have enough to put down a deposit.'

'Just ignore him,' said Samantha.

'I always do,' said Jessica, standing up. 'Must dash, Pops, we're off to the ICA to see an exhibition of ceramics Richard thinks looks promising.'

'And can still afford,' added Richard. 'But if you do have two thousand to invest, sir, I would recommend—'

Samantha laughed, but Richard looked as if he was already regretting his words.

'Bye, Pops,' said Jessica. She bent down, kissed her father on the forehead and slipped an envelope into his inside pocket, hoping Richard wouldn't notice.

Richard thrust out his hand and said, 'Goodbye, sir. It was nice to meet you.'

'Goodbye, Richard. I hope you enjoy the exhibition.'

'Thank you, sir,' said Richard as Samantha accompanied them both to the door.

While Seb waited for her to return, he took the envelope out of his pocket, opened it and extracted his own cheque for a thousand pounds. First time he'd ever been outbid by the under-bidder.

'I think I could have handled that better,' suggested Seb when Samantha returned to the drawing room.

'That's an understatement, even by British standards. But I'm more interested in what you thought of Richard.'

'Nice enough chap. But no one will ever be good enough for Jessie.' He paused for a moment before adding, 'I've been wondering what to give her for her twenty-first. Perhaps I ought to buy her a house?'

'That's the last thing you're going to do.'

'Why not?'

'Because it will simply remind Richard that he's penniless and will only make him feel beholden to you. In any case, Jessica is every bit as stubborn as you are. She'd turn the offer down, just as she did your two thousand.'

Seb handed Samantha the cheque, which only made her laugh even louder, before suggesting, 'Perhaps we should allow them to lead their own lives. We might even be surprised how well they get on without us.'

'But I only meant—'

'I know what you meant, my darling, but I'm afraid your daughter trumped you,' she said as the phone began to ring.

'Ah, I have a feeling that will be Richard wanting to know if I'd be willing to raise my offer to four thousand.'

'More likely to be your mother. I told her we were meeting Jessica's new boyfriend for the first time, so she's bound to want to know what we think.' She picked up the phone.

'Good evening, Mrs Clifton. It's John Ashley.'

'Hello, John. Has the bank burnt down?'

'Not yet, but I do need a word with Seb fairly urgently.'

'The bank's burnt down,' said Samantha, handing the phone to her husband.

'You wish. John, what can I do for you?'

'Sorry to bother you this late, chairman, but you asked

me to alert you if Miss Lombardo presented any more large cheques.'

'How much this time?'

'Forty-two thousand.'

'Forty-two thousand pounds?' Seb repeated. 'Hold up the payment for now, and if Victor doesn't turn up tomorrow, I'll have to speak to our legal team. And, John, go home. As my wife keeps reminding me, it's outside banking hours, so there's nothing more you can do about it tonight.'

'A problem, my darling?' asked Samantha, sounding genuinely concerned.

'Yes, I'm afraid so. Do you remember that woman we saw dining with Victor at the Caprice?' he said, picking the phone back up and beginning to dial.

'How could I possibly forget?'

'Well, I think she's taking him to the cleaners.'

'Are you calling Victor?'

'No, Arnold Hardcastle.'

'That bad?'

'That bad.'

◄◦►

'Hi, Jessie, I'm glad you were able to make it,' he said, giving her a hug.

'There's no way I would have missed it, Grayson.'

'Congratulations on winning the Founder's Prize,' he said. 'I bet it won't be long before a West End gallery is showing your work.'

'From your lips to God's ears,' said Jessica as the artist turned away to talk to another student.

'What do you really think?' whispered Richard, as they strolled around the gallery.

'It's a great show, even if I'm not sure about the teddy bear.'

'I wasn't talking about his teddy bear. How do you think the meeting with your parents went?'

'As I told you, Mom thought you were dishy. You're a lucky girl, were her exact words.'

'I'm not sure your father felt the same way.'

'No need to worry about Pops,' said Jessica as she stared at a magnificent vase. 'Once Mom starts to work on him, he'll come round.'

'I hope so, because it won't be too long before we have to tell him.'

◄o►

The chairman, the chief executive and the bank's in-house lawyer were seated around an oval table in Sebastian's office at eight o'clock the following morning.

'Any sign of Victor?' was Seb's first question.

'No one's seen him since Friday night,' said John Ashley. 'He told his secretary he was going on a business trip but would be back in time for the board meeting.'

'But that's not for another ten days,' said Seb. 'Doesn't Carol have any idea where he is?'

'No, and he didn't leave a contact number.'

'That's unlike Victor,' said Seb.

'Carol told me he's never done it before.'

'Curiouser and curiouser.'

'Do you think the time has come to call in Barry Hammond?' suggested Ashley. 'I'm sure it wouldn't take him long to track Victor down, and also to find out everything there is to know about Miss Candice Lombardo.'

'No, we can't have a private detective investigating

the deputy chairman of the bank,' said Seb. 'Is that understood?'

'Yes, chairman. But Miss Lombardo presented another cheque yesterday for immediate clearance,' said Ashley as he opened her growing file.

'How much this time?' asked Arnold.

'Forty-two thousand,' said Ashley.

'Do you have any idea what it's for?'

'No, chairman, I do not,' replied Ashley.

Seb studied a balance sheet that had never been in the black and was about to utter a single word to let his inner team know exactly how he felt, but thought better of it.

'What's our legal position?' he asked, turning to the bank's in-house lawyer.

'If the account is in funds, or the guarantor is good for that amount, we have no choice but to clear the cheque within forty-eight hours.'

'Then let's hope Victor returns soon, or at least contacts us in the next couple of days.'

'Isn't there a paper trail of any sort?' asked Arnold. 'Phone calls, credit cards, hotel bills, plane tickets, anything?'

'Nothing so far,' said Ashley. 'His secretary has instructions to call me the moment she hears from him, but I'm not hopeful, because I have a feeling that if we do find Victor, Miss Lombardo won't be far behind.'

'There's one other person who might know where he is,' said Arnold.

'Who?' asked Seb.

'His wife.'

'Absolutely not,' said Seb. 'Ruth is the last person I want contacted under any circumstances.'

'In which case, chairman,' said Arnold, 'we have no

choice but to clear the latest cheque within forty-eight hours, unless you want me to report the whole matter to the Bank of England and ask if we can hold up any further payments until Victor returns.'

'No, allowing the Old Lady of Threadneedle Street to wash our dirty linen in public would be worse than telling Ruth. Clear the cheque, and let's hope Miss Lombardo doesn't present another one before Victor shows up.'

◄○►

'She's what?' said Sebastian.

'Pregnant,' repeated Samantha.

'I'll kill him.'

'You'll do nothing of the sort. In fact, when you next see Richard, you'll congratulate him.'

'Congratulate him?'

'Yes, and leave them both in no doubt how delighted you are.'

'Why the hell would I do that?'

'Because the alternative doesn't bear thinking about. To lose your daughter and never be able to see your grandchild. Just in case you've forgotten, you've experienced something similar before, and I don't need to go through that again.'

'Are they going to get married?' asked Sebastian, changing tack.

'I didn't ask.'

'Why not?'

'Because it's none of my business. Anyway, I'm sure they'll let us know when they're good and ready.'

'You're being very calm, in the circumstances.'

'Of course I am. I'm looking forward to being a grand-mother.'

'Oh my God,' said Seb. 'I'm going to be a grandfather.'

'And to think the *FT* described you as one of the sharpest minds in the City!'

Sebastian grinned, took his wife in his arms and said, 'I sometimes forget, my darling, how lucky I am to have married you.' He switched on the light on his side of the bed and sat up. 'We ought to give my mother a call and warn her she's about to become a great-grandmother.'

'She already knows.'

'So was I the last person to be told?'

'Sorry. I needed to get all the troops on side before you heard the news.'

'This just hasn't been my week,' said Seb, turning the light out.

—◦—

'I've found out what the forty-two thousand pounds was for, chairman,' said John Ashley.

'I'm all ears,' said Seb.

'It's a down payment on a building in South Parade that used to be an escort agency.'

'That's all I need. So who's the agent?'

'Savills.'

'Well, at least we know the chairman.'

'I've already had a word with Mr Vaughan. He tells me he'll be presenting a cheque signed by Miss Lombardo, in full and final settlement for the property, later today, and politely reminded me that if the sale doesn't go through, Miss Lombardo will lose her deposit.'

'Let's hope Victor is back in time for the board meeting, otherwise by the end of next week she'll probably have taken over the Playboy Club.'

43

'WHAT'S THE MEANING of the word "martinet"?' asked Freddie, looking up from his prep.

'A stickler for discipline,' replied Karin. 'I think you'll find the word derives from the French.'

'How come your English is so good, Karin, when you grew up in Germany?'

'I always enjoyed languages when I was at school, so when I went to university I studied Modern Languages and became an interpreter, which is how I met Giles.'

'Have you thought about what you're going to read when you go up to university?' asked Giles, looking up from his evening paper.

'PPC,' said Freddie.

'I'm aware of politics, philosophy and economics,' said Karin, 'but I've never heard of PPC.'

'Politics, philosophy and cricket. It's a well-known degree course at Oxford.'

'Yes, but not for martinets,' said Giles, 'and I suspect that were you to look up the word in the Revised Oxford Shorter, you'd find that Lieutenant Colonel Martinet has been replaced by Margaret Thatcher as the primary source.'

'Take no notice of him,' said Karin. 'He'll use any excuse to have a go at the Prime Minister.'

'But the press seem to think she's doing rather a good job,' said Freddie.

'Much too well for my liking,' admitted Giles. 'The truth is, we had her on the ropes until the Argentinians invaded the Falklands, but ever since then, even though the bullets are still coming at her from every direction, like James Bond, she always seems to duck at the right moment.'

'And what about the Under Secretary of State for Health?' asked Freddie. 'Will she have to duck now you're back on the front bench?'

'The bullets are just about to hit her,' said Giles with some relish.

'Giles, behave yourself. It's your sister you're talking about, not the enemy.'

'She's worse than the enemy. Don't forget that Emma's a disciple of the blessed Margaret of Grantham. But when she presents the government's latest NHS bill to the Upper House, I intend to dismantle it clause by clause, until she'll consider resignation a blessed relief.'

'I should be careful if I were you, Giles,' said Karin. 'I suspect that having served as the chairman of a major hospital, Emma just might be better informed about the health service than you are.'

'Ah, but you forget the debate won't be taking place in a hospital boardroom, but on the floor of the House of Lords, where I've been lying in wait for some time.'

'Perhaps you'd be wise to heed Grace's warning,' said Karin, 'that Emma might trip you up on the details, because unlike most politicians she's actually been at the coalface.'

'I do believe you're a closet Tory,' said Giles.

'I most certainly am not,' said Karin. 'I came out of the closet years ago, and it was Emma who converted me.'

'Traitor.'

'Not at all. I fell in love with you, not the Labour Party.'

'For better or worse.'

'Worse in that particular case.'

'I'm sorry to interrupt you, but I only wanted to know the meaning of the word "martinet".'

'Ignore Giles,' said Karin. 'He's always the same just before a major debate, especially when his sister's involved.'

'Can I come and watch?' asked Freddie.

'Depends which party you're going to support,' said Giles.

'The party that convinces me it has the better policy.'

'That's original,' said Karin.

'Perhaps now's not the time to tell you that I've joined the Young Conservatives,' said Freddie.

'You've done what?' asked Giles, reeling back and clinging on to the mantelpiece.

'And it gets worse.'

'How can it possibly get worse?'

'We've just held a mock election at school, and I stood as the Tory candidate.'

'And what was the result?' demanded Giles.

'You don't want to know.'

'He not only won by a landslide,' said Karin, 'but he now wants to follow in your footsteps and become a Member of Parliament. Just a pity he won't be sitting on your side of the House.'

A silence followed that few government ministers

had ever managed to impose upon the Rt Hon. the Lord Barrington of Bristol Docklands.

—◄◦►—

'When Mr Kaufman arrives, Tom, would you ask him to drop into my office before the board meeting?'

'Of course, sir,' said the doorman, as he saluted the chairman.

Seb made his way quickly across the lobby to the lifts. Although eight hadn't yet struck, when he stepped out at the top floor John Ashley and Arnold Hardcastle were already waiting for him in the corridor.

'Good morning, gentlemen,' said Seb, striding past them and into his office. 'Please, have a seat. I thought we should discuss tactics before Victor arrives – assuming he does arrive. Let's start with you, John. Any further news?'

Ashley opened a file that was becoming thicker by the day. 'The cheque for £320,000 has been presented. However, Mr Vaughan has agreed that we needn't clear it immediately as we're still within the settlement period.'

'That's considerate of him,' said Seb, 'but then we have been a reliable customer for many years. What do you think we should do, John, if Victor fails to turn up?'

'Call in Barry Hammond and instruct him to track Victor down wherever he is, because I've no doubt he'll also find the girl there too.'

'That has its own risks,' suggested Arnold.

'Outweighed, in my opinion,' said John, 'by the consequences of allowing her to milk Victor dry.'

'An unfortunate metaphor,' said Seb, checking his watch. 'He's cutting it fine.'

There was a gentle tap on the door and all three of

them looked up expectantly. The door opened and Rachel entered the chairman's office.

'Some of the directors have already arrived and are waiting for you in the boardroom,' said his secretary as she handed a copy of the agenda to Seb.

'Is Mr Kaufman among them, Rachel?'

'No, chairman, I haven't seen him this morning.'

'Then I suggest we join our colleagues,' said Seb, after glancing at the agenda. 'I propose that we say nothing about Miss Lombardo until we've had a chance to speak to Victor privately.'

'Agreed,' said the CEO and the bank's legal advisor in unison.

All three men rose without another word, made their way out of the chairman's office and headed for the boardroom, where they joined their colleagues.

'Good morning, Giles,' said Seb, who hadn't called his uncle by his first name until he'd become chairman. 'Am I to understand that you and my mother are no longer on speaking terms, now the NHS bill has been given its first reading?'

'That is correct, chairman. The only discourse we will have in the future is across the despatch box.'

Seb smiled, but couldn't stop himself from continually glancing towards the door. The other directors took their places around the boardroom table but the chair at the far end of the room remained unoccupied. Like his mother, Seb believed in starting board meetings on time. He checked his watch. One minute to nine. He took his seat at the head of the table and said, 'Good morning, gentlemen. I will ask the company secretary to read the minutes of the last meeting.'

Mr Whitford rose from his place on the right of the

chairman and delivered the minutes as if he were reading the lesson at his local church.

Seb tried to concentrate but kept glancing in the direction of the door, although he wasn't hopeful, as he'd never known Victor to be late for a board meeting. When Mr Whitford sat down, Seb forgot to ask his fellow directors if they had any questions. He simply mumbled, 'Item number one,' and was about to call on the chief executive to present his monthly report when the boardroom door was flung open and a flustered deputy chairman rushed in.

Even before he'd taken his seat, Victor said, 'I apologize, chairman. My flight was delayed because of fog. We must have passed over this building a dozen times before we were allowed to land.'

'It's not a problem, Victor,' said Seb calmly. 'You've only missed the reading of the minutes of the last meeting, and I was about to move on to item number one, the government's new banking regulations. John?'

Ashley opened a file and looked down at the copious notes he had prepared and the précis he was about to share with his colleagues. 'It seems that bankers,' he began, 'are now ranked alongside estate agents and Members of Parliament as the least trusted members of the community.'

'Then all I have to do is become an estate agent,' said Giles, 'and I'll have managed all three.'

'What's the bottom line?' said Seb, after the laughter had died down.

'We can expect further scrutiny into the bank's daily affairs, and far tougher inspections from the regulatory bodies, along with a string of new regulations. Geoffrey

Howe is determined to show he's a new broom cleaning up the City.'

'Conservative governments always are, but it's usually forgotten after a few well-chosen homilies from the chancellor at the lord mayor's banquet.'

Seb found his mind drifting again, as the directors began to voice their predictable views, the one exception being Giles, who even now he could never second-guess. He snapped back to the real world when he realized his fellow directors were all staring at him.

'Item number two?' prompted the company secretary.

'Item number two,' said Seb. 'Lord Barrington has just returned from Rome, and I believe he has some rather exciting news to share with us. Giles?'

Giles briefed the board on his recent visit to the Eternal City, where he'd held meetings with Mr Menegatti, the chairman of the Cassaldi Bank, with a view to the two institutions forming a long-term partnership. His report was followed by a discussion among the directors, which Seb summed up with the recommendation that Giles, along with a select team, should take the discussions to the next stage and find out if a substantive proposal for a merger could be agreed on that both chairmen would feel able to recommend to their boards.

'Congratulations, Giles,' said Seb. 'We'll look forward to your next report. Perhaps now we should move on to item number three.' But his mind began to wander again as he considered the only item that would be on the agenda when he later had a private meeting with his deputy chairman. Although he had to admit that Victor looked a damn sight more relaxed than he felt.

Seb was relieved when the company secretary finally asked, 'Any other business?'

'Yes,' announced Victor, from the far end of the table. Seb raised an eyebrow. 'Some of my colleagues may have been wondering where I've been for the past ten days, and I feel I owe you all an explanation.' Certainly three of the directors agreed with him.

'When I became deputy chairman,' Victor continued, 'among the responsibilities the chairman gave me was to look into how the bank dealt with its charitable donations. I'm bound to say I assumed that would not be a demanding task. However, I couldn't have been more wrong. I quickly discovered that the bank simply doesn't have a policy, and that by the standards of our competitors we're not only found wanting but, frankly, mean. I would not have realized just how mean if Lady Barrington hadn't approached me to ask for the bank's support when she was running the marathon. When she produced her list of sponsors, I felt ashamed. She'd raised more money from Barclays, Nat West and Dr Grace Barrington than she managed from Farthings Kaufman. That also caused me to take a greater interest in the charity she was supporting.'

The deputy chairman had captured the attention of the entire board.

'The charity concerned sends missions to Africa where its distinguished heart surgeon, Dr Magdi Yacoub, operates on young children who would otherwise have no hope of survival.'

'What exactly is a mission?' asked Mr Whitford, who had been writing down the deputy chairman's every word.

'A mission comprises five people – a surgeon, a doctor, two nurses and a manager, all of whom give their services for nothing, often sacrificing their holidays to carry out this vital work. Lady Barrington suggested I meet a Miss

Candice Lombardo, who is an active member of the charity's board, so I invited her to join me for dinner.' Victor smiled at the chairman.

'Why do I know that name?' asked the company secretary.

'Miss Lombardo,' said Clive Bingham, 'was voted the most desirable woman on the planet by the readers of *GQ* magazine and, if the tabloids are to be believed, she's currently having a fling with Omar Sharif.'

'I have no idea if that's true,' said Victor. 'All I can tell you is that when we had dinner, it quickly became clear how committed she was to the cause. Miss Lombardo invited me to join her on a trip to Egypt to witness first-hand the work Dr Yacoub and his team were carrying out in that country. That's where I've been for the past ten days, chairman. And I confess, I spent much of my time either fainting or being sick.'

'The deputy chairman fainted?' said Clive in disbelief.

'On more than one occasion. I can assure you, watching a young child having their chest cut open isn't for the faint-hearted. By the time I got on the plane to come home, I was resolved to do more, a great deal more. As a result of that trip, I will be recommending to the board that we take on the role of being the charity's bankers, with no charges. I have already agreed to become its honorary treasurer.'

'To use your words, a great deal more,' said Seb. 'What else can the bank do to help?'

'We could start by making a substantial contribution to the Marsden charitable trust, so they can continue their work without having to live from hand to mouth.'

'Do you have a sum in mind?' asked Giles.

'Half a million a year for the next five years.' There

were one or two gasps from around the table before Victor continued, 'Which I know the board will be pleased to learn qualifies for forty per cent tax relief.'

'How do you think our shareholders will react to us giving such a large amount to charity?' asked John Ashley.

'If Mr Kaufman were to address the AGM,' suggested Seb, 'I suspect they'd say it isn't enough.'

One or two of the board members nodded, while others smiled.

'But we would still have to explain how the money is being spent,' said the company secretary. 'After all, that would be no more than our fiduciary duty.'

'I agree,' said Victor, 'and if I am allowed to address our shareholders on the subject at the AGM, I'm sure I wouldn't need to remind them that recently the bank made over eleven million pounds on the Harrods take-over by Mr Al Fayed. However, I must confess that without the board's approval, I made a down payment on a property in South Parade behind the Royal Marsden, so the charity can set up its headquarters near the hospital. I was able to pick it up at a knock-down price, because the premises had previously been used by an escort agency.'

'Why didn't you give the board advance notice of the purchase?' asked Seb. 'A phone call would have been quite sufficient, so our executive directors could have discussed your proposal before today's board meeting. Instead, you appear to have presented us with a fait accompli.'

'I apologize, chairman, but I failed to mention that Princess Diana, a friend of Dr Yacoub's, was also on the trip to Egypt, and we were asked by her security team not to reveal our location or the names of anyone else on the trip.'

'Quite right,' said Giles. 'We don't need to telegraph the IRA.'

'And I assumed,' continued Victor, looking directly at Seb, 'that if a real emergency were to arise, you wouldn't have hesitated to call my wife, the one person who knew exactly where I was.'

Three of the directors nodded in agreement.

'Finally,' said Victor, 'I know you'll all be delighted to hear that Professor Yacoub will be holding a press conference at the Marsden next Thursday to announce that Princess Diana has agreed to be the charity's patron.'

'Bravo,' said Clive. 'That can only be good for the bank's image.'

'That's not my sole purpose for wanting to support such a worthwhile cause,' said Victor sharply.

'Possibly not,' said Arnold, 'but while the chancellor is still thrashing about, it won't do us any harm.'

'Perhaps you'd write up a proposal for our consideration at next month's board meeting,' said Seb, 'and distribute it early enough for us to give it some serious thought.'

'I drafted an outline summary while I was circling above you this morning, chairman, and once I've completed it, I'll send copies to all board members.'

Several directors were nodding, as Victor closed the file in front of him.

'Thank you,' said Seb. 'Now all we have to decide is the date of the next meeting.'

Diaries were consulted and, once a date had been agreed, Seb brought the meeting to a close.

'Could you spare me a moment, Victor,' he said, as he gathered up his papers.

'Of course, chairman.' Victor followed Seb out of the

room, down the corridor and into the chairman's office. He was just about to close the door behind him when he noticed that John Ashley and Arnold Hardcastle were following close behind.

Once all four of them were seated around the oval table, Seb tentatively began by saying, 'One or two of us became quite concerned, Victor, when during your absence three cheques were presented for clearance by a Miss Lombardo, whom Arnold, John and I had never heard of.'

'Never heard of?' said Victor. 'Which planet have you been living on?'

When none of them attempted to defend themselves, the penny dropped.

'Ah,' he said, looking like a man who had a straight flush, 'so you all assumed—'

'Well, you must try to see it from our perspective,' said Arnold defensively.

'And to be fair,' said Victor, 'I don't suppose Miss Lombardo makes the front page of the *FT* that often.'

The other three directors burst out laughing.

'I confess I didn't have the board's approval to purchase the building and, fearing that we might lose it while it was still at such a low price, I allowed Miss Lombardo to open an account, which I guaranteed.'

'But that doesn't explain the five thousand pounds she paid for a mink coat from Harrods,' said John Ashley, a little sheepishly.

'A birthday present for Ruth that I didn't want her to know about. By the way, is that why you were trying to get in touch with me?'

'Certainly not,' said Seb. 'We just wanted you to know

that Giles may have pulled off a major coup in Rome, before you read about it in the press.'

'Good try,' said Victor. 'But I've known you far too long, Seb, to fall for that one. I'll tell you what I'll do. I won't mention the subject again, as long as you back my proposal to support the charity at the next board meeting.'

'That sounds like blackmail.'

'Yes, I do believe it is.'

'I should have listened to my wife in the first place,' mumbled Seb.

'That might have been wise, all things considered,' said Victor. 'I wasn't planning to mention to the board that Samantha winked at me when you were making your ridiculous exit from the Caprice.'

HARRY AND EMMA
CLIFTON

1986–1989

44

WHEN HARRY WOKE, he tried to recall a dream that didn't seem to have had an ending. Was he yet again the captain of the England cricket team about to score the winning run against Australia at Lord's? No, as far as he could remember, he was running for a bus that always remained a few yards ahead of him. He wondered what Freud would have made of that. Harry questioned the theory that dreams only ever last for a few moments. How could the scientists possibly be sure of that?

He blinked, turned over and stared at the fluorescent green figures on his bedside clock: 5.07. More than enough time to go over the opening lines in his mind before getting up.

The first morning before starting a new book was always the time when Harry asked himself why. Why not go back to sleep rather than once again embark upon a routine that would take at least a year, and could end in failure? After all, he had passed that age when most people have collected their gold watch and retired to enjoy their twilight years, as insurance companies like to describe them. And Heaven knows, he didn't need the money. But if the choice was resting on his laurels or embarking on a new adventure, it wasn't a difficult decision. Disciplined, was how Emma described him; obsessed, was Sebastian's simple explanation.

For the next half an hour, Harry lay very still, eyes closed, while he went over the first chapter yet again. Although he'd been thinking about the plot for more than a year, he knew that once the pen began to move across the page, the story could unfold in a way he wouldn't have predicted only a few hours before.

He'd already considered and dismissed several opening lines, and he thought he'd finally settled on one, but that could easily be changed in a later draft. If he hoped to capture the readers' imagination and transport them into another world, he knew he had to grab their attention with the opening paragraph, and certainly by the end of the first page.

Harry had devoured biographies of other authors to find out how they went about their craft, and the only thing they all seemed to have in common was that there is no substitute for hard work. Some mapped out their entire plot even before they picked up a pen or began to tap away on a typewriter. Others, after completing the first chapter, would then make a detailed outline of the rest of the book. Harry always thought himself lucky if he knew the first paragraph, let alone the first chapter, because when he picked up his pen at six o'clock each morning, he had no idea where it would lead him, which was why the Irish said he wasn't a writer, but a seannachie.

One thing that would have to be decided before setting out on his latest journey, was the names of the main characters. Harry already knew the book would open in the kitchen of a small house in the back streets of Kiev, where a young boy, aged fifteen, perhaps sixteen, was celebrating his birthday with his parents. The boy must have a name that could be abbreviated, so that when readers were following the two parallel stories, the name alone would immediately tell them if they were in New York or London. Harry had considered Joseph/Joe – too associated with an evil dictator; Maxim/Max – only if he was going to be a general; Nicholai/Nick – too royal, and had finally settled on Alexander/Sasha.

The family's name needed to be easy to read, so readers didn't spend half their time trying to remember who was who, a problem Harry had found when tackling *War and Peace*, even though he'd read it in Russian. He'd considered Kravec, Dzyuba, Belenski, but settled on Karpenko.

Because the father would be brutally murdered by the secret police in the opening chapter, the mother's name was more important. It needed to be feminine, but strong enough for you to believe she could bring up a child on her own, despite the odds being stacked against her. After all, she was destined to shape the character of the book's hero. Harry chose Dimitri for the father's name, and Elena for the mother – dignified but capable. He then returned to thinking about the opening line.

At 5.40 a.m., he threw back the duvet, swung his legs out of bed and placed his feet firmly on the carpet. He then uttered the words he said out loud every morning before he set off for the library. 'Please let me do it again.' He was painfully aware that storytelling was a gift that should not be taken for granted. He prayed that like his hero, Dickens, he would die in mid-sentence.

He padded across to the bathroom, discarded his pyjamas, took a cold shower, then dressed in a T-shirt, tracksuit bottoms, tennis socks and a Bristol Grammar

School 2nd XI sweater. He always laid out his clothes on a chair before going to bed, and always put them on in the same order.

Harry finally put on a pair of well-worn leather slippers, left the bedroom and headed downstairs, muttering to himself, 'Slowly and concentrate, slowly and concentrate.' When he entered the library he walked across to a large oak partner's desk situated in a bay window overlooking the lawn. He sat down in an upright, red buttoned-back leather chair and checked the carriage clock on the desk in front of him. He never began writing before five minutes to six.

Glancing to his right he saw a clutch of framed photographs of Emma playing squash, Sebastian and Samantha on holiday in Amsterdam, Jake attempting to score a goal, and Lucy, the latest member of the family, in her mother's arms, reminding him that he was now a great-grandfather. On the other side of the desk were seven rollerball pens that would be replaced in a week's time. In front of him a 32-lined A4 pad that he hoped would be filled with 2,500 to 3,000 words by the end of the day, meaning the first draft of the first chapter had been completed.

He removed the top from his pen, placed it on the desk beside him, stared down at a blank sheet of paper and began to write.

She had been waiting for over an hour, and no one had spoken to her.

◄○►

Emma followed a routine every bit as disciplined and demanding as her husband's, even if it was completely different. Not least because she wasn't her own mistress.

When Margaret Thatcher had won a second term, she had promoted Emma to minister of state at the Department of Health, in acknowledgement of the contribution she had made during her first term of office.

Like Harry, Emma often recalled Maisie's words, that she should strive to be remembered for something more than just being the first woman chairman of a public company. She hadn't realized when she accepted that challenge that it would pit her against her own brother, whom Neil Kinnock had shrewdly selected to shadow her. It didn't help when even the *Daily Telegraph* referred to Giles as one of the most formidable politicians of the day, and possibly the finest orator in either House.

If she was going to defeat him on the floor of the House, she accepted that it would not be with some witty repartee or a memorable turn of phrase. She would have to rely on blunter instruments: complete command of her brief, and a grasp of detail that would convince her fellow peers to follow her into the Contents lobby when the House divided.

Emma's morning routine also began at six o'clock, and by seven she was at her desk in Alexander Fleming House, signing letters that had been prepared the day before by a senior civil servant. The difference between her and many of her parliamentary colleagues was that she read every single letter, and didn't hesitate to add emendations if she disagreed with the proposed script or felt a crucial point had been overlooked.

Around eight a.m., Pauline Perry, her principal private secretary, would arrive to brief Emma on the day ahead; a speech she would be making at the Royal College of Surgeons that evening needed the odd tweak here and there before it could be released to the press.

At 8.55 a.m., she would walk down the corridor and join the Secretary of State for the daily 'prayer meeting', along with all the other ministers in the department. They would spend an hour discussing government policy to make sure they were all singing from the same hymn sheet. A casual remark picked up by an alert journalist could all too easily end up as a front-page story in a national newspaper the following day.

Emma was still mercilessly teased about the headline, MINISTER SUPPORTS BROTHELS, when she'd said in an unguarded moment, 'I have every sympathy with the plight of women who are forced into prostitution.' She hadn't changed her mind, but had since learnt to express her views more cautiously.

The main topic for discussion that morning was the proposed bill on the future of the NHS, and the role each one of them would play in seeing any legislation through both Houses. The Secretary of State would present the bill in the Lower House, while Emma would lead for the government in the Upper House. She knew this would be her biggest challenge to date, not least because her brother would, to quote him, be lying in wait.

At eleven a.m., she was driven across Westminster Bridge to the Cabinet Office to attend a meeting to consider the financial implications for the government of keeping to pledges the party had made in the last election manifesto. Some of her colleagues would have to make sacrifices when it came to their pet projects, and each minister knew that just promising to cut costs in their department by being more efficient wouldn't suffice. The public had heard the paperclips solution once too often.

Lunch with Lars van Hassel, the Dutch minister for health, in the privacy of her office; no civil servants in attendance. A pompous and arrogant man, who was quite brilliant, and knew it. Emma accepted that she would learn more in an hour over a sandwich and a glass of wine with Lars than she would from most of her colleagues in a month.

In the afternoon, it was her department's turn to answer questions in the Lords, and although her brother landed the occasional blow, no blood was spilt. But then, Emma knew he was saving his heavy artillery for when the NHS bill came before the House.

Questions were followed by a meeting with Bertie Denham, the chief whip, to discuss those members who sat on the government benches but had voiced misgivings when the white paper on the bill was first published. Some sincere, some ill-informed, while others who had sworn undying loyalty to the party if they were offered a peerage suddenly discovered they had minds of their own if it resulted in favourable coverage in the national press.

Emma and the chief whip discussed which of them could be bullied, cajoled, flattered, and in one or two cases bribed with the promise of a place on a parliamentary delegation to some exotic land around the day of the vote. Bertie had warned her that the numbers were looking too close to call.

Emma left the chief whip's office to return to the ministry and be brought up to date on any problems that had arisen during the day. Norman Berkinshaw, the general secretary of the Royal College of Nursing – Emma could only wonder how much longer it would be before a woman held that post – was demanding a 14 per cent pay rise for his members. She had agreed to a meeting with him, when she would point out that if the government gave way to his demands, it would bankrupt the NHS.

But she knew only too well that her words would fall on deaf ears.

At 6.30 p.m. – but by then she would probably be running late – Emma would attend a drinks party at the Carlton Club in St James's, where she would press the flesh of the faithful and listen intently to their views on how the government should be run, a smile never leaving her face. Then she would be whisked off to the Royal College of Surgeons, with just about enough time to check over her speech in the car. More emendations, more crossings out, then finally underlining the key words that needed to be emphasized.

Unlike Harry, Emma needed to be at her best in the evening, however exhausted she felt. She'd once read that Margaret Thatcher survived on only four hours' sleep a night, and was always at her desk by five o'clock in the morning, writing notes to ministers, constituency chairmen, civil servants and old friends. She never forgot a birthday, an anniversary or, as Emma had recently experienced, a card of congratulations on the birth of a great-granddaughter.

'Never forget,' the Prime Minister had added as a postscript, 'your dedication and hard work can only benefit Lucy's generation.'

Emma arrived home at Smith Square just after midnight. She would have phoned Harry, but she didn't want to wake him, aware that he would be up at six in the morning, working on chapter two. She retired to the study to open another red box, delivered while she was having dinner with the president of the Royal College of Surgeons. She sat down and began working on the first draft of a speech that she knew might well define her entire political career.

'My lords, it is my privilege to present to the House for its consideration, the second reading of the government's NHS bill. Let me begin by saying . . .'

45

'WHAT BROUGHT THIS ON?' Emma asked as they left the house for their evening walk into Chew Magna.

'You know I had my annual check-up recently,' said Harry. 'Well, I received the results this morning.'

'Nothing to worry about, I hope?' said Emma, trying not to sound anxious.

'All clear. It seems I ticked all the boxes except one, and although I've stopped jogging, Dr Richards is pleased that I'm still walking for an hour every morning.'

'I only wish I could say the same,' said Emma.

'Your diary secretary would make sure it was never possible. But at least you try to make up for it at the weekend.'

'You said every box except one,' Emma said as they walked along the driveway towards the main road.

'He says I have a couple of small lumps on my prostate. Nothing to worry about, but it might be wise to deal with it in the not-too-distant future.'

'I agree with him. After all, you can have an operation nowadays, or a course of radiotherapy, and be back to normal in a few weeks.'

'I only need another year.'

'What do you mean?' said Emma, stopping in her tracks.

'By then I should have finished *Heads You Win*, and fulfilled the terms of my contract.'

'But knowing you, my darling, by then you'll have another half a dozen ideas racing around in your head. Dare I ask how this one's going?'

'Every author believes their latest work is the best thing they've ever done, and I'm no exception. But you don't really have a clue until you read the reviews or, as Aaron Guinzburg says, three weeks later, when you find out if the tills are still ringing up sales once the initial hype is over and you only have word of mouth to rely on.'

'To hell with Aaron Guinzburg. How do *you* feel?' pressed Emma.

'It's the best thing I've ever done,' said Harry, beating his chest with bravado, only to add, 'Who knows? But then, are you able to be realistic about how your speech is coming along?'

'There's only one thing I can be sure about. My colleagues will let me know how I've done the moment I sit down. They won't wait three weeks to tell me.'

'Is there anything I can do to help?'

'You could get hold of a copy of Giles's speech so I can find out what I'll be up against.'

'Have a word with Karin. I'm sure she could lay her hands on a copy.'

'That's exactly what Seb suggested, and I told him that if Giles ever found out, I wouldn't be the only person he wasn't speaking to.'

'Giles's speech,' said Harry, 'will be like Falstaff in full flow, lots of grandiose ideas, most of them impractical, and certainly unaffordable, along with one or two golden nuggets that you'll be able to steal, and possibly even implement before the next election.'

'You're a crafty old thing, Harry Clifton. You would have made a formidable politician.'

'I would have made a dreadful politician. To start with, I'm not altogether sure which party I support. It's usually the one in opposition. And the thought of having to expose myself to the press, let alone the electorate, would be enough to make me become a hermit.'

'What guilty secret are you hiding?' mocked Emma, as they walked on towards the village.

'All I'm willing to admit is that I intend to go on writing until I drop, and frankly there are enough politicians in this family already. In any case, like a typical politician, you haven't answered my question. How's your speech coming on?'

'Well enough, but I'm worried it's a bit dull and workmanlike at the moment. I think I've dealt with most of my colleagues' reservations, even if one or two of them still remain unresolved. Frankly the speech needs a big idea that will keep Giles in his place, and I've been hoping you might find the time to read it and give me your honest opinion.'

'Of course I will. Though I suspect Giles is every bit as anxious as you are and would like nothing better than to get his hands on a copy of your speech. So I wouldn't be too worried.'

'Can I ask another favour?'

'Anything, my darling.'

'Promise me you'll go and see a specialist, otherwise I'll worry,' said Emma as they linked arms.

'I promise,' said Harry, as they passed the parish church and turned down a public footpath that would lead them back across the meadows to the Manor House. 'But in return, I expect something from you.'

'That sounds rather ominous.'

'It's just that I'd sleep more easily if we both updated our wills.'

'What's brought this on?'

'The realization that I'll be seventy next year and will have fulfilled the Maker's contract, not to mention the birth of a great-granddaughter. It would be irresponsible of us not to make sure our affairs are in order.'

'How morbid, Harry.'

'Possibly, but it shouldn't be avoided. It isn't my will that's the problem because, other than a few gifts to charities and old friends, I've left everything to you, which, according to Seb, is both sensible and at the same time tax advantageous. But both of us should start giving gifts to the children, and as long as we live for another seven years, they won't be liable for any tax. However, the real problem, he tells me, is your will.'

'Unless I die before you, darling, then all your best-laid plans . . .'

'That's unlikely, because I think you'll find that actuaries, like bookies, usually get the odds right. It's how they make their living. Insurance companies currently work on the assumption that women will outlive their husbands by seven years. The average man will live to the age of seventy-four, while their wives will carry on to eighty-one.'

'There's nothing average about you, Harry Clifton, and in any case, I've already planned to die about a fortnight after you.'

'Why a fortnight?'

'I wouldn't want the vicar to find the house untidy.'

Harry couldn't stop grinning. 'Be serious for a moment, my darling. Let's assume we're typical. As I'm a year older than you, you should survive me by eight years.'

'Bloody statistics.'

'Nevertheless, I think it's time for you to update your will, with a view to minimizing the children's inheritance tax liability, which is still at forty per cent, despite Mrs Thatcher's promises.'

'You've thought very seriously about this, haven't you, Harry?'

'The thought of cancer is a wake-up call that shouldn't be ignored. In any case, I read the small print in the Prudential's life policy and couldn't find any reference to immortality.'

'I hope we're not going to have this conversation too often.'

'Once a year should suffice. But I'll feel happier when I know your will is in order.'

'I've already left the Manor House to Sebastian and most of my jewellery to Samantha, Jessica and Lucy.'

'What about Jake?'

'I don't think he'd look good in a pearl necklace. In any case, I have a feeling he has inherited all his father's worst traits and will end up a multimillionaire.'

Harry took her hand as they headed back to the house.

'On to more pleasant matters,' he said. 'Where would you like to spend your summer holidays this year?'

'On a small island in the Indian Ocean where none of my colleagues will be able to find me.'

◅◦►

'We haven't seen Harry and Emma for weeks,' said Karin. 'Why don't we invite them over for lunch on Sunday?'

'I have no intention of fraternizing with the enemy,' said Giles, tugging at the lapels of his dressing gown, 'until the final vote has been cast and the Tories have been defeated.'

'Oh, for heaven's sake, Giles. She's your sister.'

'We only have my parents' word for that.'

'So when can I expect to see them again?'

'Not until the captains and the kings have departed.'

'What are you talking about?'

'Do you think, for one moment, that Wellington would have considered dining with Napoleon the night before Waterloo?'

'It might have been a damned sight better for everyone concerned if he had,' said Karin.

Giles laughed. 'I have a feeling Napoleon might have agreed with you on that.'

'How much longer do we have to wait before we discover which one of you is to be exiled on St Helena?'

'Not much longer. A provisional date for the debate has been pencilled into the parliamentary calendar for a week on Thursday.'

'Dare I ask how your speech is going?'

'Never better. I think I can safely say it will be greeted with the waving of order papers and prolonged and rapturous applause.' Giles paused. 'Actually, I haven't got a clue, my darling. All I can tell you is that I've never worked harder on a speech.'

'Even if you win the argument, do you really have any chance of defeating the government while it has a built-in majority?'

'A very real chance. If the crossbenchers and Liberals join us in the lobby, it will be a close-run thing. I've also identified about a dozen Tories who are not at all happy with the bill, and are still wavering. If I can convince some of them to cross the floor, or just abstain, it will be neck and neck.'

'But surely the Conservative whips will be working overtime cajoling, threatening and even bribing any possible rebels?'

'That's not quite so easy to pull off in the Lords, where the whips don't have too many jobs to offer, promotions to hint at or honours to dangle in front of ambitious young politicians. Whereas I can appeal to their vanity by claiming they are courageous, independent men of conscience, who place what is good for the nation ahead of what is good for their party.'

'What about the women?' demanded Karin.

'It's much harder to bribe women.'

'You're a scoundrel, Giles Barrington.'

'I know, my darling, but you have to understand that being a scoundrel is simply part of a politician's job description.'

'If you were to win the vote,' said Karin, sounding serious for the first time, 'would that mean Emma might have to resign?'

'All's fair in love and war.'

'I hope you've got some better clichés than that in your speech.'

'Traitor,' said Giles, as he put his slippers on, disappeared into the bathroom and turned on the hot water. He looked in the mirror, which was rapidly steaming up, and declared, 'How can the minister pretend to understand the plight of a young mother in Darlington, Doncaster or Durham?

'Which one do you think?' he asked, his voice returning to normal.

'Darlington,' said Karin. 'Emma's unlikely ever to have been there.'

'—or the hardships suffered by a miner from South Wales, who spends half his life down a pit, or a crofter in the Highlands, who begins work at four in the morning. For these are the very people who rely on their local hospital when they fall sick, only to discover that it's been closed by those decent, caring Tories opposite, who aren't interested in saving lives, just saving pennies.'

'So they can build a bigger, better-equipped hospital just up the road?' suggested Karin.

'How can the right honourable lady begin to understand . . .' continued Giles, ignoring his wife's interruption.

'How long are you going to be in there, Giles?'

'Stop heckling, woman. I've just begun my peroration.'

'And I need to go to the loo, now.'

Giles came out of the bathroom. 'And you dare to accuse me of underhand tactics,' he said, brandishing his shaving brush at her.

Karin didn't reply, but glared at her half-shaven husband and retreated into the bathroom.

Giles picked up the latest copy of his speech from the bedside table and replaced Durham with Darlington.

'And how can the right honourable lady hope to understand—' he leant down and crossed out hope, replacing it with begin, as the bathroom door opened.

'The minister of state just might remind the noble lord that she fully understands, as she had the privilege of chairing one of the largest NHS hospitals in the country for seven years.'

'Whose side are you on?' demanded Giles.

'I won't make up my mind until I've heard both sides of the argument,' said Karin. 'Because so far, I've only listened to one side, several times.'

'Love, honour and obey,' said Giles, returning to the bathroom to finish shaving.

'I didn't promise to obey,' said Karin, just before the door was closed.

Karin sat on the end of the bed and began to read Giles's speech. She had to admit, it wasn't half bad. The bathroom door swung open and a fully shaven Giles reappeared.

'It's time to discuss more pressing matters,' he said. 'Where shall we go on holiday this year? I thought perhaps a few days in the South of France. We could stay at La Colombe d'Or, visit the Matisse museum, drive along the Corniche coast, even spend a weekend in Monte Carlo.'

'Berlin.'

'Berlin?' repeated Giles, sitting down beside her on the bed.

'Yes,' said Karin, sounding serious. 'I have a feeling it won't be long before that barbaric wall finally comes down. Thousands of my countrymen and women are standing on the Western side in silent protest every day, and I'd like to go and join them.'

'And so you shall,' said Giles, placing an arm around her shoulder. 'I'll give Walter Scheel a call as soon as I get to the office. If anyone knows what's happening behind the scenes, it will be him.'

'I wonder where Emma will be going on holiday this year?' said Karin as she returned to the bathroom.

Giles waited for the door to shut before he said quietly, 'The island of St Helena, if I have anything to do with it.'

46

'I MUST CONFESS, Sir Harry, that I have never read any of your books,' said the Harley Street specialist, as he looked across the desk at his patient. 'My colleague Mr Lever, however, is an ardent fan. He was disappointed to hear that you've chosen to have an operation rather than a course of radiotherapy, which is his particular field of expertise. Can I begin by asking if that is still the case?'

'It most certainly is, Mr Kirby. I've discussed it at length with my GP, Dr Richards, and my wife, and they're both of the opinion that I should opt for an operation.'

'Then my next question,' said Kirby, 'and I think I already know the answer, is whether you would prefer to go private or have the operation done on the NHS?'

'On that particular decision,' said Harry, 'I wasn't given a lot of choice. If your wife has chaired an NHS hospital for seven years, and gone on to become a minister of health, I have a feeling going private would constitute grounds for divorce.'

'Then all we need to discuss is the timing. I've studied your test results and agree with your GP that while your PSA level remains around six, there is no need for alarm. But as it has been increasing steadily year by year, it might be wise not to hold off the operation for too much longer. With that in mind, I'd like to book you in for some time in the next six months. That will have the added bonus that no one will be able to suggest that you jumped the queue because of your connections.'

'Frankly, that would suit me as well. I've just completed the first draft of my latest novel, and I plan to hand in the manuscript to my publishers just before Christmas.'

'Then that's one problem settled,' said Kirby, as he began to turn over several pages of a large desk diary. 'Shall we say January eleventh at ten o'clock? And I suggest you clear your diary for the following three weeks.'

Harry made a note in his diary, placed three asterisks at the top of the page, and put a line through the rest of the month.

'I do most of my NHS work at Guy's or St Thomas's,' Kirby continued. 'I presume that as Tommy's is just over Westminster Bridge from your home, it would be more convenient for you and your wife.'

'Indeed it would, thank you.'

'Now, there is one small complication that has arisen since your last consultation with Dr Richards.' Kirby swung his chair round and faced a screen on the wall. 'If you study this X-ray,' he said, pointing a thin pencil beam of light on to the screen, 'you will observe that the cancer cells are currently confined to one small area. However, if you look more carefully,' he added, magnifying the image, 'you will see that one or two of the little miscreants are attempting to escape. I intend to remove every one of them before they spread to other parts of your body, where they will be able to do far more damage. Although we have recently developed a cure for prostate cancer, the same cannot be said for the bones or liver, which is where these little blighters are heading.'

Harry nodded.

'Now, I expect, Sir Harry, you may well have some questions of your own.'

'How long will the operation take, and how quickly will I recover?'

'The operation usually takes three to four hours, after which you will experience a fairly unpleasant fortnight, but the average patient is pretty well back to normal after three weeks at most. You will be left with little more than half a dozen small scars on your stomach that will quickly fade, and I would expect you to be back at your desk writing within a month.'

'That's reassuring,' said Harry. He hesitated before asking tentatively, 'How many times have you performed this particular operation?'

'Over a thousand, so I think I've got the hang of it by now,' said Kirby. 'How many books have you written?'

'Touché,' said Harry, standing up to shake hands with the surgeon. 'Thank you. I look forward to seeing you again in January.'

'No one looks forward to seeing me again,' said Kirby. 'But in your case, I consider it a privilege to have been chosen as your surgeon. I may not have read any of your books, but I had just started my first job as a registrar at UCH when you made your speech to the Nobel Prize Committee in Stockholm on behalf of Anatoly Babakov.' He removed a pen from an inside pocket, held it in the air and said, 'The pen is mightier than the sword.'

'I'm both flattered and appalled in equal measure,' said Harry.

'Appalled?' said Kirby, a look of surprise on his face.

'Flattered that you remember my speech, but appalled that you were a young registrar at the time. Am I that old?'

'Certainly not,' said Kirby. 'And when I'm finished with you, you'll be good for another twenty years.'

—◦—

'What do you think?' whispered Emma.

'I can't pretend it would have been my first choice as Jessie's entry for the RA School's gold medal,' admitted Richard.

'Nor mine. And to think she could have entered one of her traditional portraits, which would surely have given her a chance of winning.'

'But it is a portrait, Mama,' said Sebastian.

'Seb, it's a giant condom,' whispered Emma.

'It is indeed, but you have to look more closely to see its real significance.'

'Yes, I must confess I've missed its real significance,' said Emma. 'Perhaps you'd be kind enough to explain it to me.'

'It's Jessie's comment on mankind,' said Samantha, coming to Seb's rescue. 'Inside the condom is a portrait of modern man.'

'But that's a—'

'Yes,' said Harry, unable to resist any longer. 'It's an erect penis in the place of the man's brain.'

'And his ears,' said Emma.

'Well done, Mama, I'm glad you worked that one out.'

'But look more closely at the eyes,' said Samantha, 'and you'll see two images of naked women.'

'Yes, I can see them, but why is the man's tongue poking out?'

'I can't imagine, Mother,' said Seb.

'But at three thousand pounds,' continued Emma, still unconvinced, 'will anyone buy it?'

'I intend to,' said Seb.

'That's very loyal of you, my darling, but where on earth will you hang it?'

'In the banking hall, so everyone can see it.'

'Sebastian, it's a giant condom!'

'It is indeed, Mother, and I suspect one or two of our more enlightened customers might even recognize it as such.'

'And no doubt you can also explain the title to me,' said Emma. '*Every Seven Seconds*?'

Sebastian was saved when a distinguished-looking gentleman appeared by their side.

'Good evening, minister,' he said to Emma. 'May I say how delighted I am to see you and your husband at the RA.'

'Thank you, Sir Hugh. We wouldn't have missed it.'

'Is there a particular reason you interrupted your busy schedule to join us?'

'My granddaughter,' said Emma, gesturing towards *Every Seven Seconds*, unable to hide her embarrassment.

'You must be very proud,' said the former president of the RA. 'It is to her credit that she has never mentioned her distinguished grandparents.'

'I suspect that if your father is a banker and your grandmother a Tory politician, it's not something you would want to share with your artistic friends. But then I doubt if she's ever told you we have two of your water-colours hanging in our home in the country.'

'I'm flattered,' said Sir Hugh. 'But I confess I wish I had been born with your granddaughter's talent.'

'That's kind of you, but can I ask you for your candid opinion of Jessica's latest work?'

The PPRA took a long look at *Every Seven Seconds*, before saying, 'Original, innovative. Stretches the boundaries of one's imagination. I would suggest it is influenced by Marcel Duchamp.'

'I agree with you, Sir Hugh,' said Sebastian, 'which is precisely the reason I'm going to buy the picture.'

'I'm afraid it's already been sold.'

'Someone's actually bought it?' said Emma incredulously.

'Yes, an American dealer snapped it up as soon as the show opened, and several other customers, like you, have been disappointed to find it had already been sold.'

Emma was speechless.

'Please, will you excuse me, because it's time to announce the winner of this year's gold medal.' Sir Hugh gave a slight bow before leaving them to walk over to the stage at the far end of the room.

Emma was still speechless when a couple of photographers began taking pictures of her standing beside the painting. A journalist turned a page of his notepad and said, 'May I ask, minister, what you think of your granddaughter's portrait?'

'Original, innovative. Stretches the boundaries of one's imagination. I would suggest it was influenced by Marcel Duchamp.'

'Thank you, minister,' said the journalist, writing down her words before hurrying away.

'You are not only shameless, Mama, but your audacity stretches the boundaries of one's imagination. I'll bet you'd never heard of Duchamp before today.'

'Let's be fair,' said Harry, 'your mother never behaved like this before she became a politician.'

There was a gentle tap on the microphone, and everyone turned to face the stage.

'Good evening, ladies and gentlemen. My name is Hugh Casson, and I'd like to welcome you to the Royal Academy School's exhibition. As chairman of the awards panel, it is now my privilege to announce the winner of this year's gold medal. I usually preface my words by saying what a difficult decision it has been for the judges, and how unlucky the runners-up were, but not on this occasion, because the panel was unanimous in awarding this year's gold medal to—'

◄○►

'You must be so proud of your granddaughter,' said the Permanent Secretary when she joined the minister in her office the next morning. 'She'll be among such illustrious company.'

'Yes, I read the details in this morning's papers, and all the different interpretations of the picture, but tell me, Pauline, what did you make of it?'

'Original, innovative, and it stretches the boundaries of one's imagination.'

'That's all I need,' said Emma, not attempting to hide her sarcasm. 'But I'm sure I don't have to remind you that it's a giant condom, which the *Sun* featured on its front page.'

'And that condom got more coverage than the government's entire PR campaign for safer sex, which as I'm sure you remember, minister, you launched last year.'

'Well, I did manage the odd headline when I said I

hoped the campaign would be penetrative,' said Emma with a smile. 'Anything else, Pauline?'

'I've just read the latest version of your speech for next Thursday's debate, minister.'

'And it sent you to sleep?'

'I did find it a little prosaic.'

'A polite way of saying it was dull.'

'Well, let's say that an injection of humour wouldn't do any harm.'

'Especially as humour is my brother's forté.'

'It just might make a difference if the press are right in suggesting it's going to be a close-run thing.'

'Can't we rely on the facts to persuade the waverers?'

'I wouldn't count on it, minister. And I think you ought to know that the PM has asked what plans we have in place should we lose the vote.'

'Has she indeed? Then I'd better go over the speech yet again this weekend. The irony is that if it wasn't my brother I was up against, I'd be asking him to add the odd bon mot.'

'I'm sure he'd like to,' said Pauline, 'but no doubt that's why Kinnock gave him the job in the first place.'

'Hardly subtle,' said Emma. 'Anything else?'

'Yes, minister, I wonder if I might discuss a personal matter with you.'

'That sounds rather serious, Pauline, but yes, of course.'

'Have you been following the latest research to come out of the States concerning DNA?'

'Can't say I have,' said Emma. 'My red boxes provide me with quite enough reading as it is.'

'It's just that I felt the most recent breakthrough in the field might interest you.'

431

'Why?' said Emma, genuinely puzzled.

'Scientists can now prove conclusively if two people are related.'

'How did you know?' asked Emma quietly.

'When someone is appointed as a minister to the Crown, we prepare a file on them, so that if the press contact us about their past, we are at least forewarned.'

'And have the press been in touch?'

'No. But I was at school when the trial was held in the House of Lords that passed judgement on whether your brother or Harry Clifton was the first born, and therefore the lawful heir to the Barrington title and estates. All of us at Berkhamsted High thought it was very romantic at the time, and were delighted when their lordships came down in favour of your brother, making it possible for you to marry the man you loved.'

'And now I would finally be able to discover if their lordships' judgement was correct,' said Emma. 'Give me a little time to think about it, because I certainly wouldn't be willing to go ahead without Harry's blessing.'

'Of course, minister.'

'On a lighter note, Pauline, you said you kept a file on me. Does that mean you have a file on every other minister?'

'We most certainly do. However, that does not mean I would be willing to divulge which of your colleagues is a transvestite, who was caught smoking marijuana in Buckingham Palace, and which law lord likes to dress up as a policeman and go on night patrols.'

'Just one question, Pauline. Are any of them among the waverers?'

'Sadly not, minister.'

47

ALTHOUGH MOST OF their lordships had made up their minds how they would vote long before the House assembled for the crucial debate, both Emma and Giles accepted that the fate of the bill now rested in the hands of a dozen or so peers who were yet to be persuaded either way.

Emma had risen early that morning and gone through her speech once again before leaving for the department. She rehearsed several of the key paragraphs out loud, with only Harry as her audience, and although he made some excellent suggestions, she reluctantly accepted that the responsibility of government didn't allow her the freedom of rhetorical hyperbole that Giles so enjoyed in opposition. But then his single purpose was to embarrass the government when the House divided. Hers was to govern.

When Emma arrived at her office in Alexander Fleming House, she was pleased to find her diary had been cleared so she could concentrate on the one thing uppermost in her mind. Like a restless athlete preparing for an Olympic final, how she spent the last few hours before the race might well decide the outcome. However, in politics there are no prizes for second place.

For the past week, she had tried to anticipate any awkward questions that might arise during the course of the debate, so nothing could take her by surprise. Would Field Marshal Montgomery prove to be right? Nine-tenths of a battle is won in preparation long before the first shot is fired.

Emma was shaking as she climbed into the ministerial car to be driven across the river to the Palace of Westminster. On arrival, she retired to her room, accompanied by a ham sandwich and a black coffee. She went over her speech one more time, adding a couple of minor changes, before making her way to the chamber.

—<o>—

As Big Ben struck twice, the Lord Speaker took his place on the Woolsack, so the day's business could begin.

The Right Reverend Bishop of Worcester rose from the bishops' bench, to conduct prayers for the assembled House. Worcester, like his fellow peers, was well aware of the significance of today's debate, and the fact that although there were over a thousand hereditary peers who had the right to attend proceedings, along with six hundred life peers, the chamber could only hold around five hundred, so it was no surprise that the benches were already packed.

Home Office questions were first on the order paper, but few peers were interested in the answers, and a gentle hum of chatter descended on the House while they waited for the main event.

Giles made his entry towards the end of questions, and was greeted warmly by his colleagues, like a heavyweight boxer before he steps into the ring. He took his seat in the only remaining place on the front bench.

Emma appeared a few moments later, and was greeted equally warmly as she made her way along the government front bench before taking her seat next to the leader of the House.

When questions came to an end, the Lord Speaker indicated that the main business of the day could begin. Lord Belstead rose slowly from his place, put his speech on the despatch box and with all the confidence of a man who had held several offices of state, delivered the opening salvo on behalf of the government.

Once he had delivered his opening remarks, Lord Cledwyn, equally familiar with his surroundings, rose to reply from the opposition benches.

There then followed a series of speeches from the back benches, which Emma and Giles, like the rest of the House, listened to with varying degrees of interest. Everyone was clearly waiting to hear the contributions from the Rt Hon. Lord Barrington of Bristol Docklands, who would be summing up on behalf of the opposition, and the Rt Hon. Baroness Clifton of Chew Magna, who would put the case for the government.

Neither Emma nor Giles left the chamber at any time during the debate, both eschewing a break for supper as they continued to listen to their colleagues' contributions, while making the occasional note when a particular point was well argued.

Although gaps on the red benches appeared between the hours of seven and nine, Emma and Giles knew the stalls would fill up long before the second-act curtain was due to rise. Only John Gielgud making his last West End appearance in *Best of Friends* could take such a packed house for granted.

By the time the final speaker rose to make his contribution from the back benches, the only empty seat was on the throne, which was only ever occupied by the monarch when she delivered the Queen's speech at the opening of Parliament. The steps below the throne and in the aisles between the red benches were packed with noble lords who had been unable to secure a seat. Behind the bar of the House, at the far end of the chamber, stood several members of the House of Commons, including the Secretary of State, who had promised the Prime Minister that everything had been done to ensure that the bill would be passed so the government could make progress with its heavy legislative programme, for which time was fast running out. But from the looks on the faces of those attendees from the Lower House, they were equally unsure of the outcome.

Emma glanced up at the Distinguished Strangers' Gallery to see members of her family seated in the front row, but they were also members of Giles's family, and she suspected that they were equally divided. Harry, Sebastian and Samantha unquestionably supported her, while Karin, Grace and Freddie would back Giles, leaving Jessica to hold the casting vote. Emma felt they only mirrored the feelings of her fellow peers.

When Lord Samuels, an eminent former president of the Royal College of Physicians, sat down having delivered the last speech from the cross benches, a buzz of expectation went up around the chamber.

If Giles was nervous when he got to his feet, there was no sign of it. He gripped the sides of the despatch box firmly and waited for silence before delivering his opening line.

'My lords, I stand before you this evening painfully aware that the fate of the National Health Service rests in our hands. I wish I was exaggerating, but I fear I am not. Because tonight, my lords, you, and you alone, will decide if this dreadful bill' – he waved the order paper high above his head – 'will become law, or simply a collector's item for those interested in the footnotes of history.

'I do not have to remind your lordships, that it was the Labour Party, under Clem Attlee, which not only founded the NHS, but has been defending its very existence ever since. Whenever this country has had to suffer the travails of a Conservative administration, it has been Labour's responsibility to ensure that the NHS survives attack after attack from the infidels storming its hallowed gates.'

Loud cheers erupted from behind him, which allowed Giles to turn a page of his script and check the next sentence.

'My lords, I am ashamed to admit,' he continued, with an exaggerated sigh, 'that the latest of these infidels is my own kith and kin, the Baroness Clifton of Chew Magna.'

Both sides of the House joined in the laughter, while Emma wished she had been bestowed with the gift to switch from grave pronouncement to light humour in a moment, and at the same time to carry the House with her.

Giles spent the next twenty minutes dismantling the bill line by line, concentrating particularly on those clauses about which Tory waverers had expressed concerns. Emma could only admire the skill with which her brother heaped praise on the statesmanlike contributions of the few Tories who remained undecided, before adding, 'We can only hope that those men and women of conscience display the same courage and independence of mind when the time comes to enter the division lobby, and do not at the last moment cast their true beliefs aside, hiding behind the false mask of party loyalty.'

Even by Giles's standards, it was a formidable performance. Colleagues and opponents alike were on the edge of their seats as he continued, like Merlin, to cast his spell over a mesmerized House. Emma knew she would have to break that spell and drag her colleagues back to the real world if she hoped to win the vote.

'Let me end, my lords,' said Giles, almost in a whisper, 'by reminding you of the power you hold in your hands tonight. You have been granted the one opportunity to throw out this flawed and counterfeit bill, which, were it to become law, would spell the end of the National Health Service as we know it, and stain the memory of its glorious past, and of those good old days.'

He leant across the despatch box and looked slowly up and down the government front bench before saying, 'This bill proves only one thing, my lords: dinosaurs are not only to be found in the Natural History Museum.' He waited for the laughter to die down before he lowered his voice and continued, 'Those of you who, like myself, have studied this bill word for word, will have noticed that one word is conspicuously absent. Search as I might, my lords, nowhere could I find the word "compassion". But why should that come as a surprise, when the minister opposite, who will shortly present this bill, has herself personally denied hard-working nurses a living wage?'

Cries of 'Shame!' came from the opposition benches, as Giles stared across at his sister. 'And you don't have to read between the lines to understand that the government's real purpose in this bill is to replace the word "National" with "Private", because its first priority is to serve those who can afford to be sick, while leaving on the scrap heap those of our citizens who are unable to bear the cost. That is, and always has been, the overriding philosophy of this government.

'My lords,' said Giles, his voice rising in a crescendo, 'I invite you to vote decisively against this iniquitous bill, so those same citizens can continue to enjoy the security of a truly national health service, because I believe that when it comes to our health, all men –' he paused and stared across the despatch box at his sister – 'and women, are born equal.

'My lords, I don't ask you, I beg you, to let your views be clearly heard by our fellow countrymen when you cast your votes tonight, and soundly reject this bill.'

He sat down to resounding cheers and the waving of order papers from behind him, and silence from the benches opposite. When the cheers finally died down, Emma rose slowly from her seat, placed her speech on the despatch box and gripped its sides firmly in the hope that no one would see just how nervous she was.

'My lords,' she began, her voice trembling slightly, 'it would be churlish of me not to acknowledge the performance of my noble kinsman, Lord Barrington, but performance it was, because I suspect that when you read his words in Hansard tomorrow, you will see that his speech was long on rhetoric, short on substance and devoid of facts.'

A few muted 'Hear, hear's could be heard from her colleagues seated behind her, while the members opposite remained silent.

'I spent seven years of my life running a large NHS

hospital, so I don't have to prove that I am just as concerned about the future of the National Health Service as anyone sitting on the benches opposite. However, despite all the passion mustered by the noble lord, the truth is that, in the end, someone has to pay the bills and balance the books. The NHS has to be funded with real money, and paid for with the taxes of real people.'

Emma was delighted to see a few heads nodding. Giles's speech had been well received, but it was her responsibility to explain the finer details of the proposed legislation. She took their lordships through the substance of the bill clause by clause, but was unable to kindle the flame of passion that her brother had ignited so successfully.

As she turned another page, she became aware of what her grandfather, Lord Harvey, once described as losing the attention of the House, that moment when members become listless and begin chattering among themselves. Far more damning even than jeering or cries of 'Shame'.

She glanced up to see an elderly peer nodding off, and when, moments later, he began to snore, the members seated on either side of him made no attempt to wake him, as they were all too clearly enjoying the minister's discomfort. Emma realized the minutes were slipping away before the House would be asked to divide and the votes would be counted. She turned another page. 'And now I would like to acknowledge the backbone of the NHS, our magnificent nurses, who—'

Giles leapt to his feet to interrupt the minister, and in doing so strayed on to enemy territory. Emma immediately gave way, allowing her brother to command the despatch box.

'I am grateful to the noble lady for giving way, but may I ask, if she considers nurses are doing such a magnificent job, why are they only receiving a three per cent pay rise?' Convinced that Emma was now on the ropes, he sat down to loud cries of 'Hear, hear!'

Emma resumed her place at the despatch box. 'The noble lord, if I recall his words correctly, demanded a fourteen per cent pay rise for nurses.' Giles nodded vigorously. 'So I am bound to ask him where he expects the government to find the extra money to pay for such an increase?'

Giles was quickly back on his feet, ready to deliver the knockout blow. 'It could start by putting up taxes for the highest earners, who can well afford to pay a little more to assist those less fortunate than themselves.' He sat down to even louder cheers, while Emma waited patiently at the despatch box.

'I'm glad the noble lord admitted that would be a start,' she said, picking up a red file that a Treasury official had handed her that morning, 'because a start is all it would be. If he is asking this House to believe that the Labour Party could cover a fourteen per cent pay rise for nurses simply by raising taxes for those earning forty thousand pounds a year or more, let me tell him this, he would require a tax hike to ninety-three per cent year on year. And I confess,' she added, borrowing her brother's brand of sarcasm, 'I hadn't realized that a tax rate of ninety-three per cent was Labour Party policy, because I didn't spot it in their manifesto, which I read word for word.'

Emma could hear the laughter coming from behind her, even if she couldn't see her colleagues jabbing their fingers at her brother and repeating, 'Ninety-three per cent, ninety-three per cent.'

Like Giles, she waited for silence before adding, 'Perhaps the noble lord would tell the House what other ideas he has for covering the extra cost?'

Giles remained seated.

'Might I be allowed to suggest one or two ways of raising the necessary funds that would help him to reach his target of fourteen per cent?'

Emma had recaptured the attention of the House. She turned a page of the Treasury memo inside the red file. 'For a start, I could cancel the three new hospitals planned for Strathclyde, Newcastle and Coventry. That would solve the problem. Mind you, I'd need to close another three hospitals next year. But I am not willing to make that sacrifice, so perhaps I should look at some other departments' budgets and see what my colleagues have to offer.'

She turned another page.

'We could cut back on our plans for new universities, or withdraw the three per cent increase in the old age pension. That would solve the problem. Or we could cut back on our armed forces by mothballing the odd regiment. No, no, we couldn't do that,' she said scornfully, 'not after the noble lord spoke so passionately against any cutbacks in the armed forces budget only a month ago.'

Giles sank further into his seat.

'And remembering the noble lord's distinguished record in another place, as a Foreign Office minister, perhaps we could close half a dozen of our embassies. That should do the trick. We could even leave him to decide which ones. Washington? Paris? Moscow perhaps?

Beijing? Tokyo? I'm bound to ask, is this another Labour Party policy they forgot to mention in their manifesto?'

Suddenly the government benches were alight with laughter and cheering.

'No, my Lord Speaker,' continued Emma once the house had fallen silent again, 'the truth is, words are cheap, but action comes more expensive, and it's the duty of a responsible government to consider priorities and make sure it balances the books. That undertaking was in the Tory manifesto, and I make no apology for it.'

Emma was aware that she only had a couple of minutes left, and the cheering of her delighted colleagues was eating away at her time.

'I must therefore tell the House that I consider education, pensions, defence and our role in world affairs every bit as important as my own department. But let me assure your lordships, when it comes to my own department, I fought the Treasury tooth and nail to keep those three new hospitals in the budget.' She paused, raised her voice and said, 'This morning the Chancellor of the Exchequer agreed that the nurses will be awarded a six per cent pay rise.'

The benches behind her erupted in prolonged cheers.

Emma abandoned the final pages of her script and, looking directly at her brother, said, 'None of this, however, will be possible if you follow the noble lord into the Not Contents lobby tonight and vote against this bill. If I am, as he suggests, an infidel storming the hallowed gates of the National Health Service, then I must tell him that I intend to open those gates to allow all patients to enter. Yes, my lords, free at the point of use, to quote his hero Clement Attlee. And that is the reason, my lords, I do not hesitate to urge you to join me in the real world and support this bill, so that when I return to my department tomorrow morning, I can set about making the necessary changes that will ensure the future of the National Health Service and not allow it to languish in the past, along with my noble kinsman, Lord Barrington, who will presumably still be reminiscing fondly about the good old days. I, my lords, will be telling my grandchildren, and also my great-granddaughter, about the good new days. But that will only be possible if you support this bill, and join me in the Contents lobby tonight. My lords, I beg to move the second reading.'

Emma sat down to the loudest cheer of the night, while Giles sat slumped back, aware that he shouldn't have raised his head above the parapet, but should simply have feigned boredom and allowed Emma to dig her own grave. She glanced across the chamber at her brother, who raised a hand, touched his forehead and mouthed the word 'Chapeau'. Praise indeed. But both of them were well aware that the votes still had to be counted.

When the division bell rang, members began to make their way towards the corridors of their conviction. Emma entered the Contents lobby, where she spotted one or two fence-sitters and waverers casting their vote. But would it be enough?

Once she had given her name to the teller seated at his high desk, ticking off each member, she returned to her seat on the front bench and joined in the inconse-quential chatter that always rises like hot air from both sides while members wait for the whips to return and deliver the verdict of the House.

A hush descended on the chamber when the four gentlemen ushers lined up and marched slowly towards the table at the centre of the chamber.

The chief whip held up a card and, once he'd double-checked the figures, declared, 'Contents to the left, four hundred and twenty-two.' Emma held her breath. 'Not Contents to the right, four hundred and eleven. The Contents have it. The Contents have it.'

Cheers erupted from the benches behind Emma. As she made her way out of the chamber, she found herself surrounded by supporters telling her they had never doubted she would win. She smiled and thanked them.

She finally managed to break away and join Harry and the rest of the family in the peers' guest room, where she was delighted to find Giles opening a bottle of champagne. He filled her glass and raised his own.

'To Emma,' he said, 'who not only won the argument but also the battle, as our mother predicted she would.'

Once the rest of the family had departed, Harry, Giles, Emma, Karin and Freddie – his first glass of champagne – walked slowly back to their home in Smith Square. Emma climbed into bed exhausted, but an intoxicating mix of adrenaline and success made it impossible for her to sleep.

–◆–

The following morning, Emma woke at six, her cruel body clock ignoring her desire to go on sleeping.

Once she had showered and dressed, she hurried downstairs, looking forward to reading the reports of the debate in the papers while enjoying a cup of tea, and perhaps even a second slice of toast and marmalade. The papers were already laid out on the dining table. She read the headline in *The Times* and collapsed into the nearest chair, her head in her hands. That had never been her intention.

LORD BARRINGTON RESIGNS AFTER
HUMILIATING DEFEAT IN THE LORDS

Emma knew that 'resigned' was a parliamentary euphemism for sacked.

48

THE END

HARRY PUT DOWN his pen, leapt in the air and shouted 'Hallelujah!', which was what he always did whenever he wrote those two words. He sat back down, looked up at the ceiling, and said, 'Thank you.' Another ritual fulfilled.

In the morning, he would send copies of the script to three people, so they could read *Heads You Win* for the first time. Then he would suffer his annual neurosis, while he waited to hear their opinions. But just like him, they all had their own routines.

The first, Aaron Guinzburg, his American publisher, would leave his office and go home the moment the manuscript landed on his desk, having given clear instructions that he was not to be disturbed until he had turned the last page. He would then call Harry, sometimes forgetting what time it was in England. His view could often be discounted because he was always so enthusiastic.

The second was Ian Chapman, his English publisher, who always waited until the weekend before he read the book, and would call Harry first thing on Monday morning to offer his opinion. As he was a Scotsman who was unable to hide his true feelings, this only made Harry more apprehensive.

The third, and by far the most intuitive of his first readers, was his sister-in-law, Grace, who not only offered her disinterested opinion, but invariably accompanied it with a ten-page written report, and occasionally, forgetting he was not one of her pupils, corrected his grammar.

Harry had never considered Grace to be an obvious William Warwick fan until in an unguarded moment she admitted to a penchant for racy novels. However, her idea of racy was Kingsley Amis, Graham Greene (the ones he described as entertainments) and her favourite, Ian Fleming.

In return for her opinion, Harry would take Grace to lunch at the Garrick, before accompanying her to a matinee, preferably by her favourite racy playwright, Terence Rattigan.

Once the three manuscripts had been despatched by courier, the agonizing wait began. Harry's three readers had all been warned that *Heads You Win* was a departure from his usual fare, which only made him more anxious.

He had considered allowing Giles, who had a lot more time on his hands lately, and Sebastian, his most ardent fan, to also be among the first to read his latest manuscript, but decided not to break with his usual routine. He would allow them to read the final draft over Christmas, after his line editor had suggested any changes.

Miss Eileen Warburton, a spinster of this parish, was a woman Harry suspected lived alone in a basement flat and, like Mole, didn't emerge until spring. During those winter months, she would spend her time toiling away on her authors' hapless scripts, correcting their mistakes, some of which were so inconsequential no one else would ever have noticed them. While others, howlers, as she liked to describe them, had they gone uncorrected, would have caused a thousand irate letters to end up on the author's desk, pointing out his stupidity. Miss Warburton never allowed Harry to forget that Geneva was not the capital of Switzerland, and that the *Titanic* had sunk on April 15th, not 14th.

In a moment of flippant bravado, Harry had once reminded her that in Flaubert's *Madame Bovary*, the heroine's eyes changed from black to brown to blue and back to black again in less than a hundred pages.

'I never comment on books I haven't edited,' she said, without any suggestion of irony.

Emma would be among the last to read the manuscript, when it was in proof form. Everyone else would have to wait until publication day before they could get their hands on a copy.

Harry had planned to spend a relaxing weekend once the book was finished. On Saturday afternoon, he and Giles would drive over to the Memorial Ground and watch Bristol play their old rivals Bath. In the evening, he would take Emma to the Bristol Old Vic to see Patricia Routledge in *Come for the Ride*, followed by dinner at Harvey's.

On Sunday, he and Emma had been invited by Giles and Karin to lunch at Barrington Hall. They would later attend evensong, when he would spend most of the sermon wondering which page his three readers were on. As for an unbroken night's sleep, that would not be back on the agenda until all three had called and given their opinion.

When the phone rang, Harry's first thought was that

it was too early for any of them to have finished the book. He picked it up to hear Giles's familiar voice on the other end of the line.

'Sorry to mess you about, Harry, but I won't be able to join you for rugby on Saturday, and we'll also have to postpone lunch on Sunday.' Harry didn't need to ask why, because an explanation followed immediately. 'Walter Scheel called earlier. The East Germans have opened the floodgates at last, and their citizens are pouring across the border. I'm calling from Heathrow. Karin and I are about to board a flight to Berlin. We're hoping to get there before they start knocking the wall down, because she and I plan to be part of the demolition crew.'

'That's the most wonderful news,' said Harry. 'Karin must be delighted. Tell her I'm envious, because when people ask where were you on the day the wall came down, you'll be able to tell them. And if you can, bring me back a piece.'

'I'm going to have to take an extra suitcase,' said Giles. 'So many people have made the same request.'

'Just remember, you'll be witnessing history, so before you go to bed each night, be sure to write down everything you've experienced that day. Otherwise you'll have forgotten the details by the time you wake up.'

'I'm not sure we'll be going to bed,' said Giles.

━◄◦►━

'May I ask why you're carrying a hammer in your bag, sir?' asked a vigilant security officer at Heathrow.

'I'm hoping to break down a wall,' Giles replied.

'I wish I could join you,' said the officer, before zipping up the overnight bag.

When Giles and Karin climbed aboard the BA plane

half an hour later, it was as if they had gatecrashed a party rather than joined a group of passengers who would normally be fastening their seatbelts prior to receiving safety instructions from a zealous air hostess. Once the flight had taken off, champagne corks were popping, and passengers chatted to their neighbours as if they were old friends.

Karin held on to Giles's hand throughout the entire flight, and she must have said, 'I just can't believe it' a dozen times, still fearful that by the time they landed in Berlin, the party would be over and everything would have returned to normal.

After two hours that seemed like an eternity the plane finally touched down, and the moment it had taxied to a halt, the passengers leapt out of their seats. The usual orderly queue that the Germans are so famed for disintegrated, to be replaced by an undisciplined charge as the passengers rushed down the steps, across the tarmac and into the airport. Tonight, no one would be standing still.

Once they had cleared customs, Giles and Karin headed out of the terminal in search of a taxi, only to discover a heaving mass of people with the same thought in mind. However, to Giles's surprise, the line moved quickly, as three, four, or even five passengers piled into each cab, all of them heading in the same direction. When they finally reached the front of the queue, Giles and Karin joined a German family who didn't need to tell the driver where they wanted to go.

'Englishman, why you come to Berlin?' asked the young man squeezed up against Giles.

'I'm married to an East German,' he explained, placing an arm around Karin's shoulder.

'How did your wife escape?'

'It's a long story.' Karin came to Giles's rescue, and it took her three slow miles of unrelenting traffic, speaking in her native tongue, before she came to the end of her tale, which was greeted with enthusiastic applause. The young man gave Giles a new look of respect, although he hadn't understood a word his wife had said.

With a mile to go, the taxi driver gave up and stopped in the middle of a road that had been turned into a dance floor. Giles was the first out of the car and took out his wallet to pay the driver, who said simply, 'Not tonight,' before swinging round and heading back to the airport; another man who would tell his grandchildren about the role he'd played the night the wall came down.

Hand in hand, Giles and Karin weaved their way through the exuberant crowd towards the Brandenburg Gate, which neither of them had seen since the afternoon Karin had escaped from East Berlin almost two decades ago.

As they drew closer to the great monument, built by King Frederick William II of Prussia, ironically as a symbol of peace, they could see ranks of armed soldiers lined up on the far side. Giles thought about Harry's suggestion that he should write down everything he witnessed, for fear of forgetting the moment, and wondered what his brother-in-law would have considered the appropriate word to describe the expressions on the soldiers' faces. Not anger, not fear, not sadness; they were simply bemused. Like everyone dancing around them, their lives had been changed in a moment.

Karin stared at the soldiers from a distance, still wondering if it was all too good to be true. Would one of them recognize her, and try to drag her back across the border even now?

Although a united people were celebrating all around her, she remained unconvinced that life wouldn't return to normal when the sun rose. As if Giles could read her thoughts, he took her in his arms and said, 'It's all over, my darling. You can turn the page. The nightmare has finally come to an end.'

An East German officer appeared from nowhere and barked out an order. The soldiers shouldered their weapons and marched off, which caused an even louder roar of approval. While everyone around them danced, drank and sang ecstatically, Giles and Karin made their way slowly through the crowd towards the graffiti-covered wall, on top of which hundreds of revellers were dancing, as if it were the grave of a hated foe.

Karin stopped and touched Giles's arm when she spotted an old man hugging a young woman. It was clear that, like so many people on that unforgettable night, they were finally being reunited after twenty-eight years apart. Laughter, joy and celebration were mingled with tears, as the old man clung on to the granddaughter he had thought he would never meet.

'I want to stand on top of the wall,' declared Karin.

Giles looked up at the twelve-foot-high monument commemorating failure, on which hundreds of young people were having a party. He decided it wasn't the moment to remind his wife that he was nearly seventy. This was a night for shedding years.

'Great idea,' he said.

When they reached the foot of the wall, Giles suddenly knew what Edmund Hillary must have felt when faced with the final ascent of Everest, but two young Sherpas, who had just descended, cupped their hands and made the first rung of a ladder, so he could take their place on the summit. He couldn't quite make it, but two other young revellers reached down and yanked him up to join them.

Karin joined him a moment later and they stood, side by side, staring across the border. She was still unwilling to believe she wouldn't wake up and find it was all a dream. Some East Germans were attempting to climb up from the other side, and Karin stretched down to offer a young girl a hand. Giles took a photograph of the two women, who'd never met before, hugging each other as if they were old friends. A photograph that would end up on their mantelpiece in Smith Square to commemorate the day East and West returned to sanity.

From their lofty position, Giles and Karin watched a flood of people flowing downstream to freedom, while the guards, who only the night before would have shot anyone attempting to cross the border, just stood and stared, unable to comprehend what was happening all around them.

Karin was finally beginning to believe that the genie had escaped from the communist bottle, but it took her another hour to summon up the courage to say to Giles, 'I want to show you where I lived.'

Giles found the descent from the wall almost as difficult as clambering up it had been, but with the help of several outstretched hands, he somehow managed it, though he needed to catch his breath once his feet had touched the ground.

Karin took his hand and they battled against a one-way stampede of human traffic as she led him slowly towards the border post. Thousands of men, women and children, carrying bags, suitcases, even pushing prams laden with their life's possessions, were heading in one direction, leaving their old lives behind, clearly unwilling to consider returning in case they should find themselves trapped once again.

After they'd passed under the red and white barrier and left the West, Giles and Karin joined a trickle of citizens who were heading in the same direction as themselves. Karin hesitated, but only for a moment, when they passed the second barrier and found themselves on East German soil.

There were no border guards, no snarling Alsatians, no thin-lipped officials to check that their visas were in order. Just an eerie, unoccupied wilderness.

There were also no taxi queues, as there were no taxis. They passed a little group of East Germans kneeling in silent prayer, in memory of those who'd sacrificed their lives to make today possible.

The two of them continued to weave their way through the crowds that were melting away with each step they took. It was well over an hour before Karin finally stopped and pointed towards a group of identical grey tenement buildings that stood in a grim line, reminding her of a past life she'd almost forgotten.

'This is where you lived?'

She looked up and said, 'The nineteenth floor, second window on the left is where I spent the first twenty-four years of my life.'

Giles counted until he reached a tiny curtainless window on the nineteenth floor, second from the left, and couldn't help recalling where he'd spent the first twenty-four years of his life: Barrington Hall, a townhouse in London, the castle in Scotland in which he spent a few weeks every summer, and then of course there was always the villa in Tuscany should he need a break.

'Do you want to go up and see who's living there now?' he asked.

'No,' said Karin firmly. 'I want to go home.'

Without another word, she turned her back on the towering blocks of grey concrete and joined those of her countrymen who were heading towards the West, to experience a freedom that she had never taken for granted.

She didn't once look back as they walked towards the border, although a moment of anxiety returned as they approached the crossing point, but it quickly evaporated when she saw some of the guards, jackets unbuttoned, collars loosened, dancing with their newly made friends, no longer from East or West, now simply Germans.

Once they had passed under the barrier and were back in the West, they found young and old alike attempting, with sledgehammers, crowbars, chisels and even a nail file, to dismantle the 96-mile-long monstrosity piece by piece. The physical symbol of what Winston Churchill had described as the Iron Curtain.

Giles unzipped his bag, took out the hammer and handed it to Karin.

'You first, my darling.'

EMMA CLIFTON

1990–1992

49

'It's that time of the year,' said Emma as she raised a glass of mulled wine.

'When we all throw our toys out of the pram,' said Giles, 'and refuse to join in with any of your games?'

'It's that time of the year,' repeated Emma, ignoring her brother, 'when we raise a glass in memory of Joshua Barrington, founder of the Barrington Shipping Line.'

'Who made a profit of thirty pounds, four shillings and tuppence in his first year, but promised his board he would make more in the future,' Sebastian reminded everyone.

'Thirty-three pounds, four shillings and tuppence, actually,' said Emma. 'And he did make more, a lot more.'

'He must have turned in his grave,' said Sebastian, 'when we sold the company to Cunard for a cool sixty-eight million.'

'Mock you may,' said Emma, 'but we should be grateful to Joshua for all he did for this family.'

'I agree,' said Harry, who stood, raised his glass and said, 'To Joshua.'

'To Joshua,' declared the rest of the family.

'And now to business,' said Emma, putting down her glass.

'It's New Year's Eve,' protested Giles, 'and you seem to forget you're in my house, so I think we'll have a year off.'

'Certainly not,' said Emma. 'Only Lucy will be spared this year.'

'But be warned, young lady,' said Harry, smiling at his great-granddaughter, who was fast asleep in her mother's arms, 'your reprieve is only temporary.'

'That is correct,' said Emma, as if Harry hadn't been joking. 'The time has come for everyone to tell us their New Year's resolutions.'

'And the brave ones,' said Harry, 'will remind us of last year's.'

'Which I've recorded in this little red book,' said Emma, 'just in case anyone's forgotten.'

'Of course you have, Chairman Mao,' said Giles, refilling his glass.

'Who'd like to go first?' said Emma, once again ignoring her brother.

'I'm looking for another job,' said Samantha.

'Still in the art world?' asked Harry.

'Yes. The Wallace Collection is advertising for a deputy director, and I've applied for the position.'

'Bravo,' said Grace. 'The Courtauld's loss will be the Wallace's gain.'

'It's just the next step on the ladder,' said Sebastian. 'My bet is that by this time next year, Samantha's New Year's resolution is to be chairman of the Tate.'

'So what about you, Seb? What will you have achieved by this time next year?'

'I intend to go on annoying my aunt Grace by making her more and more money.'

460

'Which I can then distribute to more and more worthy causes,' said Grace.

'Don't worry, Victor's already seeing to that, as Karin will confirm.'

'I read Mr Kaufman's report,' said Grace, 'and it does great credit both to you and to the bank, Sebastian.'

'Praise indeed,' said Emma, making a note before looking across at her sister. 'As you're one of the few among us who has a tick by her name every year, Grace, what have you got planned for the next twelve months?'

'Seven of my young charges are hoping to be offered a place at university this year, and I am determined that all seven of them will achieve it.'

'What are their chances?' asked Harry.

'I'm confident that the four girls will all make it, but I'm not so sure about the boys.'

Everyone laughed except Grace.

'My turn, my turn!' demanded Jake.

'Now, if I remember correctly,' said Emma, 'last year you wanted to leave school. Do you still want to?'

'No,' said Jake firmly. 'I want Mom to get that job.'

'Why?' asked Samantha.

'Because then I won't be late for school every morning.'

'From out of the mouths of babes and sucklings,' said Harry, unable to hide a smile.

Samantha reddened, while the rest of the family burst out laughing. 'Then I'd better have two resolutions this year,' she managed eventually. 'One for me, and one for Jake.'

'As Giles seems unwilling to join in this year,' said Emma, 'how about you, Karin? Will you be running another marathon?'

'Never again. But I have joined the committee of the Marsden charitable trust, and I'm hoping the family will finance a mission. That doesn't include Sebastian, by the way.'

'Does that mean I'm off the hook this year?'

'No,' said Karin. 'I've convinced Victor that the bank should finance its own mission, the Farthings Kaufman Mission.'

'What's that going to cost me?'

'It will cost the bank twenty-five thousand pounds,' said Karin, 'but then I'm expecting you to finance your own mission.'

Sebastian was about to protest when Grace said, 'And Giles and I would also like to finance a mission, the Barrington Mission.' Giles smiled at his sister and bowed.

'As will Emma and I,' said Harry, which caused the rest of the family to start applauding.

'I dread to think what your resolution will be next year,' said Sebastian.

'I haven't finished with this year yet,' said Karin.

'Sebastian, Jessica, Richard, Lucy and I will be delighted to join you,' said Samantha, 'and finance our own mission.'

Sebastian looked to the heavens and said, 'Joshua Barrington, you've got a lot to answer for.'

'Well done, Karin,' said Emma as she wrote down the details in her red book. 'Follow that, Jessica,' she added, smiling at her granddaughter.

'I'm hoping to be shortlisted for the Turner Prize.'

'I can't imagine why,' said Grace. 'Turner would never have won the Turner Prize.'

'That would be quite an achievement, young lady,' chipped in Harry.

'And if she is,' said Richard, 'she'll be the youngest artist ever to have been shortlisted.'

'Now that is worth achieving,' said Grace. 'What are you working on at the moment?'

'I've just begun a series called *The Tree of Life*.'

'Oh, I love trees,' said Emma, 'and you've always been so good at landscapes.'

'It won't be that kind of tree, Grandmama.'

'I don't understand,' said Emma, 'a tree is a tree.'

'Unless it's symbolic,' suggested Harry, smiling at his granddaughter.

'And what's your resolution, Grandpops? Is your book going to win the Booker?'

'Not a hope,' said Grace. 'That prize will never be awarded to a storyteller, more's the pity. But I can tell you all, because I'm the only person in this room who's read it, that Harry's latest novel is by far his most accomplished work to date. He's more than fulfilled his mother's hopes, so he can take a year off.'

Harry was taken by surprise. He'd planned to tell the family he'd be having a major operation in January, but that there was no need to worry because he'd only be out of action for a few weeks.

'What about you, Emma?' said Giles. 'Are you planning to be PM by this time next year?'

'I don't think so,' said Emma. 'But I do intend to be even more of an infidel next year than I was last year,' she added, putting her glass down on the table, and spilling a little wine.

'What's an infidel?' asked Jake.

'Someone who votes Conservative,' said Giles.

'Then I want to be infidel. But only if Freddie's an infidel too.'

'I most certainly am,' said Freddie.

> 'I often think it's comical—
> How Nature always does contrive—
> That every boy and every gal—
> That's born into the world alive—
> Is either a little Liberal—
> Or else a little Conservative!'

'Lyricist?' demanded Grace.

'W. S. Gilbert.'

'Which operetta?'

'*Iolanthe*,' said Freddie, 'and as I'm already an infidel, I've decided to come up with a new resolution this year.'

'But you haven't scored that century at Lord's yet,' Giles reminded him.

'I still intend to, but by this time next year, I will have changed my name.'

Freddie's unexpected announcement left everyone, even Jake, speechless.

'But I've always liked Freddie,' Emma eventually managed. 'I think it rather suits you.'

'Freddie's not the name I want to change. From January first, I'd like to be known as Freddie Barrington.'

The round of applause that followed left Freddie in no doubt that the family approved of his New Year's resolution.

'It's a simple enough procedure,' said Grace, ever practical. 'You only have to sign a deed poll and Fenwick will be a thing of the past.'

'I had to sign a lot more forms to achieve that,' said Giles, shaking hands with his son.

The phone began to ring and a moment later Markham appeared.

'It's Lord Waddington on the phone,' he said.

'The prince of infidels,' said Giles. 'Why don't you take the call in my study, Emma?'

'It must be serious for him to call me on New Year's Eve,' said Emma.

'The call is not for you, my lady,' said Markham. 'He asked to speak to Lord Barrington.'

'Are you sure, Markham?'

'Quite sure, my lady.'

'Then you'd better go and find out what he wants,' said Emma.

If Jessica and Freddie had caused silence, a phone call from the leader of the Lords caused the rest of the family to all start talking at once. They didn't fall silent until the door opened and their host reappeared. They all looked at him in anticipation.

'Well, that's sorted out my New Year's resolution,' was all Giles had to say.

◄o►

'You're going to have to tell them at some point,' said Emma, as she and Harry walked back to the Manor House early the next morning.

'I'd intended to yesterday afternoon, but Grace rather upstaged me, not to mention Freddie and Giles.'

'Giles couldn't hide how delighted he was by Freddie's decision.'

'Did he tell you why Lord Waddington wanted to speak to him?'

'Not a word.'

'You don't think he could be crossing the floor and joining the infidels?'

'Never. That's just not his style. But now you've handed in the book, is there anything else you have to do before going into hospital?'

'I wish I could do that.'

'Do what?'

'Change the subject without having to include a link line. You'd never get away with it in a book. In real life, when two people are having a conversation, they switch back and forth without thinking about it, sometimes even in mid-sentence. Scott Fitzgerald wrote a short story recording a real-life conversation, and it was unreadable.'

'How interesting. Now answer the question.'

'No,' said Harry. 'Now that the line editor has done their damnedest, there's not a lot more I can do before the book is published.'

'What did the redoubtable Miss Warburton catch you out on this time?'

'I had a New York detective reading the Miranda Rights to a prisoner three years before they came into force.'

'Oops. Anything else?'

'Colons that should have been semi-colons, and it appears I use the expression "no doubt" too often throughout the book. Something else everyone does in normal life, but you can't get away with it in a novel.'

'Will you be going on any book tours this time?'

'I expect so. Most readers will assume it's another William Warwick novel, and I'll have to disabuse them of that. And in any case, Aaron is already lining up a tour of the States for me, and my London publishers are pressing me to visit the Bombay Book Festival.'

'Does the timing work? It all sounds quite demanding.'

'It's all rather convenient, actually. I check into St Thomas's in a couple of weeks' time, and by the time the novel is published, I should have fully recovered.'

'Once you're out of hospital, I don't think you should come down here. Stay in London where Karin, Giles and I can fuss over you. In fact I've already warned my department I'll be away for at least a couple of weeks.'

'I think Giles might be away for a lot longer than that.'

'What makes you say that?'

'There's a rumour doing the rounds that our ambassador in Washington will be retiring in the spring.'

50

THE OFFICE WAS smaller than he'd expected, but the magnificent wood panelling and fine oil portraits of his predecessors left him in no doubt of the historic importance of his new role.

His duties had been carefully explained to him by Commander Rufus Orme, his private secretary. Like the monarch, he may have had little real power in his new position, but immense influence. Indeed, when it came to state occasions he followed in the Queen's footsteps, with the Archbishop of Canterbury and the Prime Minister a pace behind.

He was assisted by a small, well-trained team who would take care of his every need, although he wondered how long it would take him to get used to someone helping him get dressed. His valet, Croft, would appear at the same hour every day to perform a ceremony that needed to be timed to the second.

He began to take off his clothes until he was standing in only his vest and pants. He felt quite ridiculous. Croft helped him into a white shirt that had been freshly ironed earlier that morning. A starched white collar was attached to a stud in the back of the shirt, followed by a frilly lace

468

neckerchief where a normal man would wear a tie. He didn't need to look in the mirror. Croft was his mirror. The valet then turned his attention to a long black and gold silk gown that was draped on a wooden mannequin in a corner of the room. He lifted it carefully and held the gown up so the new recipient could place his arms in the long gold sleeves. Croft stood back, checked his master, then dropped to his knees to help him into a pair of shiny, brass-buckled shoes. He stood up again and removed a full-bottomed wig from the mannequin's wooden head, before transferring it to the head of the Lord Chancellor. Croft stood back once again and made a slight adjustment, just a fraction to the left.

Croft's final task was to place the great chain of office that dated back to 1643 over his head, not letting go of it until it was resting securely on Giles's shoulders. That was the moment at which Giles recalled from his schooldays that three of his predecessors had been executed in the Tower of London.

Once dressed, he was finally allowed to glance at himself in the long mirror. He looked ridiculous, but had to admit, if only to himself, that he loved it. The valet bowed. His task completed, he left without another word.

As Croft departed, Commander Orme walked in. Orme would never have considered entering the room until the Lord Chancellor was dressed in his full regalia.

'I've read today's order paper, Orme,' he said. 'Is there anything I should be concerned about?'

'No, my lord. Questions today will be answered by the minister of state for health. There may well be some robust exchanges on the subject of AIDS, but nothing you need concern yourself with.'

'Thank you.' He glanced at his watch, aware that at seven minutes to the hour, he would leave his office in the North Tower and set off on his journey to the Prince's Chamber.

The door opened again, this time to allow a young page to make his entrance. He bowed low, moved quickly behind him and picked up the hem of his long robe.

'Thirty seconds, my lord,' said Orme, moments before the door opened again to allow the Lord Chancellor to set out on the seven-minute journey through the Palace of Westminster to the House of Lords.

He stepped out on to the red carpet and progressed slowly along the wide corridor. Members of the House, door keepers and badge messengers stood to one side and bowed as he passed, not to him, but to the monarch he represented. He maintained a steady pace, which he had practised the day before when the House was not in session. Commander Orme had emphasized that he must be neither too fast nor too slow if he was to arrive in the Prince's Chamber just moments before Big Ben struck twice.

As he proceeded down the north corridor, he could have been forgiven for wondering how many of his colleagues would be in the chamber to greet him when he took his seat on the Woolsack for the first time. Only then would he discover how his surprise appointment had been received by his fellow peers.

On a normal day, there would only have been a handful of members present. They would rise from their places as the Lord Chancellor entered the chamber, give a slight bow, and remain standing while his old friend, the Bishop of Bristol, conducted daily prayers.

He felt more and more nervous as he continued to place one foot in front of the other, and his heartbeat reached another level when he stepped on to the blue and gold carpet of the Prince's Chamber with ninety seconds to spare. He turned right and made his way down the long red-carpeted corridor to the far end of the House, before he could finally make his entrance. As he reached the Members' Lobby, in which the public were standing in silence, he heard Big Ben's first chime echoing around the building.

On the second chime, two doormen in full evening dress pulled open the great doors of the chamber to allow the new Lord Chancellor to enter the Upper House. He tried not to smile when he saw what a theatre producer would have called a full house. In fact, several of his colleagues had had to stand in the aisles, while others sat on the steps of the throne.

Their lordships stood as one as he entered the chamber and greeted him with loud cries of 'Hear, hear!' and the traditional waving of order papers. Giles later told Freddie that his colleagues' welcome was the greatest moment in his life.

'Even better than escaping from the Germans?'

'Just as terrifying,' Giles admitted.

While the Bishop of Bristol conducted prayers, Giles glanced up at the Distinguished Strangers' Gallery, to see his wife, son and oldest friend looking down at him. They couldn't hide the pride they felt.

When the bishop had finally blessed his packed congregation, their lordships waited for the Lord Chancellor to take his place on the Woolsack for the first time, then resumed their seats once Giles had settled and arranged his robes. He couldn't resist pausing for a moment before he nodded in the direction of the Rt Hon. the Baroness Clifton, to indicate that she could rise to answer the first question on the order paper.

Emma stood to address the House.

'My lord chancellor,' she began. 'I know the whole House will want to join me in congratulating you on your appointment, and to wish you many happy years presiding over the business of the House.'

The cries of acclamation came from all sides of the chamber as Giles bowed to his sister.

◄○►

Question number one.

Emma turned to face the cross benches.

'I can assure the noble lord, Lord Preston, that the government is taking the threat of AIDS most seriously. My department has set aside one hundred million pounds for research into this terrible disease, and we are sharing our findings with eminent scientists and leading medical practitioners around the globe in the hope of identifying a cure as quickly as possible. Indeed, I should add that I am travelling to Washington next week, where I will be meeting with the Surgeon General, and I can assure the House that the subject of AIDS will be high on our agenda.'

An elderly gentleman seated on the back row of the cross benches stood to ask a supplementary question.

'I am grateful for the minister's reply, but may I ask how our hospitals are coping with the sudden influx of patients?'

Giles sat back and listened with interest to the way his sister dealt with every question that was thrown at her, recalling his own time on the front bench. Although there was the occasional hesitation, she no longer needed to constantly check the brief prepared by her civil servants. He was equally impressed that she now had total command of the House, something some ministers never mastered.

For the next thirty minutes, Emma answered questions on subjects that ranged from cancer research funding, to assaults on A&E staff following football matches, to ambulance response times to emergency calls.

Giles wondered if there was any truth in the rumours being whispered in the corridors that if the Conservatives won the next election, Margaret Thatcher would appoint her as leader of the House of Lords. Frankly, if that were to happen, he didn't think any of his colleagues in the Upper House would be surprised. However, another rumour that had recently been echoing around the corridors of power was that a Tory backbencher was preparing to challenge Thatcher for the leadership of the party. Giles dismissed the idea as speculation, because although the lady's methods were considered by some in her party to be draconian, even dictatorial, Giles couldn't imagine that the Tories would even consider removing a sitting prime minister who had never lost an election.

'I can only tell the noble lord,' said Emma, when she stood to answer the final question on the order paper, 'that my department will continue to sanction the sale of generic drugs, but not before they have undergone the most rigorous testing. It remains our aim to ensure that patients will not have to pay exorbitant prices to drug companies whose priority often seems to be profit, and not patients.'

Emma sat down to loud 'Hear, hear!'s, and when a

Foreign Office minister rose to take her place in order to open a debate on the Falkland Islands, she gathered up her papers and hurried out of the chamber, as she did not wish to be late for her next appointment with the gay rights campaigner Ian McKellen, who she knew held strong views on how the government should be handling the AIDS crisis. She was looking forward to telling him how much she'd enjoyed his recent performance as Richard III at the National Theatre.

As she left the chamber, she stumbled and dropped some papers, which a passing whip picked up and handed back to her. She thanked him, and was about to hurry on when a voice behind her called out, 'Minister, I wonder if I might have a word with you?'

Emma turned to see Lord Samuels, the president of the Royal College of Physicians, chasing after her. If she had made a blunder during question time, he wasn't the kind of man who would have embarrassed her in the chamber. Not his style.

'Of course, Lord Samuels. I hope I didn't make some horrendous gaffe this afternoon?'

'Certainly not,' said Samuels, giving her a warm smile. 'It's just that there is a subject I would like to discuss with you, and wondered if you could spare a moment.'

'Of course,' repeated Emma. 'I'll ask my private secretary to give your office a call and arrange a meeting.'

'I'm afraid the matter is more urgent than that, minister.'

'Then perhaps you could join me in my office at eight tomorrow morning?'

'I'd prefer to see you privately, away from the prying eyes of civil servants.'

'Then I'll come to you. Just tell me when and where.'

'Eight o'clock tomorrow morning, in my consulting rooms at 47A Harley Street.'

—<o>—

Emma was well aware of the unpleasant and, some suggested, personal antagonism between the president of the Royal College of Physicians and the president of the Royal College of Surgeons, concerning the merger of Guy's, St Thomas's and King's into one NHS trust. The physicians were in favour, the surgeons against. Both declaring, 'Over my dead body.'

Emma had been careful not to take sides, and asked the department to prepare a brief that she could consider overnight, before her meeting with Lord Samuels. However, back-to-back meetings, some of which overran, prevented her from reading the brief before she climbed into bed just after midnight. But she was so tired she found it hard to concentrate on the details, and soon fell into a deep sleep.

—<o>—

The following morning, Emma reopened the red box even before she'd made herself a cup of tea.

The 'Tommy's, Guy's, King's' brief still rested on top of a dozen other urgent files, including a confidential DNA report by two distinguished American academics. She already knew the results of their initial findings, and now at last she felt able to share the good news with Harry.

Emma jumped up, grabbed the phone on the sideboard and dialled Harry at the Manor House.

'This better be good,' he said, 'because Alexander is just about to decide whether to jump in the crate going to America or the one going to England.'

'It's good, better than good,' said Emma. 'The DNA report shows that Arthur Clifton was without doubt your father.'

There was a long silence before Harry shouted, 'Hallelujah, that is indeed good news. I'll put a bottle of champagne on ice so we can celebrate when you get home this evening.'

'America,' said Emma, and put the phone down. After taking several phone calls during breakfast, she still hadn't had a chance to consider the arguments for and against Lord Samuels' proposal before her driver pulled up outside the front door at 7.25 a.m. It was going to be another back-to-back day.

Emma read the detailed submissions from both presidents during her journey across London, but hadn't come down in favour of either side by the time her car pulled into Harley Street. She placed the file back in the red box and checked her watch: 7.57. She hoped the discussion wouldn't go on for too long, as she needed to be back at the department for a meeting with the new chairman of the BMA, a firebrand who, she had been warned by her Permanent Secretary, believed all Tories should be drowned at birth. What Pauline described as the King Herod solution.

Emma was about to press the bell of No. 47A when the door was opened by a young woman.

'Good morning, minister. Let me take you through to Lord Samuels.'

The president of the Royal College of Physicians rose as the minister entered the room. He waited until she was seated before offering her coffee.

'No, thank you,' said Emma, who didn't want to waste any more time than necessary, while trying not to give the impression that she was in a hurry.

'As I explained yesterday, minister, the matter I wish to discuss with you is personal, which is why I didn't want us to meet in your office.'

'I fully understand,' said Emma, waiting to hear his arguments in favour of Guy's and St Thomas's being joined at the hip with King's.

'During question time yesterday' – Ah, thought Emma, so I must have made some blunder after all, which he was kind enough not to raise in the chamber – 'I noticed that when you paused to take a drink, you spilt some water over your papers. You then answered the question without referring to your notes so no one noticed, although it was not for the first time.'

Emma wondered where all this was leading, but didn't interrupt.

'And when you left the chamber, you stumbled and dropped some papers.'

'Yes, I did,' said Emma, her mind now racing. 'But neither incident struck me as important at the time.'

'I hope you're right,' said Samuels. 'But may I ask if you've recently found it difficult to grasp objects like cups, your briefcase, even your pen when you're signing letters?'

Emma hesitated, before saying, 'Yes, now that you mention it. But my mother always accused me of being clumsy.'

'I also noticed that you hesitated on a couple of occasions while you were addressing the House yesterday. Was that because you were considering your reply, or was your speech in some way restricted?'

'I put it down to nerves. My brother is always warning me never to relax when I'm at the despatch box.'

'Do your legs sometimes feel weak, so you need to sit down?'

'Yes, but I am nearly seventy, Lord Samuels, and I'd be the first to admit I ought to take more exercise.'

'Possibly, but I wonder if you would allow me to conduct a short neurological examination, if only to dismiss my own concerns.'

'Of course,' said Emma, wanting to say no, so she could get back to her office.

The short examination took over an hour. Lord Samuels began by asking Emma to take him through her medical history. He then listened to her heart and checked her reflexes with a patella hammer. Had those tests proved satisfactory, he would have apologized for troubling her and sent her off to work. But he didn't. Instead, he went on to assess the cranial nerves. Having done so, he moved on to a close study of her mouth, looking for fasciculation of the tongue. Satisfied that he was far from satisfied, Lord Samuels said, 'The examination I'm about to conduct may be painful. In fact, I hope it is.'

Emma made no comment when he produced a needle and proceeded to stick it into her upper arm. She immediately reacted with a yelp, which clearly pleased Samuels, but when he repeated the exercise on her right hand, she did not respond.

'Ouch!' she said as he stuck the needle into her thigh, but when he proceeded to her lower calf, she might as well have been a pincushion, because she felt nothing. He moved on to her back, but Emma often couldn't tell when he was sticking the pin in her.

While Emma put her blouse back on, Lord Samuels returned to his desk, opened a file and waited for her to join him. When he looked up, she was sitting nervously in front of him.

'Emma,' he said gently, 'I'm afraid that what I'm about to tell you is not good news.'

51

WHEN A MINISTER resigns because of some scandal, the press dip their pens in the blood and make the most of it. But if they have to surrender their seals of office because of illness, a very different attitude prevails, especially when the minister in question is both liked and respected.

The traditional letters between a prime minister and a colleague who has to resign unexpectedly were exchanged, but on this occasion no one could have missed the genuine regret felt on both sides.

It has been the most exciting job I've ever done in my life, and a privilege to serve in your administration.

The Prime Minister wrote in response, *Your exceptional contribution to public life, and unstinting service to your country, will not be forgotten.*

Neither the Prime Minister nor the departing minister of state mentioned the reason for Emma's sudden departure.

The senior physician in the land had never known a patient to take such news with more dignity and composure. The only sign of human frailty Emma revealed expressed itself as he accompanied her to her car, when for a moment she leant on his arm. She only made one request of him, to which he agreed without hesitation.

Lord Samuels remained on the pavement until the minister's car was out of sight. He then returned to his office and, as she had requested, made three telephone calls to three people to whom he'd never spoken before: the Lord Chancellor, the Prime Minister and Sir Harry Clifton.

One of them broke down and wept, and was quite unable to respond, while the other immediately cleared her diary, explaining to her staff that she wished to visit a friend. Both of them, Lord Samuels concluded, were cut from the same cloth as the great lady who had just left his consulting rooms. But the call he was most dreading was the one he had put off until last.

As gently as he could, Lord Samuels told Harry that his wife had motor neurone disease, and could only hope to live for another year, eighteen months at the most. The gentle man of letters could find no words to express his feelings. After a long silence, he eventually managed, 'Thank you, Lord Samuels, for letting me know,' before putting the phone down. It was some time before he recovered sufficiently to accept that one of them needed to remain strong.

Harry left *Heads You Win* in mid-sentence, and drove himself to the station. He was back in Smith Square long before Emma arrived.

When Emma left the department for the last time, she was driven home to find Harry waiting for her on the doorstep. Neither spoke as he took her in his arms. How little needs to be said when you've been together for more than fifty years.

By then, Harry had phoned every member of the

family to let them know the devastating news before they read about it in the press. He had also written half a dozen letters, explaining that, for personal reasons, he was cancelling all his existing engagements and would not be accepting any new ones, whether social or professional.

◄○►

The following morning, Harry drove Emma down to their home in Somerset so they could begin their new life. He made up a bed in the drawing room so she wouldn't have to climb the stairs, and cleared everything from his desk in the library, so she could set about answering the sackfuls of letters that were arriving by every post. Harry opened each one and placed them in separate piles: family, friends, colleagues, those who worked for the NHS, with a special pile for young women up and down the country, of whom until then Emma had not even been aware, who not only wanted to say thank you, but again and again mentioned the words 'role model'.

There was another particularly large pile that lifted Emma's spirits every time she read one of them. Those of her colleagues who did not share her political persuasion, but wanted to express their admiration and respect for the way in which she had never failed to listen to their views, and had on occasions even been willing to change her mind.

Although her postbag didn't diminish for several weeks, Emma replied to each and every person who had taken the trouble to write to her, only stopping when she no longer had the strength to hold her pen. After that, she dictated her replies to Harry, who added 'scribe' to his many other responsibilities. However, she still insisted on checking every letter before adding her signature. When, in the fullness of time, even that became impossible, Harry signed them on her behalf.

Dr Richards dropped in twice a week, and kept Harry informed of what he should expect next, although the old GP admitted that he felt quite helpless because there was little he could do other than show sympathy and write out endless prescriptions for pills that he hoped would ease Emma's pain.

For the first few weeks, Emma was able to enjoy a morning walk around the grounds with Harry, but it was not long before she had to lean on his arm, then rely on a walking stick, before finally succumbing to a wheelchair that Harry had bought without her knowing.

During those early months, Emma did most of the talking, never failing to express her strongly held views on what was happening in the world, although she now only picked it up second-hand from the morning papers and the evening news on television. She delighted in watching President Bush and Mrs Thatcher signing a peace treaty with Chairman Gorbachev in Paris, finally bringing the Cold War to an end. But only a few days later she was horrified to learn that some of her old parliamentary colleagues back in London were plotting to remove the PM from office. Did she need to remind them that the Iron Lady had won three elections in a row?

Emma rallied enough to dictate a long letter to Margaret, making her views clear, and was astonished to receive an even longer reply by return of post. She wished she was still in Westminster, where she would have roamed the corridors letting her colleagues know exactly what she thought of them.

Although her brain remained sharp, her body continued to deteriorate, and her ability to speak became more restricted with each passing week. However, she never failed to express her joy whenever a member of the family appeared and took their turn to wheel her around the garden.

Little Lucy would chatter away, keeping her great-grandmother up to date on what she'd been doing. She was the one member of the family who didn't fully understand what was happening, which made their relationship very special.

Jake was now in long trousers and pretending to be very grown-up, while her nephew Freddie, in his first year at Cambridge, was quiet and considerate, and discussed current affairs with Emma as if she was still in high office. She would have liked to live long enough to see him take a seat in the House of Commons, but knew that wouldn't be possible.

Jessica told her grandmother as she pushed her wheelchair around the garden that her *Tree of Life* exhibition would be opening soon, and that she still hoped to be shortlisted for the Turner Prize, but added, 'Don't hold your breath!'

Sebastian and Samantha drove down to Somerset every weekend, and Seb tried gallantly to remain cheerful whenever he was in his mother's presence, but he confided to his uncle Giles that he was becoming as anxious about his father as he was his mother. *Harry's running himself into the ground* were the words Giles wrote in a letter to his sister Grace that evening.

Giles and Karin spent as much time as they could at the Manor House, and regularly phoned Grace, who was torn between her responsibilities to her pupils and her sister's wellbeing. The day school broke up for the summer holidays, she took the first train to Bristol. Giles picked her up at Temple Meads and warned her just how much their sister had deteriorated since she'd last seen her. Grace was well prepared for Emma's condition, but the shock came when she saw Harry, who had become an old man.

Grace began to nurse them both, but when Giles next visited, she warned him that she didn't think Emma would see the autumn leaves fall.

—◦—

The publication of *Heads You Win* came and went, making no impact on the Cliftons' daily lives. Harry did not travel to America for his planned eleven-city tour, nor did he visit India to address the Bombay Literary Festival.

During this period, he only went up to London once, not to visit his publisher, or to speak at the Foyle's literary lunch, but to tell Roger Kirby that he wouldn't be rescheduling his prostate cancer operation, as he wasn't willing to be out of commission for any length of time.

The surgeon was sympathetic, but warned, 'If the cancer escapes from your prostate and spreads to your bowel or liver, your life will be in danger. Tell me, Harry, have you had any sharp pains in your back recently?'

'No,' Harry lied. 'Let's discuss it again, when . . .'

Harry had one more task to carry out before he could return to the Manor House. He had promised Emma he would pick up a copy of her favourite novel from Hatchards, so he could read a chapter to her every evening when she became too ill to leave her bed. When he got out of the taxi in Piccadilly, he didn't notice the window in which only one book was displayed, with a banner that proclaimed:

THE PUBLISHING SENSATION OF THE YEAR

He walked into the bookshop and once he'd found a hardback copy of *The Mill on the Floss*, he handed over a ten-pound note to the young woman behind the counter. She placed the book in a bag, and as he turned to leave she took a closer look at the customer, wondering for a moment if it was possible.

She crossed to the central display table, picked up a copy of *Heads You Win* and turned to the author's photograph on the back flap, before peering through the window at the man who was climbing into a taxi. She had thought for a moment it might be Harry Clifton, but looking at the photograph more closely, she realized the unshaven man with dishevelled grey hair she had just served was far too old. After all, the photograph had been taken less than a year ago.

She returned the book to the top of the table of best-sellers, where it had been for the past eleven weeks.

◄○►

When Emma was finally confined to her bed, Dr Richards warned Harry that it could now only be a matter of weeks.

Although Harry rarely left her alone for more than a few minutes, he found it hard to bear the pain she had to endure. His wife was now barely able to swallow anything but liquids, and even the power of speech had deserted her, so she had begun to communicate by blinking. Once for yes, twice for no. Three times please, four times thank you. Harry pointed out to her that three and four were somewhat redundant, but he could hear her saying *good manners are never redundant*.

Whenever darkness crept into the room, Harry would switch on the bedside light and read her another chapter, hoping she would quickly fall asleep.

◄o►

After one of his morning visits, Dr Richards took Harry to one side.

'It won't be long now.'

For some time, Harry's only concern had been how much longer Emma would have to suffer. He replied, 'Let's hope you're right.'

That evening, he sat on the edge of the bed and continued reading. *'This is a puzzling world, and Old Harry's got a finger on it.'*

Emma smiled.

When he came to the end of the chapter, he closed the book and looked down at the woman who had shared his life, but who clearly no longer wanted to live. He bent down and whispered, 'I love you, my darling.' Four blinks of the eyelids.

'Is the pain unbearable?' One blink.

'It won't be much longer now.' Three blinks, followed by a pleading look.

He kissed her gently on the lips. 'I have only ever loved one woman in my life,' he whispered. Four blinks. 'And I pray it will not be long before we see each other again.' One blink, followed by three, followed by four.

He held her hand, closed his eyes and asked a God of whose existence he was no longer sure to forgive him. He then picked up a pillow before he could change his mind, and looked at her one more time.

One blink, followed by three.

He hesitated.

One blink, repeated every few seconds.

He lowered the pillow gently on to Emma's face.

Her hands and legs twitched for a few moments before she fell still, but he continued to press down. When he finally lifted the pillow, there was a smile on her face as if she was enjoying her first rest in months.

Harry held her in his arms as the first of the autumn leaves began to fall.

—◦—

Dr Richards dropped by the following morning, and if he was surprised to find that his patient had died during the night, he did not mention it to Harry. He simply wrote on the death certificate *Died in her sleep as a result of Motor Neurone Disease*. But then he was an old friend, as well as the family doctor.

Emma had left clear instructions that she wanted a quiet funeral, attended only by family and close friends. No flowers, and donations to the Bristol Royal Infirmary. Her wishes were carried out to the letter, but then she had no way of knowing how many people looked upon her as a close friend.

The village church was packed with locals, and others who were not quite so local, as Harry discovered when he shuffled down the aisle to join the rest of the family in the front pew and passed a former prime minister seated in the third row.

He couldn't recall a great deal about the service, as his mind was preoccupied, but he did try to concentrate when the vicar delivered his moving eulogy.

After the coffin was lowered into the ground and the rough sods of earth had been cast upon it, Harry was among the last to leave the graveside. When he returned to the Manor House to join the rest of the family, he found he couldn't recall Lucy's name.

Grace kept a close eye on him as he sat quietly in the drawing room where he'd first met Emma – well, not exactly met.

'They've all gone,' she told him, but he just sat there, staring out of the window.

When the sun disappeared behind the highest oak, he stood, walked across the hall and slowly climbed the stairs to their bedroom. He undressed and got into an empty bed, no longer caring for this world.

—◦—

Doctors will tell you, you can't die of grief. But Harry died nine days later.

The death certificate gave the cause of death as cancer, but as Dr Richards pointed out, if Harry had wanted to he could have lived for another ten, perhaps twenty years.

Harry's instructions were as clear as Emma's had been. Like her, he wanted a quiet funeral. His only request was to be buried beside his wife. His wishes were adhered to, and when the family returned to the Manor House after the funeral, Giles gathered them all together in the drawing room and asked them to raise a glass to his oldest and dearest friend.

'I hope,' he added, 'that you'll allow me to do one thing that I know Harry wouldn't have approved of.' The family listened in silence to his proposal.

'He most certainly wouldn't have approved,' said Grace. 'But Emma would have, because she told me so.'

Giles looked in turn at each member of the family, but he didn't need to seek their approval, because it was clear that they were as one.

HARRY ARTHUR CLIFTON

1920–1992

52

HIS INSTRUCTIONS couldn't have been clearer, but then they'd been at it since 1621.

The Rt Hon. Lord Barrington of Bristol Docklands was to arrive at St Paul's Cathedral at 10.50 on the morning of April 10th, 1993. At 10.53, he would be met at the north-west door by the Very Reverend Eric Evans, canon in residence. At 10.55, the canon would accompany the Lord Chancellor into the cathedral, and then they would proceed to the front of the nave where he should land – the canon's word – at 10.57.

As eleven a.m. struck on the cathedral clock, the organist would strike up the opening bars of *All people that on earth do dwell*, and the congregation would rise and sing, the dean assured him. From that moment until the final blessing by the dean, the memorial service would be in the safe hands of the Rt Reverend Barry Donaldson, the Bishop of Bristol, and one of Harry's oldest friends. Giles would only have one role left to play on the ecclesiastical stage.

He had spent weeks preparing for this single hour, because he felt it had to be worthy of his oldest friend and, equally important, that it would have been approved of by Emma. He had even carried out a practice run from Smith Square to St Paul's at exactly the same time the previous week, to make sure he wouldn't be late. The journey had taken 24 minutes, so he decided he would leave home at 10.15. Better to be a few minutes early, he told his driver, than a few minutes late. You can always slow down, but London traffic doesn't always allow you to speed up.

◄○►

Giles rose just after five on the morning of the memorial service, as he knew he wouldn't be able to get back to sleep. He slipped on a dressing gown, went down to his study and read the eulogy one more time. Like Harry with his novels, he was now on the fourteenth draft, or was it the fifteenth? There were a few changes, the occasional word, one added sentence. He felt confident he could do no more, but he still needed to check the length.

He read it through once again without stopping, just under fifteen minutes. Winston Churchill had once told him, 'An important speech should take an hour to write for every minute it took to deliver, while at the same time, dear boy, you must leave your audience convinced it was off the cuff.' That was the difference between a mere speaker and an orator, Churchill had suggested.

Giles stood up, pushed back his chair and began to deliver the eulogy as if he were addressing an audience of a thousand, although he had no idea how large the congregation would be. The canon had told him that the cathedral could hold two thousand comfortably, but only managed that on rare occasions, such as the funeral of a member of the royal family, or a memorial service for a prime minister, and not even all of them could guarantee a full house.

'Don't worry,' he had added, 'as long as six hundred turn up, we can fill the nave, block off the chancery and it will still look packed. Only our regular worshippers will be any the wiser.'

Giles just prayed that the nave would be full, as he didn't want to let his friend down. He put down the script fourteen minutes later, then returned to the bedroom, to find Karin still in her dressing gown.

'We ought to get going,' he said.

'Of course we should, my darling,' said Karin, 'that is, if you're thinking of walking to the cathedral. If you leave now, you'll be there in time to welcome the dean,' she added before disappearing into the bathroom.

While Giles had been going over his speech downstairs, she had laid out a white shirt, his Bristol Grammar School tie, and a dark suit that had come back from the cleaners the previous day. Giles took his time dressing, finally selecting a pair of gold cufflinks Harry had given him on his wedding day. Once he'd checked himself in the mirror, he paced restlessly around the bedroom, delivering whole paragraphs of his eulogy out loud and constantly looking at his watch. How long was she going to be?

When Karin reappeared twenty minutes later, she was wearing a simple navy blue dress that Giles had never seen before, adorned with a gold portcullis brooch. She'd done Harry proud.

'Time to leave,' she announced calmly.

As they left the house Giles was relieved to see that Tom was already standing by the back door of the car.

'Let's get moving, Tom,' he said as he slumped into the back seat, checking his watch again.

Tom drove sedately out of Smith Square as befitted the occasion. Past the Palace of Westminster and around Parliament Square before making his way along Victoria Embankment.

'The traffic seems unusually heavy today,' said Giles, once again looking at his watch.

'About the same as last week,' said Tom.

Giles didn't comment on the fact that every light seemed to turn red just as they approached it. He was convinced they were going to be late.

As they drove past the mounted griffins that herald the City of London, Giles began to relax for the first time, as it now looked as if they would be about ten minutes early. And they would have been, but for something none of them had anticipated.

With about half a mile to go and the dome of the cathedral in sight, Tom spotted a barrier across the road that hadn't been there the previous week when they'd carried out the practice run. A policeman raised his arm to stop them, and Tom wound down his window and said, 'The Lord Chancellor.'

The policeman saluted and nodded to a colleague, who lifted the barrier to allow them through.

Giles was glad they were early because they were moving so slowly. Crowds of pedestrians were overflowing from the pavement and spilling on to the road, finally causing the car to almost come to a halt.

'Stop here, Tom,' said Giles. 'We're going to have to walk the last hundred yards.'

Tom pulled up in the middle of the road and rushed to open the back door, but by the time he got there, Giles and Karin were already making their way through the crowd. People stood aside when they recognized him, and some even began clapping.

Giles was about to acknowledge their applause, when Karin whispered, 'Don't forget they're applauding Harry, not you.'

They finally reached the cathedral steps and began to climb up through a corridor of raised pens and pencils, held high by those who wished to remember Harry not only as an author, but as a civil rights campaigner.

Giles looked up to see Eric Evans, canon in residence, waiting for them on the top step.

'Got that wrong, didn't I,' he said, grinning. 'It must be an author thing, always more popular than politicians.'

Giles laughed nervously as the canon escorted them through the north-west door and into the cathedral, where those who had arrived late, even if they had a ticket, were standing at the side of the nave, while those who didn't were crammed at the back like football fans on a crowded terrace.

Karin knew that Giles's laughter was a cocktail of nerves and adrenaline. In fact, she had never seen him so nervous.

'Relax,' she whispered, as the dean led them down the long marble aisle, past Wellington's memorial and through the packed congregation, to their places at the head of the nave. Giles recognized several people as they made their slow progress towards the high altar. Aaron Guinzburg was sitting next to Ian Chapman, Dr Richards with Lord Samuel, Hakim Bishara and Arnold Hardcastle representing Farthings, Sir Alan Redmayne was next to Sir John Rennie, while Victor Kaufman and his old school chum Professor Algernon Deakins were seated near the front.

But it was two women, sitting alone, who took him by surprise. An elegant old lady, who bowed her head as Giles passed, was seated near the back, clearly no longer wishing to be acknowledged as a dowager duchess might have expected to be, while in the row directly behind the family was another old lady who had travelled from Moscow to honour her late husband's dear friend.

Once they had taken their places in the front row, Giles picked up the order of service sheet that had been prepared by Grace. The cover was adorned with a simple portrait of Sir Harry Clifton KBE that had been drawn by the most recent winner of the Turner Prize.

The order of service could have been chosen by Harry himself, as it reflected his personal tastes: traditional, popular, with no concern about being described as romantic. His mother would have approved.

The congregation was welcomed by the Rt Rev. Barry Donaldson, the Lord Bishop of Bristol, who led them in prayers in memory of Harry. The first lesson was read by Jake, whose head could barely be seen above the lectern.

'1 Corinthians 13. *If I speak in the tongues of men or of angels . . .*'

The choir of St Mary Redcliffe, where Harry had been a chorister, sang *Rejoice that the Lord has risen!*

Sebastian, as the new head of the Clifton family, walked slowly up to the north lectern to read the second lesson, Revelation 21, and only just managed to get the words out.

'*And I saw a new heaven and a new earth: for the first heaven and the first earth were passed away; and there was no more sea . . .*' When he returned to his place in the front pew, Giles couldn't help noticing that his nephew's hair was starting to grey at the temples – which was only appropriate, he reflected, for a man who had recently been elected to the court of the Bank of England.

The congregation rose to join all those outside the cathedral in singing Harry's favourite song from *Guys and Dolls*, 'Sit Down, You're Rockin' the Boat'. Perhaps for the first time in the cathedral's history, cries of 'Encore' rang out both inside and out; inside, where the Salvation Army were led by Miss Adelaide representing Emma, while outside were a thousand Sky Mastersons playing Harry.

The dean nodded, and the choir master raised his baton once again. Giles was probably the only person who didn't join in when the congregation began to sing, *And did those feet in ancient times* . . . Becoming more nervous by the minute, he placed the order of service by his side and clung on to the pew, in the hope that no one would see his hands were shaking.

When the congregation reached, *Till we have built Jerusalem* . . . Giles turned to see the dean standing by his side. He bowed. It must be 11.41.

Giles stood, stepped out into the aisle and followed the dean to the pulpit steps, where he bowed again, before leaving him with *In England's green and pleasant land* echoing in his ears. As Giles turned to climb the thirteen steps, he could hear Harry saying, *Good luck, old chap, rather you than me.*

When he reached the pulpit, Giles placed his script on the small brass lectern and looked down on the packed congregation. Only one seat was empty. The last line of Blake's masterpiece having been rendered, the congregation resumed their places. Giles glanced to his left to see the statue of Nelson, his one eye staring directly at him, and waited for the audience to settle before he delivered his opening line.

'This was the noblest Roman of them all.

'Many people over the years have asked me if it was obvious, when I first met Harry Clifton, that I was in the presence of a truly remarkable individual, and I have to say no, it wasn't. In fact, only chance brought us together, or to be more accurate, the alphabet. Because my name was Barrington, I ended up in the next bed to Clifton in the dormitory on our first day at St Bede's, and from that random chance was born a lifelong friendship.

'It was clear to me from the outset that I was the superior human being. After all, the boy who had been placed next to me not only cried all night, but also wet his bed.'

The roar of laughter that came from outside quickly spread to those inside the cathedral, helping Giles to relax.

'This natural superiority continued to manifest itself when he crept into the washroom. Clifton had neither a toothbrush nor toothpaste, and had to borrow from me. The following morning, when we joined the other boys for breakfast, my superiority was even more apparent when it became clear that Clifton had never been introduced to a spoon, because he licked his porridge bowl clean. It seemed a good idea to me at the time, so I did the same. After breakfast, we all trooped off to the Great Hall for our first assembly, to be addressed by the headmaster. Although Clifton clearly wasn't my equal – after all, he was the son of a docker, and my father owned the docks, while his mother was a waitress, and my mother was Lady Barrington. How could we possibly be equals? However, I still allowed him to sit next to me.

'Once assembly was over, we went off to the classroom for our first lesson, where yet again Clifton was sitting next to Barrington. Unfortunately, by the time the bell sounded for break, my mythical superiority had evaporated more quickly than the morning mist once the sun has risen. It didn't take me much longer to realize that I would walk in Harry's shadow for the rest of my life, for he was destined to prove, far beyond the tiny world we then occupied, that the pen is indeed mightier than the sword.

'This state of affairs continued after we left St Bede's and progressed to Bristol Grammar School, when I was placed next to my friend once again – but I must admit that I only gained a place at the school because they needed a new cricket pavilion, and my father paid for it.'

While those outside St Paul's laughed and applauded, decorum allowed only polite laughter inside the cathedral.

'I went on to captain the school's first eleven, while Harry won the prize for English and an exhibition to Oxford. I also managed to scrape into Oxford, but only after I'd scored a century at Lord's for Young MCC.'

Giles waited for the laughter to die down before he continued.

'And then something happened that I hadn't been prepared for. Harry fell in love with my sister Emma. I confess that at the time I felt he could have done better. In my defence, I wasn't to know that she would win the top scholarship to Somerville College, Oxford, become the first female chairman of a public company, chairman of an NHS hospital and a minister of the Crown. Not for the first time, or the last, Harry was to prove me wrong. I wasn't even the superior Barrington any more. This is perhaps not the time to mention my little sister Grace, then still at school, who went on to become Professor of English at Cambridge. Now I am relegated to third place in the Barrington hierarchy.

'By now I had accepted that Harry was superior, so I made sure that we shared tutorials, as I had planned that he would write my essays, while I practised my cover drive. However, Adolf Hitler, a man who never played a game of cricket in his life, put a stop to that, and caused us to go our separate ways.

> *'All the conspirators save only he*
> *Did that they did in envy of great Caesar.*

'Harry shamed me by leaving Oxford and joining up even before war had been declared, and by the time I followed him, his ship had been sunk by a German U-boat. Everyone assumed he'd been lost at sea. But you can't get rid of Harry Clifton quite that easily. He was rescued by the Americans, and spent the rest of his war behind enemy lines, while I ended up in a German prisoner-of-war camp. I have a feeling that if Lieutenant Clifton had been in the next bunk to me at Weinsberg, I would have escaped a lot sooner.

'Harry never talked to me or anyone else about his war, despite his having been awarded the prestigious Silver Star for his service as a young captain in the US Army. But if you read his citation, as I did when I first visited Washington as a foreign minister, you'd discover that with the help of an Irish corporal, a jeep and two pistols, he convinced Field Marshal Kertel, the commanding officer of a crack panzer division, to order his men to lay down their arms and surrender. Shortly afterwards, Harry's jeep was blown up by a land mine while he was travelling back to his battalion. His driver was killed, and Harry was flown to the Bristol Royal Infirmary, not expected to survive the journey. However, the gods had other plans for Harry Clifton that even I would not have thought possible.

'Once the war was over and Harry had fully recovered, he and Emma were married and moved into the house next door, although I confess a few acres still divided us. Back in the real world, I wanted to be a politician, while Harry had plans to be a writer, so once again we set out on our separate paths.

'When I became a Member of Parliament, I felt that at last we were equals, until I discovered that more people were reading Harry's books than were voting for me. My only consolation was that Harry's fictional hero, William Warwick, the son of an earl, good-looking, highly intelligent and a heroic figure, was obviously based on me.'

More laughter followed, as Giles turned to his next page.

'But it got worse. With every new book Harry wrote, more and more readers joined his legion of fans, while every time I stood for election, I got fewer and fewer votes.

> *He only in a general honest thought*
> *And common good to all, made one of them.*

'And then, without warning, as is fate's capricious way, Harry's life took another turn, when he was invited to be the president of English PEN, a role in which he was to display skills that would be the envy of many who consider themselves to be statesmen.

'PEN assured him that it was an honorary position and shouldn't be too demanding. They clearly had no idea who they were dealing with. At the first meeting Harry attended as president, he learned about the fate of a man few of us had ever heard of at the time, who was languishing in a Siberian gulag. Thanks to Harry's sense of justice, Anatoly Babakov became a household name, and part of our daily lives.'

This time the cheering inside and outside the cathedral went on and on, as people took out their pens and held them high in the air.

'Thanks to Harry's relentless determination, the free world took up the great Russian writer's cause, forcing that despotic regime to give in and finally release him.'

Giles paused and looked down at the packed congregation, before he added, 'And today, Anatoly Babakov's wife, Yelena, has flown from Moscow to be with us, and to honour the man who had the courage to challenge the Russians in their own back yard, making it possible for her husband to be released, win the Nobel Prize and join those giants of literature who live on long after we have been forgotten.'

This time it was over a minute before the applause died down. Giles waited until there was total silence before he continued.

'How many of you present here today are aware that Harry turned down a knighthood because he refused to be so honoured while Anatoly Babakov was still languishing in prison? It was his wife Emma who, several years later, when the palace wrote a second time, convinced him he should accept, not in recognition of his work as a writer, but as a human rights campaigner.

'I once asked this modest, gentle man what he

considered to be his greatest achievement: topping the bestsellers lists around the world, becoming a knight of the realm or making the world aware of the genius and courage of his fellow author, Anatoly Babakov? "Marrying your sister," was his immediate reply, "because she never stopped raising the bar, which pushed me to greater and greater heights." If Harry was ever boastful, it was only in the pride he took in Emma's achievements. Envy never entered his thoughts. He only delighted in other people's success.

> 'His life was gentle, and the elements
> So mixed in him that Nature might stand up

'In our family, we have a tradition that every New Year's Eve we each reveal our resolution for the coming twelve months. Some years ago, Harry admitted somewhat diffidently that he was going to try and write a novel that would have been admired by his mother, who was his most exacting critic. "And you, Giles," he asked, "what's your New Year's resolution?" "I'm going to lose a stone," I told him.'

Giles waited for the laughter to die down, as he placed one hand on his stomach, while holding up a copy of *Heads You Win* in the other for all to see.

'I put on another five pounds, while Harry's book sold a million copies in the first week after publication. But he would still have considered it more important that his sister-in-law Grace, a former professor of English at Cambridge, hailed it as a masterpiece of storytelling.'

Giles paused for a moment, as if reflecting, before he continued. 'They tell me Harry Clifton is dead. I suggest that whoever dares to repeat that slander should look at the bestseller lists around the world, which prove he's still very much alive. And just as he was about to receive the accolades and garlands that would acknowledge his life's achievements, the gods decided to step in and remind us that he was human, by striking down the person he most loved.

'When Harry first learned of Emma's tragic illness and had to face the fact that she only had a year to live, like every other obstacle that life had placed in his path he faced it head on, even though he accepted that this was a battle that could yield no victory.

'He immediately dropped everything, even his pen, in order to devote himself to Emma, and do everything in his power to lessen her pain. But none of us who lived with them through those final days fully realized the toll and strain that pain was inflicting on him. Within a few days of Emma's death, in an ending worthy of one of his novels, he was to die himself.

'I was at his bedside when he died, and had rather hoped that this man of letters might deliver one final, memorable line. He didn't let me down. "Giles," he said, clutching me by the hand, "I've just come up with an idea for a new novel." Tell me more, I said. "It's about a boy born in the back streets of Bristol, the son of a docker, who falls in love with the daughter of the man who owns the docks." And what happens next, I asked. "I've no idea," he said, "but I'll have the first chapter ready by the time I pick up my pen tomorrow morning."'

Giles looked up towards the heavens and said, 'I can't wait to read it.' Trying desperately to hold himself in check, the words no longer flowing, he turned to the last page of his eulogy, determined not to let his friend down. Ignoring the text, he said quietly, 'It is true that Harry requested a quiet exit from life's stage, and I ignored his wishes. I am no Mark Antony,' said Giles, looking down at the congregation, 'but I believe the Bard's words apply every bit as much to Harry as they did to the noble Brutus.'

Giles paused for a moment, before he leant forward and said, almost in a whisper,

> *'His life was gentle, and the elements*
> *so mixed in him that nature might stand up*
> *and say to all the world, This was a man!'*

THE END

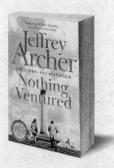

1

14 July 1979

'YOU CAN'T BE serious.'

'I couldn't be more serious, Father, as you'd realize if you'd ever listened to anything I've been saying for the past ten years.'

'But you've been offered a place at my old college at Oxford to read law, and after you graduate, you'll be able to join me in chambers. What more could a young man ask for?'

'To be allowed to pursue a career of his own choosing, and not just be expected to follow in his father's footsteps.'

'Would that be such a bad thing? After all, I've enjoyed a fascinating and worthwhile career, and, dare I suggest, been moderately successful.'

'Brilliantly successful, Father, but it isn't your career we're discussing, it's mine. And perhaps I don't want to be a leading criminal barrister who spends his whole life defending a bunch of villains he'd never consider inviting to lunch at his club.'

'You seem to have forgotten that those same villains

paid for your education, and the lifestyle you presently enjoy.'

'I'm never allowed to forget it, Father, which is the reason I intend to spend my life making sure those same villains are locked up for long periods of time, and not allowed to go free and continue a life of crime thanks to your skilful advocacy.'

William thought he'd finally silenced his father, but he was wrong.

'Perhaps we could agree on a compromise, dear boy?'

'Not a chance, Father,' said William firmly. 'You're sounding like a barrister who's pleading for a reduced sentence, when he knows he's defending a weak case. But for once, your eloquent words are falling on deaf ears.'

'Won't you even allow me to put my case before you dismiss it out of hand?' responded his father.

'No, because I'm not guilty, and I don't have to prove to a jury that I'm innocent, just to please you.'

'But would you be willing to do something to please me, my dear?'

In the heat of battle William had quite forgotten that his mother had been sitting silently at the other end of the table, closely following the jousting between her husband and son. William was well prepared to take on his father but knew he was no match for his mother. He fell silent once again. A silence that his father took advantage of.

'What do you have in mind, m'lud?' said Sir Julian, tugging at the lapels of his jacket, and addressing his wife as if she were a high court judge.

'William will be allowed to go to the university of his choice,' said Marjorie, 'select the subject he wishes to study, and once he's graduated, follow the career he wants to pursue. And more important, when he does, you will give in gracefully and never raise the subject again.'

'I confess,' said Sir Julian, 'that while accepting your wise judgement, I might find the last part difficult.'

Mother and son burst out laughing.

'Am I allowed a plea in mitigation?' asked Sir Julian innocently.

'No,' said William, 'because I will only agree to Mother's terms if in three years' time you unreservedly support my decision to join the Metropolitan Police Force.'

Sir Julian Warwick QC rose from his place at the head of the table, gave his wife a slight bow, and reluctantly said, 'If it so please Your Lordship.'

◄o►

William Warwick had wanted to be a detective from the age of eight, when he'd solved 'the case of the missing Mars bars'. It was a simple paper trail, he explained to his housemaster, that didn't require a magnifying glass.

The evidence – sweet papers – had been found in the waste-paper basket of the guilty party's study, and the culprit wasn't able to prove he'd spent any of his pocket money in the tuck shop that term.

And what made it worse for William was that Adrian Heath was one of his closest pals, and he'd assumed it would be a lifelong friendship. When he discussed it with his father at half term, the old man said, 'We must hope that Adrian has learnt from the experience, otherwise who knows what will become of the boy.'

Despite William being mocked by his fellow pupils, who dreamt of becoming doctors, lawyers, teachers, even accountants, the careers master showed no surprise when William informed him that he was going to be a detective. After all, the other boys had nicknamed him Sherlock before the end of his first term.

William's father, Sir Julian Warwick Bt, had wanted his son to go up to Oxford and read law, just as he'd done thirty years before. But despite his father's best efforts, William had remained determined to join the police force the day he left school. The two stubborn men finally reached a compromise approved of by his mother. William would go to London University and read art history – a subject his father refused to take seriously – and if, after three years, his son still wanted to be a policeman, Sir Julian agreed to give in gracefully. William knew that would never happen.

William enjoyed every moment of his three years at King's College London, where he fell in love several times. First with Hannah and Rembrandt, followed by Judy and Turner, and finally Rachel and Hockney, before settling down with Caravaggio: an affair that would last a lifetime, even though his father had pointed out that the great Italian artist had been a murderer and should have been hanged. A good enough reason to abolish the death penalty, William suggested. Once again, father and son didn't agree.

During the summer holidays after he'd left school, William backpacked his way across Europe to Rome, Paris, Berlin and on to St Petersburg, to join long queues of other devotees who wished to worship the past masters. When he finally graduated, his professor suggested that he should consider a PhD on the darker side of Caravaggio. The darker side, replied William, was exactly what he intended to research, but he wanted to learn more about criminals in the twentieth century, rather than the sixteenth.

◄○►

At five minutes to three on the afternoon of Sunday, 5 September 1982, William reported to Hendon Police College in north London. He enjoyed almost every minute of the training course from the moment he swore allegiance to the Queen to his passing-out parade sixteen weeks later.

The following day, he was issued with a navy-blue serge uniform, helmet and truncheon, and couldn't resist glancing at his reflection whenever he passed a window. A police uniform, he was warned by the commander on his first day on parade, could change a person's personality, and not always for the better.

Lessons at Hendon had begun on the second day and were divided between the classroom and the gym. William learnt whole sections of the law until he could repeat them verbatim. He revelled in forensic and crime scene analysis, even though he quickly discovered when he was introduced to the skid pad that his driving skills were fairly rudimentary.

Having endured years of cut and thrust with his father across the breakfast table, William felt at ease in the mock courtroom, where instructing officers cross-examined him in the witness box, and he even held his own during self-defence classes, where he learnt how to disarm, handcuff and restrain someone who was far bigger than him. He was also taught about a constable's powers of arrest, search and entry, the use of reasonable force and, most important of all, discretion. 'Don't always stick to the rule book,' his instructor advised him. 'Sometimes you have to use common sense, which, when you're dealing with the public, you'll find isn't that common.'

Exams were as regular as clockwork, compared to his days at university, and he wasn't surprised that several candidates fell by the wayside before the course had ended.

After what felt like an interminable two-week break following his passing-out parade, William finally received a letter instructing him to report to Lambeth police station at 8 a.m. the following Monday. An area of London he had never visited before.

<o>

Police Constable 565LD had joined the Metropolitan Police Force as a graduate but decided not to take advantage of the accelerated promotion scheme that would have allowed him to progress more quickly up the ladder, as he wanted to line up on his first day with every other new recruit on equal terms. He accepted that, as a probationer, he would have to spend at least two years on the beat before he could hope to become a detective, and in truth, he couldn't wait to be thrown in at the deep end.

From his first day as a probationer William was guided by his mentor, Constable Fred Yates, who had twenty-eight years of police service under his belt, and had been told by the nick's chief inspector to 'look after the boy'. The two men had little in common other than that they'd both wanted to be coppers from an early age, and their fathers had done everything in their power to prevent them pursuing their chosen career.

'ABC,' was the first thing Fred said when he was introduced to the wet-behind-the-ears young sprog. He didn't wait for William to ask.

'Accept nothing, Believe no one, Challenge everything. It's the only law I live by.'

During the next few months, Fred introduced William to the world of burglars, drug dealers and pimps, as well as his first dead body. With the zeal of Sir Galahad, William wanted to lock up every offender and make the world a better place; Fred was more realistic, but he never once attempted to douse the flames of William's youthful enthusiasm. The young probationer quickly found out that the public don't know if a policeman has been in uniform for a couple of days or a couple of years.

'Time to stop your first car,' said Fred on William's second day on the beat, coming to a halt by a set of traffic lights. 'We'll hang about until someone runs a red, and then you can step out into the road and flag them down.' William looked apprehensive. 'Leave the rest to me. See that tree about a hundred yards away? Go and hide behind it, and wait until I give you the signal.'

William could hear his heart pounding as he stood behind the tree. He didn't have long to wait before Fred raised a hand and shouted, 'The blue Hillman! Grab him!'

William stepped out into the road, put his arm up and directed the car to pull over to the kerb.

'Say nothing,' said Fred as he joined the raw recruit. 'Watch carefully and take note.' They both walked up to the car as the driver wound down his window.

'Good morning, sir,' said Fred. 'Are you aware that you drove through a red light?'

The driver nodded but didn't speak.

'Could I see your driving licence?'

The driver opened his glove box, extracted his licence and handed it to Fred. After studying the document for a few moments, Fred said, 'It's particularly dangerous at this time in the morning, sir, as there are two schools nearby.'

'I'm sorry,' said the driver. 'It won't happen again.'

Fred handed him back his licence. 'It will just be a warning this time,' he said, while William wrote down the car's number plate in his notebook. 'But perhaps you could be a little more careful in future, sir.'

'Thank you, officer,' said the driver.

'Why just a caution,' asked William as the car drove slowly away, 'when you could have booked him?'

'Attitude,' said Fred. 'The gentleman was polite, acknowledged his mistake and apologized. Why piss off a normally law-abiding member of the public?'

'So what would have made you book him?'

'If he'd said, "Haven't you got anything better to do, officer?" Or worse, "Shouldn't you be chasing some real criminals?" Or my favourite, "Don't you realize I pay your wages?" Any of those and I would have booked him without hesitation. Mind you, there was one blighter I had to cart off to the station and lock up for a couple of hours.'

'Did he get violent?'

'No, far worse. Told me he was a close friend of the commissioner, and I'd be hearing from him. So I told him he could phone him from the station.' William burst out laughing. 'Right,' said Fred, 'get back behind the tree. Next time you can conduct the interview and I'll observe.'

◄○►

Sir Julian Warwick QC sat at one end of the table, his head buried in the *Daily Telegraph*. He muttered the occasional tut-tut, while his wife, seated at the other end, continued her daily battle with the *Times* crossword. On a good day, Marjorie would have filled in the final clue before her husband rose from the table to leave for Lincoln's Inn. On a bad day, she would have to seek his advice, a service for which he usually charged a hundred pounds an hour. He regularly reminded her that to date, she owed him over £20,000. Ten across and four down were holding her up.

Sir Julian had reached the leaders by the time his wife was wrestling with the final clue. He still wasn't convinced that the death penalty should have been abolished, particularly when a police officer or a public servant was the victim, but then neither was the *Telegraph*. He turned to the back page to find out how Blackheath rugby club had fared against Richmond in their annual derby. After reading the match report he abandoned the sports pages, as he considered the paper gave far too much coverage to soccer. Yet another sign that the nation was going to the dogs.

'Delightful picture of Charles and Diana in *The Times*,' said Marjorie.

'It will never last,' said Julian as he rose from his place and walked to the other end of the table and, as he did every morning, kissed his wife on the forehead. They exchanged newspapers, so he could study the law reports on the train journey to London.

'Don't forget the children are coming down for lunch on Sunday,' Marjorie reminded him.

'Has William passed his detective's exam yet?' he asked.

'As you well know, my dear, he isn't allowed to take the exam until he's completed two years on the beat, which won't be for at least another six months.'

'If he'd listened to me, he would have been a qualified barrister by now.'

'And if you'd listened to him, you'd know he's far
more interested in locking up criminals than finding ways
of getting them off.'

'I haven't given up yet,' said Sir Julian.

'Just be thankful that at least our daughter has followed in your footsteps.'

'Grace has done nothing of the sort,' snorted Sir
Julian. 'That girl will defend any penniless no-hoper she
comes across.'

'She has a heart of gold.'

'Then she takes after you,' said Sir Julian, studying
the one clue his wife had failed to fill in: *Slender private
man who ended up with a baton.* Four.

'Field Marshal SLIM,' said Sir Julian triumphantly.
'The only man to join the army as a private soldier and
end up as a field marshal.'

'Sounds like William,' said Marjorie. But not until the
door had closed.

2

WILLIAM AND FRED left the nick just after eight to set out on their morning patrol. 'Not much crime at this time of day,' Fred assured the young probationer. 'Criminals are like the rich, they don't get up much before ten.' Over the past eighteen months William had become used to Fred's oft-repeated pearls of wisdom, which had proved far more useful than anything to be found in the Met's handbook on the duties of a police officer.

'When do you take your detective's exam?' asked Fred as they ambled down Lambeth Walk.

'Not for another year,' replied William. 'But I don't think you'll be getting rid of me quite yet,' he added as they approached the local newsagent. He glanced at the headline: 'PC Stephen Walker killed in the line of duty'.

'Such a tragic accident,' said Fred. 'Poor bloke.' He didn't speak again for some time. 'I've been a constable all my life,' he eventually managed, 'which suits me just fine. But you—'

'If I make it,' said William, 'I'll have you to thank.'

'I'm not like you, Choirboy,' said Fred. William feared that he would be stuck with that nickname for the rest of his career. He preferred Sherlock. He had never admitted to any of his mates at the station that he had been a choirboy, and always wished he looked older, although his mother had once told him, 'The moment you do, you'll want to look younger.' Is no one ever satisfied with the age they are? he wondered. 'By the time you become commissioner,' continued Fred, 'I'll be shacked up in an old people's home, and you'll have forgotten my name.'

It had never crossed William's mind that he might end up as commissioner, although he felt sure he would never forget Constable Fred Yates.

Fred spotted the young lad as he came running out of the newsagent's. Mr Patel followed a moment later, but he was never going to catch him. William set off in pursuit, with Fred only a yard behind. They both overtook Mr Patel as the boy turned the corner. But it was another hundred yards before William was able to grab him. The two of them led the young lad back to the shop, where he handed over a packet of Capstan to Mr Patel.

'Will you be pressing charges, sir?' asked William, who already had his notebook open, pencil poised.

'What's the point?' said the shopkeeper, placing the cigarette packet back on the shelf. 'If you lock him up, his younger brother will only take his place.'

'It's your lucky day, Tomkins,' said Fred, clipping the boy around the ear. 'Just make sure you're in school by the time we turn up, otherwise I might tell your old man what you were up to. Mind you,' he added, turning to William, 'the fags were probably for his old man.'

Tomkins bolted. When he reached the end of the street he stopped, turned around and shouted, 'Police scum!' and gave them both a 'V' sign.

'Perhaps you should have pinned his ears back.'

'What are you talking about?' asked Fred.

'In the sixteenth century, when a boy was caught stealing, he would be nailed to a post by one of his ears, and the only way he could escape was to tear himself free.'

'Not a bad idea,' said Fred. 'Because I have to admit I can't get to grips with modern police practice. By the time you retire, you'll probably have to call the criminals "sir". Still, I've only got another eighteen months to go before I collect my pension, and by then you'll be at Scotland Yard. Although,' Fred added, about to dispense his daily dose of wisdom, 'when I joined the force nearly thirty years ago, we used to handcuff lads like that to a radiator, turn the heat full on, and not release them until they'd confessed.'

William burst out laughing.

'I wasn't joking,' said Fred.

'How long do you think it will be before Tomkins ends up in jail?'

'A spell in borstal before he goes to prison, would be my bet. The really maddening thing is that once he's locked up he'll have his own cell, three meals a day and be surrounded by career criminals who'll be only too happy to teach him his trade before he graduates from the University of Crime.'

Every day William was reminded how lucky he'd been to be born in a middle-class cot, with loving parents and an older sister who doted on him. Although he never admitted to any of his colleagues that he'd been educated at one of England's leading public schools before taking an art history degree at King's College London. And he certainly never mentioned that his father regularly received large payments from some of the nation's most notorious criminals.

As they continued on their round, several local people acknowledged Fred, and some even said good morning to William.

When they returned to the nick a couple of hours later, Fred didn't bother to report young Tomkins to the desk sergeant, as he felt the same way about paperwork as he did about modern police practice.

'Feel like a cuppa?' said Fred, heading towards the canteen.

'Warwick!' shouted a voice from behind them.

William turned round to see the custody sergeant pointing at him. 'A prisoner's collapsed in his cell. Take this prescription to the nearest chemist and have it made up. And be quick about it.'

'Yes, sarge,' said William. He grabbed the envelope, and ran all the way to Boots on the high street, where he found a small queue waiting patiently at the dispensary counter. He apologized to the woman at the front of the queue before handing the envelope to the pharmacist. 'It's an emergency,' he said.

The young woman opened the envelope and carefully read the instructions before saying, 'That will be one pound sixty, constable.'

William fumbled for some change, which he gave to the pharmacist. She rang up the sale, turned around, took a packet of condoms off the shelf and handed it to him. William's mouth opened, but no words came out. He was painfully aware that several people in the queue were grinning. He was about to slip away when the pharmacist said, 'Don't forget your prescription, constable.' She passed the envelope back to William.

Several amused pairs of eyes followed him as he slipped out into the street. He waited until he was out of sight before he opened the envelope and read the enclosed note.

Dear Sir or Madam,
I am a shy young constable, who's finally got a girl to come out with me, and I'm hoping to get lucky tonight. But as I don't want to get her pregnant, can you help?

William burst out laughing, put the packet of condoms in his pocket and made his way back to the station; his first thought: I only wish I did have a girlfriend.

3

CONSTABLE WARWICK SCREWED the top back onto his fountain pen, confident he had passed his detective's exam with what his father would have called flying colours.

When he returned to his single room in Trenchard House that evening, the flying colours had been lowered to half mast, and by the time he switched off his bedside lamp, he was sure he would remain in uniform and be on the beat for at least another year.

'How did you do?' the station officer asked when he reported back on duty the following morning.

'Failed hopelessly,' said William, as he checked the parade book. He and Fred were down to patrol the Barton estate, if only to remind the local criminals that London still had a few bobbies on the beat.

'Then you'll have to try again next year,' said the sergeant, unwilling to indulge the young man. If Constable Warwick wanted to wallow in self-doubt, he had no intention of rescuing the lad.

◄○►

Sir Julian continued sharpening the carving knife until he was confident blood would run.

'Six months, possibly a year. I'll have to wait for a vacancy to arise in another patch.'

'Perhaps you'll go straight to Scotland Yard?' said his father, raising an eyebrow.

'That's not possible. You have to prove yourself in another division before you can even apply for a job at the holy grail. Although I will be visiting the Yard tomorrow for the first time.'

Sir Julian stopped carving. 'Why?' he demanded.

'I'm not sure myself,' admitted William. 'The super called me in on Friday and told me to report to a Commander Hawksby at nine on Monday morning, but he didn't give any clue why.'

'Hawksby ... Hawksby ...' said Sir Julian, the lines on his forehead growing more pronounced. 'Why do I know that name? Ah yes, we once crossed swords on a fraud case when he was a chief inspector. An impressive witness. He'd done his homework and was so well prepared I couldn't lay a glove on him. Not a man to be underestimated.'

'Tell me more,' said William.

'Unusually short for a policeman. Beware of them; they often have bigger brains. He's known as the Hawk. Hovers over you before swooping down and carrying all before him.'

'You included, it would seem,' said Marjorie.

'What makes you say that?' asked Sir Julian, as he poured himself a glass of wine.

'You only ever remember witnesses who get the better of you.'

'Touché,' said Sir Julian, raising his glass as Grace and William burst into spontaneous applause.

THE CLIFTON CHRONICLES

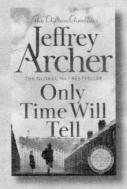

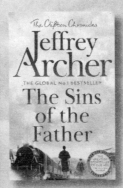

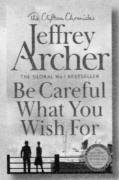

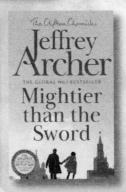

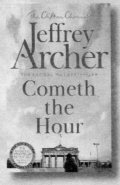

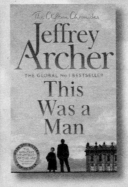

THE
WILLIAM WARWICK
NOVELS

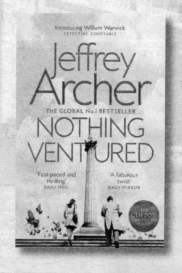

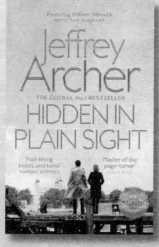

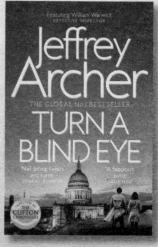

JEFFREY ARCHER
THE MASTER STORYTELLER

International bestseller Jeffrey Archer took the world by storm with the global phenomenon *Kane and Abel*, a novel which has been read over 100 million times, introduced the world to William Lowell Kane and Abel Rosnovski and spawned two sequels.

Have you read them yet?

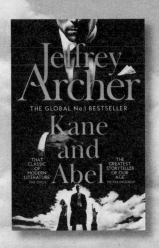

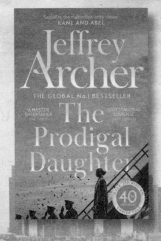

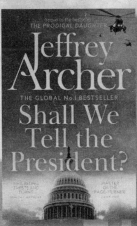

JEFFREY ARCHER
THE MASTER STORYTELLER

The internationally bestselling author delights with
these standalone novels, which showcase his imagination,
his wit and his unrivalled storytelling ability.

Have you read them all yet?

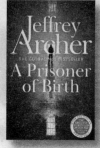
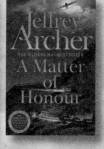
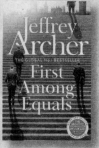
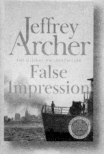

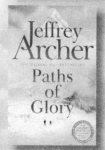
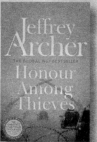
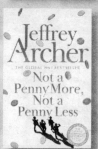
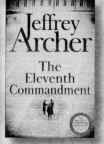